MONEY POWER LOVE

Joss Sheldon

www.joss-sheldon.com

Copyright © Joss Sheldon 2017

ISBN-13: 978-1976365119
ISBN-10: 1976365112

EDITION 1.0

First published in the UK in 2017.

Cover design by Marijana Ivanova Design.

Edited by Cynthia Parten and Madness Jones.

Proofread by Jayne Clifford-Greening and Roxann Acosta

"Let us control the money of a nation, and we care not who makes its laws."

HOUSE OF ROTHSCHILDS

INSPIRED BY REAL EVENTS

WRITTEN WITH FICTICIOUS LICENCE

BOOK ONE

NATURE AND NURTURE

THE END

"Endings are not always bad. Most times they're just beginnings in disguise."
KIM HARRISON

Picture the scene, if you will...

Our three heroes are sitting in a traditional British pub. They do little to stand out. If you were to see them, you probably would not give them a second glance.

The first man sips half a pint of cheap ale. He is still on his second drink, despite his companions being on their fourth.

The second man, drinking whisky, spreads himself out across the booth. He takes up more space than the other two men combined.

The third man, mulling over the fine notes in his glass of claret, twirls a diamond-encrusted ring around his index finger.

These three men were once three babies, born on three adjacent beds, a mere three seconds apart. Their mothers had screamed in unison as they endured what were not so much three separate sets of labour pain, but one unified agony; an agony so immense, they all agreed it was three times greater than any pain womankind had ever known.

These three men were once three toddlers, who lived in three adjacent houses, which were each three metres wide. Each house had three windows. All three families shared a single latrine.

These three men had once been three teens. They had been three adults. You get the picture...

But these men are not toddlers, nor are they teens. Age has wizened them, serpentine scales have cut craggy ravines from their skin, grey has replaced colour, and baldness has replaced hair.

Their shared nature has not been forgotten; at times, it has been so strong that they have felt each other's emotions, as if those emotions were their own. They have always looked the same, and have often acted in a similar manner.

Yet nurture has triumphed over nature. Cast adrift by the whimsy of circumstance, our three heroes have been shaped by three very different sets of events, and three very different sets of people.

As a result, they have spent their lives chasing three very different goals.

This man here, his fingers moist with warm beer, has spent his life chasing love. This man, throwing back whiskies with conscious indifference, has spent his life chasing power. And this man, well, you must have guessed it by now. This man, with his diamond ring, has spent his life chasing money.

But to leave it there simply would not do. So let's start, as all good stories should, back at the very beginning…

THE CAULDRON

"The fire inside me burned brighter than the fire around me."
JOSHUA GRAHAM

Our story begins at three minutes past three, on the morning of the third of March, sometime in the late 1700s.

Everything was aflame, ablaze, and drenched in smoke. But the flames were too hot to feel, the blaze too bright to see, and the smoke too fragile to mount a case against the moonless sky.

Three terraced houses, built from one set of bricks, were falling victim to an infinity of flames. Three families, of common stock, were taking their final breaths.

How did this fire begin?

It would be easy to blame Mayer's father. Coming home late from the pub, intoxicated, with an alcohol soaked hunger, he placed a hunk of bread and the remains of a lamb shank in his oven. Turning to look for more liquor, he tripped over his toe, stumbled, fell, and knocked himself unconscious. There he remained, cradled in Azrael's arms, whilst bread turned to flames and meat turned to fury; spitting charcoal-flecked sparks out across the room.

But to lay the blame solely with that man would be to ignore the role played by Hugo's father. Whilst Mayer's father was stumbling, drunk, around his larder, Hugo's father was sound asleep; wrapped in a quilt he had inherited from a reclusive aunt. But that did not stop his flapping arm from knocking over the gas lamp on his bedside table. Nor did it stop that lamp from smashing onto the floor; igniting the clothes, tally sticks and books which had been scattered there during a night of frenzied copulation. Fuel sped across the floorboards, and flames gave chase.

Whilst Mayer's father was tripping, and Hugo's father was flapping, Archibald's father was pacing. Aimlessly wandering from one room to another, this would not have been an issue, had it not been for the fact that he was asleep. In his mind, he was doing his family's laundry; collecting their dirty undergarments and placing them in a bucket of soapy water. In reality, he was putting those clothes in a fire. When he sleepwalked back to bed, he left a trail of burning garments in his wake. Blazing socks joined the dots between blazing jumpers. Flaming knickers touched flaming shirts.

Whilst three fathers could have shouldered the blame for that fire, little Hugo could not. Asleep in his cot, Hugo's mind was consumed by his dreams. Those dreams were soon consumed by the flames. Hugo saw himself lighting fires in every room: Lighting lamps, torches, ovens and stoves. His dreams were so lifelike, so real, that Hugo was convinced he had lit those fires himself.

His family fell, unconscious, into the embrace of toxic smoke; smiling at death with angelic faces. But Hugo awoke with a jolt. Rattled by a sixth sense, his torso bolted forwards and his lungs thumped into his ribs; propelling him onto the floor, where he instinctively crawled outside.

Archibald and Mayer were also compelled by this impulse, which they felt in the same way, at the very same time. They too were jolted awake, thrown from their cribs, and propelled to crawl outside.

They reached the street, three seconds after the other, in the order they had been born.

*****

By the time their parents and siblings had turned to ash, and the cinders of their homes had ceased to glow, our three heroes were surrounded by adults.

Archibald and Mayer answered every question they were asked. As a result, they were soon rehoused; Archibald with an uncle and aunt; Mayer with a woman who just happened to be passing.

But, overcome by an unbearable sense of guilt, Hugo was struck dumb. No matter how hard they tried, no-one could prise a word from his lips. The offer of sweet toffee, normally reserved for Christmas, could not encourage him to speak. Kisses, cuddles, pats, back rubs, tears, smiles, jokes, and other assorted pleas had no effect. Hugo refused to hold the stuffed toy which was thrust into his hands. He refused to react in any way.

Unable to help himself, no-one was able to help Hugo. The crowd shrugged, sent him to a distant workhouse, and departed the scene.

*****

United by birth, our three heroes had been divided by tragedy. Their lives were about to head in three very different directions...

BUCKINGHAM TOWERS

*"There are people who have money and
people who are rich."*
COCO CHANEL

So, what of Mayer?

Mayer would never forget the lightness he felt when he first entered Buckingham Towers; the semi-detached Camden townhouse his adopted parents called home. He felt like an alien, incapable of comprehending the new planet onto which he had stepped.

His eyes wandered from the upholstered settees to the inlaid cabinets; to the paraphernalia of gentility; the chintz and chinoiserie, doilies and drapes.

To Mayer, the dark, oak doors seemed older than time and heavier than space. The fact that every child in that house had their own bedroom seemed like wanton luxury. Even Molly, the house cat, was fed a better diet than Mayer had been accustomed to.

Mayer could barely comprehend what he was seeing.

Open mouthed, he allowed himself to be led inside. He said "Thank-you", rubbed the pins and needles from his feet, and collapsed.

*****

Abe, Mayer's adopted father, had not been born into such luxury. The son of a wheat farmer, he passed a modest childhood in the company of donkeys and dung.

If you had asked Abe for the secret of his success, he would have told you it came down to two important factors.

"The first," he would shout, "was hard work. You can never work hard enough.

"And the second," he would continue, "was even more hard work!"

Yet, whilst hard work was no doubt a factor in Abe's ascent, chance played an even greater role.

Abe was born in the village of Hillmorton; a sleepy idyll where mills flecked the earth like daffodils in spring. Whenever he sold his wheat to those mills, his father carried Abe on his shoulders, which endeared him to the local millers.

During the harvest, Abe was sent to stay in London with his aunt; the wife of a baker, who introduced him to the other bakers in his guild.

As soon as he was old enough to carry a rake, Abe started to work with his father.

And, when he was not working, he passed his time in the company of Ole Jim Diamond; a family friend who had a penchant for telling vivid tales about countries he had never visited, and battles he had never fought. Ole Jim's life had actually been somewhat prosaic; a shipbuilder in the navy, he had retired to Hillmorton to take care of his elderly mother; but that did not stop him from spinning a good yarn.

It was thanks to these connections that Abe was able to profit from the opening of the London canal.

In return for a share in his business, Abe convinced Ole Jim Diamond to build him a barge. Because they had known Abe all his life, and could therefore trust him, the local millers were happy to sell him flour on credit. Using the canal and his barge, Abe transported that flour to London, where he sold it to the bakers in his uncle's guild. Those men were keen to buy whatever flour they could, to satisfy the increasing demand for bread in that expanding metropolis.

Abe reinvested his profits. By the time his wife adopted Mayer, he owned a whole fleet of barges, and supplied almost every bakery in north London. He was a respected merchant, with a small fortune to his name.

Yet, had it not been for his father's and uncle's connections, the opening of a canal, and the growing demand for bread, Abe would have remained a humble farmer.

Still, that was not the way he told it. According to Abe, his rise was due to two factors, and two factors alone: "Hard work and hard work".

*****

Whilst Abe built empires in suburbia, his wife became the empress of their home. Sadie was a strong monarch, with sturdy thighs and a stout personality. She ruled in a manner which even Abe was not brave enough or stupid enough to challenge.

Like Abe, Sadie was a farmer's child. Unlike Abe, she was well aware of her good fortune. This made her all the more determined to maintain her newfound position.

Whilst her husband toiled like an ordinary member of the working poor, Sadie lived an aristocratic life of idle luxury. She invested in books with titles such as "How to Behave" and "Hints from a Lady". She read how to act at dinner parties and in public, how to shake hands and bring conversations to an end, how to dress herself and adorn her home.

She scoured the pages of "Sam Beeton's Magazine" for items to buy, believing that owning fine things would impress her peers and profit her nation:

"I say, this modern economy of ours requires two things. Supply and demand! Men must work hard to supply nice things, and women must work hard to demand them.

"If we left it to the men, nothing would ever get bought. And then where would we be? I tell you, being a consumer is a patriotic duty. It's because of us that expensive fabrics have to be imported from India. We keep the wheels of empire turning!"

Sadie had enjoyed a similar conversation before adopting Mayer, when her friend, Mrs Winterbottom, had opined:

"It's the responsibility of the wealthy to help those with less than themselves. It really does soothe one's conscience to know one is not *only* spending one's money on oneself."

Sadie nodded along in agreement.

When her carriage passed by the smoking remains of Mayer's home, those words rang loud in her ears. Without thinking, she disembarked, swooped down on Mayer, lifted him up by his collar, and dropped him inside her carriage.

"I'll take this one," she said, as if selecting a puppy. And that, as they say, was that.

*****

Mayer reminded Sadie of herself as a child; helpless and in need of good fortune. This had a dual effect. A part of Sadie loved Mayer; she wanted to raise him up, just as she had been raised. But a part of her hated him; he was a constant reminder of the humble origins she had worked so hard to forget.

Sadie adopted Mayer out of love; a desire to do something truly kind. She housed, fed and clothed him. Such acts of philanthropy were a mainstay of the middle-class existence she had worked so hard to embrace. But respectable members of the middle-class did not associate *too* closely with the poor. So Sadie kept her distance; she did not speak to Mayer once in all their years together.

This left Mayer feeling as though he was just another object in Sadie's collection, bought to boost her status, like a piano or a pony. He felt like a stranger in another family's home.

Whilst that family dined together, taking their silver cutlery and fine food for granted, Mayer ate with Maggs, the housekeeper, in the funerary darkness of the pantry. It was Maggs, not Sadie, who dressed Mayer as a gentleman's son; in a beaver-hat, surtout coat and black necktie; and it was Maggs who walked Mayer to school.

When Mayer was told he was to receive an education, he had asked if he would be attending the same private school as his adopted brothers. Sadie responded with a look of condescension which was so violent it teetered on the brink of outright war. She did not issue a verbal reply.

But Mayer still appreciated his Church School. Whilst the lessons were basic, taught by the older pupils rather than by the teacher, Mayer realised he was learning more than he would have done had he lived with his birth family. None of his blood relations had ever received any education at all.

Nor did Mayer mind that school's emphasis on religion. In fact, religion was the one thing which brought his adopted family together. Each night, just before bed, they gathered in the evening room, drew the curtains, lit a candle, and prayed as one. For Mayer, it was the only time he felt like a member of the family. And for Mayer, that was enough.

LAMBETH MARSH

*"Kindness is the language which the deaf
can hear and the blind can see."*
MARK TWAIN

So, what of Archibald?

Archibald was adopted by his Uncle Raymondo and Aunt Ruthie.

Two things should be noted, when it comes to that shopkeeper and his wife. Firstly, they were old. Archibald could not be sure how old they were, but he was certain they were antique. Uncle Raymondo, with his long white beard and hearty laugh, reminded Archibald of every image he had ever seen of God himself. Aunt Ruthie smelled of lavender.

The second thing to note, was that despite their advanced years they had never had any children. It was not for want of trying. Theirs had been a healthy love, but not a fruitful one.

Ruthie and Raymondo had tried to conceive, day and night, ever since they married, aged fourteen. On realising their predicament, they tried every remedy in the book. Raymondo was circumcised. He ate curds and meat. Aunt Ruthie tried vaginal steaming, using a brew of rosemary, lavender, oregano, marigold, basil and rose. They made love in the dark and beneath the glow of a hundred candles, inside and outside, in the presence of both northerly and southerly winds.

Nothing worked.

Raymondo was sure the blame lay with Ruthie, who was sure it lay with him. But both husband and wife were too kind to blame their partner. In fact, they each admitted fault, to soothe their spouse's conscience. They each believed their partner's confession, which confirmed their own belief in their innocence.

Whoever was to blame, they grew sure of one thing: They would never sire a child.

Then, out of the blue, Archibald arrived on their doorstep. For Raymondo and Ruthie, it was the miracle of all miracles. They felt as though God had finally answered their prayers. They celebrated with ale, which they shared amongst their neighbours, and they lavished young Archibald with all the love and affection they had been saving for years.

*****

Archibald's childhood played out in three arenas: His home, his uncle's shop and his village, Lambeth Marsh; a sleepy hamlet on the south bank of the River Thames.

Lambeth Marsh was a patchwork of market gardens and boggy ditches; held together by the family's shop, a church and a pub, "The Three Horseshoes". Raymondo visited that place each evening, sat Archibald on his knee, lit his pipe and played cribbage. Archibald held his uncle's cards. The other villagers congratulated him whenever Raymondo won, and ribbed him whenever he lost, as if it was Archibald and not his uncle who was playing.

Whereas that pub was the centre of evening life, it was Raymondo's shop which united the community during the day. Everyone popped in. They spent a little time picking up the things they needed, but could not produce themselves, and a lot of time nattering about village life.

They spoke about the weather, the harvest, and the key issues of the day; about how London was crawling out towards them, about the new factories which were popping up, and about the botanical gardens, which were still viewed with suspicion, even though they had been open for almost two decades.

Archibald listened to those conversations, sat by his uncle's feet, whilst playing with his one wooden toy; a figurine made by Bobby Brown, the village carpenter. Bobby had not asked for anything in return, but Raymondo had still issued him with store credit, and allowed him to take a pack of candles the next time he popped in.

Raymondo tried to convince Archibald that figurine was a soldier. "Bang! Bang!" he joked, bending his fingers into the shape of a gun. But Archibald insisted that it was a lady. He dressed it up in any scraps of cloth he could find, and made it a head of hair using the remains of an old mop.

Archibald also enjoyed playing with the other villagers his age. He was never one for rough and tumble, but he soon became a favourite amongst the girls.

"You're a regular Casanova," Ruthie joked, whenever she wasn't saying "I love you" or "Whose Auntie's favourite little boy? You are. Yes you are!"

Aunt Ruthie was a jack of all trades. She worked in the shop when Raymondo was away, taught Archibald to read and write, and maintained their small home.

That place possessed all of life's necessities, but few of its luxuries. There were walls, but no wallpaper; floors, but no rugs; a roof, but no ceiling; windows, but no curtains; shelves, but no cupboards; pots, but no pans. Uncle Raymondo owned a bible, but even that lacked a cover. His ink pot contained just one type of ink: Black. There was one fireplace, which blazed cheerily, a single knife, and a solitary chair which the family took it in turns to use. Other than that, there was not a single atom of furniture in their home. Ruthie had once bought a doormat, but had decided it was too much of an extravagance, and so chopped it up into squares which she used to scrub the floor.

*****

Archibald was given an outfit made from Raymondo's one frock coat, which Ruthie cut apart with her one pair of scissors, and sewed back together using a borrowed needle. After much debate, they agreed to buy Archibald a new set of underwear. The only other item of clothing he was given was Raymondo's hat, which was so large it came down over his eyes.

Archibald liked these clothes, but he did not love them. He *loved* using Ruthie's one piece of make-up; an eyeliner she had not touched in over a decade. Unaware of social conventions, and indifferent to gender stereotypes, Archibald took an enormous amount of pleasure from using that eyeliner to make himself look pretty.

He stopped using it as soon as Ruthie told him off:

"Now, now, my love; boys don't wear make-up."

Instead of using that eyeliner, Archibald put on Ruthie's Sunday dress. For him, it was a compromise; he was still being true to himself, exploring his feminine side, but he was also respecting Ruthie's wishes. He loved Ruthie so much that he would have done anything to please her.

It was not enough. When she saw him in that dress, Ruthie flew into a rage, and threw their only wooden spoon towards their only wooden door. Then she hugged Archibald for several minutes; smothering him with an abundance of oppressive love:

"Oh, I am sorry. I love you more than anything in the world, my little miracle child. Yes I do! Oh, yes I do!"

Archibald never wore women's clothing again.

*****

Such was Archibald's youth.

He slept under a desk, next to a pile of coals, from where he could hear the sound of cocks crowing and wheels turning. He spent his mornings at home, his afternoons at the shop, and his evenings in the pub. He had few possessions, but he was loved by many people. And that, for Archibald, was enough.

ST MARY MAGDALEN'S

"The rich have become richer and the poor have become poorer."
PERCY SHELLEY

So, what of Hugo?

Whereas Mayer was schooled in the ways of individualistic consumption, and Archibald in the ways of communal life, Hugo was simply left alone.

He was dumped, unceremoniously, on the doorstep of the St Mary Magdalen Workhouse, Bermondsey, like Moses in the rushes. He lay there in the shadows, whilst sewage crept up towards his feet.

When, in later life, he was asked about his time at St Mary Magdalen's, Hugo would struggle to give specific details. He would remember the sheer quantity of children, but would be unable to recall their faces. He would remember the pain, but not the punishments; the fatigue, but not the work. One thing, however, would stick with him: The unremitting stench of that place. He would still be able to smell the malodorous fumes emanating from the urinals, and the bittersweet rankness of the deadhouse. Simply being asked about that place would make Hugo want to vomit.

That smell was the last thing he remembered all those years later. It was the first thing he noticed when he arrived.

*****

"Well I suppose we'll have to take youse in," the Drillmaster said, looking just as unimpressed as he sounded.

"I'm sorry," Hugo replied. Bearing the guilt of his family's demise, he was happy to receive any sort of welcome at all.

"Just don't expect an easy ride boy. Everyone has to pull their weight here; young and old alike. We shan't be tolerating no slackers! This ain't no place for no goldbrickers."

"Yes sir. I'm grateful sir. I'm ever so sorry sir. I really don't deserve your kindness."

"True that. Tut, tut, true that. Tut, tut, tut, tut, tut."

The Drillmaster led Hugo through a fever-nest of an infirmary in which tuberculosis, cholera and general decay were eating their way through the decrepit bodies of the capital's poor. He led Hugo through a tall set of prison gates, past a sign which read "God is love", and into the infant nursery, where he shaved Hugo's hair and threw him into a uniform made of brown drugget.

Cracked walls looked down on the cracks in the floorboards with a lofty sort of scorn.

Babies cried, toddlers coughed, and children clung, screaming, to the last possessions of deceased parents; to chipped crockery, faded dresses, ledgers, candlesticks and quills.

Hugo was shown to his bed: A narrow orange crate, stuffed with straw, which he would have to share with two other boys.

The Drillmaster turned and left.

*****

One day passed in pretty much the same manner as the next, and one hour was spent in pretty much the same place as the last: Their dorm. The orphans at St Mary Magdalen's only ever left that place to attend chapel.

The food was so pitiful it left Hugo fearing he would eat another boy; washing, using water from the chamber pot, was so ineffective that he avoided it if he could; and the work was so tedious it made him doolally.

The boys in Hugo's dorm were made to pick oakum fibres out of rope. It was hard work. It was meant to be hard, to discourage people from entering a workhouse in the first place. But it was worthwhile, as the Drillmaster was at pains to point out:

"You're serving your county, helping the navy like this. Only way a bunch of gutter rats like you ever will. Tut, tut, too right. Tut, tut, tut, tut, tut."

*****

At times, Hugo grew angry. At times, he grew resigned.

He told himself he did not deserve any better; that he was a despicable child who had murdered his family. He told himself he could not expect any better; that he was doing penance for his crimes. And he told himself that if he did want anything better, he would have to earn it; work was good for him; the Drillmaster did care; his was a tough sort of love.

"Sorry", he said each time he was told off. Only "Sorry", never anything more.

In his mind, he was apologizing to the family he believed he had killed. But he never spoke of such matters, for fear of being sent to the hangman. As a result, the Drillmaster assumed he was saying "Sorry" for his lacklustre work, which confirmed his belief that Hugo needed to be disciplined.

He was flogged whenever he dropped his rope. He was whipped whenever he sneezed. When he was punched by Stevie Davidson, the skew-whiff child who shared his bed, they were both made to scrub the nursery floor. As soon as they had finished, the Drillmaster knocked over two scuttles of coal and made them start again.

Hugo did not complain, boys were punished for complaining; and Hugo felt he deserved that punishment because he had wet their bed, and therefore incited Stevie to punch him.

Hugo believed he deserved every punishment which came his way. But, at the same time, he also felt a subtle nagging; a voice which told him he could do better; that anyone could do better than that.

Such was Hugo's youth: Born in guilt and lived in confusion.

For Hugo, it was not quite enough.

MUDLARKING

"Please sir, replied Oliver, I want some more."
CHARLES DICKENS

Hugo held out his empty bowl:

"Please sir, can I have some more?"

"Why of course, dear boy!" the Drillmaster replied. "Tut, tut, too right."

Hugo waited, but nothing happened:

"Please sir, can I have some more gruel?"

"Of course you can, young squire. You can have anything you want; crumpets with cream cheese, afternoon cat-lap at the Ritz, caviar and foie gras. Why, my lord, I dare say you could wash it down with a glass of the finest champagne in Christendom. All you need do is go and get it."

"Go where sir?"

"Anywhere! Anywhere but here. We've fed you enough, and it's cost us more than your work has ever made. Tut, tut, too true. What are you: A man, who seeks his own living? Or a plant, who expects it to be brought to him?

"Go on! Pack your bags and bugger orf. Go get your lobster frittata with smoked salmon. Tut, tut, tut, tut, tut."

*****

Hugo was thrown out of the workhouse in much the same fashion he was thrown into it all those years before: Ingloriously.

He trudged out onto Bermondsey's muck-paved streets.

To his left were the tanneries, hide dressers and skin sellers whose premises clung to the south bank of the Thames. To his right were a line of chemical works, and the noxious ditches they produced.

There were people, so many people. And there were rats, so many rats; the sort which startled horses, the sort which would try to bite you, and the sort which would actually bite you. Hugo gave them all a wide berth.

*****

Tired and hungry, Hugo needed help. It came in the form of a muddy little creature with mud-caked hair, mud-covered clothes, mud in her shoes and mud in her pockets. Perhaps that girl warmed to Hugo's appearance; he was a sooty shade of drab himself. Or, perhaps, she just took pity on our pathetic hero. We shall never know.

What was indisputable, however, was that she did call out:

"Wha' a blazin' sight for sore eyes if evers I saws one. Corr blimey guvnor. Wha' ahvs we 'ere then? Well, well, well. Jiminy crickets!"

She ran her muddy finger down Hugo's cheek:

"Wells then? Don' ya speak Mr Crickets?"

Hugo looked into her muddy eyes and tried to reply. He failed. He bowed his head, inhaled, and mustered all the strength he could find. Finally, he was able to exhale six measly words:

"Sorry. I'm ah Hugo. What are you?"

"Wha' am I? Wha' am I, Mr Ah Hugo Crickets? Dearie me. Do Ize looks like a 'What' to you?"

"Sorry."

"Ah, that youse are, Mr Ah Crickets. That youse are!"

"Wells, young cricketty, Ize is a scavenger. Or a mudlark, as wees likes to call ourselves. Wees scavenge, we does. Wees find wha'evers treasure we can in the mud o' low tide, and sells it on to who evers might buy it."

"I see."

"But Ize don't thinks that's what youse is worried about now, is it Mr Ah Crickets? Methinks youse is more interested in some grub for your belly, and some singsong for your gullet."

"Some food? Yes. Sorry."

"I thoughts as much. Ah yes. As soon as Ize seen ya, Ize thoughts to myselves, 'Now 'eres be a lad who needs 'imself some food.'

"Wells, Mr Ah Crickets, today is your lucky day. Wees gots ourselves some jellied eels, straights off da back o' Mr Ribbett's truck, yes we did. Your lucky day indeed!"

Hugo grinned.

The girl continued:

"My name's Delilah, by da way, but my friends all call me Dizzy. Youse can call me Delilah."

*****

Hugo ate his jellied eels with ferocious delight. To him, they tasted better than caviar and foie gras. They were not just dinner, they were a family homecoming.

The home to which Hugo came was an abandoned barge, with sacks for bedding and crates for beds. Reeds peeked in through the panelling and rootworms infested the boards.

Hugo's new family consisted of Dizzy and two Irish youths, Izzy and Jo, whose parents had been sent to America as indentured servants.

"White slaves," Izzy said. "Debt slaves. Let's go the whole hog and call them what they are. Or, at least, what they were. They've probably kicked the bucket by now."

Izzy was a majestic example of the power of dress. She had turned her shabby vest and raggedy blazer into an outfit which almost resembled a waistcoat and frock. Her crusty hair had been combed in such a manner it seemed to shine, as if moulded by beeswax, and the dust which circled her eyes had all the elegance of cheap mascara.

From a certain angle, Izzy could have passed as a nobleman's daughter. From another, she looked like a beggar. As is the way with abandoned children; people without a past, connections or status; Izzy was able to appear as a member of any class at any time.

Jo, on the other hand, looked like a regular tramp. His corduroy trousers contained more holes than a piece of Emmental, his vest had grown yellow through constant wear, and his socks were nothing more than collections of loosely connected threads.

But, whatever you may think of their appearance, there was warmth in those children's hearts. It poured from them as they sang gypsy songs; "The Dark Eyed Sailor", "The Female Cabin Boy" and "Gentle Annie"; songs which had been sung by waifs and strays for countless generations.

After they sang, they talked. And, after quite some time, they broached the subject of theft.

Hugo did not mind that his food had been stolen, only that his belly had been filled, but he was determined to earn an honest crust himself.

"Aye, we all start off that way," Jo replied. "But there'll come a week when you don't eat a crumb. That'll have you changing your mind, just as quick as the wind."

"Ah, leave him alone, wills ya?" Dizzy rollocked. "If this 'ere Mr Ah Crickets don't wanna pilfer, so bees it. Leastways, he's a skinny lil' devil; there's no way in 'ell he'd be able to swimmy away from da traps."

Everyone chortled apart from Hugo.

"By da by," Dizzy continued. "This 'ere mudlarkin' malarkey ain't for evers; Ize for one plan to go to sea just as soon as Ize find a captain who'll 'ave me; but it keeps us fed for nows."

*****

Hugo's first day in the mud started at sunrise. It started in filth, and it advanced in excrement.

Hugo took particular care to tiptoe around the pools of raw sewage which washed up against the banks of the River Thames. Dizzy skipped right through them.

Hugo almost screamed when he saw a dead cat, half rotten, and infested with flies. Dizzy just laughed, picked it up, and threw it aside.

"Mr Ah Crickets," she sang. "Now wha' are youse like? Cat got your tongue 'as he?"

She laughed to herself as she skipped ahead.

Hugo gave chase, like an apprentice following his master.

It was in this fashion, knee-deep in mud, that Dizzy and Hugo filled their bags with scraps of iron, canvas and fat. Whenever a bargeman dropped a lump of coal, Hugo was quick to grab it. He scurried through the mud to collect the rope and copper which fell from boats. And, when the tide came in, he filled a basket with the wood chips which washed ashore.

By the end of the day, his legs had been cut to ribbons, his body had browned, and his arms felt hollow:

"What now?"

"Now wees go to work."

"Work? I thought we'd been working all day."

"All day? The day's still young, Mr Ah Cricketty. Dearie me, youse really is as green as da spring grass. My oh blimey my! Come on chuckaboo, we needs to be gettin' on our rounds."

They walked to Limehouse, where they sold all the rivets and washers they had scavenged. The marine dealers in that part of town were always keen to buy such things. Then they knocked on doors, selling coal and wood chips to any family who needed fuel.

By the time they were done, the sky was full of stars and their pockets were full of pennies. They bought themselves some bread, and retired for a night full of songs and sandwiches.

*****

They were the best of times. They were the worst of times.

Mud-filled days bled into song-filled nights.

Hugo did not have toys and had little time for games. He did, however, collect things he could never keep; snowflakes, which melted; conkers, which rotted; dormice, which escaped; and frogs, which leapt away.

Hugo and his friends survived. Their earnings were meagre, but they could usually afford to eat, and what they lacked in income they made up for in independence; they had each other, and they did far better than the elderly mudlarks, who were unable to keep up with their pace.

In the winter, there were barely ten mudlarks on their stretch. Without much competition, times were good. In the summer, however, they were joined by another fifteen souls. Life got tough.

Most of the other mudlarks were the children of coal whippers; robust Irishmen who earned money for lugging coal onto the vessels moored in Newlands Quay. Hugo envied their clothes. Their trousers were patched, whilst his were full of holes. They had shirts with collars, caps with peaks, and real jumpers. Hugo had to insulate his clothes with old newspaper.

Such was Hugo's life.

Whilst he was slow to speak, he was quick to observe things such as these. He watched the labourers as if they were actors on a stage; loading and unloading vessels; their muscles bulging, their backs stooped, and their brows drenched with sludge. He watched lumpers, porters, heavers, riggers, packers and pressers; men with the strength and endurance of an ox, but less in the way of an education. And he watched the thieves; the dredgermen who pilfered coal, the smugglers who dodged import duties, the river pirates who snuck out at night, and the lighter-men who guided ships off course in order to rob them.

Hugo learnt from all those scallies, but he did not put his lessons into practise. For as long as he had the means to survive, he saw no need to steal himself.

*****

No-one wants to be a bad person, but not everyone has the opportunity to be good.

So it was with Hugo. He had gone eight days without eating, and Proverbs Chapter Six was ringing in his ears:

"People do not despise a thief if he steals to satisfy his hunger when he is starving."

'Would it be so bad?' he asked himself. *'Really? I'm just a wretched little mudlark after all; a fire-starter who murdered his family. Would becoming a thief really make me any worse than I already am? Could I truly expect to amount to anything better?'*

Hugo was famished. He could feel his muscles disintegrate and his heartbeat jitter. A lack of vitamins was turning his skin a pale shade of yellow; leaving him short of breath and lethargic. He felt compelled to act whilst he still had the strength...

*****

During the year in which Hugo had been a mudlark, he had noticed a group of shipbuilders who took material, such as fabric or cord, at the end of each shift. Their foreman never stopped them.

When Hugo investigated, he discovered that those men had not been paid in months. They had been granted permission to take those items as interest on the wages they were owed.

Curious, Hugo kept watch, keen to see what they would take. He saw a carpenter named Honest Jim, who only ever took the smallest items; a bit of cloth or wood, never anything more. And he saw a joiner called Crafty Chris, who took whatever he could. Hugo saw him take benches, troves, ladders, and a sail from a dingy.

Hugo spied on those ship builders, imagining what they might do with the items they took. It was by such spying that he finally saw them get paid. Only they were not paid with coins. Pennies, shillings and pounds, which contained precious metals such as silver and gold, had been in short supply for as long as anyone could remember. So, to tide them over, those ship builders were paid with branded nails. Hugo considered this bizarre, until it was explained to him that the local establishments accepted those nails in lieu of real coins. They knew they would be repaid just as soon as the shipyard had the cash.

It was with this knowledge that Hugo embarked Honest Jim's boat. With a broom in one hand and a cloth in the other, he offered to sweep the deck, as he often did when times were tough.

The foreman, as always, gave him short shrift:

"I ain't got two coins to rub together me-self. How d'ya think I'm gonna pay a cadger like you?"

The foreman turned his back in a gesture of mock offence. And Hugo, seizing the opportunity, grabbed a handful of nails from his desk.

"You're a mean old one," he shouted as he disembarked. "A right old bad 'un!"

Hugo had acted without thinking, which was probably for the best. If he had thought about it, he might have stopped himself, and he might have starved.

As it was, he headed straight for Brown's Bakery, where he exchanged his nails for three loaves of bread. Mrs Brown looked at him with a judgmental frown which verged on a guilty sentence, but she knew his nails were as good as coins, and so thought better than to ask any questions.

Hugo and his friends ate together that night.

"Youse has paid us back for them eels, youse has," Dizzy told him. "Ize knews youse would. Ize saids so. Oh yes, Mr Ah Cricketty, as sure as houses Ize did!"

*****

Once he had started, Hugo could not stop. He stole every time he went for three days without eating.

He began on the docks, where he climbed aboard boats and grabbed anything he could; wool, sugar and cotton from the colonies; headfasts, wires and chains from the boats themselves. Sometimes he sold wood chips, accepting stolen rope as payment. At other times, he simply stuffed that rope up his shirt.

Wracked with guilt, Hugo felt even more wretched than before. He called himself a *'Fire Starter'*, *'Gutter Rat'* and *'Thief'*. He whispered the word "Sorry" whenever he stole.

Hugo was confused. He drew a fuzzy line between theft and graft; never entirely sure where one ended and the other began:

'Am I not stealing when I find things in the mud? Am I not working when I'm stealing? Both put food in my belly. Is that not the most important thing?'

Hugo could not be sure. What was certain was this: Hugo's theft spread from riverbank to town, and from town to townhouse.

Sallying forth in search of food, he dived into the crowds at public executions, knocked property from people's hands, picked it up, and then disappeared into the heart of the hullabaloo.

He jumped over the brick walls which surrounded the gardens in Kensal Green, Camden Town, and Kensington, before stealing the laundry which had been hung out to dry.

What he could eat, he ate; what he could not eat, he sold to a pawnbroker; and what he could not sell to a pawnbroker, he sold on the street.

*****

Once, whilst stealing laundry from a Camden townhouse, Hugo saw a child who reminded him of himself. As if peering into a sorcerer's mirror, he felt he was seeing a life which might have been his.

That child was sitting on a windowsill, alone, with a book in his hand; abandoned by the rest of his family, who could be seen through a different window.

He seemed lonely.

Hugo felt his loneliness.

His blood turned to ice and his feet turned to run.

*****

In certain societies, both in Europe and the Middle East, it is the culture not to harm anyone with whom a person has shared bread or salt.

At times, this mundane custom can lead to scenarios which verge on the absurd.

This was the case with an Arab house robber who, having filled his bags with bounty, stuck his finger in a jar to see if it contained sugar. On tasting it, he realised it was salt. Having shared the homeowner's salt, he felt duty bound to return every item he had stolen.

Like that robber, it would be wrong to consider Hugo amoral; he had an ethical code of his own. Hugo only stole when he had gone for three days without food. He never stole from the poor, elderly or homeless; from other mudlarks, beggars or thieves.

But of all of Hugo's rules, he was most loyal to one: The Eleventh Commandment: "Though shall not get caught".

Getting caught was a private matter in Georgian London.

Victims and onlookers were expected to capture thieves and pass them on to a "Constable"; a volunteer who escorted them to a "Justice of the Peace"; a man who prosecuted them if their victims could prove their guilt.

In addition, watchmen roamed the streets at night; searching for fires and petty crimes. It was for this reason that Hugo only ever stole whilst hidden by clear daylight.

Such a tactic worked. In fact, Hugo only came close to being caught once during his three years of thieving.

Seen slipping a screw into his pocket, a deckhand sounded the Hue and Cry:

"Stop! Thief! Stop the thief!"

Everyone turned.

A ship squealed.

Another ship covered the dock in steam.

Hugo fled; his feat rapping an allegro beat on the deck, *tap-a-tap-tap*, as his hands sliced open the air.

Four men gave chase, each of whom was larger than the last, and each of whom was more determined. The first was the son of an overweight mother, the second owned a three-legged cat, and the third was missing two toes.

The fourth, who wore an eye patch, reached out to grab Hugo.

Hugo dived into the Thames.

Splashing like a river rat, he crashed into a locket, thrown overboard by a shunted lover; a frazzled sack, which had once contained tea; a message in a bottle; a complete set of cow's teeth; and an Anglo-Saxon spearhead, which had not been touched for millennia.

His final pursuer jumped into the river, with his eyes closed and his fingers pinching his nose. He too flapped through the mud. Silt slithered inside the deepest recesses of his crotch, sludge weighed heavy against his thighs, and miasmic slime seemed to burn his skin alive.

The sporadic, muffled light began to recede; the river darkened and the water cooled.

For a moment, it seemed as though Hugo would be caught.

As his pursuer's fingers skimmed his foot, Hugo's heart beat with such ferocity it created ripples in the mud, which encouraged a frog to leap aside and a dragonfly to awake from its slumber. Hugo's face turned a fiery shade of red, and his hands lost all their colour.

That moment did not last for long.

After years of mudlarking, Hugo had grown accustomed to the ways of the mud; able to flow with its rhythm and bend to its needs. He accelerated away from his pursuer, who panted so much that purple phlegm oozed out of his mouth.

"Sorry," Hugo whispered as he disappeared from sight; hidden by flotsam and jetsam, barges and boats.

"Sorry," he whispered as he returned home.

"Sorry," he whispered as he slept.

"Sorry. Sorry. Sorry."

GIVING CREDIT WHERE IT'S DUE

"Financial terms became indistinguishable from moral ones."
DAVID GRAEBER

As Uncle Raymondo shrank, Archibald grew into the space he vacated, learning more about their shop each year. No longer an infant, more interested in figurines than financial figures, he discovered how they sourced supplies.

Raymondo introduced Archibald to their suppliers whenever he visited the docks. Together, they picked up rice from India, whisky from Scotland, tobacco from the Caribbean, and items from all across England.

Archibald also accompanied his uncle when he sourced items from local producers; stocking up on Mrs Harding's honey, Ms Hulme's apple pies, and Miss Herbert's shoelaces.

Relations between these people were cordial; Raymondo seldom paid the other villagers, and they seldom paid him when they took items from his shop.

Like at the docks, coins were in short supply in Lambeth Marsh; they appeared from time to time, but they were not used on a daily basis. Instead, people ran up debts. If, come harvest, one party still owed another, those debts were repaid. Most of the time, however, such formalities were not required.

It was as Raymondo often put it:

"Offering credit and taking on debts is a social duty. It keeps us all united."

It was a philosophy he both preached and practised.

Raymondo allowed Lambeth Marsh's market gardeners to take items on credit. He recorded what they had taken, but only took payment, either in produce or cash, once the harvest had been reaped.

Such arrangements, which had been the norm for centuries, also worked in reverse. Griggs, who was a part-time thatcher as well as a market gardener, repaired Raymondo's roof, and then took items from Raymondo's shop when the need arose. Dicky, who was a part-time bricklayer, fixed Raymondo's walls on a similar basis. The part-time barber, John Day, cut the family's hair. Ted the cobbler fixed their shoes.

Even The Three Horseshoes had a tab in Raymondo's name.

Raymondo was either a creditor or a debtor to everyone in his village, and that was just the way he liked it. His debts and credits compelled his kinsfolk to maintain good relations. In fact, had a villager tried to pay with coins, Raymondo would have probably been offended.

"What have I done to upset you?" he might have asked. "Why do you wish to sever the ties which unite us?"

Only servants, beggars, harlots, thieves, fortune-tellers, minstrels, and women of ill repute were deemed unworthy of credit. But such characters were scarce in Lambeth Marsh.

Strangers also had to pay with coins and, as the botanical gardens grew in popularity, those people did begin to visit the shop. If Raymondo was unable to give them change, he issued an IOU which they could redeem at a later date. Those notes were usually spent at The Three Horseshoes, as if they were coins, before passing from hand to hand, and ending up back at Raymondo's shop.

Raymondo used coins to pay his taxes and donate to the church. But he was happy to accept branded nails as payment from the dockers, since he could use them to buy supplies at the docks, and he was happy to set up tabs for the migrant workers who were arriving in Lambeth Marsh to build an ironworks.

This was the cause of the only argument Raymondo and Ruthie ever had.

"Who are they?" Ruthie complained. "What are they doing here with their whatnots and their thingies? No, we shouldn't give them credit. They can't *all* be trusted."

"We must!" Raymondo protested. "We must embrace them, and help them to integrate, just like the villagers helped my grandfather when he first moved here."

"Your grandfather was just one man. A swarm of people are marching on Lambeth Marsh right now. It's an invasion! Some of them are bound to bad 'uns, it stands to reason."

Archibald shared his aunt's opinion; he did not like the new migrants, who teased him every day; but Raymondo was insistent:

"No! This is how my father ran things, it's how his father ran things, and so long as I live it'll be how I run things. This dog is too old to learn new tricks. We welcome people here, be there one of them or one thousand, and that's that! I'll not have a woman tell me what to do. The shame!"

Ruthie fainted.

Raising her hand to her forehead, her knees buckled, her legs swayed, and her body collapsed, limp limbed, into their only fireplace. Their only pile of cinders puffed up into the air. Their only poker toppled over.

'Clang!'

Archibald gasped.

Raymondo helped Ruthie to her feet and gave her a hug which lasted for hours.

*****

Credit relations were based on trust, that trust was maintained by goodwill and, when it came to generating goodwill, Raymondo had his very own signature move.

Each year, on the seventeenth of January, Raymondo and Ruthie marched around the village, taking long steps with straight legs, ringing a bell, and shouting, "Wassail! Wassail! Wassail!"

It was a strange custom, dating from pagan times, which Raymondo's grandfather brought with him when he moved from Cornwall; dragged to Lambeth Marsh by the incessant pounding of his lovesick heart, and determined to marry Raymondo's grandmother.

"Waes hael", in Old English, simply meant "Be well". So, when Uncle Raymondo shouted "Wassail", he was wishing good health to his brethren. And, when those villagers replied, "Drinc hael", meaning "Drink and be healthy", Uncle Raymondo was quick to oblige. He went from door to door, filling villagers' tankards with the spiced ale his family had brewed.

Archibald was keen to help; skipping from between houses, pouring drinks, and leading the songs which erupted as soon as the villagers gathered on the common.

So it was that wassailing passed down from Raymondo to Archibald, just as it had passed down to Raymondo. And, so it was, that Archibald's family endeared itself to the community; winning the trust it needed to survive.

*****

Archibald's family were not the only ones who endeared themselves in a unique way.

Ms Hulme led the festivities each Shrove Tuesday. Ahead of the Lent fast, she gathered all the sugar, meat and dairy products in the village, before cooking them in a giant pan. "Pancake Day", as it was known, became a regular event. Aproned housewives held cooking contests on the common, men downed ale, and children raced around with painted faces.

At other times, villagers arranged community events together. They hosted a travelling circus each June, and put on boxing matches twice a year. Puppet shows always drew the crowds, as did the annual village fair.

Of all such activities, however, it was Morris dancing which titillated Archibald the most.

Archibald loved to dress up in a skimpy white suit he borrowed from a neighbour; tying bells to his knees and handkerchiefs to his wrists. He loved bounding around the maypole with gay abandon. A shiver ran down his spine whenever he brushed up against another dancer, and his heart jumped whenever he was grabbed by the hand. He was never as happy as whilst in the midst of a sidestep or a forward lunge, a galley or a do-si-do.

Ruthie responded in three ways whenever she saw Archibald dance.

She muttered to herself: "Oh Archie, what are you like?"

Then she called out: "You show 'em my love!"

Then, when it was over, she told Archibald: "I love you my boy. You light up my life."

Their routine did not change until more migrants moved to the village.

"I luuurv you," they mocked. "Lover boy! Lover boy!"

Then: "Go dancer boy, you sissy."

Then: "Real men don't dance, they fight!"

If she was near, Ruthie would give Archibald a hug:

"Don't worry about them, my love, they're all mouth and no trousers."

At first, her words were enough to appease Archibald. In time, however, his bullies' jibes began to chafe. They were the last thing he heard when he went to sleep, and the first thing he heard when he awoke.

Archibald tried to make amends. He repressed his personality. He stopped dancing, binned his Morris dancer's costume, and suppressed his little outbursts of joy de vivre. But even this was not enough to placate his bullies. Their jibes continued.

TALLY HO

"Money is a social convention; it has no intrinsic value which comes before its use. Instead, its value is created by its constant exchange and use."
JENS WEIDMANN

Sadie barely acknowledged Mayer's existence.

"Well," she explained to Mrs Winterbottom. "Children should be seen but not heard."

Sadie saw her adopted son on a regular basis. But, if she did hear him, she did not react in a way which showed it.

Relations with Abe were somewhat different. Mayer's adopted father was seldom seen; he spent most of his time working, fox hunting and playing polo. But, when he was seen, he was most certainly heard.

Abe was a loud man. Even his clothes were loud. He owned over a thousand yellow waistcoats, each a shade brighter than the last; he tucked his breeches inside knee-high socks, which were so white they could blind a man; and his dandyish blazers were the talk of the town.

Georgian fashion was moving towards the mundane; most men were dressing in drab shades of grey. Abe, quite clearly, had not received the memo.

But it was his voice, more than his attire, which truly screamed. Abe's words were full bodied, his speech projected over everyone in his vicinity, and his laugh rumbled on like volcanic thunder.

The rare occasions he spent with Mayer were deafening. But Mayer cherished those moments, which made him feel like he had a father. Even though Abe called him "May", a name he despised, Mayer appreciated the affection with which Abe spoke. He appreciated Abe's words of fatherly wisdom, and the boiled sweets which Abe passed his way.

So Mayer's heart pounded when Abe placed his hand on his shoulder and led him outside.

It was a crisp winter's morning. The paths were coated with a light dusting of snow and an even lighter dusting of frozen leaves. The black railings which surrounded Camden's squares, and the black lamps which lined its streets, made that place feel like a black and white wonderland.

Abe spoke in a voice which was so loud it encouraged a hundred birds to flee:

"Today, my son, you become a man."

"A man?"

"A man! I'm giving you the greatest gift anyone can give."

"A gazillion pounds?"

"No. An opportunity! An opportunity to make something of yourself.

"May, my other boys have received expensive educations. They'll be successful, but they'll never be satisfied. They'll always want more, because they'll always be plagued by doubt, asking themselves, 'Did I really earn this?'

"Well, May, you'll never have that problem. There'll be no handouts for you, no charity; your success will be earned by your own sweat and tears. And I'll tell you this: There's nothing more satisfying than knowing you're a self-made man. Just look at me; I'm living proof! I tell you, it's the best feeling in the world. You'll never have the morbs again!"

Mayer was unsure if he was being helped or insulted.

He trudged on through the snow.

Together, Abe and Mayer formed a single silhouette; two dimensional; trapped in timelessness and united by their differences.

They stepped up into a bakery, where Abe embraced the head baker and then shouted at Mayer:

"Zebedee here is one of my oldest friends. Why, I do believe I was about your age when I first met him. He was as red-faced then as he is now!"

Both men chuckled. Abe chuckled so loudly it caused an elderly lady to drop her bags.

Mayer remained silent, which allowed him to observe two things about Zebedee. The first was his chest: Zebedee's belly was as soft as a brioche roll, his breasts protruded like cottage loaves, and his torso was so large it made his arms look like baguettes, even though they were rather sturdy. Zebedee seemed to be more bread than man.

The second thing Mayer noticed was just how red Zebedee was. It would be easy to compare his face to the colour of an overcooked lobster, but that would not do it justice. Zebedee's face was not just bright, it was fluorescent. His hands were not just florid, they were aflame. The rest of his body, however, was covered by a white uniform, which made him look like a barber's pole.

As though he could tell what Mayer was thinking, Abe was quick to continue:

"Zebedee is a good man. If you do as he says he'll help you to prosper, just as he helped me when I started out. But, at the end of the day, it's up to you. If you want to succeed in life, you need two things: Hard work and hard work. There's no such thing as a free lunch.

"Take this opportunity, May. Grab it by the balls!"

Zebedee nodded.

Abe left.

Mayer began his apprenticeship.

*****

Zebedee's bakery was a majestic mix of mechanistic furnaces and dust clouds; all brassy, black and grey. Every inch of space was packed full with shelves of bread, tables of dough, lines of customers, and throngs of underpaid bakers.

"It's the only way," Zebedee insisted. "Yes, yes, yes, yes, yes. All and sundry are opening bakeries these days. All and sunny sundry; driving prices down and whatnot. It's war! We need to keep our costy costs down or we'll go out of business. Plonk. Ca-putty-put!"

Zebedee's bakers often worked eighteen-hour shifts, exposed to heat which left them exhausted and flour which irritated their lungs. Heart diseases and apoplectic seizures were not uncommon.

But Mayer was not a baker. Thanks to Abe's relationship with Zebedee, he had been given a position as a baker's man, much to the chagrin of his more experienced colleagues. It was Mayer's role to deliver bread to Zebedee's customers and then take payment.

Mayer would have liked to accept coins but, born of another time, Zebedee was naturally suspicious of such things:

"Money? No, no, no, no, no. Coins? No, no, no, no, no. Banknotes? Bits of paper, and whatnot, with squiggles and lines, and what-have you? No, no, no, no, NO!!! Ahum. Tut. Spittle-spattle.

"Let me tell you about such wiff-waffery. You see, the problems with coins, is that they'se always being debased; coin-clipped and whatnot. You never know what you're getting; gold coins what contains fools' gold, silver what has been mixy mixed with common metals, and all sorts of coins what has been shaved smaller than they ought to be. They can't be trusted. No, no, no, no, no.

"You not hear about those coiners what was caught the other year? The Halifax lot?

"And don't get me started on those bankers. Those rascals of the royal mint! You can't trust them neither. They've got numbers dripping out their earholes! Dubious skilamalinks the lot of them. Never trust a man in a suit. Well, apart from your father, he's a good sort; a noisy bugger, but a good egg.

"Yes. Where was I? Oh, coins. No, don't accept coiny coins or notes. No, no, no, no, no. Always ask for a trusty old tally stick. Now you know where you are with a tally stick. Point of honour.

"Always ask for a tally stick, backed by real gold, or for real gold and

silver what has been verified by Mr Bronze. There's a good lad. Now go and do your jobby job. Time and tide wait for no man."
*****

The tally stick was a throwback to another time. But, then again, so was Zebedee. Neither of his age, nor of his society, he was a living, breathing reminder of the road once travelled.

That road had started, in leafy hamlets and fortified towns, many centuries before.

In such times, tally sticks were created to acknowledge the existence of a debt. Debtor and creditor would take a length of wood, cut notches to indicate the amount which was owed, and then split it into two parts which could be reconnected like pieces of a puzzle.

The creditor took one half, known as the "Stock", which was emblazoned with the debtor's seal. The creditor, therefore, was known as the "Stock holder".

The debtor took the other half, which was known as the "Ticket Stub".

Stock and stub acted as a contract; an agreement that the stub holder would repay their debt to the stock holder; either in gold, silver, goods or services.

Tally sticks were used to pay wages to workers and taxes to the state. People used them to buy and sell items, as if they were coins. They were, after all, an IOU; a pledge by whoever issued the stock to pay gold to whoever happened to possess it. The stock, therefore, had a value in gold, and so could be spent as if it was actual gold.

Tally sticks were used as the de facto currency across Europe following the fall of the Roman Empire. Their popularity began to wane in the 1400s, when paper became affordable and literacy improved. Instead of using sticks, people started to write debt contracts on paper. Like with the tally, those contracts were ripped in half, which created credit notes; the forbears of the modern banknote.

But the tally stick's decline was slow. Even in the early 1800s, they were still used by most baker's men. Mayer was going to have to become accustomed to them, whether he liked it or not...
*****

Mayer kept Zebedee's tallies on a string, which he attached to his belt.

Made from short lengths of hazel or willow, a standardised system of crosses and Vs were cut from their sides to signify different amounts. They were backed up by legislation to prevent fraud.

Mayer loaded his cart with bread and went on his rounds. Whenever he made a delivery, he cut a notch in his customer's stub, and an equivalent notch in his corresponding stock. Normally, customers settled their debts once their tally was filled with notches; paying Mr Bronze, Zebedee's jeweller, who verified their silver and gold. Some customers, however, settled their debts in other ways.

Davey Boy, who had worked in the bakery since before anyone could remember, took Mr Smith's tally as part of his pay. Mr Smith was Davey Boy's landlord, and accepted those tallies as part payment of Davey Boy's rent. Zebedee used Mr Bloodworth's tally to buy vegetables at that man's greengrocery, and Mr Godwin's tally to buy supplies at that man's shop.

Mayer came to know these men. Just as Abe before him, he took advantage of his circumstances to establish a network of acquaintances. And, just like Abe, he did everything he could to win their trust.

He started by looking into the person's eyes. This was crucial for three reasons: Firstly, it showed assurance; secondly, it showed humanity; and thirdly, it showed stature. Most baker's men looked down at their feet; a sure sign of inferiority. In making eye contact, Mayer refused to be bowed. It was as if he was saying that he, one day, would be the equal of the people he served. And that, in turn, earned him their respect.

Whilst making eye contact, Mayer shook his customer's hand. His was a firm grip, but not a powerful one; protective but not aggressive. He shook hands in an enthusiastic manner, which made the other person feel that Mayer was genuinely excited to see them.

Then came the pièce de résistance: Mayer's smile.

If Mayer's handshake made his acquaintances feel warm, his smile made them feel positively ablaze. Mayer's smile was broad and expressive, which made it seem spontaneous and therefore genuine, even though it was just part of his act. Mayer had spent hours perfecting that smile, standing in front of his mirror; making his cheeks stretch outwards, his eyebrows jut upwards, and his head nudge forwards. It was a tough ask, he had looked rather clownish at first, but his hard work eventually bore fruit. His smile had a powerful effect on everyone he met.

Then the small talk began.

Mayer always asked the other person how they were feeling. If this did not get them talking, he would speak about the weather, or rekindle a previous conversation:

"How was the operation?"

"Did your nephew pass his exam?"

"Have the prices of potatoes started to fall?"

Mayer did not care about such things, but his customers did, and the fact that Mayer showed an interest won him their respect. He was a good listener, who encouraged his acquaintances to speak about themselves, and who reacted in a way which made them feel important; nodding, raising his eyebrows, and asking further questions. He looked as though he was hanging on their every word.

In this manner, Mayer was taken into the confidence of almost everyone he met; all the merchants, magistrates and middle men; doctors, dealers and assorted do littles. Some of these characters shall grace our tale. In time, we shall come to meet the likes of Bear the barber, Big Bob the porter, and Randel the roguish shoeshine. But of all the acquaintances Mayer made, two alone were his favourites. It was Mr Orwell and Mr Bronze who would have the biggest effect on his life...

*****

Mr Orwell, who was shrunken but not shrivelled, possessed the bittersweet aromas of pipe smoke and old age. He was a retired teacher. In his mind, he still was a teacher; one who engaged in Socratic Dialogue to encourage his students to think for themselves.

"How much bread would you like, Mr Orwell?" Mayer asked when they met.

"How much do you think I'd like?"

"Hmm. I don't know."

"Would you be so kind as to think about it?"

"Okay."

"And?"

"I still don't know."

"Can you look around?"

Mayer looked around.

"What do you see?"

"A table, Mr Orwell. A chair. A bed. A plate."

"What's the common theme?"

"There's one of everything."

"And what does this tell you?"

"That you'd like one loaf of bread."

Mayer handed Mr Orwell a small bloomer. A part of him was perturbed by the peculiar nature of that man's discourse. A part of him loved that very same eccentricity.

The next day, Mayer visited Mr Orwell again. He made eye contact, shook hands, and smiled his hard-earned smile. Then he tried to engage in small talk:

"How are you today, Mr Orwell?"

"How do I look?"

"Tired."

"Why do I look tired?"

"Because your eyes are dark."

"And what causes dark eyes?"

"Staying up late."

"Now why would I stay up late?"

"I don't know."

"Would you care to look around?"

Mayer looked around.

"What do you see?"

"One of everything."

"One of most things. And lots of what?"

"Lots of books."

"How many books?"

"Hundreds."

"Thousands?"

"Yes."

"And?"

"And, Mr Orwell?"

"Why do I have bags under my eyes?"

"Because you stayed up late to read?"

"So, how am I?"

"One part fatigued and one part informed. Happy but tired."

"By Jove, I think he's got it! Well done that man! Now, let's move on to the important business of the day. Tell me, do you like reading?"

"Yes, Mr Orwell, more than anything in the world."

"Well then, would you care to borrow a book?"

Mayer smiled, and this time his smile was genuine.

Books had been a refuge for Mayer ever since he had learnt to read. For him, novels offered a portal into a never-never land into which he could escape whenever he felt abandoned. And, living with a family that barely acknowledged his existence, this was an all too regular occurrence. Mayer spent countless hours reading; sitting on a windowsill which overlooked a garden full of laundry. He imagined that the characters in those books were people he knew in real life; picturing Sadie as a wicked witch and Abe as a Roman politician. By the time he turned ten, he had read every book in Buckingham Towers, without discrimination; incapable of telling good from bad or tasteful from tawdry. By the time he turned twelve, he had read those books so many times that he was able to recite whole sections from memory, much to the annoyance of the servants who were forced to listen. So the chance to borrow books from Mr Orwell felt like a godsend.

"Thank-you," he said, whilst running his finger along a row of leather-bound editions. "Can I borrow this one?"

"Does night follow day?"

"Yes, Mr Orwell."

"Well?"

Mayer nodded, took that book, read it in a single sitting, returned the next day, and left with another book.

So it continued.

Mr Orwell was the best teacher Mayer ever had.

Mayer was the only friend old Mr Orwell had left.

*****

Mayer was also fond of Mr Bronze; the one goldsmith who Zebedee trusted to verify his customers' coins. Mayer delivered Mr Bronze three loaves of bread each day. He waited in line, whilst his eyes watered with greed; mesmerized by Egyptian jade, Australian opal, medieval relics, lapis lazuli shaped like eggs, diamonds as big as plums, and an assortment of golden trinkets which glowed so much they haloed Mr Bronze's customers.

But it was not Mr Bronze's shop which warmed Mayer's heart. It was his personality.

Mr Bronze had an aura which made you want to believe every word he said. Everything about him seemed relaxed; his chest was always open and his arms always hung by his side. He was never flustered; he was known to be happy but never ebullient, sad but never distraught. His emotions showed his humanity, but they never overwhelmed him.

Then there was his schedule. You could set your watch by it. Mr Bronze ate the same breakfast at twenty-three minutes past six each morning; two slices of toast, one with marmalade and one with honey. He shaved, with the grain, from right to left, at thirty-one minutes past the hour. He dressed seven minutes later; always wearing a pressed shirt and a bronze bow tie. He kissed his wife on the same spot, just above the cheekbone, and left home at exactly six minutes to seven. He always opened his shop at seven o'clock; never a second earlier, and never a second late.

Mayer left his tallies with Mr Bronze, so Zebedee's customers could pay him directly. Mr Bronze verified their silver and gold, before locking it in his safe; a sturdy old colossus which had survived three attempted robberies without sustaining so much as a scratch.

Whenever Zebedee bought flour from Abe, rather than pay Abe directly, he got Mr Bronze to move the requisite amount of gold from his pouch into Abe's.

The fact that Abe also had a sack of gold in that sturdy vault, may explain why Mayer warmed to Mr Bronze. But there was more to it than that. Something beyond reason. Mayer had no idea why he liked Mr Bronze so much, it was simply so.

*****

These people added colour to Mayer's days. But his life, in general, chugged on with monotonous blandness. Mayer was unfulfilled.

Of slight frame, he was not built for physical labour. Whilst his role was less demanding than that of a baker, it still required Mayer to walk for several miles each day, come hell or high water, pulling a cart full of bread. He felt like a mule. His heels blistered and his soles turned to stone.

Having grown up surrounded by the finer things in life, Mayer considered himself to be above such travails. His education had encouraged him to dream. His expectations had soared.

Still, he found solace in the rise of his adopted father. Abe had once toiled in his father's fields, in much the same manner that Mayer had been forced to toil. Abe had taken his opportunities and attained a lofty position. Mayer was convinced that he would do the same.

CRIME AND PUNISHMENT

"Man grows used to everything, the scoundrel!"
FYODOR DOSTOYEVSKY

Hugo was seen stealing on two more occasions.

The second time, like the first, he was seen in the act. Nimble footed, with a turn of pace and a penchant for a shimmy, he was able to escape his pursuers. But, on turning into an alley, he was not able to escape the arms of a suited man.

"My, my," that man chuckled in a melodious voice. "Well, well. What do we have here? A cured sausage I see, and I dare say you stole it, judging by the speed of your feet."

"I did not!" Hugo protested in a voice which betrayed him.

"Now, now. It does not behove one to tell porky pies."

Hugo tried to squirm free.

The suited man continued:

"You have two options, and escape doesn't appear to be one of them. Now the first option is to go to the magistrate, who is likely to chop your hand off. The second is to attend the Ragged School."

Hugo was baffled:

"School sir? What sort of a punishment is that?"

The suited man chuckled:

"Punishment? No, no. It's an opportunity!"

"Sorry."

"So?"

Hugo nodded.

The suited man led Hugo on, gripping his hand firmly enough to ensure he did not flee, yet gently enough to give the impression of affection. Together, they marched through Whitechapel, penned in by stalls which were stuffed full with a cacophony of brushes, chimney ornaments, children's toys, common jewellery, Sheffield cutlery and plated goods.

After being buffeted one way and bumped the other, they emerged in a small cobbler's workshop which smelled of baked potatoes. The counter was covered in tools. The floor was covered with children.

"I've got another one for you, John Pounds," the suited man announced.

"You're the goose which keeps on laying," Pounds replied. "A regular production line!"

The suited man smiled, ruffled Hugo's hair and left.

Hugo waited, bored and impatient, whilst the other pupils read the bible, copied lines from the bible, and arranged their bibles in piles. He considered it a small price to pay to save his hand.

When the lesson finished, Mrs Pounds entered and offered Hugo a baked potato. Perplexed, he took the biggest one, before sharing his sausage with the other children.

Surprising even himself, Hugo returned a week later. Receiving a meal in return for sitting through a boring lesson seemed like good business to him.

So began Hugo's education. He did not learn much, but it was a start, and it meant that he never had to steal on a Sunday.

*****

The third time Hugo was seen stealing, he was not so lucky.

Unlike the previous two occasions, he was not caught in the act. There was barely any act at all. Hugo had simply found a pocket watch on the floor, following a public execution, and picked it up.

Such were the crowds at those events, bodies jostled against bodies, and items often fell to the ground. When people dispersed, they left behind them a cornucopia of rubbish and rich pickings. Hugo was always eager to search for hidden treasure amongst the debris.

But a person simply cannot eat a pocket watch, and so Hugo went to visit Mr Loansmith, his regular pawnbroker.

On opening the door, the pocket watch clasped firmly between his fingers, Hugo felt a hand on his shoulder. Before he knew it, he had been spun around and hauled back out onto the street.

The pawnshop's door creaked on its hinges; sullen and sour. Impatient carriages roared by, chip paper blew against Hugo's shins, and a long shadow engulfed him. Then he heard a voice:

"Well, what do we 'ave 'ere then?"

"Nothing sir."

"Don't look like nothing. It looks very much like a pocket watch, if I'm not mistook."

"Well, yes sir. Sorry sir."

The shadowy man tapped his copy of the London Times:

"Now it says 'ere that a pocket watch just like that was stolen at yesterday's execution. Said watch belonged to a certain Mr Toodlepip. Now if your watch is the item in question, it'll 'ave Mr Toodlepip's name engraved inside. What d'ya say you open it and see?"

Hugo opened the watch.

"Ah! Just as I'd done thought it. You can see 'is name right there, clear as day. Mister Jay Kay Toodlepip. Oh yes. Which means you must be the culprit what thieved it."

"No, I found it, honest to God. I didn't nick it sir. I swear!"

The man consolidated his grip on Hugo's shoulder:

"Found it, you say? Didn't nick it?"

"Yes sir. Sorry sir. I picked it up off the floor. It was there amongst the rubbish."

"Picked it up off the floor, did you? Just lying there, was it? A common excuse if ever I 'eard one. There ain't no magistrate in the land who ain't 'eard that one before. And there ain't no magistrate in the land who'd give it credence neither. Do you think we was born yesterday?"

"No sir."

"Well then, don't be trying to 'uggle-fuggle us."

"But it's the truth."

"The truth is Mr Toodlepip 'ad 'is watch stolen and you've been caught red 'anded. Don't look good, now does it?"

Hugo bowed his head.

"Here's what I'm gonna to do: I'm gonna give you two options. Option one: I take you to the magistrate, who'll 'ang you and give me forty nicker as a reward."

"Hang me? I thought thieves got their hands chopped off."

"Sakes alive! What are you, a lawyer? You thought wrong. Now listen to me, option one is the 'angman's noose. They'll 'ang you for anything these days, 'cos they'se just so fond of 'angings.

"Option two is that you pay me the forty nicker yourself."

"I don't have forty pounds."

"Well, then youse'll 'ave to work for me to earn it."

"Work for you sir? What as?"

"Why, as a thief of course. That's what you are, ain't it?"

Hugo shrugged.

"So, what's it to be? Your guts for garters or my generous employ. Come on, chop chop, I ain't got all day."

Hugo was dizzy with confusion. He felt as though he was at the centre of a pantomime which had no beginning, middle nor end.

"Okay," he finally choked. "If it saves my life, I'll be your thief."

"A fine choice indeed! There's a good lad. Now what's your name?"

"Hugo sir. Who are you?"

"The name's Jonathan Wild. Wild by name, wild by nature. I be the greatest thief taker there ever was!"

*****

A "Thief Taker" was a private detective, employed by wealthy individuals to reclaim their stolen property.

In several cases, those victims chose not to prosecute the thieves who robbed them. Some did not want to be responsible for the death of a fellow being. Others, robbed in brothels and gambling dens, did not want the details to be made public.

Sometimes, however, thief takers did send thieves to court. This earned them the respect of the community, and up to forty pounds in cash. They earned rewards for returning stolen items, they earned commissions for acting as mediators between thieves and their victims, and they made money by operating their own team of thieves.

*****

Jonathan Wild was a tall, ugly man. His head was shaped like a punctured football; perfectly spherical but for a few flattened patches. His cleft lip dragged his mouth up towards his nostrils.

The son of a herb seller, he started life an honest man. In search of his fortune, he migrated to London where he fell on hard times. Imprisoned for debt, he became a prison snitch; a double timer who charged his jailors for information about his fellow inmates, and who charged those inmates for protection from their jailors. He lent out the money he earned, and charged interest on those loans, which earned him enough money to buy his freedom.

Whilst still languishing in jail, Wild was given "The liberty of the gate"; a position which permitted him to go into town each night to catch thieves. He spent a small portion of his time engaged in that activity, and a much larger portion of his time in the arms of a prostitute named Mary Milliner.

It was to Milliner that Wild returned upon his release. A low-level gangster herself, she taught Wild the tricks of her trade, and introduced him to the high rankers of the underworld.

Wild soon discarded Milliner, although not before cutting off her ear to mark her as a harlot. He did not, however, discard the lessons Milliner had taught him. He became a fence, a seller of stolen goods, and used the money he earned to bribe prison guards; getting them to release thieves into his employ.

Wild had two faces:

To society, he was as a *thief taker*. Daily newspapers portrayed him as a white knight, the "Thief Taker General", who kept thieves and degenerates at bay; returning property to its rightful owner, and sending over sixty thieves to the gallows.

To the underworld, however, Wild was a *thief maker*; a man who controlled almost every thief in the city. He protected his thieves, in return for a healthy cut of their earnings, and he got them to give testimony against any thief who refused to fall under his command.

Whenever one of his thieves riled him, Wild put a cross by their name in his little black book. If that thief riled him again, Wild added a second cross. He sold anyone who had been "Double Crossed" to the Crown for hanging. In this manner, he maintained absolute control.

*****

This, then, was the man to whom Hugo owed his life.

Or was it?

Unbeknownst to Hugo, Wild had not been working for Mr Toodlepip. There probably never was a Mr Toodlepip. It is a rather curious name.

That watch, a worthless thing, had been left amongst the rubbish by one of Wild's thieves; a youngster with the smarts of an alley-cat and the swagger of a miniature horse.

"The name's Wilkins," he said when introducing himself. "That's my one and only name: Wilkins. Or, if you prefer, Wilkins Wilkins. It serves as a first name, and it serves as a second. I don't need no other. If I had two names, someone'd only come and pinch one."

"My name is Hugo."

"Hugo who?"

"Hugo Crickets, I guess. Although I only really have one name too. You can call me Hugo Hugo if you like."

"Don't get chuffin' cocky with me, *Rob-Roy*. If Crickets be your name, I shall call you Hugo, and that'll be that."

Wilkins was indefinable. It would have been easy to assume he was Caucasian, but his skin had been discoloured by so much guilt and grime that he could have passed for a member of almost any race. His height suggested he was about thirteen years old, a little older than Hugo, but he had the tiny fingers of a six-year-old, and the dead eyes of a centurion. His attire was something else. He appeared like a gentleman who had been buried beneath the earth for many centuries. His majestic blue blazer was full of worm holes; his breeches, though crisply pressed, had faded with dust; and his pointy shoes, which he polished to the point of obsession, had been slashed from several angles and pockmarked by gravel and grit.

Wilkins never told Hugo that he had planted the lost watch. He never told Hugo that he had followed him home, slept near his barge, and turned him over to Wild the following morning. He thought such things were better left unsaid.

Wilkins did, however, introduce Hugo to his new life.

He moved Hugo to a lodging house behind Spitalfields Market, without giving him the chance to say "Goodbye" to Dizzy, Izzy or Jo. Then he led Hugo into a room which was littered with assorted beggars and thieves, naked and clothed; spread out across the floor, and spread out across each other.

There was method to the madness. Keeping his thieves together enabled Wild to manage them. It also enabled them to teach each other the tricks of their trade.

That place was a hub of sociability; evenings were spent telling tales, and nights were spent drenched in liquor. Hugo soon felt at home, although he did feel guilty for abandoning his friends.

"Wretch", he whispered to himself as he slept. "Rat". "Thief". "Killer". "Sorry".

*****

"I ain't never seen no-one so green," Wilkins told Hugo during their first day on the streets. "Corr blimey guvnor! You're telling me you just push stuff out of people's hands?"

Hugo nodded.

"And they don't notice?"

Hugo shrugged.

"Well knock me down with a feather. You ain't never gonna get me to do that. Now listen here, the first chuffin' rule of thieving is this: Don't never let the mark know they've been robbed. If they don't know it, they ain't gonna kick up a fuss. Clever, eh?"

Hugo nodded. And, like a good student, he listened keenly to what his teacher had to say.

By the end of the day, they had perfected their first routine. Hugo approached shoppers with his hands cupped, his arms outstretched, and his eyes full of tears.

"Please ma'am," he begged. "I'm ever so hungry. Please spare a ha'penny for a lump of bread."

As the mark gazed at Hugo, or tried to step around him, their mind drifted from the shopping they were holding. Wilkins walked by, lifted an item from their bag, and strolled off without breaking his stride.

Most of the time the mark was oblivious. Even on the rare occasions they did notice, Wilkins was always long gone. They never realised he was in league with Hugo.

On their first day together, Hugo and Wilkins used this tactic to steal two clocks, a china teapot and a silver necklace. The next day they stole ten items. Their haul grew by the day.

In time, they switched roles. They popped up in every district in London; in the hustle and bustle of the East End, the pomposity of Mayfair, and the craggy dens of Soho; in Dark Entry, Cat's Hole, and Pillory Lane.

When they were done, they passed their loot on to Wild, who scoured the daily papers to see if the theft had been announced. If it had, he returned the item, declared himself a hero, and claimed his reward. If it had not, he advertised it in his lost property office, where items could be reclaimed for a fee.

"If you continue like this," he rejoiced. "You'll be the greatest thieves that ever walked the land!"

*****

Hugo and Wilkins were not the greatest thieves that ever walked the land. But, as the months turned into years, they did start to branch out; creating new scams, behind Wild's back, and keeping all the money they made.

They kept things fresh.

Once, they stole a cage of brown finches from a pet shop on the Old Kent Road. Using dye and make-up, which they also stole, they made those birds look like goldfinches; with yellow feathers and tails unlike anything London had ever seen. They sold them on Regents Street for a tidy sum.

Another time, they stole a bag of brass rings embedded with fake diamonds, which they pretended to find on the street.

"A diamond ring!" Wilkins would exclaim to win people's attention. "I don't *Adam-and-Eve* it. But no jeweller would buy a precious thing like this from me. They'd take one look at me, assume I stole it, and pack me off to the clink."

Occasionally, a passer-by, keen to turn a quick profit, would offer to buy the ring. Hugo and Wilkins were only too happy to take their money.

Hugo questioned their actions each day, but Wilkins was always persuasive:

"With a face like that, you could steal broaches from old grannies in church and get away with it. That sort of angelic innocence shouldn't go to waste."

This left Hugo conflicted; having to choose between doing right by his friend and doing right by their victims; between satisfying his hunger and satisfying his soul. His emotions remained a blur.

Hugo liked that he had found something he was good at; it filled him with pride. But his guilty conscience grew by the day; he felt for his victims and judged himself harshly. He chewed his nails until there was barely anything left; he shuddered, involuntarily, several times an hour; and he muttered in a voice which only he could hear: "Swindler". "Hustler". "Crook". "Sorry. Sorry. Sorry."

*****

Hugo and Wilkins got caught.

They had been performing one of the oldest tricks in the book, the "Pig in a Poke"; showing off a healthy piglet before wooing the crowds:

"Sir, ma'am, there ain't never been a pig like this one. This ain't your average hog. This little fella can oink like a boar. He can roar, roar, roar! You can tell he's gonna grow; gonna give you pork chops, bacon and more. Well, I wouldn't be surprised if he learns how to mop your own floor! Sir, ma'am, this is the bargain of the century; it's gonna go down in folklore. 'Cos I ain't asking for a shilling, not even for eight pence, not even for six. Sir, ma'am, I'm gonna give you this piglet for four!"

Hugo and Wilkins attracted a steady flow of customers. Hugo took their payment and passed the piglet to Wilkins, who switched it for a stray cat, which he put in a sack and passed on to their mark.

They repeated this trick fourteen times before Wild found out.

"Pig in a poke!" he scolded; throwing a mug across the room. "Pig in a blimming poke! What do you think this is, the seventeen blimming 'undreds?

"You're nothing. You're worse than nothing. You're negative! You, *boys*, are set apart.

"You think this wouldn't get back to me? I 'ave eyes in the walls. Even the lampposts work for me! This is my city, you 'ear me? Even the rats know my name.

"Pig in a blimming poke. I've sent men to the gallows for less."

Wild brought his cane crashing down upon his desk.

Wilkins straightened his back and puffed chest.

Hugo wet his pants.

"Pig in a blimming poke. My, my. I ought to wop the pair of you."

Wild took his little black book from his pocket, found the correct page, and scrawled a cross next to Wilkins and Hugo's names:

"You've both been single crossed, and you know what 'appens to anyone who double crosses me!

"Pig in a blimming poke. Pig. In. A. Blimming. Poke."

*****

Hugo and Wilkins left Wild's office and took to the streets, which seemed to be filled with two types of people; drunk people and sober people. Some of the sober people were pouring water over some of the drunks, to sober them up. The drunks looked annoyed.

Hugo was too shaken to steal, but Wilkins did manage to lift a set of ivory chess pieces, a silver-plated tray, a pair of candlesticks and a snakeskin bag.

Neither spoke a word of what had happened.

Wilkins wore a brave face and an obstinate demeanour. Hugo, on the other hand, wore a look of rabbit-eyed fear. He was overcome by prophetic visions; of the hangman, cloaked in death's black cape; of himself, bowing his head; of the trapdoor opening, his body falling, the crowd cheering, jeering and leering.

A cold flush usurped him, a fever took hold, he froze, and then he burned. His stomach churned, his knees buckled, he fell to the floor and dry wretched.

"Hugo Hugo! Hugo Crickets! Get up on your feet, you wally. You look like a right chuffin' plonker."

Hugo stumbled away from his companion.

Stumbling and slipping, he fell through the doors of Saint Pancras Church; that sturdy old bastion of piety and pretension. Using the pews to drag himself forwards, but struggling to grip hold of their backs, he crashed down onto the stony tiles. He slivered on like a lizard, with his arms akimbo and his belly against the floor.

The church bells rang: '*Ding dong. Ding dong. Ding dong.*'

Hugo pulled himself onto the altar. With Jesus above him and the slaughterer's slab below, he clasped his hand together to pray.

He projectile vomited.

The Vicar shrieked:

"Oi! Get out of here you blasphemous wretch!"

Hugo fled. Running from that place, as if running from his sins, and running from his very existence; running, running, running; he ran out through the wooden doors and straight into a wooden cart.

Bread rolls flew right, loaves shot left, buns bounced and baguettes blasted up into the air. As those doughy creations filled the sky, Hugo crashed into Mayer.

Mayer felt Hugo's anguish, guilt and fear as if those emotions were his own:

"It's okay, my brother, we're going to fix this."

He embraced his long-lost friend, holding him tight, until the fine autumn rain had soaked right through their clothes.

DIVIDE AND RULE

*"Absolute power corrupts absolutely, but
absolute powerlessness does the same.
It's not the poverty, it's the inequality we
live with every day that will turn us insane."*
AKALA

Things would never be the same again.

When the ironworks opened in Lambeth Marsh, the multitudes came calling; pulled by the lure of work, and pushed off their lands by the Enclosure Acts.

For centuries, families across the nation had been living in villages just like Archibald's. As farmers, they were masters of their own smallholdings, able to produce most of the things they needed. They worked when they wanted, how they wanted, and had hundreds of holidays a year. Theirs was no utopia; adverse weather could have a devastating effect, their lifestyles were rudimentary, and a good chunk of their produce had to be paid to the lord of the manor. But those people controlled their destinies; they were free individuals and members of strong communities.

Then, thanks to four thousand acts of parliament, one sixth of the nation's land was taken from peasant smallholders and converted into large farms; "Enclosed" by hedges, and owned by a tiny number of individuals, including many of the politicians who had voted for those acts.

Common land disappeared. Millions of people had the basis of their independent livelihoods and autonomous lifestyles snatched away. Entire communities were obliterated.

Villagers were left with two stark options: They could continue farming, as wage labourers on someone else's farm, or they could leave their villages, and work as wage labourers in someone else's factory; toiling for fifteen hours a day, without the holidays which defined their culture.

Such a fate befell the McDavishes; a ginger haired, whisky swilling, log throwing, porridge guzzling, poetry reciting, kilt wearing, dry humoured, rambunctious family from Aberdeenshire. Every member of that family had beards, even the womenfolk. They all had enormous guts and stomping feet.

When the "Highland Clearances" turned huge swathes of Scotland into sheep farms and deer reserves, the McDavishes had been left with no choice but to leave home. Similar fates befell the Chapmans of Norfolk, the Reeves of the Black Country, and the Parkers of Dorset.

Other families moved to Lambeth Marsh in search of a more metropolitan life. As London grew outwards, it swallowed Archibald's village, which metamorphosed into a city suburb: "Lambeth".

Then there were families such as the Donaldsons. Hailing from the South Midlands, it was easy to spot a Donaldson, on account of the rightwards kink in their noses. Even people who had married into that family seemed to possess this peculiar facial feature.

The Donaldsons were hand-lace makers who had been forced to close their family business when factories began to produce cheap lace. They had planned to move to Australia, but had fallen in love with Lambeth, and showed no sign of moving on.

Likewise, the Rawlinsons moved from East Anglia when the wool industry collapsed, under pressure from factories in Lancashire. Families of potters, furniture makers, brewers and millers all followed in their footsteps.

Lambeth's natives became a minority fringe.

*****

Uncle Raymondo welcomed the new migrants with open arms. He loved their strange cultural quirks; their random accents and eccentric diets. He feasted on the exotic dishes they introduced; delicacies such as Lancashire hotpot, Scottish haggis and Yorkshire pudding. He appreciated their business; offering them credit as if he had known them all his life.

Archibald, on the other hand, was not so enamoured.

The migrants had no history in Lambeth; no reputations to uphold, no ties to other villagers, and no status in local society. So, whilst the older generation were busy at work, their offspring jostled for position. Like lions on the prowl, they took it upon themselves to make a show of their prowess.

All too often, Archibald was their prey.

Whilst the natives had grown to love him for his idiosyncrasies, Archibald's personality made him an easy target for newcomers. This boy with a penchant for bright colours, who skipped as often as he walked, existed outside their comfort zones. And there really is nothing which makes small-minded people as uncomfortable as other people who are ever so slightly different to them.

Archibald had been called a "Sissy" since the first migrants arrived. As new migrants joined them, the name calling grew to epic proportions. Each new migrant youth took it upon themselves to berate Archibald, as if it were a rite of passage:

"Gongoozler."

"Stamp crab."

"Bog washer."

"Snaggletooth."

"Totty one-lung."

"Double-breasted water-butt smasher!"

"Cumberworld! All you do is take up space."

"Jollocks! Bugger off and hedge-creep somewhere else."

"Gnashgab! I bet your genitals look like a throttled-prawn."

This is not to say that Archibald did not have friends, the other natives did come to his defence, but they also felt lost and alone, walking through life in a daze. The owners of the ironworks were building houses on top of their market gardens, their traditional way of life was evaporating in front of their eyes, and their futures were shrouded in uncertainty.

The natives attached locks to their doors, closed their curtains at night, forbid their infants from playing in the streets, followed an informal curfew, stopped picking up litter, and cancelled community events.

The Three Horseshoes was a refuge for those people; an ageless relic which spoke of times gone by. Its homemade ale, moonshine gin, roaring fire and shove ha'penny board had not changed in living memory. But The Three Horseshoes was a one off. When Archibald retreated from that place, he also retreated into himself.

Archibald had an outstanding ability for assimilating indignities, but even he could not stop his humiliations from taking up so much space in the vault of his personality that the rest of his character was squeezed. In his mind, he was still the same person, but in the real world he was not. He stopped wearing colourful clothes, lost the spring in his step, and stopped playing with his figurine. He did everything he could to fit in; to look normal, act normal and sound normal. But he barely spoke; he was courteous to his customers, but he was never loquacious; he engaged in small talk, but his heart was never in it. Sometimes he daydreamed. Sometimes he did not think of anything at all.

*****

Uncle Raymondo continued to shrink. His arms retreated into their sleeves, his trousers hung over his ankles, and he had to add a new hole to his belt. Only his beard seemed to grow, upwards and outwards, merging with his eyebrows and hair. His head became a giant ball of grey wool, pierced only by two tiny pupils.

He sent Archibald on a mission:

"Son, have you seen old what's his name?"

"'What's his name'?"

"You know, what d'ya call him."

"I'm afraid you're going to have to be more specific."

"Ol' doohickey! Come on, you know who I mean."

"I'm sorry to say I don't."

"Thingy! Thingamabob! Thingamajig!"

"Eh?"

"Big fella. Gut like a barrel of fish. You know, the ginger one. Always got oats in his beard. Ah, you know who I mean. The chubby chappie who's always reciting poetry."

"Oh, I suppose that could be any of the McDavishes."

"Yep, that's the one!"

"Who?"

"McDavishes. You seen him recently?"

"Not for at least a month, no."

"Strange?"

"I guess."

"You guess?"

"Oh, it's just that I was sort of enjoying the peace and quiet."

"Indeed. But McDavishes has got quite some tab; a pound and a shilling if I'm not mistook. Now what's the point in allowing someone to rack up such a debt if they never come to visit? The whole point in extending credit is to keep yourself in peoples' good books, maintain relationships and whatnot. The least he could do is pop by and say 'Hello'."

Archibald frowned.

"Son, do an old man a favour: Go and see that he's okay."

"Who?"

"McDavishes! What have I been going on about all this time?"

"Which of the McDavishes?"

"Yes, that's the one. Now be a good lad. Off you trot."

*****

Assuming Raymondo had been referring to Hamish McDavish, the patriarch of the McDavish clan, Archibald went to the ironworks where he worked.

"I'm sorry to bother you, but have you seen ol' Hamish?" he asked Donald Donaldson; a boy whose nose bent askew at an almost impossible angle.

"Sorry pipsqueak," Donaldson replied. "I can't help you there."

"I don't mean to disturb you fellas, but I was just wondering if you'd seen the McDavishes?" Archibald asked the Chapmans and Reeves, who just murmured or shrugged.

"Hey, Griggs!" Archibald cheered. "I don't suppose you've seen the McDavishes?"

"The McDavishes?" the former thatcher replied. "I'm afraid not. They ain't been seen around these parts for months. I dessay they're long gone by now."

"Gone? I'm not sure I understand."

"Ain't much to get. They'se not here. They've gone."

Unable to fathom what he was hearing, Archibald went to the McDavishes' cottage, which he soon discovered had been occupied by a new family of migrants. Archibald was bamboozled. He had heard of families moving to Lambeth, but never of a family leaving. He had heard of people building new houses, or passing them on to their children, but never of people passing them on to strangers.

In a heady state of disbelief, he asked after the McDavishes in the four pubs which had opened in Lambeth, as well as the new post office, school, bakery, butcher's shop and greengrocery.

Some people said the McDavishes had moved back to Scotland, others that they had gone to work in another factory. One person said they thought the family had emigrated, another that they had joined the merchant navy. They all spoke fondly of the McDavishes, but they did not seem to care that they had left. The McDavishes did not have a history in Lambeth, so the fact they had no future did not take anyone by surprise.

After twelve different people had spoken in a similar manner, Archibald finally accepted the truth.

"A pound and a shilling," he muttered. "We've been robbed! I just don't know what things have come to when a man can disappear without honouring his debts. Damn migrants, with their grubby coins. I reckon they should all be made to assimilate."

*****

It hit Uncle Raymondo hard:

"I don't get it. That's not how people behave in Lambeth Marsh."

Raymondo spent a whole day scratching his beard, tutting and spitting. Then he went to sleep, woke up, and continued on as if nothing had happened; convinced that the whole situation had been so bizarre it could never possibly happen again.

It happened again.

Whilst the Donaldsons gave up on their plan to emigrate, the Browns did just that; leaving without settling their tab. Then, at harvest time, the Davenports stopped frequenting Raymondo's shop. They used the new stores which had opened in Lambeth instead of repaying Raymondo.

Those stores only accepted coins. Shopkeepers and customers made one off transactions, without any obligation to meet again. It was impersonal, but it saved those shopkeepers from unpaid debts. Their shops flourished, whilst Raymondo's floundered.

This was the situation until the ironworks set up a truck system. Rather than pay their employees with coins, they paid them with tokens which could only be spent in factory-owned shops. Overnight, Raymondo lost hundreds of customers, many of whom did not repay their debts.

In order to balance the books, Ruthie had to sell the family's one table, one chair and one curtain:

"If things continue like this, my love, we'll have to sell our ceiling and floor!"

Archibald cringed.

"Oh don't you look at me like that. Whatever happens, you'll always have us; we'll always love you, my little miracle child."

*****

"Be a good lad. Go and get some what-do-you-call-thems from what's his face."

"Some 'What-do-you-call-thems'?"

"Yes, two boxes will do. And get some doohickeys, doodahs and dojiggers whilst you're at it. There's a trooper."

Archibald nodded.

He had understood that "What-do-you-call-thems" were candles, because Raymondo had nodded at the empty spot where the candles were usually kept. In the same manner, he deduced that "Doohickeys"

JOSS SHELDON | 57

were pencils and "Doodahs" were soap, all of which could be sourced at the docks.

Archibald did not know what "Dojiggers" were, but he decided not to ask, believing it would cause his uncle more pain than it was worth. Raymondo was fighting a losing battle with time; falling asleep every hour, sometimes mid-sentence, and taking up to fifteen minutes to walk to the shop.

Archibald put on his sheepskin jacket and went to meet Jim McCraw at the docks.

McCraw was an old family friend whose whisky was the stuff of legend. His blazer, whilst in the contemporary style, had a single tartan pocket, as if to pay homage to his Scottish roots. His grey mane contained a single lock of ginger hair.

"Aye Laddie," he told Archibald. "We've everythin' yoose desire, an' it'd be a pleasure tae serve ye. But oor supplies ahr askin' fur cash, an' sae we're gonna need ye tae pay up front. It's doin' ma dinger, but whit can I dae?"

Archibald nodded and turned to leave.

"Oh, an' one lest wee thingy," McCraw called out. "If ye could be a saint an' get yer ol' man tae settle his debt, that'd be gran; it'd keep an ol' mukker in hoose an' home."

This request blindsided Archibald, who had never known McCraw to request payment in such a manner. McCraw and Raymondo had always wiped the slate clean after the harvest, with a big family dinner and a night spent drinking Scotch. But Archibald did not feel he should challenge McCraw. He had been brought up to respect his elders, and so he just smiled, nodded, and returned to the shop.

When he arrived, empty handed, he gave his uncle a tender hug. Then he told him what had happened.

"I'll get the supplies tomorrow," he concluded. "I guess there'll be a way."

But Archibald's levity had little effect on his uncle.

Raymondo's fingers shook, a dry tear formed in his eye, and the remaining colour drained from his skin. His speech was lethargic:

"McCraw. My old friend McCraw? He wants to cancel my debt? To break off relations? Heaven forbid. Why has everyone forsaken me?"

Raymondo's coronary artery tightened around his heart, which succumbed without resistance. Lacking the strength to grasp his chest, his head tipped over his knees and his body tumbled forwards. He was dead before his skull hit the tiles. He shrank. Puff! And that was it. The back cover slammed shut on the book of his life.

Archibald froze.

Time froze.

When Ruthie entered and asked how long Raymondo had been in that state, Archibald could not comprehend the question.

"It's Friday the thirteenth," he replied; paralysed; unable to react as Ruthie grabbed a bottle of white spirit, glugged it down, and stabbed herself in the throat. By the time Archibald heard her last words, he was already covered in blood, and Ruthie had already collapsed on top of Raymondo.

Those words glided through the air in slow motion, before diving into Archibald's ear:

"I love you Archie. I always will."

The church bells rang: *'Ding dong. Ding dong. Ding dong.'*

Ruthie's words echoed: *'I love you. I love you. I love you.'*

Archibald fell into a set of shelves, and projectile vomited over his jacket.

*****

Archibald was traumatized, grief-stricken, inconsolable, distraught and depressed.

His loved ones had died, horrifically, in front of his very own eyes. He had seen his community disintegrate, and he had been bullied himself.

These events would have a significant effect on Archibald; causing his personality to develop in a profoundly different way from Hugo and Mayer.

He would never be the same again.

*****

Of all the emotions which gazumped Archibald back then, two affected him more than any other: Fear and guilt.

He feared for himself.

He had inherited Raymondo's debts, without inheriting the goodwill that man commanded. As a result, he knew he was just a single encounter away from being thrown into a debtors' prison.

Debtors prisons were worthy of fear. They were overcrowded places where starvation was sure to consume you if disease did not, where inmates had to work so hard they collapsed with exhaustion, and where release was little more than a passing fantasy.

With this in mind, Archibald sold his family's house and almost everything they owned. He moved into the shop; working there during the day, and sleeping on the floor at night. He settled his debts. But he remained in a state of fearful nausea; worried that prices would increase, his customers would abandon him, and he would be forced to sell the shop.

He felt guilty for Raymondo and Ruthie's deaths:

'I should've kept my conversation with McCraw a secret'.

'I should've challenged McCraw when I had the chance'.

'I should've stopped my uncle from extending credit to outsiders'.

To lose one set of parents was unfortunate, but to lose two sets felt like utter negligence.

*****

Enfeebled and isolated, Archibald stumbled through those grey mourning days.

The other villagers tried to console him, but Archibald was cold to their touch and indifferent to their words. He went through the motions, but did so without any lustre. To him, the world had lost its shine. His feet lost their shimmy and his skin lost its shimmer.

Archibald still visited The Three Horseshoes, where he socialised with the other natives. But there was less melody in the raillery, less devilment in the ale, less motion in the madness, less mystery in each impulse, less passion in each song, less lust in each dance, less warmth in each body, less hunger in each gut, less conviction in each quarrel, less sex in each embrace, less love in each handshake, less magic in each kiss, and less salt in each tear.

Less, less, less. Less of everything. Less heart, less soul, less spirit. Everything seemed watered down. Everything seemed hollow.

The only thing there seemed to be an abundance of was time. Archibald dedicated himself to killing it. He retreated into his mind, becoming so oblivious to the world that he almost tripped over a rooster, and actually tripped over a gypsy who was reading palms. His existence would have probably ended had life not been imposed on him by a constant stream of customers; by the ironing lady, the woman who smelled of pilchards, the beggars who smelled of sewers, the nuns who liked to gossip, the organ grinder who hummed in his sleep, the man who collected empty bottles, and the scally who searched through his bins. As if he had lost the ability to speak, Archibald opened his mouth when those people approached, but he seldom made a sound. His thoughts rang so loud they rendered him mute.

*****

After several months had passed, Archibald felt a sudden determination to snap out of his malaise. He took the bony fish he had bought for his dinner, gripped its tail between his nails, and flicked its skull up against the spot where his eyebrows met. He shook his head, emitted a warbled sound, opened his eyes so wide they bulged, and then slapped himself again.

He repeated this process until his fish was flat and his forehead was covered in guts.

"Aha!" he exclaimed. "I feel that could do it."

He grabbed his vomit-encrusted coat and headed for that day's executions, believing that nothing could end his own suffering quite like witnessing the suffering of a man who was even more wretched than himself.

It was in this mood of jolly morbidity that Archibald headed for Newgate Street.

That place was already jam-packed by the time Archibald arrived. Lords and ladies perched atop padded thrones on hastily erected gantries, whilst the hoi polloi squeezed into the street below; a space where attendance was free of charge and almost free of air. The first thing Archibald saw when he arrived was the asphyxiated body of a buxom spinster, which was being dragged away unconscious.

Surrounding this scrimmage, costermongers were selling just about anything which could be eaten, to just about anyone who could eat. Their rickety barrows were overflowing with ice-cold oysters and burning hot eels; pies and puddings, crumpets and cough-drops, ginger-beer and gingerbread; pea soup, battered fish, sheep's trotters, pickled whelks, baked potatoes, ice lollies, cocoa, and peppermint water.

On the other side of the road was the tall brick wall of Newgate Prison. In front of that wall was a tall brick stage, upon which the gallows stood erect. And, hanging from those gallows, was the body of Thomas White; a sixteen-year-old boy who had been found guilty of committing homosexual acts. His corpse seemed to be making faces at everyone in the crowd.

The static blur of a million rumbling conversations filled the air. The hollers and huzzas began to build. Then there was silence; a deathly hush.

Two large windows creaked open, and one shackled man stumbled through; back bent, legs unsteady, hair untamed, face unwashed and unshaved.

The crowd gasped in unison, sucking down every last drop of air. A vacuum opened above them. The floor shuddered below.

'Snap!'

A roar of thunder shattered the glassy atmosphere.

'Boo!' 'Scum!' 'Wretch!' 'Devil's spawn!' 'Die! Die! Die! Die! Die!'

Whipped up in the collective ebullience of it all, Archibald could not help but join in; booing in time with each boo, stamping in time with each stamp, hollering, howling, hooting, hissing and heckling.

The condemned man stumbled onto the lip of the stage, where he slurred his final words:

"You, you people, you are my people, yes you are. So it is. So it izzy is. Now 'ere's the thing: All I ever did. All I ever did from days one and days two and so forth. Alls I ever did, I did do for you."

'Boo!' 'Hiss!' 'Evil!' 'Wicked!' 'Die! Die! Die! Die! Die!'

"Now youse all may boo, and boo so it is. And I shall not say not to boo. Boohoo! It's true that you boo! Hehe. But all I ever did, I did it for you.

"So 'ere I shall die. Bye bye! Tah-ra! Toodle pip! But I shall die as your 'umblest servant. A servy-ervant, so I am. I tell no word of a lie. I ain't selling you a dead dog. I'm every little wee thing that you did make me. You-hoo! Boohoo! Woo, a woo, a woo!"

'Liar!' 'Cheat!' 'Phony!' 'Fake!' 'Die! Die! Die! Die! Die!'

There was melody to the malice. There was song in the scolding. Archibald did not so much chant in time with the crowd, but croon along with their macabre anthem.

The condemned man was led onto the scaffold.

Archibald serenaded him with song.

The noose crowned his neck.

Archibald harmonized a chorus of bittersweet abuse.

The trapdoors swung open.

Archibald's cries reached an epic crescendo.

The crack of the condemned man's neck gazumped Archibald's guilt and fear, replacing those grisly emotions with a wave of euphoria he found hard to explain. As if surfing on clouds of fairy dust, he felt weightless and hollow and free. Ecstasy ruptured his misery and elation ravished his malaise.

As the condemned man swung; asphyxiated, bloated and blue; so Archibald swayed, delirious, overcome by a shared sense of delight.

*****

Archibald's euphoria remained with him as he turned into Warwick Lane.

It did not remain for much longer. Clenched fingers on his shoulders wrung the levity from his step, an uppercut to his abdomen made him choke on his pride, and a backhanded slap forced him to spit out the last remnants of his delight.

Before he knew what had happened, his body had been turned and his back had been pressed up against a wall. He stood face to face, and nose to crooked nose with Donald Donaldson; swallowing the oysters on that youth's breath; his belly filling with rancid flesh.

Two other youths stepped out of the shadows, cracking their knuckles and gnashing their teeth. They each had putrid odours of their own.

"Orphan boy," Donaldson mocked in a voice which was both whiny and vainglorious. "Killed any more parents this week?"

Archibald did not respond.

His attacker's fingernails clamped his throat, pierced his skin, and squeezed his larynx; inflicting a devilish sort of pain which was both physical and emotional; choking his neck, and shunting every last remnant of joy from his soul:

"Two sets of parents not good enough for you, eh?"

The other two migrants joined in:

"Gigglemug!"

"Parent killer!"

Donaldson shook his head:

"I expect you'll soon be up on the scaffolding yourself. Well, if we don't finish you first."

He fisted Archibald's stomach so deeply that knuckles penetrated lungs and air fired out of Archibald's mouth. Winded, Archibald gagged. And, as he gagged, two youths stepped into the mottled light.

"Three on three," they said with jolly assurance. "That's a fair fight. What do you say?"

Donaldson shuddered.

Archibald squinted. He looked at the first youth and then at the second:

'*Are they me? They look like me. But they can't be. Can they? No, it's simply not possible. A ghost! A Hugo! Mayer? No. I don't believe it. It can't possibly be true.*'

ALL TOGETHER NOW

"A spirit stronger than war was at work that night,
December 1914 cold, clear and bright,
Countries' borders were out of sight,
When they joined together and decided not to fight,
All together in No Man's Land."
THE FARM

Time and space seem to have an inverse relationship: As time extends, so space seems to contract.

At least that was the case with our three heroes. Uprooted from their native soil, they were planted in three very different locations; separated by just a few miles, yet segregated by the vastness of London; by a multitude of townhouses and trenches; tinkers, tailors and taverns.

The very idea they might be reunited seemed beyond absurd.

But, as time expanded, so the space between them seemed to contract. The older they grew, the smaller London appeared.

Like three weighty objects, sucked in by the force of their gravitational fields, they were destined to collide...

*****

In Hugo's lodging house lived a boy who everyone called "Bib", on account of how much he dribbled. He never did wear a bib, since he did not want to fuel the taunting, but it would have been for the best if he had. His collar was covered in the entrails of dried spittle, and his neck was coated in crispy saliva.

What Bib lacked for in hygiene, he made up for in innocence. Like Hugo, he was thrust into a life of thieving against his will. Unlike Hugo, he had never taken to it.

After just three weeks in the job, Bib had walked into a shop, walked out with a set of forks, walked into the shop's owner, and been walked straight to Newgate Prison.

It took Hugo quite some time to mention this to Mayer. When he first crashed into his friend's cart, his thoughts were jumbled and his speech was a blur:

"Mayer! Hugo! Orphanage. Barge. Rope. Then I was caught by the thief taker general. Sorry. We only ate gruel at St Mary Magdalen's. But brass screws are worth more than mucky threads. So I ate a rat once. But most of the time I was covered in mud. And then it rained, a fine sort of rain. But that's what friends are for."

"Slow down," Mayer replied, whilst rescuing whatever loaves he could.

"Sorry."

"It's fine, brother. Look, I've got to deliver this bread, but I could do with some company. Why don't you join me, and bring me up to date as we go?"

Hugo nodded, took a deep breath, and told Mayer about his life.

*****

"So, what happened to Bib?" Mayer asked.

"He went out and never returned. Anyway, this morning I overheard Wild. It turns out Bib had been sent to the clink. Wild was making plans to break him out."

"Break him out?"

"Yeah, it ain't so uncommon. Wild has plenty of contacts at Newgate; he plays the system like a game of skittles."

Mayer thumbed his chin:

"When is this prison break set to take place?"

"At midnight, give or take."

"Hmm. In that case, brother, meet me outside the Old Bailey at half past eleven. I think I can free you from this Wild fellow once and for all."

*****

Hugo shot back into the shadows as soon as he saw the two people by Mayer's side.

To Mayer's right walked the spherical figure of Mr Justice, the jovial magistrate to whom Mayer delivered bread. Mr Justice was a fine blend of obesity and pomposity; a vintage concoction of blubber and refinement, who had the vocal range of an opera singer and the gait of a sumo wrestler.

On hearing Bib's story, Mr Justice had insisted on bringing the second man, Mr Strong; a no-nonsense night watchman, as chiselled as a chiffonier, and as dark as a moon-free midnight; cloaked, as he was, in a black raincoat which stretched from his leather boots up to his oily beard.

Mr Strong's reputation preceded him, which may explain why Hugo was quick to hide.

"Psst," Mayer whispered. "Don't worry, we're here to help."

Hugo tiptoed forwards.

"Come, brother, you're no use to us there."

Hugo emitted a nervous laugh.

Mayer led him by the hand.

They took up their positions; Mayer with Mr Justice at one end of Limeburner Lane, and Hugo with Mr Strong at the junction of Bishop's Court.

Squeezed in between two buildings, they hid in silence. Hugo was fearful of incriminating himself, and Mr Strong was in no mood to converse with a scrawny child.

They hid in the driest air and they hid in the stoic night; disturbed not by the scuttling rats nor by the rustling leaves; indifferent to the pallid lamplight and the distant stars.

They waited: Eyes focussed. Feet ready. Hearts pumping. Breath controlled.

They waited: Skin frostbitten. Lips chapped. Fingers numb. Eyes dry. Hair stiff.

They waited.

A ghost sang a song of sombre remorse.

They waited.

A cat shot out into the road. It froze as quickly as it appeared, statuesque; its eyes fixed on the gutter; its legs ready to pounce.

They waited.

They leapt into action. Springing. Bounding. Feet pounding. Legs lifting. Heads bowed.

Wild and Bib were sprinting up the Old Bailey, chased by Mayer, with Mr Justice lagging behind; panting, wheezing and gagging.

Strong and Hugo blocked the road.

Bib jinked one way, Wild the other.

Strong and Hugo stepped in together.

Bib ran free.

Wild turned, palmed Mayer to the ground, and accelerated away. He readied himself to sidestep the lumbering figure of Mr Justice. In doing so, he stalled for the briefest of moments. It was a moment too long. Strong dived through the air and bundled Wild to the ground.

Hugo dived on top of them.

"Chops ahoy!" screamed Mr Justice; holding his arms out wide; ready to add his prodigious hulk to the heap of flesh before him.

"Nooooo!!!" screamed Wild, Strong and Hugo.

Mr Justice looked genuinely upset.

Hugo and Strong looked genuinely relieved.

Mayer limped towards them. As he approached, he saw Mr Strong bind Wild's arms and lead him away. He felt euphoric.

Hugo felt mesmeric.

Mr Justice felt like his lungs were about to implode.

*****

An arrest is nothing without a guilty verdict, and a guilty verdict is nothing but uncertain when one is talking about a man with as much cunning as Jonathan Wild. So, when Wild was hauled up in front of the Old Bailey, Mayer did not rest on his laurels. He marched triumphantly into that chamber and demanded to introduce a witness.

On hearing this bombastic request pour forth from such a scrawny boy, fleet of step and shrill of voice, the judge's lips froze together. He was unable to reply.

Mr Bronze ambled forwards, with his chest open, his lips slightly parted, and his arms hanging loose by his side:

"I have come to give honest testimony, that this man, whom I'm told goes by the name of Jonathan Wild, did return stolen jewels to me and did request a fee. Said jewels did consist of: Two rubies, red; a diamond, cut; and a ring, gold."

"And why, ahum, is this alarming?" the judge asked. "This man is a thief taker. It's his job to return stolen items."

Mr Bronze broke into a modest smile. His eyes opened and closed in the manner of a Siamese cat, and his countenance flushed with monastic modesty. He neither looked perplexed nor placid, flustered nor flat.

"I did see the thief who stole these items," he said, pensively; mulling over the words which tripped from his tongue. "And I did see him the day after those items were returned, on the corner of Stanhope Street, receiving a payment from Jonathan Wild."

"Why didn't you, ahum, apprehend him there and then?"

"Ah, that would have been a fine thing. I did sound the Hue and Cry but, alas, they were as quick as greased lightning and soon did slip into the never never. An arrest, I'm sorry to say, did prove beyond our humble means."

The judge nodded.

Mr Bronze left in search of tea. It was twelve minutes past ten; the time at which Mr Bronze always drank a cup of tea.

Wild shouted at his shadow:

"Piffle! Poppycock! Podsnappery! This man's words are like piss from a parted penis; they spray all over the place, but leave no mark on their target. Let 'im prattle. But I pray, pay no heed to 'is pompous perjury; this pyramid of poop; this plentiful pile of foul platitudes."

Hugo choked.

Mayer rubbed his back.

They both knew that Wild's outburst might have been granted credence if that had been the end of the story. Fortunately for them, it was far from the end of the story. It was a watershed moment; the moment at which a plug was removed, and a torrent of witnesses brought forth a flood of allegations.

Sitting in the gallery, Hugo and Mayer gazed on in wonderment as those people took to the stand. There were men in top hats and women in head scarves, elderly folk with walking sticks and middle-aged folk with canes; the rich and the not so rich, the respectable and the not so respectable, the beautiful and the downright repulsive.

They spoke of stolen silver and gold, pilfered heirlooms and keepsakes, sentimental souvenirs that had gone missing, and long-lost antiques which had suddenly reappeared. They spoke of fees and bribes and charges.

Granted immunity, prison guards spoke of Wild's duplicity, gang members of his threats, and thieves of his blackmail. Together, they formed a queue which stretched around the block.

"Ahum," the judge concluded once they had all given testimony. "Guilty!"

He brought his gavel down upon its sounding block, and then coughed for a full seven minutes.

*****

Hugo needed to see Wild's execution with his own eyes before he could believe he was actually free.

So it was that he pushed through the crowds on Newgate Street, with the smell of fried fish in his nostrils, the friction of a thousand bodies on his skin, and Mayer by his side; more out of a sense of duty than any genuine desire to see that morbid event:

"I wouldn't miss it for the world, my brother. We're in this together!"

By the time Wild appeared, he had already tried to take his own life. His body had rejected most of the laudanum he gulped down, but enough remained in his system to slur his speech:

"So 'ere I shall die. Bye bye! Tah-ra! Toodle pip! But I shall die as your 'umblest servant. A servy-ervant, so I am. I tell no word of a lie. I ain't selling you a dead dog. I'm every little wee thing that you did make me. You-hoo! Boohoo! Woo, a woo, a woo!"

'Liar!' 'Cheat!' 'Phony!' 'Fake!' 'Die! Die! Die! Die! Die!'

Serenaded by these bloodthirsty howls, Wild was led onto the scaffold. The noose crowned his neck, the trapdoors swung open, and Wild fell through.

The crack of Wild's neck brought Hugo an exquisite sort of euphoria, which he found easy to explain. It was the euphoria of liberation. As if surfing on clouds of fairy dust, he felt weightless, hollow and free.

In the spirit of brotherly love, Mayer experienced these very same emotions, at the very same time. He felt Hugo's elation, as if it was *he* who had been granted his freedom. He cheered and sang with Hugo. They swayed together, overcome by a shared sense of delight.

"Thank-you!" Hugo cheered. "I'm in your debt. I only pray that I'll be able to repay you someday; it'd be an honour and a duty."

Mayer smiled, placed his arm around Hugo's shoulder, and led him away.

*****

Within moments, they both felt a devilish pain. It was a physical pain, which shot across their abdomens, and it was an emotional pain, which shunted every last remnant of joy from their souls.

As if compelled by a tender force, they both turned into Warwick

Lane. They walked ahead, unsure why they were walking, and they spoke, unsure why they were speaking:

"Three on three. That's a fair fight. What do you say?"

Hugo and Mayer had stepped between the victim of an attack and his three assailants. They looked at those youths; at their leader, whose nose was so twisted they could not quite believe it was real; and at his two henchmen, who both smelled of rotten fish.

Then they looked at the victim:

'Is he me? He looks like me. But he can't be. Archibald? No, it can't possibly be true.'

The boy with the crooked nose thumped Mayer's stomach.

Mayer stood firm:

"My turn?"

The assailants took a step backwards.

Mayer shooed them away with a pompous flick of his hand:

"And don't you pick on this lad again."

He turned to face the victim:

"Archibald? Is that really you?"

Archibald smiled.

Hugo laughed.

Mayer hugged them both.

BOOK TWO

LOVE, LUST AND LUDUS

UNITED WE STAND

"We were all humans until race disconnected us, religion separated us, politics divided us, and wealth classified us."
ANONYMOUS

The years which followed were happy years. They were pugnacious years. But, most importantly, they were formative years. Our three heroes grew older and wiser, but things, in general, progressed in an unspectacular fashion. As is the rhythm of life, most years tend to be replicas of the years which preceded them. These years are lived, they are loved, but they deliver little in the way of flashpoints.

If one thing defined those years, it would be the relationships which emerged between Hugo, Archibald and Mayer, who made a point of meeting each other at least once a month.

Together, after so much time apart, two things were abundantly clear: Just how similar they looked, and just how different they had become.

They all had shoulder length brown hair, brown eyes, square shoulders, back hair shaped like angels' wings, chests which were wider than their waists, and eyebrows which almost merged in the middle. They all leaned slightly to the right, and they all had asymmetrical nostrils.

They all bore a striking resemblance to Hugo's father, although none of them realised this fact, since none of them could remember that man.

But, whilst their looks united them, their upbringings divided them. Their different relationships with power and money had caused their lives to diverge.

Archibald had been the victim of big power; the power of the government, which effected mass migrations; and the power of industry, which transformed Lambeth Marsh. Born into a world of debt relations, cash had been imposed upon his village, and his community had crumbled. As a result, Archibald had retreated inside his mind, becoming a meek and feeble imitation of his former self.

Hugo had also been a victim of power; the power of the individual. Held captive by the whims of a drillmaster and a thief taker, his life had rarely been his own. Money was always scarce. But Hugo had been resurrected; his oppressor had been banished and, in the meantime, he had learnt how to be as cunning as Jonathan Wild, as mean as the drillmaster, and as opportunistic as Wilkins.

Finally, we have Mayer. Mayer had first-hand experience of the power of circumstance; of being lifted up into high society and being dumped back down in his place; of being endowed with a network of contacts he had done nothing to earn, and of working hard without earning a reward. He had learnt about tally sticks, coinage and gold. And he had learnt to play the game; to follow society's rules, go through the motions, and present a respectable face to the world.

So, if money and power had divided our three heroes, what then of love? Love had united them. Love would bring them together…

*****

"Love" is an unsatisfactory word. It can mean so many things, in so many situations, that it barely means anything at all.

The Greeks knew this all too well. So, rather than settle for one word, "Love", they used different words to refer to different types of love.

We shall encounter these words over the course of this modest tome. But, at this stage of our tale, it would be remiss to mention more than one: Philia.

Philia, put simply, is the comradely love which exists between family members and close friends. Born on the battlefield of life, of shared roots or experiences, it is typified by loyalty; of thinking of one's brethren before thinking of one's self.

It was philia which united our three heroes; compelling Mayer to rescue Hugo from Jonathan Wild, and compelling them both to save Archibald from his bullies. Born on three adjacent beds, to mothers who experienced one set of labour pains, they too had felt each other's pain, and had been moved by an irresistible urge to help their long-lost friend.

Philia had united them. And, carrying this momentum forward, it would be philia which would bring them together. Each would help another…

*****

Mayer helped Hugo.

Having saved him from a life of petty crime, Mayer felt duty-bound to provide Hugo with a better life. Fortunately, he had established a network of contacts which enabled him to do just that.

In the first instance, he introduced Hugo to Mr Orwell.

"And what do we have here?" the retired teacher asked when they arrived.

"This is Hugo."

"And why do I have the pleasure of young Hugo's company?"

"We were hoping you'd be kind enough to educate him."

"I see. And why, I pray, did you think that?"

"Because you love to teach and he'd love to study."

Orwell smiled. Mayer smiled. Hugo looked confused.

Theirs would go on to become a mutually beneficial relationship; one which brought Mr Orwell some much needed company, and Hugo some much needed education. In time, Hugo would become a model pupil, with unnatural abilities when it came to the natural sciences.

Mr Orwell refused to accept payment, but Mayer could tell that he needed it; his cupboards were almost bare. So, Mayer asked Zebedee to take Mr Orwell's tally as part of his wages; effectively giving him free bread in return for his lessons.

This made Mayer feel great, which made Hugo feel great, which made Mr Orwell ask a hundred more questions.

Hugo, on the other hand, struggled to articulate his gratitude:

"I... I... I don't know what to say. I... I... I..."

"Don't worry about it," Mayer replied. "It's nothing."

"It's everything; rescuing me from Wild, ensuring he was hung, and getting me an education; I'm in your debt."

"Hmm. Well, maybe one day you'll be kind enough to repay me."

"It'd be an honour. A debtor had a duty to repay their debts."

"Perhaps. But a creditor has a duty to their debtor too; a duty to ensure their debtor has the means with which to pay."

"Sorry?"

"Come with me. There's someone else I'd like you to meet."

*****

London's streets were a potpourri of all the lifestyles Hugo was leaving behind; a smorgasbord of splendid squalor and industrious opportunism.

A boy in brown rags was earning a ha'penny for holding horses whilst their driver ate his lunch. Teens in flat caps were selling newspapers, shouting "Read all about it! Read all about it!" A mother and her toddler were collecting dog turds to sell on to a tannery. A young woman was collecting cigar butts to repackage and sell on as new.

Mayer and Hugo passed an ashen faced seven-year-old, whose clothes contained more holes than material. She was sweeping a path through the clay, grit, rain and horse muck which covered the street, and scrounging for pennies in return.

Thieves were thieving.

Children were begging, the elderly were begging, and women were begging; holding out the babies they had borrowed for the day. Some had been blinded, others maimed, so as to maximize their effect on both heartstrings and purse-strings.

Mayer and Hugo passed those people, walked into a barber's shop, and walked into Hugo's new life; a life surrounded by sharp scissors and even sharper knives; hair clippings, nail clippings, and a barber who appeared to be more bear than man.

That barber was a colossus; a man mountain of muscle and gristle, whose head almost touched the ceiling, and whose shadow almost covered the floor. His mane shimmered in the sepia light, his shoulder blades protruded from his back, and his blackened nose extended from his face.

"This is Bear," Mayer said. "He's one of my best customers."

"I bet he is," Hugo mumbled.

"What?"

"Nothing."

Bear and Mayer embraced.

Mayer's flesh squeezed out of all the wrong places:

"It's raining cats and dogs."

"It never just rains, it pours."

Bear turned to face Hugo:

"So, you're the lad who wants an apprenticeship?"

"I am?"

"You are."

"I see."

"You're everything Mayer said you were."

"I am?"

"You are. Now here's your indenture. It guarantees me seven years' of labour. In return, I'll keep you housed, fed and clothed. I'll have you learn the ropes good and proper. I'll allow you to keep your tips. Ha! Tips! But I'll not pay you a brass farthing. You hear me boyo?"

Hugo nodded. He physically shrunk. A part of him thought that he was being trapped by another malicious master. A part of him felt that he did not deserve anything better.

"It's all bravado," Mayer whispered in his ear. "Don't worry about him, brother; he's more teddy bear than grizzly bear; his bark is worse than his bite."

Hugo was unconvinced, but he signed the contract nonetheless. He was far too scared to refuse.

*****

Hugo helped Archibald.

"Punch me!" he yelled.

Archibald shook his head.

"Punch me, mother ducker!"

Archibald puckered his lips.

"Punch me, you crazy ass country bumpkin, or I'll punch you myself."
Archibald stood firm.

Hugo thumped him.

"Punch me! Punch me! Punch me! Or I'll punch you so many times you'll either punch me back or collapse. And then I'll punch you on the floor. And then I'll punch you *into* the floor."

Archibald winced. He took a tepid breath, and he took an even more tepid punch.

"Again," Hugo bellowed. "Harder! Imagine I'm your bully. Punch me! Imagine I'm old bent nose. Thump me! Imagine I'm calling you names. Finish me off! Fight back! Shake a flannin, you lowdown good-for-nothing hoot nanny. Have some goddamn self-respect!"

Archibald feathered Hugo's torso with a set of powder-puff punches.

"Sissy! Pansy! Milksop!"

Archibald found his rhythm. Careful not to hurt Hugo, he ricocheted punches off his midriff, and landed blows to his breast. His head bobbed, his feet skipped, a shiver ran down his spine, and colour returned to his face.

"That's more like it. Now you're talking my language!"

Archibald grinned.

Hugo led Archibald outside:

"I'm taking you to a wrestling gym. They'll soon have you wiping the floor with your bullies. No-one will dare mess with Archibald the Great. King Archibald of Lambeth Town!"

* * * * *

Archibald helped Mayer:

"I feel you should probably come with me."

"Why?"

"Oh, it's just that I'd like you to meet someone in the pub."

"The pub?"

"The pub!"

Archibald took Mayer to The Three Horseshoes, where he bought him a pint of frothy ale. At a mere one percent proof, it was barely alcoholic. But, drunk by children and adults alike, it was the most popular drink in town, on account of it being dirt-free, unlike the so-called "Drinking water".

Mayer had never seen a pub quite like The Three Horseshoes. For sure, it looked the same as every other pub in town; the bar was made from the same polished wood, and the floor was covered in the same mix of spit and sawdust; it possessed a ubiquitous smell of stale ale; it sounded of rambunctious revelry and untapped angst. But there was something unique about that place; a collective energy; a wondrous sense of camaraderie.

"This here is Sammy," Archibald said. "And this is Mayer."

Mayer shook Sammy's hand in his enthusiastic manner.

"Sammy here is in charge of the factory's bakery. I think he has the final say when it comes to buying flour."

Archibald gave Mayer a piercing look, which Mayer did not quite understand.

"Hmm," he replied. "I'll drink to that. Cheers!"

Mugs clinking, beer drinking, Mayer treated Sammy the same way he treated all his new acquaintances. He made eye contact to show his assurance, humanity and stature; he engaged his broad, expressive smile; and he delved into his repertoire of small talk. He chatted about the pub, the ale, Lambeth, factory life, village life, family life, and life in general; he nattered about how it was always either too wet or too dry, too hot or too cold, too windy or too still; and he asked about Sammy's life.

Sammy was the son of Mrs Harding, the lady who supplied honey to Archibald's shop. Their family had lost their market garden, but they had kept their bees, whose hives they had placed on their roof. As a result, their cottage disappeared beneath a cloud of honey bees each day at dawn. It was quite the spectacle. Some people made detours just to see it. Others made detours to avoid it.

Archibald finally pulled his friend to one side:

"It's just... I think you once told me you're an outcast in your own home, didn't you?"

"I did."

"So, I guess you need to endear yourself to your family, right?"

"Right."

"Well, your old man sells flour north of the river. This guy needs flour south of the river. Maybe you could make it happen. If you help your father, things might improve at home."

Mayer placed his palm on his friend's shoulder:

"That's a sweet thought, brother, but it's not my place to interfere in Abe's business."

Archibald shrugged:

"Oh, maybe not, but I suppose you could make it your place, I guess, if you want."

TIME FLIES

"Snow and adolescence are the only
problems that disappear if you ignore
them long enough."
EARL WILSON

So each friend helped another friend, this we already know. And the years which followed were unspectacular, this we have already mentioned. But we still need to discover how, exactly, our three heroes progressed.

Let us start by visiting Hugo.

Hugo started his apprenticeship on his knees; scrubbing the floor and sweeping shavings. From this lowly vantage point, back bowed and neck bent, he took it upon himself to study the other barbers. He saw the spectacle that was Giovani's dance; how that man encircled his customers, making large, slow steps, with his fingers stretched out across their crowns. He studied Randolph's lightness of hand, as his blade swept stubble from chin. He scrutinized Felix's flourishes, as he switched between dramatic pauses and frenetic bursts of activity. He surveyed Stuart's posture and Sergio's poise.

When his chance came, therefore, he was well positioned to grab it. He mastered the razor, comb, scissors and brush. He trimmed, shaved and styled with a level of aplomb that betrayed his inexperience. And, before he knew it, he had built up a regular clientele, much to the chagrin of the less popular barbers.

"Well do a better job then," Bear told them whenever they complained. "It's not my fault if you're less popular than a street-urchin."

Bear compensated for these outbursts by hugging his employees, which only made matters worse. There never did live a person who came through one of Bear's embraces unscathed. But the big man never spoke harshly to Hugo. In fact, he took quite a shine to his young apprentice. This was why, against his better judgement, he introduced Hugo to the other side of his trade: Surgery.

The evolution of barbers into surgeons was as natural as it was ancient. In possession of a set of sharp knives, and the expertise required to use them, it was natural for barbers to do more than just cut hair. They became manicurists; digging out ingrown toenails and hangnails. Then they branched out; lancing boils and infected gums, pulling teeth, castrating pets, bloodletting and performing enemas.

Hugo learnt how to perform these operations, helped in no small part by Mr Orwell's biology lessons, and a series of demonstrations which were held by the Worshipful Company of Barbers.

As Hugo became more proficient with the scalpel, he spent less time cutting hair; becoming more surgeon than barber. In time, he became more doctor than surgeon; treating everything from dysentery to venereal disease, chicken pox to piles.

Hugo's progress was aided by his unique ability to diagnose ailments, blindfolded, with just one whiff of a patient's skin. He could recognize the sharp, sweet scent of nitric oxide, which clung to people with asthma; the musky smell of Parkinson's Disease; scrofula, which smelled of stale beer; and yellow fever, which smelled of a butcher's shop. It was a talent which disappeared just as quickly as it arrived, and just as inexplicably, but not before Hugo had accrued enough expertise to survive without it. By this time, his seven-year indenture period was in its final months; he had already implemented a new system for keeping records, taken charge of the medicine cabinet, and started to insist that his patients return for check-ups. Bear had moved him into an apartment of his own, and he was earning a sizeable amount of tips.

*****

Let us now take the time to visit Archibald.

Archibald made the changes he needed to survive; abolishing debt and credit relationships, and insisting that his customers pay with coins. Migrants still gave him a wide berth, and employees of the ironworks still used the factory's shops, but the other natives frequented his store. His outgoings were modest, and so he was able to survive.

Mentally, however, Archibald was a wreck. Enfeebled by the demise of everything he held dear, he was held captive by his mind; by images of Raymondo's death, Ruthie's suicide, and his bullies' taunts. His personality was unable to flourish.

There was just one thing which offered Archibald respite from his mental illness: Cumberland and Westmorland wrestling.

In that sport, wrestlers take up their starting position; chest to chest, with chins on shoulders and arms interlinked. The umpire calls "Wrestle", and the participants tussle each other to the ground.

Archibald loved dressing up in an outfit that accentuated his muscles, which were beginning to bulge. He loved his long johns, which caressed his thighs, and his embroidered vest, which gave him an air of flamboyance. He loved comparing himself to his manly opponents. He loved grabbing those men, gripping their flesh, and inhaling their breath. He loved being held, manhandled, and thrown to the ground.

Archibald became a proficient wrestler, just as his sport gained mass appeal. Hundreds of people began to attend events in Lambeth's new theatre, where Archibald won almost as often as he lost. He attended events all across south London, but it was the annual Good Friday Festival on Kensington Common which would come to be the highlight of his year.

Thousands of people attended that event; feasting and making merry. They filled the temporary stands, in a state of intoxication and lewdness. They hollered, howled and hooted.

The first time Archibald entered the main competition, he was defeated in a matter of seconds. The crowd threw rotten cabbages in his general direction. Unperturbed, he returned the next year, when he made it to the second round. On his third visit, he won three fights. On his fourth, he walked away with four shillings in prize money.

His wallet grew a little and his muscles grew a lot.

It was at this point that the bullying stopped for good. Perhaps it was because Archibald had grown stronger than his tormentors. Or, perhaps, it was simply a matter of maturity. Wedded to the workplace, Archibald's bullies no longer had the time to torment him.

Archibald grew so muscular, in fact, that on his fifth visit he was accused of being too heavy to fight. He stripped naked, displaying himself like Adam to Eve, but the scales still betrayed him. So he gathered up a handful of fur coats from the crowd, wrapped them around his torso, and sprinted for a full five miles. By the time he returned, his body had shed so much water that he was able to make the cut. He won eight of his nine bouts that year, which earned him the princely sum of five shillings.

His ripped body earned him a little admiration from the ladies, his finesse earned him a little respect from the men, and his successes earned him a little spending money. This pleased him, but it only pleased him a little. He still missed his uncle and aunt, he still felt cast adrift, and he still lived like a prisoner; trapped inside his mind, and unable to be true to himself.

*****

And now let us now visit Mayer.

After many sleepless nights, and many restless days, Mayer finally approached Abe. It was not the ordeal he had feared. Abe took kindly to his advances, and pounced upon the opportunity to do business south of the river. But neither was it the revolutionary development Mayer had envisioned. He remained a second-class citizen at home. Abe, whilst grateful, was never around to show his gratitude. Sadie, meanwhile, was always lurking; ready to put Archibald in his place.

Life in Zebedee's bakery also continued as before. Aided by the training he received from Mr Orwell, Mayer did take on some extra responsibilities; managing the books, stock-checking and ordering supplies. But he spent the majority of his time on the streets, delivering bread and cutting notches from tallies. Whilst he enjoyed the fresh air and the chance to make acquaintances, he did feel unfulfilled.

There was one man, however, who noticed Mayer's exploits: Mr Bronze. That jeweller saw Abe's sack of gold grow fat, and soon learnt of the role Mayer had to play.

Abe's was not the only pouch which grew fat during those years; Mr Bronze was accruing so many gold coins that he had to buy a second safe. This piqued Mayer's interest. So, keen to discover the secret of that man's success, he did everything he could to endear himself to Mr Bronze; he brought him a present every Christmas, he asked about his daughters, and he visited his wife when she was ill. But he never asked for anything in return, and so he never got anything in return. His life continued on as before.

THE POWER OF LOVE

"Love will tear us apart."
JOY DIVISION

Our three heroes met in their usual spot, in Covent Garden's piazza; surrounded by portico houses, undulating arcades, market stalls and bohemians of every imaginable variety. They sipped their drinks, chatted, and gazed at the ladies who were sitting at the adjacent tables.

It was late spring, that radiant season when young ladies bloom; casting off their winter robes and revealing themselves to sun and sundry.

Three friends, born three seconds apart, saw one such lady three seconds after the other. But they fell for her at exactly the same time, when she turned and glanced in their direction. That serendipitous gesture marked the beginning of a devastating love which would still be wreaking havoc many decades later.

This was not the brotherly love, philia, which had brought our three heroes together. This was "Eros"; sexual passion and desire; a fiery, frightening, irrational love which took hold of them, possessed them, and would turn them into foes.

Their love was one and the same: Felt in the same places; in the base of the stomach and the balls of the feet; in fingers, lungs and toes. Felt in the same ways; leaving them short of breath and light of mind; restless with limerence and raging with lust. Felt like one hapless love, held by one single person, who just happened to have three separate bodies.

As soon as they saw her, they loved her. And as soon as they loved her, they felt they knew her.

But what, exactly, did they know?

They knew she was the one; that special person they had been waiting for; their soulmate. Exceptional. Extraordinary. Unlike other girls. More angel than human. More divine. More refined.

They knew this. They were sure of it. They could see it with their very own eyes.

So, what, exactly, could they see?

Mayer, whose upbringing had grounded him in the material world, saw her body; her luminous skin, luscious curves, lavish eyebrows and luxuriant hair; the way a ringlet of that hair skimmed her shoulder and then rebounded; the perfect roundness of her face, eyes, nose, breasts and buttocks; the subtlety of her weightless dress, which hinted at hidden secrets; the bead of moisture which lingered on her lip, and the pearl which decorated her ear.

Hugo, who had learnt to look beyond external appearances, believed he saw her mind. In the way she squinted, he believed he saw her ruminations; in the way she tilted her head, he believed he saw her inclinations; and in her posture, he believed he saw her entire personality; her dreams and desires, gaiety and grace, kindness and compassion. Her expression betrayed her. Its pantheistic strength, bold and bodacious, spoke volumes; telling Hugo that she demanded the extraordinary, implored the fantastical, and absorbed every ounce of the world's magnificence.

Archibald, who lived in the world of his mind's imagination, was sure he had seen that girl's soul; her Platonic form, removed from her mortal self. Unburdened by truth or reality, his love was metaphysical. Like a jolt to the heart, it was earth-shattering. He sucked her in; consuming her, without being sure what it was, exactly, that he was consuming.

*****

Three young men felt the same love at the same time, but they had seen their amore in three different ways and, as a result, their responses diverged.

Archibald felt as though their souls had already united. He did not feel a need to act, nor did he have the capacity to act; he was far too weak and feeble. He simply sat there, hoping beyond hope that his mere presence would be enough to win the girl's heart.

Hugo knew he needed to act. He did not, however, feel a need to act right away. He decided to study the girl, like he studied science, and to use his wits, as if he were a thief or a mudlark once more. To do this, he needed time to plot and plan. He did not believe he could succeed, his low self-esteem kept him too modest for such fancies, but he felt compelled to try. That girl had stolen his heart, and he felt that he owed it to himself to at least try to steal hers.

But for Mayer, to have seen her, was to want her, was to go and get her.

Unlike Archibald, Mayer knew he needed to act. And, unlike Hugo, he felt compelled to act right away. Lust overpowered him, testosterone overwhelmed him, and his emotions overthrew him. His legs propelled him towards the girl.

He found himself standing before her, without being entirely sure how he had arrived there.

Never one to let an opportunity pass, Mayer unleashed the full force of his repertoire: He gazed into the girl's eyes. He almost drowned in them. He tried to shake her hand, but she pulled away. He smiled, but he only managed to cringe.

The nerves! Mayer had never experienced anything like it. He opened his mouth, ready to unleash a marvellous array of small-talk, but his tongue betrayed him. He was could only blurt out three measly words:

"Be my girl."

"No", the girl replied without even thinking. It was a gut reaction; a shield held high to Cupid's arrow. "How bodacious! I have no interest in a double-breasted tot-hunter like you."

"Well then," Mayer shot back. "I have no interest in a pompous princess like you!"

He turned, theatrically, and returned to his friends.

*****

Watching from a distance, Hugo and Archibald became aware of their shared intentions. Still, they did not find solace in Mayer's failure; they felt his pain, patted his back, and kept their feelings to themselves.

Archibald, for his part, actually envied Mayer's chutzpah. He would have liked to have approached the girl himself, but was far too shy. When she looked their way, he had bowed his head; his heart full, his eyes blind, his lips mute, and his feet immovable.

Hugo, on the other hand, was streetwise; accustomed to tricky situations. Educated in the school of hard knocks, he was a schemer, a dreamer, a player, and a go-getter who knew what he had to do.

"Don't fear," he told Mayer. "I'll put in a good word. You'll win her over another time. I mean, look at you. How could any girl resist?"

He chuckled and Mayer reciprocated. Then he turned to face the girl, caught her eye, doffed his cap, smiled, and strolled towards her:

"It's an honour and a pleasure to meet you."

The girl blushed.

"Please don't judge my friend harshly ma'am, he's as good as they come. I'm sure you'd see that if you were kind enough to give him a chance."

The girl tilted her head, looked at Mayer and smiled.

Hugo returned to his friends, put his hands on their shoulders, and gestured for them to leave:

"To the pub?"

"To the pub!"

PLAYING IT BY THE BOOK

"The young man knows the rules, but the old man knows the exceptions."
OLIVER WENDELL HOLMES JUNIOR

Left alone in his room, Mayer was able to reflect on that day's events. He realised he could not treat his flame as if she were a professional acquaintance; he could not be embarrassed by nerves and nausea again. He would have to raise his game, and learn a whole new set of rules: The rules of love. Or, to be more specific, the rules of courting.

These, he would come to discover, were clearly defined...

Young ladies, known as "Debutantes", sought matches at London's summer balls. At those balls, if a bachelor was from a lower social stratum, he could only approach a girl if he was invited. If he was her equal, he could make an approach, but only with the permission of her chaperone. The debutante used her fan to signal her intentions; holding it with her right hand to wave a man over, or with her left hand to wave him away; opening it as a sign of interest, or closing it as a sign of indifference; fanning quickly to show she was single, or slowly to show she was engaged.

Mayer had seen a ticket to such an event in his flame's handbag. Golden and gilded, it revealed her intent to attend the Opening Ball at the Almack Rooms in St. James.

Mayer had all the ammunition he needed.

He approached Big Bob, one of his customers, who was a porter for the wine merchant that supplied the Almack Rooms. He was not, however, big. Far from it. Big Bob stood at a mere four feet six inches. He was stocky and, as a result, he was strong, but it was easy to peer over his head, and even easier to lose him in a crowd.

Big Bob was fond of Mayer. When his wife fell ill, Mayer had extended him credit, and delivered his bread for a full two years before requesting payment. When his wife died, he had persuaded Zebedee to provide free food for the wake.

Big Bob felt he owed Mayer. So when Mayer asked him to source a ticket, he was more than happy to oblige.

Mayer needed just one more thing: A dinner suit. To get one tailor made would have cost him the best part of five pounds; money he simply did not have. Nor was he acquainted with any tailors. So he approached Abe, whose yellow waistcoat was so bright it almost burnt a hole in his cornea:

"Please can I borrow your dinner jacket?"

Abe was inclined to say "No". If Sadie had caught him lending Mayer that outfit, which she had handpicked herself, she would have berated him for weeks. But Abe had made thousands of pounds thanks to Mayer, and felt obliged to repay the favour.

Abe paused before he answered. Then he replied in a hushed tone which took Mayer by complete surprise. Mayer had grown so accustomed to Abe's normal voice, which was loud enough to wake a corpse, that Abe's whispers made him clench his teeth and shiver:

"Okay, but only if you promise not to tell your mum. She'd string us up by our balls if she ever found out."

Mayer laughed:

"Okay, it's a deal!"

*****

Our heroine did not face either of these problems. She did not have to borrow an outfit; she had already been endowed with gowns make of silk, dresses made of lace, shoes in every colour, and accessories from across the globe. Nor did she need worry about tickets; her diary was chock-a-block with invitations to dinner parties, society lunches, brunches, balls, concerts and operas.

Our heroine had been groomed for this season since she could walk. She had been taught to sing and dance. She was familiar with every rule of etiquette. She was well schooled in the art of conversation and the art of silence. She had a large dowry, with which to entice a suitor, and an even larger wardrobe, with which to seduce him.

She only needed to dream.

She dreamt to escape the weight of her parents' expectations. She dreamt of her Prince Charming; the Romeo to her Juliet. She dreamt of Mayer; warming to his innocent idiocy in the clear light of day. And she dreamt of his friend, Archibald, whose bulging muscles had not escaped her attention.

She dreamt as she dressed for the Opening Ball; painting her lips a seductive shade of red, applying perfume designed to lure men's noses, and dressing in a way she hoped would lure their eyes. Her corset made her breasts look far larger than they actually were, and her waist far more slender. Her hat shaded her face, adding an element of mystery which was a work of pure fiction. Her whole persona was borrowed. It was all a glorious lie; a web of deception designed to ensnare the perfect man, for whom she was expected to be the most dutiful of wives.

She emitted a coquettish giggle, took her mother's hand, and boarded her carriage.

*****

Mayer was a portrait of deception himself.

His dinner suit, far removed from his normal attire, suggested wealth and status far beyond his actual station. He had spent several hours in front of the mirror, greasing and re-greasing his hair; moulding it into a helmet fit for a count. He had trimmed his eyebrows so they did not appear so bushy, used ladies' makeup to disguise the asymmetry of his nostrils, and shaved the hair off his back.

His façade was a lie. But, had you challenged him on this point, he would have argued that it was an honest lie. He would have said that peacocks preen their feathers, toucans elevate their beaks, and chameleons change colour when they try to woo a mate. For Mayer, it was the most natural of deceptions. If he was a fraud, he was an honest fraud, playing by nature's rules.

Such thoughts, however, were far from his mind as he approached the Almack Rooms. Mayer was too nervous to think of anything at all. His stomach was churning and his heart was offbeat.

To compensate, he gave himself an air of impenetrable confidence. He strode up the steps, two at a time, palmed his invitation off onto the doorman, and paced across the hall.

His image reflected from a hundred chandeliers.

He reached the opposite corner and stopped dead. To simply stand there, motionless, would have appeared foolish. So Mayer continued on, jinked behind some drapes, and entered a gambling room, where he frittered away half of his evening and most of his money.

By the time he emerged, the hall had filled with music and country dancing. The air had filled with the scents of tulips and clammy women, the tumultuous tapping of bachelors' prowling feet, and the flirtatious chatter of marriage negotiations.

Mayer saw his love, made eye contact with her mother, and bowed; hoping she would invite him over. She did not.

He looked at the girl herself, hoping she would open her fan. She did not.

Mayer retreated to the toilet to compose himself, before striding back into the hall. He looked at the mother again. She ignored him again. He looked at the girl. She closed her fan.

Mayer retreated to the supper room, took a slice of cake, and then returned to the hall, where he ate it as slowly as he could; spying on his amore from afar. He made that cake last for ninety minutes; watching, helpless, as our heroine was introduced to no less than four other suitors. Mayer did take comfort from the fact that she did not spend long with any one of them, and his heart did pound when he saw her dance. But all he could do watch, mute and distant, eating his cake one crumb at a time.

Finally, the girl's mother left the room. And, allowing his heart to lead his head, Mayer sped across the carpet.

He panted as he spoke:

"Mine eyes hath feasted on your beauteous face, and my arms shall be your sanctuary. Forgive me, my boldness wants excuse, but my duty binds me to obey you ever."

The girl's head jutted backwards, overwhelmed by Mayer's heat:

"What?"

"Come woo me, for now I'm in a holiday humour and likely enough to consent."

"Wherever do you get such lines?"

"It's Shakespeare."

"No it's not, silly."

"Is too! And I have more: I'll bathe thine lips in rosy dews of kisses. I'll chronicle your virtues. I'll pay the tribute of my love to you. Let me perish in your presence. Let me seal my vowed faith on your lips."

"Huh. Is that it?"

"I could continue…"

"You could start over. Don't you have a mind of your own, with which to think? Or a mouth of your own, with which to speak?"

"I have eyes of my own, with which to see your beauty."

"What scuzz!"

"I have ears of my own with which to hear. Tell me, what is your name?"

"My name is Lola. And you?"

"Lola! A more beautiful name has never been heard."

"You speak like a book."

"I'm Mayer."

"Well, Mayer, it's been, umm, *interesting*."

Lola turned to walk away.

"Can I just tell you, your eyes are nothing like seeds. And what's with that hair you've got going on? Wait! Where are you going? Come back, it gets better. Your face looks like a face! Write to me. Buckingham Towers, Camden. Hmm. Bye, damned wretched angel. Bye bye!"

The whole conversation lasted less than two minutes.

Mayer stayed for another two dances.

Lola spoke to another two men.

SUFFERING IN SILENCE

"The most introspective of souls are often those that have been hurt the most."
SHANNON L. ALDER

Beauty and ugliness can both be obstacles to love; ugliness can repel it and beauty can overwhelm it.

Mayer had been so overwhelmed by Lola's beauty that he had acted hastily and nervously. Archibald, on the other hand, had been so overwhelmed that he was unable to act at all.

So, if he was too feeble to approach Lola, what could he do?

He could imagine her.

He saw Lola in the faces of passers-by and in the shapes of mischievous clouds; reflected in puddles and windows. Wherever he looked, there she was. Whenever he closed his eyes, he saw her. He saw her lavish eyebrows and luxuriant hair; the perfect roundness of her face and nose.

But he did not see Lola in the flesh, and so the image in Archibald's mind began to fade. He struggled to recreate the angle of her jaw and the depth in her eyes. He could not quite remember the number of curls in her hair or the line which formed where her neck met her shoulders.

Desperate to halt this slide, he redrew Lola's image in his mind. Then he sketched it. He drew thousands of images; each less lifelike than the last, and each more angelic. He covered a wall with those sketches, which he covered with a sheet whenever he opened his shop.

He lost his mind in a sea of dopamine and testosterone, in which no thought was too sublime nor too desperate, no feeling too powerful or pathetic.

His thoughts were intoxicated by the sweet ambrosia of impossible dreams.

Those impossible dreams brought certain sorrow.

Archibald imagined Lola's personality; building palaces in his mind for a queen of his own invention. He came to know her, without knowing her at all. He imagined their courtship, wedding, marriage, children, old age, deathbeds, and joint ascent to heaven. It was glorious. Archibald's whole being filled with pure joy. He wanted to scream out with ecstatic passion and skip through the streets.

But, at the very same time, he fell into a pit of self-despair; hating himself for his inability to act; facing the fact that Lola would never be his. It was an unimaginable agony. He felt as though his veins had been clogged with ball-bearings, and his intestines had been tied up in a thousand tiny knots.

BREAKING THE RULES

"The urge to destroy is also a creative urge."
MIKHAIL BAKUNIN

Hugo was sure of two things:

One: He was not worthy of a girl like Lola.

Two: He had to have her, no matter what it took.

He did not believe he deserved Lola. He was a penniless apprentice, with no social standing; a former gang member, mudlark and workhouse boy; a thief and a parent-killer. She, on the other hand, was from the higher echelons of society. There was no way he could win her by fair means; he would have to play foul.

He did not *want* to play dirty, he *had* to play dirty; he did not have a choice.

And so he became a regular snollygoster; both clever and unscrupulous...

*****

It started that day in Covent Garden. Leaving his friends in the pub, drunk on beer and gin, Hugo returned to the café, drunk on love. He watched Lola from afar, waited for her to finish her tea, hailed a Hackney coach, and ordered its driver to follow Lola's carriage.

His mind was full of Lola. He caught his reflection in a shop window, and saw that it was also obsessed with her.

His horse-drawn carriage rattled past half-built squares and incomplete buildings, rubbish and rubble, before pulling up in front of a tall terraced house on Hill Street, Mayfair. Built from Bath stone, that building was a majestic example of pomp and pomposity, with chiselled cherubs lounging on various ledges, and gilded patterns creeping out across the house-front. Miniature pine trees, trimmed into perfect cones, decorated narrow balconies. Each window was over eight feet tall.

Hugo returned the following morning.

Urged on by a merciless resolve to triumph over his ignorance, he waited; spying Lola's father, who appeared to be a doctor; her mother, who appeared not to be much of anything; her two brothers and her entourage of servants.

When she emerged, Hugo trailed Lola, cloaked by London's ubiquitous fog. Made of ash and cinders, that fog was pervasive, acrid, thick, dull and grey. It made it almost impossible to see ten metres ahead, and more than possible to stalk an oblivious target.

Lola was indeed oblivious. She seemed preoccupied, alone with her thoughts; within herself rather than with herself. She did not notice anything, and so did not notice that she was being noticed.

But Hugo did notice her. Playing his own version of "Hide and Seek", he sought Lola, and then he hid from her. He hid behind books, beneath trees, beside lampposts, before bridges and by junctions; using an umbrella and a long raincoat to merge himself into the shadows.

Whenever he could, he arrived at her house at dawn; trailing her as she strolled around the Serpentine; watching her as she sat on her favourite bench, fed the ducks and read.

His love was never as severe as when Lola sat by that lake, because he was always shaken by a fear that it might float away. He had a simmering distrust of water; confusing the distant memory of his capture by Jonathan Wild with his previous life on the banks of the River Thames.

When Hugo could not arrive early, he prayed that Lola would be home in the evening, so he could follow her and her companions on their evening escapades to the shops, theatre or ballet.

As a result, Hugo got to know Lola in a way which Archibald and Mayer could only dream of. He discovered her in the unconsciousness of her actions: In the way she stood on the tips of her toes, with joyous abandon, he discovered that she had trained as a gymnast. In the way she greeted her friends, by bounding into their arms, he discovered that she knew how to dance. In the way she placed her hair behind her ears, and laughed if it came loose, he discovered her impishness. In the way she crossed her legs, dangling her shoe from her toe, he discovered that she was far too fancy-free to be familiar with erotic love.

Seeing her read, Hugo discovered Lola's taste for romantic novels, especially the works of Fanny Burney. Once, he saw her read "A Vindication of the Rights of Woman". He saw her read books in French and Spanish.

Seeing her handbag, Hugo discovered her name, which was embroidered on a pink handkerchief. A part of him believed she had intended to show him that item.

And, seeing her shop, he discovered her grace; the way she drifted through the tumult whilst her companions tangled with other shoppers; the way trout-faced hawkers serenaded her with song, "Sweets for your sweet", "Whelks for your tummy", "Come here my love and spend your money"; the way she was amused in amusement arcades, curious in curiosity shops, and overcome with unbridled glee whenever she saw a hat.

Lola's love of hats verged on the brink of addiction.

She appeared to be on a mission to buy every hat in town. She bought tall hats and wide hats, caps and bonnets, with baubles, buttons, rims, ribbons, feathers and flowers. Whenever she saw a hat, it was almost a forgone conclusion that she would buy it.

There was, however, one exception. Hugo saw Lola stop outside a small shop near Oxford Street almost every evening. She gazed into its window for minutes on end, as if in a world of her own, entranced by the only hat on display; its pink material almost translucent; its undulating rim as wide as a wheel.

Hugo believed she would have stayed in front of that shop for all eternity if she ever passed by there alone.

*****

It would be easy to judge Hugo. Unlike Mayer, he was not playing by the rules. He refused to accept that such rules existed. For him, all was fair in love and war.

Some people might have called him a "Stalker" or a "Pest". But, for once in his life, Hugo did not judge himself so harshly. In his opinion, his actions were no more dishonest than the way in which the likes of Mayer and Lola polished their appearances. Those people gave themselves false airs and graces to woo a mate. He stalked. Everyone was at it. Hugo simply believed that he was doing it better.

The alternative, to be honest and unobtrusive, like Archibald, did not bear consideration. To Hugo, it seemed idiotic; a sure-fire path to failure.

So Hugo had no guilty conscience. In fact, he actually blamed Lola for his actions:

'Who was she to seduce me thus? Who was she to steal my heart, take hold of my actions, and control my thoughts? Why couldn't she be like other girls; modest and resistible? Why did she have to enchant me, bewitch me, and goad me into following her?'

Hugo believed he was serving Lola; at her beck and call, every hour of the day; following her for *her* sake, not his own.

He was not afraid to contradict himself. He was not afraid of anything at all.

*****

Hugo became so cocksure, in fact, that he stepped closer to Lola each day. He came to recognize the different sounds she made when walking on paving slabs, brick paths and cobblestones; how to distinguish her perfume, and how to sense her presence without using his eyes. He even allowed Lola to glimpse his reflection in a puddle.

He did not always get so close. On one occasion, he lost Lola in a crowd. Rushing to catch her, he knocked a pint of beer from the hand of an intoxicated builder, and had to buy him two drinks to make amends. By the time he returned, Lola was long gone.

At other times, when the smog was light, he had to hold back. But still the trend continued. Hugo gathered more information and, with it, he gained more confidence.

Finally, he took his chance.

Lola was standing outside the shop near Oxford Street, wearing a purple frock with fuchsia spangles and a hat which shaded her face. For the first time, she had gone there alone. And, just as Hugo had predicted, it did not seem as though she would ever leave.

She had been there for fifteen minutes when it started to rain; standing with disciplined haughtiness; her chin lifted and her eyes fixed on the prize. She had remained there for a further ten minutes when a horse-drawn coach sprayed muck all over her frock.

Hugo stepped forward, through horizontal rain which doused his trousers, and vertical rain which doused the road. He wore a forced form of casualness which verged on the indolent; his shoulders perched aloof and, as if indifferent to Lola's existence, he looked over her head as he spoke:

"How ghastly."

Lola brushed herself down, greeting Hugo's concern with a modest tilt of her head.

"No, no," Hugo continued. "It jolly well doesn't do. No. Please take this. Oh, and take this for the journey home."

Hugo passed Lola his raincoat and umbrella.

"Really, I couldn't."

"Really, ma'am, I insist. I wouldn't have it any other way."

"Well then, you must promise to collect them."

"If you wish."

"I do."

"Then I will. A good day to you ma'am."

Lola curtseyed.

Hugo turned.

"Wait!"

"Yes?"

"Aren't you forgetting something?"

"Forgetting something, ma'am?"

"My address?"

"Sorry, ma'am?"

"To pick up your coat, silly."

"Oh, yes, of course."

"It's 303 Hill Street."

"Well Lola, I shall see you at 303 Hill Street."

Hugo turned, but Lola called out again:

"Hang on! How did you know my name?"

Hugo's chest contracted. He could barely open his mouth to speak:

"On yo... yo... your handkerchief, ma'am. I suh... suh... saw your name on your handkerchief."

"Oh," Lola sang, as if it was the most natural thing in the world. "How fantabulous!"

Then she skipped away.

*****

Hugo waited five days before returning to Hill Street. It was not for a lack of opportunity, nor for a lack of desire, but simply because he wanted to play things cool.

Perhaps he took this a little too far.

Whilst walking down Oxford Street, he saw Lola walking towards him. Her face softened, more with cordiality than love, but still with a certain degree of warmth.

"Hello," she said.

Hugo did not react. He walked past, with the posture of a frozen corpse, and a look of imperious indifference. He was trying to create an aura of mystery; to make Lola long for him, so that he could lead her on. It was a power play, plain and simple.

But, in lieu of that experience, Hugo decided to wait before visiting Hill Street.

So it was that he approached Lola's home the following morning. He climbed those bodacious steps, and knocked on the door with his fist. He did not trust the knocker; it just seemed a little too large, too brassy, and too unreal.

A butler opened the door. He also seemed a little too large, too brassy, and too unreal. The very idea of a having butler made Hugo feel woozy.

Hugo stepped into the hall; an expansive space, bigger than any residence he had ever called home. He felt completely lost. But, keen to fit in, he strode ahead with confident bravado and shook Lola's father's hand, whilst ignoring Lola herself.

Lola's father looked like Father Christmas. He laughed like Father Christmas. He even smelled of mince pies, mulled wine and orange peel:

"Ah! You must be Hugo. Ho! Ho! Ho! Our Lola has told us all about you."

"Well, I don't know that there's much to tell. Sorry. I'm just a humble surgeon."

"A surgeon, eh?"

"Yes sir."

"Well dash my wig; I dare say we doctors are supposed to despise you surgeons."

"We surgeons are supposed to despise you doctors."

"You are? I see. And do you?"

"Do I?"

"Do you, perchance, despise doctors?"

"No sir."

"Jolly good."

"And do you?"

"Do I?"

"Do you despise surgeons?"

"Well, I suppose that depends on the surgeon."

"Oh."

"What sort of a surgeon are you?"

"A good one."

"Ho! Ho! Ho! And what makes you such a good surgeon?"

"I care about my patients."

"And is that enough?"

"Sometimes."

"Really?"

"Well, maybe not. Sorry."

"Ho! Ho! Ho! So what else do you do?"

"I save lives sir."

"That's a big claim."

"Yes sir."

"Do you save many lives?"

"Well, maybe not."

"Ho! Ho! Ho!"

"I'd like to save more."

"Ambitious, eh?"

"No sir. I mean, yes sir. I mean, I do my best."

"Do your best?"

"Well, maybe not. I mean, I suppose I could do better. Sorry. But I always try to do better, which is what I think I meant to say."

"Ho! Ho! Ho! There's a good lad. There's many a doctor who'd do well to adopt such an approach."

Lola's father paused, tapped his lip, and led Hugo into the morning room.

"Come," he said. "Let's talk shop."

He introduced himself as "Nicholas", poured two brandies, and requested two glasses of milk from the butler. Then he talked about life, London and medicine.

Hugo observed his surroundings.

He noticed that the windows at the rear of the house were all unlatched, he noticed the maid who trailed Lola like a shadow, and he noticed Lola herself. She was eavesdropping on their conversation whilst watering the plants.

There were lots of plants. Every ledge contained a planter and every corner contained a pot. Snake plants filled the gaps between bannisters, a heart-leaf philodendron sat on a table, rubber plants adorned the fireplace, aspidistras guarded doors, and the windowsills were covered with begonias, daisies, lilies and orchids.

It was clear by the way she cared for those plants that they all belonged to Lola. Hugo thought she might have owned more plants than hats, although he was loathe to admit it. It just seemed too ludicrous to be true.

Who was this crazy lady?

Hugo found her quirks alluring. He found them utterly absurd. He wanted to distance himself from Lola, but he could not do it. Seeing the way she cared for those plants only made him want her more. Her insanity nourished his insane love. Her obsessions obsessed him. Her madness drove him mad.

He took a petal from one of Lola's rose bushes, so he could eat it to learn her flavour, said "Farewell" to Nicholas, and then departed.

CRAFT AND GRAFT

"The hardest thing of all is to find a black cat in a dark room, especially if there is no cat."
CONFUCIOUS

Mayer was in a state of constant motion; trying to do his job, trying to study, and trying to build relationships with the likes of Mr Bronze. Always trying. Always ploughing on; head bowed and back bent.

Always trying, but not always succeeding. Forgetting almost everything but Lola, Mayer missed deliveries, became careless with tallies, arrived late, arrived early, confused rolls and loaves and buns. He was obsessed. Had you challenged him, he would not have denied it. He would have looked you in the eye and said three simple words: "Love is obsession".

Bewitched by this rancorous obsession, Mayer neglected his other obligations to make the time to court Lola.

He approached her on separate three occasions...

*****

His first attempt took place back in Covent Garden. Mayer had taken to visiting the café where he first saw Lola, in the vain hope that he might see her there again.

It was, on the face of it, a fool's errand. Mayer whiled away countless hours in that establishment; drinking countless cups of tea and glancing at countless faces.

He was on the verge of giving up when Lola finally appeared, wearing stockings which reached her knees and a scarlet hat which barely reached her forehead. Again, she was flanked by her companions. And again, Mayer did not care.

Like before, he found himself propelled towards her table:

"My love for you is like Aeolus; the Greek god of the winds, who imprisoned his sons in a cave. For I'm trapped in a cave and you are my

Ariadne; here to free me!"

Lola's companions giggled with schoolgirlish clumsiness.

Mayer continued:

"I love you."

Lola replied abruptly; overwhelmed, once again, by Mayer's heat:

"Pfft. I don't care for promises of love, much less talk of the real thing. And anyway, I think you've been imagineering. Your love is not born of nature; you've created it out of thin air."

"I have! It's the best way. To be born of nature is mundane. One is born into a new day each time one awakes. One is born into a new scene every time one turns a corner. It's nothing. But to be created is magnificent. To have not existed and then to exist; to whip something up out of sheer desire, sheer will; not to let it happen, but to make it happen; well, that's exquisite. It's the biggest compliment you could have paid me. And so I say it loud, I say it true: I have created my love for you!"

"Pfft!" Lola spat. "Well, I suggest you un-create it. Your love gives me indigestion."

Mayer bowed his head. Like before, he believed he had made a fool of himself.

Like before, Lola had, in fact, warmed to Mayer's innocent idiocy; she was falling for his enthusiasm and loving the chase. But, like before, she was unable to show it.

*****

Mayer's second approach was also eerily similar to a previous encounter. It would be fair to say that he lacked a penchant for originality.

But, then again, Mayer had convinced himself that persistence was more important than creativity. His persistence, he believed, would show Lola just how much she meant to him. That, on its own, could be enough to win her heart. If not, it would eventually wear her down. Lola's resistance, he supposed, was just part of the game.

At the same time, Mayer convinced himself that his persistence was a sign of true love:

'Why else would I be so dogged, if I didn't truly love her?'

It happened like this:

As before, Mayer saw the invite to a ball in Lola's handbag. And, as before, he managed to get a ticket to that ball. As before, he borrowed Abe's dinner suit, and made himself presentable, whilst Lola did the same.

One thing, however, was different. Unlike before, this was a masked ball. Mayer wore a navy mask, replete with silver sequins, and a long beak which protruded from its nose. Lola wore a dainty purple mask, with a plume of artificial feathers attached to one side.

So began the charade.

Mayer followed Lola, whilst Lola followed Mayer. They encircled one another, dancing close and swinging away. Mayer did not think he should approach without the approval of Lola's chaperone. Lola thought the man should make the first move.

Finally, the music swung them together.

"Hello," Mayer said.

"Huh," Lola scoffed; disturbed by Mayer's jagged breathing. "Another suitor?"

"You have that many."

"A steady stream. No more than anyone else."

"And have any taken your fancy."

"One had turned my stomach."

"Do tell."

"A boy by the name of 'Mayer'."

"Hmm."

"He's craptacular."

"How so?"

"He speaks with a forked tongue, dresses like a clown, and smells of urine. You must excuse my French, but he's a real poo-poo-head. I wouldn't go near him with a barge pole"

Lola emitted a girlish giggle.

Mayer steadied himself:

"I know something of the sort."

"You do?"

"Yes, a girl by the name of Lola. She's just as foul."

"She is?"

"Yes. She hides behind false pretensions, and treats love with vicious indifference."

"Well then, I expect you'd be chuffed to bits if you never saw her again."

"Perhaps."

"Just 'perhaps'?"

"Perhaps."

"Does she make your heart flutter?"

"Every time I think of her."

"And you think of her a lot?"

"Every minute of the day."

"That's mimsy."

"It is. And are you any different?"

"Absolutely."

"You don't think of this Mayer fellow?"

"Never!"

"You don't find him appealing?"

"Appealing? No, silly; I'd rather make love to a pig."

"And yet you mentioned him right away."

"I did."

"So he must occupy your thoughts."

"Must he?"

"He must."

"Oh. Fancy that!"

Lola emitted a ditsy giggle, twirled, and floated away. Mayer followed. Whenever they separated, Lola stopped to allow Mayer to approach. Whenever he got too close, she danced away. Whenever he was about to speak, she spoke to another man. Whenever he got downhearted, she brushed up against his side.

She was utterly incapable of showing Mayer that she was flattered by his approaches. Whenever he came near, his presence completely overwhelmed her.

Mayer trailed Lola for the duration of the ball. He even followed her when she hailed a carriage.

"To 303 Hill Street," she said. And then she disappeared.

*****

A few days later, Abe asked Mayer to join him in the dining-room.

He was wearing a waistcoat which was so fluorescent it highlighted all the chinoiserie in that room, and a silken blazer which pitted burgundy patterns against golden spears.

He sat down and began to shout:

"You're a man now, May."

"I am?"

"You are."

"Hmm."

"And a man must pay his way."

"He must?"

"Yes, he simply cannot have any debts."

Having shouted himself coarse, Abe paused for breath. Then he swapped words for actions; pushing a collection of papers across the table.

A series of items were listed in Sadie's un-theatrical writing:

Sixteen years of accommodation – £320

Sixteen years of food – £103 15s 10 ½d

Use of books – £1 2s 5 ½d

Introduction to Mr Zebedee – 3d

It was all there, down to the number of potatoes Mayer had ever eaten, and every item of clothing he had ever worn. There was even a rental fee for the dinner jacket he had borrowed.

At the bottom of the last page, one value was written in large red letters:

Total Amount Owed – £453 7s 9 ½d

Mayer looked up at Abe:

"Bu… bu… but…"

"But nothing. You can pay it off at a rate of £5 a month."

"Bu… bu… But what about the money I helped you to make in south London?"

"You can stay here for two more years, then you'll have to move out. You're getting far too old for foster care."

*****

Mayer decided to repay Abe and Sadie.

'One must pay one's debts,' he told himself. *'It's the honourable thing to do.'*

This had two consequences.

One: Mayer needed to earn more. At first, he achieved this by taking on extra shifts. In time, he would earn a pay rise.

Two: Mayer needed to spend less. No longer could he afford to sup tea in Covent Garden, hoping to see Lola. No longer could he afford to attend balls.

He could not see Lola, but nor could he stop thinking of her:

'What if I leave it too long and she finds someone else? What if she forgets me? What if her father approaches another suitor? What if another suitor approaches her father? Or her mother? Or her cat?'

Mayer tore his hair out. Literally. Bare patches formed on either side of his head.

'But', he told himself, *'fortune favours the brave.'*

He put on his suit and headed for Hill Street, ready for one last roll of the dice…

*****

'Knock! Knock! Knock!'

Mayer did not have any problems with that knocker. Nor did he have any problems with the butler who opened the door.

"I beg the company of your master," he announced, as if it were the most natural thing in the world.

The butler showed Mayer into the dining room, where he waited between a peperomia and a dracaena. Scented geraniums accosted his nostrils, and African violets distracted his eyes.

After several minutes, Nicholas finally joined him. Mayer stood to attention, made eye contact, shook hands in his eager fashion, triggered his winning smile, and tried to engage in small talk:

"It's nippy out. I think a storm is brewing."

Nicholas ignored this remark:

"And what do we have here then?"

"Mayer."

"And what, dare I ask, is a 'Mayer'?"

"A Mayer is a suitor."

"A suitor?"

"Yes, my good man, a suitor!"

"Ho! Ho! Ho!"

"I don't understand."

"Everyone is a suitor these days. Everyone thinks they're suitable, even when there's so little they're actually suitable for. Most people aren't suited for anything. A law suit, perhaps, but little else."

"Hmm. Yes. You're as wise as an owl. But, you see, I really am a suitable suitor."

"A suitable suitor? Now there's a fine thing."

"Yes, I am a fine thing."

"Ho! Ho! Ho!"

"Seriously, I'd be the finest thing that ever happened to Lola."

"To Lola? To *my* Lola?"

"Yes, to your Lola."

"You've come here to court *my* Lola?"

"Yes, my good man, I have."

"You? You come in here unannounced, dressed like a merchant, without so much as a reference, and you say you're here to court *my* Lola?"

"Yes. I…"

"How vulgar! How inappropriate. How… How… How unsuitable!"

"But…"

"But nothing! I've never heard anything so preposterous in all my years."

"If you'd only give me the…"

"Away! Away with you boy. Coming here, in that pauper's suit, calling yourself a suitor. The shame. Hearts and diamonds! Be gone with you boy."

"But…"

Mayer's protestations were in vain. Nicholas had already left. His laughter could already be heard emanating from another room:

"Ho!   Ho! Ho!"

*****

A strange thing happened that week: A card arrived addressed to "Master Mayer".

No-one noticed it apart from Maggs, who knew better than to pry, and so Mayer was able to read it alone.

It was from Lola! She wanted him to take her to dinner!

Mayer could not comprehend what had happened, it defied rational explanation, and so a certain sort of nausea took hold. As if he had snorted sea water, Mayer's throat felt sickly, his nostrils congested, and his head numbed. He almost choked. But he did not complain.

Where reason failed, faith reigned:

'My persistence has paid off. I knew it would. I just knew it!'

Mayer peppered the air with punches, and hugged his pillow until it popped.

DISCOMFORT ZONE

"I think art comes from some sense of discomfort with the world."
YANN MARTEL

We left Archibald stewing in his feebleness.

We return to find him stewing in his feebleness.

Nothing has changed. But, then again, why would it? Inaction does not inspire reaction. The world does not turn for a person who suffers in silence.

Let us recap.

Archibald's love for Lola was beyond pure; an ideal untarnished by facts, undiminished by the truth, and unconstrained by base reality.

At the same time, it was paralysing. It took control of Archibald's thoughts; keeping him trapped in a world of his mind's imagination. There he remained, incapable of moving and, we should note, incapable of conceiving a way out.

Archibald did not know Lola's name, nor where he could find her.

How could he possibly woo her? It was not just a matter of will, but also a matter of means. To Archibald, the very idea of courting Lola seemed absurd.

*****

Archibald surrendered to the omnipotence of his imagination, bestowing Lola with fanciful qualities and fantastic passions; giving her an imaginary name, "Angela Gabriella"; and falling asleep at the most inopportune of moments, worn down by the most tiring of loves.

But sleep did not provide respite. If anything, Lola made more appearances in Archibald's dreams than in his waking thoughts; at one moment appearing as a native, then as a villager; as a stranger, an acquaintance, a supplier and a customer. So, when Lola and her mother *did* enter his shop, having just visited the botanical gardens, Archibald was in no doubt; he was dreaming, as he so often dreamt; imaging he was in Lola's presence, as he so often imaged himself to be. The people in front of him were not in front of him, they were not made of flesh, and could not possibly be real.

Lola could not quite believe her eyes either. She had to rub them, blink, and glare at Archibald before her mind could process the information her eyes were generating.

There he was; that fine figure of a man she had seen in Covent Garden. She had not forgotten his bulging arms or pert chest. His image had lingered on in the recesses of her mind like a tenacious ghost.

And there she was, the woman of Archibald's dreams; her hair overhanging her shoulders, her nose pointing straight, and her pinkish hat tilted to the side.

Lola and Archibald immediately felt the same pang of attraction. It was not felt in their loins; that would be a cliché. Rather, it was felt in their arms, which wanted to reach out and grab the other; their toes, which jiggled; and their hair, which fizzed with static energy.

Their eyes glazed over, their teeth chattered, and their nostrils filled with the scent of cinnamon; that aroma which, for them, was the very essence of true love.

Lola's mother approached the counter:

"Two jars of your famous honey."

Archibald passed her a jar of honey.

"Two!"

Archibald passed her another jar:

"Four pence please."

Lola's mother turned to leave.

Lola felt she had to do something, anything, to extend that blissful moment. So she gestured towards Archibald's doll, whose hat had caught her attention:

"Is that doll on your chairdrobe for sale?"

"I guess. I've had it since I was just a boy, but you can have it, if you like."

Lola giggled, tilted her head, covered her mouth and bent her knee:

"You can't just give it to me, silly."

"I can't? I'm afraid you've lost me."

"No! That's a part of your childhood."

"Oh."

Lola fluttered her eyebrows.

"I suppose I can have one made for you, if you like."

"That'd be super-duper."

Archibald smiled.

Lola fluttered her eyelids:

"Aren't you forgetting something?"

"I'm not sure."

"My address?"

"Your address?"

"So you can have the doll delivered, silly."

"Oh, yes, of course."

"It's 303 Hill Street, Mayfair, and my name is Lola."

Archibald blushed.

Lola blushed:

"And?"

Archibald raised his eyebrows.

"How much should I pay?"

"Pay?"

"I must pay something."

"You must?"

"Yes."

"Okay."

"So how much should I pay?"

"Something."

"How much, silly?"

"Anything."

"Don't be a tattle-tease."

"Oh, I didn't mean to tease you. I hope you can believe me."

"Well?"

"Maybe a penny. One pence. Two ha'pennies."

"It's not enough."

"Oh."

"Oh?"

"Well you can pay whatever is enough, I suppose."

Lola giggled.

"Here you go," she said, placing three silver shillings on the counter. "Hopefully I'll see you again?"

Lola fluttered her eyelids.

Archibald nodded like a dog.

*****

Lola!

The very sound of her name amazed him:

'*Lola! Low-lah! Loe-la! Loo-lah! Lola!*'

He rolled that word around his tongue a thousand times, and whispered it to the wind as if it were an exquisite secret:

'*Lola! Lola! Lola!*'

For Archibald, it was a magical word. It was perfection. It was bliss.

*****

Archibald was so nervous when he arrived at 303 Hill Street that he turned around and left. He circled Berkeley Square Gardens a full five times before he returned. Then he left again. He made five more laps of the square, then another five, then five more.

Lola's doll palpitated in his startled hand.

Dressed in Raymondo's suit, which was too wide at the waist and too narrow at the chest, Archibald cut a ridiculous figure. He knew it too.

Hence, his determination led him to knock on Lola's door, and his modesty made him run away.

Hidden around a corner, he saw Lola retrieve her figurine, which he had placed by on the doormat; he heard her footsteps tap like hooves on stone, and believed he smelled her perfume. But that was it; Lola did not see him; Archibald went home empty handed.

*****

Archibald kicked, slapped and cursed himself:

'*How could I be so stupid? So weak-willed? So lily livered? So feeble? Aaargh! Archibald, Archibald, Archibald!*'

He resolved to make amends, and so he returned the next day with one of his portraits. Again, it took him several attempts to pluck up the courage to knock on Lola's door. And again, he ran away as soon as he had placed his sketch on her doorstep.

He tried again the next day, and again the same thing happened. It occurred the day after that, and the day after that.

Determined not to give in, Archibald tried twice the following day, four times the day after that, and many more times during the days and weeks which followed. He visited Lola's house almost every hour, pacing around Berkeley Square Gardens in-between.

As a result, Archibald had to close his shop, which meant he lost so much money he was forced to skip meals. By the time the month was up, he had lost a stone. He had knocked on Lola's door hundreds of times, and left all his sketches, but he had not seen Lola once.

*****

Archibald adjusted his chair so it faced towards Lola's house, so many miles away; across so many streets, filled with the confusion of so much sound; and across so many squares, which would one day be filled with trees.

He dressed in Raymondo's suit, adorned his wrists with frilly cuffs, picked up his quill and began to write:

'Ever since I saw you, I knew we were destined to be.'

It was enough. Archibald did not even sign it. He simply placed it on Lola's doorstep, in the same way he had left his portraits.

So the routine rekindled.

'We are love's long-lost hope', he wrote the next day. 'We are joy unbound.'

Then: 'We are seeds and earth: Together we will make forests.' 'We are caterpillars: Together we will become butterflies.' 'We are stardust: Together we will make it to the stars.'

Like a nursling, dazzled by the light of its first spring, Archibald had aimed for the lyrical and achieved the rhetorical; each line was cornier than the last, and each note was even more desperate.

THE FINISHING TOUCHES

"Knowledge without justice ought to be called cunning rather than wisdom."
PLATO

Hugo drank brandy with Nicholas on a regular basis.

It was a relationship both parties were keen to nurture; Hugo was keen to listen, and Nicholas was keen to speak; Hugo was keen to learn, and Nicholas was keen to teach. Much to his dismay, Nicholas's sons had become lawyers, and so he came to see Hugo, a medical professional like himself, as the son he never had. Hugo, meanwhile, felt like he had finally found a father.

Lola eavesdropped on their conversations, with her eyes turned towards her aspidistras, and her ears turned towards Hugo. In this manner, she came to know Hugo; through discussions in which she never spoke, acts which she never performed, and camaraderie which she never saw.

Hugo never acknowledged Lola, which made her long to be acknowledged. She wanted to smile at Hugo, jump up and wave at him. She wanted all the attention Hugo withheld.

She scolded herself for it. Hugo was not as keen as Mayer, as handsome as Archibald, or as rich as her other suitors; his face was distinctly average and his odour was far too plebeian for her liking. Yet she still found him alluring. Why? It did not make any sense.

And so Lola alternatively reproached herself, forgave herself, reproached Hugo and forgave Hugo. She doubted the reality, and realised her doubts. She could not confide in anyone, because she did not really have anything to confide. What could she say? That she was drawn to a boy who was neither alluring nor rich, and who did not seem interested in her?

But this had been Hugo's plan all along. Hugo knew he was mundane. He also knew that mundanity could be irresistible when placed just out of reach.

Was Adam really tempted by the serpent's apple? Of course not! There were thousands of other apples in the Garden of Eden, all of which were just as juicy. But only one of those apples was forbidden. How could Adam resist?

Poor, humble and mundane; Hugo was just one apple in a vast orchard. But he had turned himself into forbidden fruit; Lola could not help but be tempted. So she listened when Hugo spoke of surgery and medicine, and she listened when he told Nicholas of a girl who had caught his eye:

"I think I'm in love."

"My boy, that's amazing!"

Hugo shrugged.

"What is it?"

"This girl. Well, you see. The thing is..."

"Yes?"

"Sorry. It's just that she's a little above my station."

"What? Ho! Ho! Ho! I'm as sure as Christ is holy that she'd be lucky to have you."

Hugo smiled:

"I hope so sir."

"I dare say I know so."

"I wish I shared your confidence. I'm sorry, really I am, but I'm just a pauper of no-account. She puts butter on bacon; sir, she's a member of your own social strata. I'd eat my own head just to make her happy, but her parents would never bless our union."

"Golly, what a bind! Ho! Ho! Ho! Can this girl really be that great?"

"'Great' doesn't come close. Sir, she puts the stars in the sky at night. She gives the sun a reason to rise. She has such profound boldness! I swear, she's stronger than most men, and larger than life itself."

"Ho! Ho! Ho! Well, if there's anything I can do, be sure to ask. Perhaps I could put in a word with her father, man-to-man, so to speak?"

"Perhaps," Hugo laughed. "Your word might just make the difference."

"Fingers crossed. Ho! Ho! Ho! Knock on wood!"

*****

Hugo had made sure Lola heard that conversation. He could not, however, be sure of her reaction:

'Being a rival for her father's attention, she must despise me. Being of good birth, she must look down on me. Being a romantic, she must adore me. Being an eccentric, she must be falling in love.'

Pessimism danced with optimism. Hope danced with despair.

Hugo knew he was just poor orphan; a thief and a parent-killer, who was unlikely to impress a girl like Lola. He knew that to stand a chance, any chance at all, he was going to have to up his game…

*****

Lola turned into the alley which connected Farm Street and Hill Street, as she did on a daily basis. Hugo had followed her there on over thirty occasions.

Before she could reach the end, a raggedy figure stepped out of the darkness. His attire was something else. His majestic blue blazer was full of worm holes, his breeches had faded with dust, and his balaclava obscured his face.

Wilkins held up his palm:

"Now, now there love. There be a toll to pay. If you wish to pass, you must hand over the king's levy. That there gold bracelet would do nicely, so it would. Yes it chuffin' well would!"

Lola stepped back; half affronted, half bemused.

"Very well," she laughed. "I won't pass."

She turned and walked back the way she had come.

"Very well!" Wilkins mocked. "And a splendid day to you ma'am. I hope it brings all the blessings in this here world."

As soon as he finished speaking, a second figure stepped out in front of Lola. His collar was covered in spittle, and his face was covered by a scarf.

"No... no... not so far," Bib stuttered. "You see, there be a toll to pay if yo... yo... you wish to pass. Thanking you kindly. Thanking you!"

Lola stepped back into Wilkins, who had followed her down the alley.

"If you wish to come this way," he repeated. "You'll have to pay with that there gold bracelet."

"And if you wi... wi... wish to come *this* way," Bib echoed. "That gold bracelet would do ve... ve... very nicely."

Lola panicked.

She had been remarkably calm up until this point, in spite of Wilkins's effrontery, so it took her by surprise when a sudden surge of fear usurped every atom in her body. Her heart raced, her breathing became erratic, and her muscles froze. She stood there, paralysed; unable to process the situation.

"That gold bracelet will do very nicely."

"Tha... tha... that there bracelet. Thanking you!"

"Oi!" Hugo shouted as he ran down the alley. "Oh no you don't! Who on earth do you think you are? Bugger off you little ruffians. Go on, skedaddle! Crawl back down whatever hole it was that spawned you."

Wilkins ran in the opposite direction.

Bib ran into Hugo.

Hugo pushed him to the ground.

"You didn't say nah... nah... nothing 'bout hurting me somethin' awful," Bib mumbled inaudibly. "That weren't neh... neh... never no part of the deal."

Hugo kicked Bib's stomach, in an attempt to nudge him away.

Bib limped away.

Lola flung her arms around Hugo. She hugged him more fervently than she had ever hugged anyone before.

"It's okay, ma'am, it's okay."

"I'm so happy to see you."

Hugo laughed:

"Well you can thank your father for that. He's the reason I was passing."

"No, don't you humble-mumble to me. *You're* my knight in shining armour, not anyone else."

Lola believed it too. She was oblivious to the fact that Hugo had manufactured that scene. But, then again, bright light is often more deceptive than darkness. Most people would rather fall for a believable lie than accept an uncomfortable truth.

*****

"Come," Hugo told Lola. "I'll walk you home."

"Thank-you, you're a gentleman. And will you talk to me?"

"Talk to you, ma'am?"

"Yes, silly, you never talk to me. When you visit, you act as though I'm a ghost."

"Sorry ma'am, but it's not for us mortals to talk to angels."

Lola blushed, took Hugo's hand, walked him home, and told her father what had happened.

"Really, Hugo Crickets! You may be below us in status, but you're well above us in deeds. I'd be proud to call you my son."

Hugo blushed.

"Come, let's chew the fat. I've just opened a vintage bottle of brandy, and I dare say it sounds like you deserve it. Ho! Ho! Ho! Let's be merry."

Nicholas led Hugo into the morning room, where they talked for all of two minutes before there was a knock at the door. After a further five minutes, Nicholas left to greet his visitor.

Hugo waited through a period of pure silence and a period of pure noise.

"You? You come in here unannounced, dressed like a merchant, without so much as a reference, and you say you're here to court *my* Lola?"

Pause.

"How vulgar! How inappropriate. How... How... How unsuitable!"

Pause.

"Away! Away with you boy. Coming here, in that pauper's suit, calling yourself a suitor. The shame. Hearts and diamonds! Be gone with you boy."

*****

Nicholas was apoplectic. His face had taken on the complexion of squashed berries, and his beard was misshapen. His normal aroma, of mince pies, had given way to the stench of unmitigated fury; of semen, chicken and burnt sugar:

"Well I never!"

"What is it?"

"It's jolly rotten, that's what it is. Some dowry thief, come to court my Lola. Can you believe it?"

"Yes sir."

"Yes?"

"She's a very courtable young lady."

"Ho! Ho! Ho!"

Lola entered:

"Oh daddy. Don't be so mean. He's harmless."

"I dare say he's dim-witted."

"He's kind."

"You like him?"

"I don't dislike him."

Nicholas shuffled, uncomfortably, as if sitting on a porcupine.

"What do you think, Hugo?"

"I suppose it should be up to Lola. She's a strong woman, and strong women always get their way in the end."

"Ho! Ho! Ho! But he is ever so inappropriate, don't you think?"

"I think Lola is afternoonified enough; she's as smart as a steel trap. If this suitor is inappropriate, it's almost certain that she'll see it."

Lola smiled, gave her father a knowing glance, and was about to speak. She paused, frowned, and turned to face Hugo:

"Don't I know you from somewhere?"

"Yes ma'am, I've visited your father on several occasions."

"No, silly, that's not it."

"It's not, ma'am?"

"No, I know you from somewhere else."

"The shop where I lent you my jacket?"

"No, that's not it."

"The alley?"

"No! Stop being such an errorist!"

"Sorry. I think we first met in Covent Garden."

"Yes, that's it! You're Mayer's buddy. You stuck up for him then, and you're sticking up for him now. Oh my, you really are a fantabulous friend!"

BEST LAID PLANS

"Self-deception is when you wind up believing what you wanted to believe all along. That's how many of us fall in love."
CLANCY MARTIN

Mayer was confused. Nicholas had been quite clear: He was not to court Lola. Lola had spurned his advances on several occasions. Why, then, had he been asked to take her out?

Mayer could not be sure.

This, however, was the least of his worries. A much more pertinent question lingered in his mind:

'Where should I take her? What should I do?'

Mayer knew he only had one chance, but he did not know how he should use it…

*****

Since committing to repaying Abe and Sadie, Mayer had restricted himself to eating three hunks of bread for his lunch. So it was that he sat down on a bench in St. Martin's Gardens, placed a handkerchief on his lap, and began to chew a crust.

Two men he did not recognize, Wilkins and Bib, sat down and began to talk:

"You smell of fu… fu… fish!"

"I do."

"You don't deny it?"

"How could I?"

"Pu… pu… pride."

"'Pu… pu… pride?' *You* speak to *me* of pride, snot boy? Talk about the pot calling the kettle black!"

"Oi!"

"Oi nothing. Tomorrow, I won't smell of fish. You, you numpty, will still be a walking, talking ball of greenies and phlegm."

Bib shook his head:

"So why do you smell of fu… fu… fish then? It's not like you."

"You'll never guess."

"Oh."

"I've been carrying seafood."

"Oh."

"Chuffin' genius, eh?"

"Not really."

"No."

"So why have you been carrying fu… fu… fish?"

"Seafood."

"Seafood."

"I got a gig for ol' Fish Breath, down at the docks. He pays me for doing deliveries, door-to-door so it is. Only when 'is other muckers is busy."

"Oh."

"There's this girl over in Mayfair. Lola they call her. Right princess.

Well, this Lola bird has a thing for oysters. And what she wants, she gets. So ol' muggins here had to lug a crate of the blighters 'cross town for her pleasure, so he did."

"And that's why you smell?"

"That's why I smell."

"Oh."

"It ain't all so bad. This Lola chick also has a thing for feathers and poetry books. I've taken her sackfuls of the things."

"They don't st... st... stink."

"They do not."

Mayer smiled. He felt as though the heavens were aligning; that this was the universe's way of saying that he and Lola were destined to be.

He finished his bread and headed back to work with a skip in his step.

Bib and Wilkins headed off to find Hugo, who paid them for staging that conversation.

*****

Lola had agreed to see Mayer for three reasons:

One: She did it to spite her father. She was a strong woman, who hated patriarchal interference.

Two: She was falling for Mayer's charm. Of all her suitors, Mayer was her favourite.

Three: She thought Archibald's notes had come from Mayer. He was the only person she knew who would be so pushy.

When Archibald wrote, 'We are seeds and earth: Together we will make forests', he had thought it was the most beautiful thing in the world. When Lola read those lines, all she could do was laugh:

'We will be forests? Oh Mayer, you're such a klutz!'

Still, any man who can make a woman laugh has half a chance, and so Lola warmed to Mayer. She thought she might even enjoy an evening in his company.

*****

'Rat-a-tat-tat. Rat-a-tat-tat'.

Lola brushed the butler aside. Her body was gowned in magenta, her head was crowned in silver, and her nose was ready for a crusade.

"Hi," she cheered.

"Hi," Mayer replied. "Isn't it lovely? The sun always shines for you."

"Oh behave, silly. It's just an average swinter day."

"Well then, it must be you that's shining bright."

"Pfft! Your head's up in the clouds."

Mayer passed Lola a bouquet of feathers, plucked from pheasants' tails, geese's shoulders and roosters' capes. They had been dyed several shades of gold and wrapped in a cone.

All told, it was a gaudy mix of opulence and ostentation. In putting it together, Mayer had spent money he did not have, to make an impression which would not last, on a girl he did not know.

He did not regret it.

"Feathers?" Lola asked.

"Feathers!"

"Feathers? *Aah-chew!*"

"Bless you!"

"Tha... Thank-... *Aah-chew!*"

"Are you okay?"

"De... Delight... *Aah-chew!*"

Lola passed those feathers to the butler before her allergic reaction could get any worse. Her nostrils were already vibrating, and her nose was already on edge:

"They're lovely. Come, let's go. I can see you have a carriage waiting."

Mayer took Lola's hand, led her down the steps, opened the carriage's door, and helped Lola to climb inside.

"So," he said once they were moving.

"So," Lola replied.

They rode on in silence, tapping their knees, until Mayer plucked up the courage to speak:

"She walks in beauty, like the night; of cloudless climes and starry skies. And all that's best of dark and bright, meet in her aspect and her eyes."

"What are you doing?"

"Reciting Byron."

"Please don't."

Lola gave Mayer's thigh a gentle squeeze.

They continued their journey, disembarked, entered a restaurant, climbed the stairs, and emerged on a secluded rooftop terrace. Buildings stood sentry on either side, turning to mist, and turning back to stone. A canopy of stars floated above them. The motion of London resonated within them. The air caressed their skin.

There was a moment of uncomfortable silence, and a moment of uncomfortable conversation. Then a waiter approached, holding a platter of oysters above his head.

"The food of love!" Mayer announced. "Come! Eat! For the love of food, and the love of all loves: Ours! Eat, my love, eat."

Lola's nose scrunched upwards, her eyes squirmed leftwards, and her stomach shrank inwards. The smell made her choke. There really was nothing she despised more than seafood; the very thought of it made her want to curl up and melt away.

She stood up:

"I… I… I can't do this. Look, you're sweet, you've gone to a lot of effort; it's lovely. I thought you were 'The One'. But this date has shown me how wrong I was. I mean: Feathers? Poetry? Oysters? Ugh! We're clearly not meant to be. We… We… We're slantindicular."

Lola stole the silence from Mayer's mouth:

"Forgive me."

She tensed her cheeks, raised her shoulders and left.

Mayer froze.

*****

Mayer was forced to accept his predicament. He refused to accept the truth.

He realised that he needed to stop courting Lola, take a time-out and regroup. But he had to go on loving her; he considered it his duty.

He was sure Lola was the one:

'*Our love is eternal. I mean, she did agree to date me. She must like me. Yes, she loves me! I just need to trust in that love.*'

SWAN LAKE

"When in doubt, be ridiculous."
SHERWOOD SMITH

Archibald kicked himself.

He knew he had to tell Lola how he felt. He knew, if he knocked on her door, he would flee. And so he decided to lure her to neutral ground.

He picked up one of his notes, folded it along its diagonal, unfolded it, and brought its corners together. He folded and unfolded that note until it had become an origami swan.

Before he knew it, he had turned all his notes into origami swans.

Then he had an idea.

*****

Lola stepped onto her doorstep, wearing a hat which was so large it shaded four square metres of the ground. She spotted a paper swan by her toe, picked it up, unfolded it, and read the message inside:

'This is the first day of the rest of our lives!'

'*Oh Mayer*', she thought. '*Don't you ever give up?*'

She saw a second swan:

'Don't ignore love, for the good of your health. Make the RIGHT choice, take a TURN for yourself.'

Lola turned right, where she found another swan, and then a fourth. They formed a trail; guiding her past grand homes, grand carriages, grand people, and gross filth.

Trees rustled, dizzy with premonitions of rain. Birds fluttered, anticipating friendly air. Ripples danced on miasmic puddles, muck congealed, and litter skipped with giddy abandon.

Lola skipped; carefree, unbound, and enthral with the game.

One swan told her: 'CROSS your heart and hope to love. THE ROAD below you, the sky above.'

Another: 'LOOK AHEAD to the future, forget the past. Time is fleeting, but we will last.'

Then: 'Eat with a FORK, or eat with a spoon. Nothing LEFT over, we'll meet very soon.'

Lola continued down Deanery Street, crossed Park Lane, and skipped through Hyde Park.

A billion blades of grass united to form one luscious carpet, and a single tree splayed apart to form a galaxy of leaves.

Lola skipped down one path and bounded down another; following those swans, reading them, refolding them, and cradling them in her blouse.

With rusty leaves caressing her ankles, and dandelion fluff in her hair, she reached a café which faced the Serpentine.

A swan sat on one of the tables:

'So here we are, this is our date. The start of our romance, and not a second too late.'

Lola perused the clientele; the elderly gentleman and his teenage wife; the lady in a moribund dress, the lord in tops and tails, the men with whiskers, and the women with wild eyes:

'*Where is he? I don't recognize anyone here.*'

She drank a cup of camomile tea. Then she drank another.

She waited. Then she waited some more.

*****

Archibald was sitting at a nearby table, hidden behind a newspaper; lacking the courage to show his face. Something was holding him back.

He did not care.

Lola was there, he was there, they were there together! In Archibald's mind, they were on a date. His heart pulsated, his brow glistened with imaginary sweat, and his nostrils tingled with tantric delight.

That saccharine aroma of cinnamon, which for him was the very essence of pure love, wafted up from his cup in steamy vapours.

Lola smelled that cinnamon. It played with her nose; making it twitch, shimmy and scrunch.

Lola smiled.

Archibald had made Lola smile! She was falling for him! He knew it, he just knew it!

He knew it was the beginning of forever. No more would they be two souls, they would be one. They would unite in marriage, in life and love. They would live together, love together, make love together, have children together, and be one together, forever and ever amen.

Archibald felt as though he was walking on air; light, free, and invincible. He did not feel a need to show himself. He did not feel a need to do anything at all.

*****

Lola was confused:

'Why go to such an effort and then just abandon me? Pfft! Men are a strange breed: Queerer than fog and much less predictable.'

Her tea turned cold.

She waited, because she wanted to wait, she wanted her mood to last, and she wanted her suitor to show. But he did not show, and so she reluctantly requested the bill.

The bill never came.

"Your bill has been paid," the waiter told her. "This is for you."

He handed Lola a swan. Full of crumples and creases, it lacked the aesthetic of her other swans, but Lola did not care. The game was on.

Reinvigorated, her pulse took on a broken beat, her feet tapped out of time, and her body swayed without rhyme or rhythm or reason. She read those scribbled words and sprang into action.

INDECENT PROPOSAL

"It's easier to fool people than to convince them that they have been fooled."
MARK TWAIN

To love is to risk.

Archibald was too timid to take that risk.

Hugo was not.

He climbed into Lola's garden, as if he was a mudlark again, and slipped into her home through an unlocked window.

All was still.

Hugo tiptoed across the giant hall, up the leafy stairs, and into Lola's bedroom; the heart of her inner-sanctum: Four posts on her bed. Four shelves on each wall. Four plants on each shelf. The scent of magnolia, sweet and fresh. The scent of virginity. The scent of flesh.

Hugo violated that space with his eyes; spotting a table covered in cosmetics, and a stack of sketches covered in lines.

He felt the love in each brushstroke as if it was his own. His heart skipped a beat and his stomach turned; his diaphragm contracted, his lungs expanded, his body buzzed, and his ears rang. He steadied himself, and then he spotted a stack of notes wedged in between some zeezee plants.

He saw beauty in their naivety. He saw pure, unadulterated humanity. The anxiety, feebleness, and hopelessness; the trembling of infatuation; the merging of hope and despair; it all spoke to him. It rekindled a feeling with which he had once been familiar; a feeling he had felt when he was turfed out of St Mary Magdalen's and when he was trapped by Jonathan Wild. One simple, complex feeling: Fear.

He felt the author's fear as if it was his own:

'*But who could write such things? Who could create such art?*'

Hugo looked for clues.

He looked at Lola's violets, roses, fuchsias and begonias; at the softness of her bed, the hardness of her furniture, and the wallpaper which went on and on and on.

Then he saw it, between four cacti. He recognized that doll straight away:

'*Archibald. Oh, dear, blessed Archibald.*'

He felt for his friend, and he felt that he had to usurp him.

Archibald had become such a fine specimen of manhood, thanks to Hugo's own encouragement, that Lola was sure to favour him. Hugo could not allow that to happen. He loved his friend, but he loved Lola more. Eros crushed philia. Hugo was determined to crush his foe.

He took a portrait and tiptoed away.

*****

An honest man follows his heart. A sensible man follows his woman.

Hugo followed Lola, literally, and so saw Archibald set out his swans.

He picked one up:

'Walk into our future, WALK STRAIGHT AHEAD. Pass leaves of green, and leaves of red.'

Hugo winced. Then he waited. Then he followed Lola to a café, where he saw Archibald.

'*Blast*', he thought. '*I'm too late.*'

As he waited for Archibald to step forward, Hugo ran his nails down the side of a tree and bit the top of his lip.

Archibald did not move.

Hugo could not believe his luck. He took a piece of paper from his satchel, wrote his own message, and folded it, using the swan he had picked up as his guide:

'Enough of tea, enough of cake. Let's feed the SWANS, down by the LAKE.'

Hugo paid Lola's bill, gave the waiter a generous tip, and asked him to give Lola the swan. Then he made his way to the bench which Lola visited each morning.

*****

Hugo stood up and smiled.

Lola turned white.

"You?" she asked.

"Me."

Lola's jaw dropped open.

Hugo passed her the sketch he had stolen.

"You?"

"Me."

"Well, really, I'm shockified."

Lola shivered.

At once it struck her. Here was a chivalrous knight who had saved her from the rain and from her muggers; a gentleman, who had stood up for his friend before making a move; a romantic, who had written her notes, drawn her pictures, and sent her on a treasure hunt; a respectable man, who had won the affection of her father; and a man on her wavelength, who had met her at her favourite bench.

Could she have hoped for anything more?

"You?"

"Me!"

Lola dropped to her knees.

"Marry me," she demanded.

"No," Hugo laughed. "You've got it all wrong. That's not how you propose."

"Oh, do excuse me, I have very little experience when it comes to proposing."

"It's okay."

Hugo got down on one knee.

"Marry *me*," he said.

"Now how is that any better?"

"Because I did it. It's a man's place to propose."

"Well, I don't care much for staying in my 'Place'. I asked first, so I deserve to be answered first. Now, Hugo Crickets, will you marry me?"

"Yes!" Hugo laughed. "Of course I will. And now, please grant me my turn: Lola, will you marry me?"

"I'll think about it."

"Oh."

The conversation paused. The clouds stopped moving. A beam of pink light highlighted the dust particles in the air, which also seemed to stop moving, as if they were waiting for an answer too.

"I've thought about it."

"And?"

"I think I'll give it a go, I'm sure it'll be sweet like strawberries and cream, and if it doesn't work out we can have a jolly good laugh about it with our friends. I'm sure it'll have us in stitches."

"Great!"

"But you must promise me one thing."

"Anything."

"Never make me eat oysters."

"I promise."

"Good. Now walk me home."

HAPPY ENDINGS

"He who does not know how to take advantage
of luck when it comes to him has no right to
complain if it passes him by."
SANCHO PANZA

Nicholas agreed to the match.

A part of him was inclined to refuse; Hugo was beneath his family, both in class and income; but he liked the boy, and the way Lola reacted when he gave her a giant pink hat told him everything he needed to know: Lola *was* in love. She had begun to suffer from impromptu onslaughts of smiling, her feet tapped whenever she sat down, and she found flowers even more fragrant than before.

"I have one request," Nicholas told Hugo.

"Yes sir."

"You must train to be a doctor. I'll not have a lowly surgeon in my family."

"Oh."

"Oh?"

"I *am* sorry, but I couldn't possibly afford to go to university."

"Well then, I suppose I'll have to pay."

"You will sir?"

"I will."

Hugo flung his arms around Nicholas.

"Ho! Ho! Ho!" Nicholas chuckled. "I have three pieces of advice for you."

"Yes sir."

"Marry a woman you don't deserve, and buy a house you can't afford. That way you'll have a reason to leave for work each morning, and a reason to return each night."

"Yes sir."

"Either admit you're wrong, even when you're not, or argue your case, and *then* admit you're wrong."

"Yes sir."

"It's the thought that counts. It helps if it's an expensive thought."

"Yes sir."

"And remember to tell your wife you love her every day. Make sure your children hear."

"That's four things."

"And here's a fifth: Don't ever question your father-in-law."

"Sorry sir."

"Ho! Ho! Ho!"

*****

"I'm getting married," Hugo told Archibald and Mayer the next time they met.

They were walking towards The Three Horseshoes, having just watched Archibald wrestle. Lambeth was in a groaning slumber; dew glistened in the half-light of dusk, and bees were moseying back to their hives.

"Congratulations!"

"Her name is Lola."

Hugo smiled. He could not help but feel elated.

Archibald and Mayer grimaced. They could not help but feel dejected.

Hugo felt their despair, and they felt Hugo's elation. They all, therefore, felt the most beautiful ambivalence. Elation neutralized despair, love neutralized hate, and they all went to the pub, where they drowned their sorrow and cheered their success, without being entirely sure if they were celebrating or mourning.

"You're both going to be my best men," Hugo said as they left. "I wouldn't have it any other way."

Archibald grabbed Hugo's shoulders and Mayer rubbed his hair. They waited for him to leave, then they turned to face each other, in sync, and uttered the very same words: "Let's drink to forget".

*****

So ended the chase.

For Archibald and Mayer, Lola had been the woman of *their* dreams. But Hugo had brushed them aside. He had become the man of *Lola's* dreams.

Mayer had been persistent, Archibald had been poetic, but Hugo had triumphed with the prosaic. He married Lola, trained to become a doctor, and moved in with his new wife.

Archibald and Mayer were forced to move on with their lives...

BOOK THREE

CONSEQUENCES

MOVING ON

"The only thing that is constant is change."
HERACLITUS

Life obliges us to be born many times.

Our three heroes had already been born on three separate occasions: When their mothers gave birth to them, when they were separated, and when they were reunited.

They were about to be born once more.

They were about to be born of money, power and love...

OF POWER

"Everything in the world is about sex except sex. Sex is about power."
OSCAR WILDE

Archibald still felt Hugo's love for Lola as if it was his own.

He hated himself for it. He hated the way he had let Lola escape, without even having the courage to approach her:

'*How could I be so weak? So feeble? So damn pathetic?*'

It was made worse by the fact that this was nothing new. Like his uncle, Archibald had always been feeble. And, just like that man, he saw himself enduring a similar fate; crushed by his peers, as the world stomped roughshod over his body.

He really was a sissy! His bullies had been right all along.

He hated that, he hated himself, and he was determined to do something about it.

'*What do I lack?*' he asked himself. '*Power! What do I need? Power! What will I seek? Power! Power, power, power!*'

It was a watershed moment; the death of his innocence, and the birth of a new, more belligerent Archibald. He resolved never to be a coward again, to never put a brake on his instincts, and never let anything or anyone get in his way.

Like a bull who had seen a matador's cape, pawing its hoof through the dust, Archibald was ready to fight.

*****

Archibald was determined to win power over two different groups of people: Men and women.

He would attempt to overpower men in the ring, outmuscling everyone who stood in his way; becoming the strongest, most revered, most brutal fighter in London.

He would attempt to overpower women in the bedroom...

*****

London was the sex capital of Europe. According to one estimate, it was home to fifty thousand prostitutes.

Starvation forced some women into selling their bodies. The aggression of pimps and chancers forced others. Some women were groomed from an early age. Others were tricked by the promise of respectable employment, and then trafficked in from France. Some were kept by men of means, some lived alone, and some dwelled in brothels.

Archibald, however, could not afford any such ladies. Like a fisherman, forced to settle for sardines when no haddock could be caught, he was left to seek love in the arms of the lowest of all working girls: The park lady.

Park ladies hid in the darkness, in bushes and woods; too ugly to show themselves in the clear light of day. They were known to do anything for a shilling. Anything at all...

*****

Archibald spotted his prey.

Shabby, in her filthy skirt, faded bonnet and old shoes; bloated, dissipated, wasted by want and suffering; that lady was not much to look at. She did not smell too pretty either. Her body seemed hostile to the approaches of both soap and water.

She was old, incapacitated and ragged; exactly the kind of woman Archibald was seeking.

The uglier the woman, he reasoned, the more handsome he would appear in comparison. The more worthless she seemed, the worthier he would seem. The weaker she was, the easier she would be to overpower.

That woman, Maggie Fletcher, had not always been so low. Born the daughter of a curate, she had worked as a governess, teaching two young girls, before eloping with the family's son. When her father-in-law died, her husband's allowance was cut. He lost his inheritance in a Parisian casino, returned home, and blew his brains out. The next day, Maggie found a letter which said their marriage had been a sham.

Maggie would have returned to her family, but her pride would not allow it. Instead, she fell for her husband's friend, who courted her, promised to marry her, and then dumped her. For ten years, she was passed from one man to another, sharing her body with anyone who cared to ask for it. Disease ravaged her, decrepitude stole her beauty, and disability stole her joy.

Maggie refused to go to the workhouse, and was too ugly to find work. She considered becoming a nun, but felt she had sinned too much to be saved, and so she became a park lady instead. She worked when she needed money, and was frugal, so that she did not need money too often.

Archibald dragged her into a bush.

"Shush," he said when she tried to speak. "I'm in charge here."

He covered her mouth, pulled his trousers down, penetrated Maggie, thought of Lola, and thrust his virginity away.

As soon as Maggie began to groan, Archibald silenced her. As soon as he began to climax, he pulled out in a panic-stricken rush, and threw four pence in Maggie's general direction. The same four pence, in fact, that he had received from Lola's mother.

He turned to leave.

"Will I see you again?" Maggie asked.

"Certainly not. I've been, I've seen, I've conquered. I have other battles to fight.

"Thank-you for your kind service, you truly are a delightful wench."

*****

Archibald was a good wrestler, but not a great wrestler; he beat his opponents, but he never overwhelmed them.

That changed.

Archibald was filled with self-hatred; furious that he had not confessed his love to Lola, stood up to his bullies, or protected Ruthie and Raymondo.

He released that rage on his opponents. Entering the zone, putting his whole being on the line, Archibald threw himself at those men. He grabbed them so hard, his fingers dug into their flesh; he lifted them so quickly, his eyes could not keep up; and he threw them so violently, the ground shuddered with discomfort.

The crowd took a collective gasp.

Archibald dominated, disposing almost every wrestler who stood in his way. It was exhilarating; adrenaline surged through his veins. It was intoxicating; lifting him higher and higher. It was enlivening. But it was not enough.

Archibald wanted more. More power, more control, more rewards. More! More! More!

He was winning almost every competition he entered, receiving a small purse each time, but he was still sleeping on the floor in his shop. He survived, but he did not thrive.

Then it happened. He was approached by a bookmaker's agent whose face was hidden, shadowed by the rim of his downturned hat; whose neck was hidden, covered by his upturned collar; and whose voice was hidden, muffled by a throaty cold.

"I can make you rich," he growled, almost silently, like a purring cat.

Archibald frowned:

"How rich?"

"Richer than you are now."

"That's not difficult."

"I'm not asking you to do anything difficult."

Archibald looked that man up and down.

Everything about him was hardened. His knuckles looked just a little too bony, and his bones protruded just a little too much. Sandpaper stubble covered his chin, jagged creases coated his lips, and gristly hair camouflaged his hands. This made him seem tough, even though he was small of stature and slight of frame. He seemed wizened, worldly even, despite having never left London.

"What do you want?" Archibald asked.

The man almost smiled:

"I want you to throw a bout."

Archibald shook his head.

"Never!" he spat. And with that he stormed away.

*****

Once more, Archibald was held prisoner by his thoughts:

'Why shouldn't I take the money? I work hard and fight well, I deserve that money, does it really matter how I get it?

'Why should I play by the rules? Powerful people don't follow other people's rules; they make their own rules; they wouldn't limit themselves to a measly prize pot, they'd take whatever money they could get.'

At first, Archibald had been wary of the man in a hat; he did not trust him, his money, or his proposal. But, the more he thought about it, the more he realised that he was being offered an opportunity to seize power.

It was an opportunity he felt obliged to take…

*****

The man in a hat appeared at Archibald's next competition.

He could tell by Archibald's steely gaze that he was interested. That look said: "Leave me alone". It also said: "Come on, what's keeping you?"

The man approached:

"You're ready."

"You're paying."

"One shilling to throw the final."

"One pound."

The man circled his tongue:

"Two shillings."

"I'm the boss, I set the price: One pound."

The man paused, looked to the side, then back at Archibald:

"Three shillings."

"No."

The man shrugged and walked away.

Archibald made mincemeat of his opponents, navigating an easy path to the final.

The man approached again:

"Six shillings."

"Ten. Next time, it'll be twelve."

"Deal."

They shook hands.

Archibald threw the fight.

The crowd howled with derision. Their sharp, hawkish boos reverberated from the rafters and resonated deep within Archibald's chest. He did not care. He held power over that crowd; the power to win and lose at will; the power to entertain and bore, delight and disappoint, surprise and stun.

It made him feel majestic, but it did not satisfy him. He still wanted more.

*****

For the first time in his life, Archibald had a little spending money. It was not much, but it was enough for him to start frequenting bawdy houses; those dens of ill repute where sex workers received bed and board in return for a large cut of their earnings; where the digs were so cheap, the sheets were only changed once a week; and where madams sat back and got rich, whilst their girls laid back and got ravaged.

When he was short of cash, Archibald allowed perverts to watch him through peepholes in the wall, in return for which he was given a discount. At other times, peeping Toms observed him through those holes without his knowledge. On one occasion, sensing this state of affairs, Archibald poked his finger through a hole in the thin, wooden partition. He came so close to blinding a man, that when he withdrew he discovered a crystallised tear on his finger. On another occasion, he was so convinced people were watching, that he thumped his fist through the wall. Archibald was thrown out for his troubles, but not before seeing the other side of that partition, where it turned out there were no perverts, just a floozy and her client; a spindly missionary whose testes were no bigger than raisins.

Archibald stumbled from Shadwell to Spitalfields, hypnotized by a Pied Piper's call of tapping heels and creaking beds. He grew fond of a girl called Brenda, who stole from all her men apart from him; a girl called Ariel, who had been bald since her madam had sold her hair; and a girl called Wendy, who eventually met another man, married him the same day, and hung up her pantyhose for good.

Every Tuesday, Archibald patronised "Queens"; a veritable museum, full of long-lost possessions. Archibald spotted all sorts of peculiar things in that place: A lizard's skeleton, a wax seal, a court summons, a military medal, a false leg, a toupee and an odd pair of braces. He also attended a venue known simply as "The Venue", until it was closed down on the evidence of a man who took its girls and set up a brothel of his own. But his favourite bawdy house was called "Paddy's Goose", and his favourite girl was called Peg.

Peg was married. She loved her husband more than anything in the world, but he was unemployable, and so Peg had to sell her body to earn money for them both. Whenever he slept with Peg, Archibald waited for her husband to collect her, so he could shake that man's hand. This gave him a tiny taste of the power he so craved.

*****

This, then, was Archibald's world.

With the drop of a coin, he could have whichever woman he chose, in whichever way he wanted. He could dominate her, make her pretend to be Lola, and even insist that she love him. He could be omnipotent for as long as his credit lasted.

Money. Power. Love.

All told, it was a glorious maelstrom of coin, control and cum: Archibald's money bought him sex, his sex imitated love, and it all served to give him an overwhelming sense of power.

But was it enough? No. Archibald wanted more.

It was not enough for him to find love in the temporary embrace of a paid harlot. He wanted to find love in the permanent embrace of a paid harlot. He wanted real love. Or, at least, something which better resembled it.

For this, Archibald needed a whole different breed of sex worker: The Sailor's Woman.

Sailors' women, as you might have guessed, were prostitutes who serviced sailors; men who returned from sea with lots of money, but very little time in which to spend it. Like Archibald, those men wanted something resembling a relationship; a monogamous fling which extended far beyond the bedroom. And, like Archibald, they were willing to pay.

*****

Archibald got a tailor to fit Raymondo's suit, before heading to a dancing room on Ratcliff Highway; a place full of orchestras and pewter pots, waltzes and polkas, sailors and sailors' women.

Those women were, in general, brazen-faced, tall, and dressed in gaudy colours. Of Germanic or Irish descent, they danced and pirouetted in a fantastical manner; with utter decorum and modest looks.

Their men wore vacant, beery expressions.

Archibald searched for the sailor's woman who most resembled Lola. Then he saw her, alone in a corner; all luminous skin and luscious curves; round eyes, breasts and buttocks. She looked at him with such hermetic gutsiness, he was convinced that Lola had taken another form in order to be his.

"Lola," he whispered. "Lola?"

He gravitated towards her:

"I... I... I..."

He could not say anything more.

"You?"

"I... I... I..."

"You'd like me to be your girl?"

Archibald nodded.

"Six shillings a day, and you'll treat me like a lady. No balum rancum, understood?"

Archibald's shook his head and smiled:

"Oi! I'm in charge here; I'm the one who makes the rules."

The woman laughed:

"Okay! I'm more than happy to play that game, so long as the pennies keep coming."

*****

Her name was Ursula.

Unlike most sailors' women, she was British.

She was not so young. But, as she once told Archibald: "An old fiddle makes the best music".

She was not so old. But, as she once told Archibald: "I'm the oldest I've ever been".

Like a star which had fallen from heaven, she flashed with

transitionary splendour and faded with spontaneous indifference. Her smile flickered and her cheeks flushed, but her icy eyes always repressed those outbursts of lost innocence.

When she was a girl, Ursula had explored the capital on a night which smelled of bonfires and beefy soup. She got lost, and asked for directions from a handsome man.

"Don't I knows you?" he asked.

"I do not suppose so. I'm quite a stranger in London."

"You're staying with someone?"

"My auntie."

"Auntie, is it? What's 'er name?"

"Lottie. Lottie Smithson."

"Well, ain't that fortunate! 'Pon my word, that is lucky. I'm gladder than ever, 'cos I knows your Aunt Lottie very well. Me an' her's great frens, leastways was, though I ain't seen her for months. Took bad, is she? Well, we're all took ill sometimes. Influenzy, is it? Lor' bless us, the influenzy! Well, youse is ever so far from your place. You must stay the night with me; we'll go down to you auntie's 'arly. She'll be ever so glad to see me; she always was fond of her frens."

This speech made sense to that young, unworldly version of Ursula, who followed the man to his house.

She felt uncomfortable as soon as they arrived, and asked to be put in a cab.

The man did not object:

"Have some white satin whilst you wait. I likes to be jolly myself and see others so."

He nudged a glass of gin in Ursula's direction:

"Mark it full, my dear. 'Ave your fill."

That drink was the last thing Ursula remembered.

She awoke with druggy hangover; her chastity stolen by the night. She cried for days and demanded to be killed; unable to face the idea of returning to her family in such a state of disgrace.

So it was that she became a sailor's woman. She drowned her sorrows in gin, her passion for the elegant subsided into a craving for the tawdry, and the bloom of youth in her cheeks was superseded by poisonous French cosmetics.

Still, every now and again, a brief spark of joy did surface on her face. Even though it vanished with supersonic speed, Archibald always saw it. He saw Lola in Ursula, even where she did not exist.

*****

Archibald treated Ursula as though she was his girlfriend; taking her to dances and matinees, on trips and walks. But, at the same time, he worked hard to maintain control. He told Ursula where to meet him, when to meet him, and what they would do. He told her how to dress; buying her the sort of clothes which Lola liked to wear. He took her back to his shop, where he whipped her, spanked her, tied her up, blindfolded her, and left her alone for hours. Then they made love. He brought Ursula to the brink of climax, and then he pulled out.

Ursula fluttered her eyelids, took Archibald's arm, and then took his money. As long as Archibald was able to pay, she was happy to play his game.

But Archibald could sense that it was him, not her, who was being played. So, rather than control Ursula with cruelty, he tried to control her with kindness. He titillated every part of her body, and gave her multiple orgasms; certain that if he could give her absolute pleasure, he would win absolute control; she would return to him for more, and would be his for as long as he wished.

Archibald was so sure he had conquered Ursula that he felt comfortable enough to open up. He told her about the fire which killed his parents, the rise of the factory, the fall of his village, his bullies, Raymondo's death, Ruthie's death, his love for Lola, and the way he had let Lola get away. He cried and smiled and fell into Ursula's arms.

Ursula listened with the patience of a saint. She rubbed Archibald's back, held him tight, and sniffed his hair. She cried when he cried, nodded when he nodded, and inhaled his dewy breath.

Like Achilles in the Iliad, Archibald was falling in love with his concubine. He even dreamt of Ursula when they were apart, just as he had dreamt of Lola. He dreamt of her as if she *was* Lola. He imagined their wedding, marriage, children, old age, deathbeds, and joint ascent to heaven.

For Archibald, it was glorious.

For Ursula, it was work.

Their relationship lasted for a little over three months. Then the wrestling season ended, Archibald's income ran dry, and Ursula left him without a second thought. To her, it was the most natural thing in the world, but to Archibald it was catastrophic. He cursed Ursula, he cursed the world but, most of all, he cursed himself:

'Where's my power? Can't I even control a whore? Come on Archibald, pull yourself together. Take control! Win yourself some frigging power!'

OF MONEY

*"Capitalism is religion. Banks are churches. Bankers
are priests. Wealth is heaven. Poverty is hell. Rich
people are saints. Poor people are sinners.
Commodities are blessings. Money is god."*
MIGUEL D LEWIS

It is natural for a person to desire the things they were not born into.
A rich man may covet a poor man's sense of community. A poor man may
covet a rich man's wealth.

With this in mind, let us now return to Mayer.

Mayer was a poor man, but he had been brought up surrounded by
wealth. It was always just out of reach, which made Mayer want it even
more.

"Money!" he sang to himself. "To want it is to know it. To know it is
to love it. To love it is to chase it. To chase it is to succumb to it. To
succumb to it is to give purpose to life."

Mayer was convinced that if he had more money, Lola would have
married him. If he could amass more wealth, she still might. He did not
concern himself with the small matter of Lola's marriage to Hugo,
because he was certain that Hugo would die. He was certain that he just
needed to bide his time.

Having realised that he had rushed in too fast when courting Lola, he
made amends by easing himself in slowly. Taking things to excess, as was
his nature, he proceeded too slowly; failing to give Lola any indication
that he was still interested in her, and waiting with penitential patience
for the right time to act.

He used that time to amass the wealth which he believed would win
Lola's heart.

*****

Mayer's logic, at first glance, may seem flawed. Lola, after all, married
a man with less money than himself. But, then again, we humans do have
a seemingly unlimited capacity for contradiction.

Perhaps it was a case of cognitive dissonance; Mayer simply refused
to accept the truth, even though it was staring him in the face; his mind
was wedded to his beliefs and incapable of change. Or, perhaps, Mayer
was being reasonable after all. Lola's case, he told himself, was an
exception. Looking around, he saw silver-haired lords with seductive
young mistresses, and overweight millionaires with harems of girls; poor

men with ugly wives, and poor women with no husbands at all. Wealth, he presumed, was a precursor to love.

He was convinced that his tactics had not been the problem; that his swagger, confidence and bravado were all vital tools in his arsenal. He was sure that it was his status which was at fault; that he needed to be more like the gentlemen he had seen at society balls.

He was determined to be wealthy like Abe, and respectable like Mr Bronze...

*****

All Mayer's hard work, geniality and sociability paid off. The friendly conversations, the interest he showed in Mr Bronze's family, Abe's pile of gold in Mr Bronze's safe, and the Christmas presents he gave Mr Bronze each year; all these things bore fruit. All that hard-earned social capital generated one giant dividend: A much better job.

Mayer left Zebedee's bakery and started to work for Mr Bronze.

*****

Mayer already knew that Mr Bronze was trustworthy, level-headed and reliable; that he could set his watch by his routine. Mayer was familiar with the gold monocle Mr Bronze attached to his blazer, the chip on his right incisor, and his straggly eyebrows. Mayer knew *of* Mr Bronze, but he very little *about* him, until the day he started to work for that man.

Mayer came to discover Mr Bronze's story.

Mr Bronze had moved to the capital as a boy, like Dick Whittington before him, in the belief that the streets were paved with gold. He had sought fame and fortune, but was more concerned with the latter.

Mr Bronze took a position as an apprentice to a goldsmith named John Silver. It was Mr Silver who taught him how to check the purity of precious metals and jewels, craft gold into shape, and make a wide variety of rings, earrings, bracelets, chains and cufflinks.

Mr Bronze considered himself a craftsman first and a shopkeeper second. Even though he spent most of his time with his customers, trading silver and gold, in his heart of hearts he was still an artist.

Eventually, he left his master to set up his own business; quickly earning himself a reputation for reliability, quality and integrity. Word spread, his business flourished, he got married, bought a house, and employed two servants.

It was this rise which inspired Mayer, who craved his master's money and status.

Fortunately for Mayer, Mr Bronze still felt he owed a debt to society; he believed he should pass his skills on to the next generation, just as Mr Silver had passed his skills on to him. This was why he recruited Mayer.

This, and the fact that Mayer was literate, which meant he could manage the books.

*****

With his new position came a new life.

Mayer left Buckingham Towers and moved into a room in Mornington Palace, a less than appropriate name for a less than splendid lodging house. According to Mrs Bradbury, the landlady, it was "Dirt cheap". According to Mayer, it was simply "Dirty".

The carpet's pattern had long since been obliterated, and its grooves were variegated with mud. The mantelpiece was covered in dirt, and the calico curtains were dirt coloured. The whole place reeked of stale tobacco. Despite being "Dirt cheap", Mayer had to pay extra for coal, which generated more dirt, and for food, which often looked, smelled and tasted of dirt.

Outside, the street suffered from monotonous tranquillity. Inside, the house suffered from incessant noise. It seemed to Mayer that not a single moment passed in which mouths did not natter or feet did not chatter. The servant was in perpetual motion; scurrying this way to deliver food, and that way to move furniture; forever at the beck and call of an insomnious bell. Elephantine snoring could be heard through every wall.

Still, he liked Mornington Palace. Mrs Bradbury was friendly and the other residents were kind, if not a little aloof. Mayer, however, spent most of his time at work or with his friends.

So it was that he visited Archibald. And, so it was, that Archibald introduced him to Jim McCraw.

"Jack Frost has been to visit," Mayer said; shaking hands in his eager fashion. "It's colder than a witches tit."

"Aye laddie," McCraw replied. "It's fair jeelit."

Mayer nodded.

McCraw continued:

"I hear ye're goldsmith?"

"Yes, my dear friend, I am."

"Well, that's jist bonnie, sae it is. We could dae wi' a goldsmith."

"You could?"

"We could, aye. Dinnae ye jus' ken it?"

"I do?"

"Aye, sonny boy, ye dae."

Mayer pondered the whisky McCraw had snuck into the pub:

"So, why do you need a goldsmith?"

"We've started importin' wine frae France. Folk be buyin' it wi' British coin, but we need French coin tae buy it oorselves. It's doin' ma dinger. Dinnae fesh yersel, but we're in wee bit of a pickle."

"I see."

"An'? Can ye be a saint an' dae us the honoor?"

Mayer tapped his lip:

"Leave it with me, my good man, leave it with me."

*****

Mayer had an idea. It would be wrong to say it was an original idea, but, then again, how many ideas are?

Mayer's idea came to him whilst conversing with McCraw, but it was inspired by a previous conversation he had with some members of his guild: "The Worshipful Company of Goldsmiths".

Those men were like friendly uncles to Mayer. They were affected by the way he looked up to them; an eager orphan in need of father figures. That affection inspired their own affection for him, quid pro quo. So, whilst Mr Bronze taught Mayer about gold and jewellery, those men brought him up to date with the more modern aspects of their trade. Amongst the knowledge they imparted was a knowledge of foreign exchange...

*****

Mayer spotted a pile of French coins in Mr Bronze's second safe. Like most of the silver and gold in that colossus, it seemed to just sit there, as if it had been abandoned.

After a cursory inquiry, Mayer deduced that those coins belonged to a certain Mr Harmer; a cloth merchant from Norfolk.

"Ah, Mr Harmer," Mr Bronze sighed. "Yes, Mr Harmer. I'm told he did hail from Norwich. He's of respectable stock; of Worstead weavers, spinners and dyers; wool combers, yard makers and regular members of the codfish aristocracy."

Mayer looked at Mr Bronze, as if to ask for more.

Mr Bronze looked at Mayer, as if to say there was no more.

"And an exporter, Mr Bronze?"

"Ah, well, he has been known to dabble. I did have it on good authority that the bulk of his trade comes from Yorkshire, Lancashire, Humberside and other assorted parts of the north."

"Not France?"

"No."

"Hmm."

"Ah, 'hmm'?"

"Hmm!"

"Should I deduce from your humming that you did approach me for an introduction?"

"You should, Mr Bronze, you should."

"And why, may I ask, did you desire the pleasure of his company?"

"For the good of both of our companies. He might just be the man to help us bring this place into the modern era."

Mr Bronze frowned, but he did not say a word. It was thirteen minutes past three, the time at which Mr Bronze always went for his afternoon stroll. He picked up his cane and left.

*****

"*Yoooo*, boy, are telling *meeee* where to sell *myyyy* cloth?" Mr Harmer squealed, stretching each vowel sound out for an improbable length of time. "*Yoooo*, boy, are telling *meeee* to export to France? What a precious strange thing. *Yoooo* boy, would make a stuffed bird laugh. What peculiarity!"

"What profitability," Mayer replied.

Mr Bronze remained still. A regular boss might have responded with fury when witnessing such audacity, but a regular boss would have had a full emotional range. Mr Bronze did not.

So, whilst no employee had ever approached a customer in that manner before, whilst *he* had never approached a customer in that manner before, Mr Bronze did not even flinch. He remained a paradigm of neutrality; neither furious nor flustered, certain nor confused. He smiled like a Buddha and allowed Mr Harmer to respond:

"Profitable, *yoooo* say? Profitable, for *whoooom*?"

"For all of us, my dear man, for all of us!"

"How *soooo*?"

"We shall guarantee to exchange whatever coins you bring back from France. This shall protect your interests in that market."

"Protect? Profit? Now you're speaking my language."

He looked at Mr Bronze:

"Where did you find this one?"

"He arrived in a bread cart."

"A bread cart?"

"A bread cart!"

*****

So it came to pass that Mr Harmer exported cloth to France, where he received French coins, which Mayer exchanged for British coins. Mayer took Mr Harmer's French coins and exchanged them with Jim McCraw.

Using his newly acquired skills, Mayer checked the silver and gold in those coins; Mr Bronze put his name to the transactions, to give them an air of respectability; then they charged Harmer and McCraw a commission.

Word soon spread. Other importers and exporters came their way, exchanged coins, and paid commissions.

Those commissions added up. A new pile of gold formed in the second safe. Unlike the other piles, it was theirs alone. And, unlike the other piles, it grew larger each day.

"Ah, I wonder what we should do with it," Mr Bronze muttered, as if talking to himself.

"Hmm,' Mayer replied. "I wonder indeed…"

*****

Mayer stayed in touch with his old workmates at Zebedee's bakery. He was of the firm belief that an acquaintance, once made, should always be kept. It was a belief which verged on the religious. Mayer even kept a ledger, in which he wrote the names of every person he had ever met, along with any details he deemed pertinent. He went through that book each year, and made an effort to meet anyone he had not seen during the previous twelve months.

This was why Mayer took Davey Boy to the pub:

"Can you hear Billy Wind out there? It's blowing some gale!"

"It's grim."

"It is. Now, dear friend, you look like you want to shoot the breeze. Come! Speak and be merry."

Davey Boy tapped the edge of a wobbly table whose top had been half-split during a drunken brawl, and whose legs had been worn down by constant use:

"Can I ask you somethin'?"

"Do you need permission?"

"D'ya need to answer every question with another question?"

"Do you?"

"Touché!"

"En garde!"

They laughed, clinked mugs, and gulped down some ale.

"A penny for your thoughts, dear friend. Tell me what's on your mind."

"I'm fed up."

"Fed up?"

"Yeah, fed up. I've given my life to that place. Like, I break my balls for Zebedee, but it's never gotten me anywhere."

"It hasn't?"

"No."

Mayer nodded sympathetically.

"I work eighteen hours a day. The heat exhausts me and the flour irritates my skin. I watch on as a steady stream of bakers suffer illnesses and seizures, thinkin' I could be next."

Mayer nodded.

"I was laid up for weeks in St. Thomas's just now; under the weather like."

Mayer nodded again.

"It's fine. I… I… I just feel I deserve more. Like, I work hard, I get results, but I don't get rewarded. You know?"

"I know. You deserve credit."

"I don't want credit, I want rewards."

"I see."

"You do?"

"No, dear friend, I'm afraid I don't."

"Eh?"

"Well, I see your predicament, but I don't see what you're asking."

Davey Boy's face softened:

"I'm askin' you to lend me a hand; take a punt; do good by an ol' mucker. What d'ya say?"

"Eh?"

"It won't take much, like. I just need enough to buy a shop, fit it out, and cover wages for a month or two. I'll have it turnin' a profit before you can say 'Abracadabra'."

"You will?"

"I will. Come on! You know me; we're as thick as thieves, us two."

"We are, dear friend, we are."

"So what d'ya say?"

"To what?"

"To lendin' me the money."

"I don't have the money."

"You don't? I thought you were a goldsmith."

"I am."

"So, goldsmiths are rich."

"Only the bosses."

"Oh. I don't suppose you could ask your boss for the funds? I'd pay 'im back, like."

"Of course."

"So?"

"We do have the money."

"And?"

"We'd have to charge you interest and secure your loan."

"So it's a deal?"

"I'll see what I can do."

Davey hugged Mayer so tightly he choked:

"You're a diamond geezer Mayer. A top dog!"

Mayer gasped for air.

*****

Mayer made a point of never working for more than forty hours a week. He believed that when it came to work, quality mattered more than quantity.

This separated Mayer from the likes of Archibald; the types of people who worked all the hours God gave them, in a shop or a gym, believing that hard graft was, in itself, somehow virtuous.

Mayer did not work hard. Any industrious pauper could work hard. For Mayer, that was a philosophy of pain, not a philosophy of gain. Mayer knew that the road to wealth lay not in working hard himself, but in getting other people to work hard for him.

Mayer did not sell cloth to the French, nor import wine from France. He left that to McCraw and Harmer, sat back, and collected their commissions.

Mayer did not choose Davey Boy's bakery, buy it, stock it, employ staff, manage those staff, sell bread, or attract new customers. He simply encouraged Mr Bronze to lend Davey Boy some of the coins they had earned whilst exchanging money, and allowed Davey Boy to do the rest.

Davey Boy grafted as hard as ever before, Mayer collected interest payments on his loan, and Mr Bronze's sack of gold grew even larger. It was as if Mayer was creating money out of nothing. He could not quite understand it. A part of him considered it to deceitful, but a larger part of him did not care.

Mayer had played things by the book all his life, and just look where it had got him! When he courted Lola, he told her, openly and honestly, that he liked her and wanted to be her man. Did it pay off? No. Lola rejected him, abandoned their date, and married Hugo. All Mayer's love, effort, longing, begging, courting and gifts; where had it gotten him? Nowhere. What had it gotten him? Nothing. What had it cost him? His innocence. Mayer came to see honesty as a burden and openness as a vice.

It was this shift in mentality which encouraged Mayer to engage in money-changing and usury.

It was this shift in mentality which encouraged Mayer to adjust his appearance; donning a tailor-suit, and attaching a gold chain to a button hole; wearing shoes made of crocodile skin, a top hat lined with red satin, and a pair of reading glasses he did not need. He grew a handlebar beard, waxed the tips of his moustache, and splashed himself with deodorant which smelled of wood-shavings. This made him look twenty years older than he was, which earned him twenty years' more respect than he deserved.

And it was this shift in mentality which would encourage Mayer's actions in love…

*****

Women often appear more attractive than other, more beautiful women, purely on account of the fact that they happen to be smiling. A smile can make a plain woman look pretty, and a pretty woman look divine.

When Mayer heard Ruby sing, as he trudged through Hampstead Heath, her voice had a similar effect.

Ruby, herself, was indeed beautiful when seen with certain eyes. There existed a certain sort of perfection in her imperfections; the kink in her nose possessed her with a sense of moreish-ness, and the asymmetry of her eyes gave her an irrational appeal. Still, she was hardly pretty. She was clothed in a curious array of colours, and her face carried an unctuous tone, as if it had been rubbed smooth with a layer of grease. Most men would have passed her without a second glance.

Not Mayer. Ruby's voice enticed him, her rhythm warmed his soul, and her pitch made him shiver. It made Ruby seem more beautiful than she actually was, and made Mayer want her more than he actually did.

He approached, stopped, removed his hat, bowed, and circled his hand through the air:

"It is a pleasure to make your acquaintance."

Ruby blushed.

"Please allow me to introduce myself; I'm a man of wealth and taste."

Ruby buried her head in her shoulder.

Mayer kicked mud up her leg:

"I'm a goldsmith banker, one of the finest around. In years to come, I'll be famous."

Ruby looked up.

"But today, I only wish to serve. Your dress is dirty, and it really wouldn't do to allow a fine young lady to go around in such a manner."

"Oh really, I'm not so 'fine'."

Mayer laughed:

"Ever was the way of the world! The problem with men, is that they always believe they're beautiful, even when they're not. The problem with women, is that they never believe they're beautiful, even when they are.

"Well, I can assure you that you are ravishing. Now, do allow me to give you my coat, and please do grant me permission to see you again."

Ruby smiled:

"Permission granted."

*****

Unbeknownst to Mayer, his actions bore an overwhelming resemblance to the methods once employed by Hugo. The similarities did not end there. He also had Ruby watched, which gave him the information he needed to woo her. He also stole Ruby's heart in a perfectly duplicitous way.

But Ruby did not steal Mayer's heart. Mayer still loved Lola, still felt Hugo's love for Lola, and still believed Lola would be his. He was convinced that Lola was his soulmate, and so felt it would be wrong to love or marry anyone else.

"Will you marry me?" he asked Ruby after three months had passed.

"Yah," she wailed with unbridled delight. "Yah, darling, yah! By George, how thrilling!"

*****

Mayer had gotten engaged, without any intention of marrying Ruby, purely for the benefits that engagement brought. In Georgian society, it was socially acceptable to be seen in public with one's fiancé, hand-in-hand, without a chaperone; betrothed couples could exchange a fleeting kiss, or visit each other at home.

Having gotten engaged, therefore, Mayer was able to take Ruby to a restaurant, where he plied her with red wine.

"I think I've had enough," she said. "I'm feeling rather lightheaded."

"Nonsense, dear girl, you just need to drink through it. Here, have a little more."

Mayer poured Ruby another glass of wine. Then he poured her another. By the time they left, she was in such a state of inebriation that Mayer had to prop her up. He hailed a cab, took her back to Mornington Palace, carried her up the stairs, laid her down on his bed and undressed her.

It was the first time Mayer had seen a naked woman, and the sight both excited and scared him. Ruby's femininity overwhelmed him, her humanity humbled him, and her carnality disgusted him.

Ruby passed out.

Mayer's eyes passed from the tender curve of her inner thigh, to her pubic mound, to her ribs, and on to her breasts.

He descended upon her unconscious form.

He stopped:

'Mayer! What have you become? You're better than this. Have some common decency. Mayer, bloody Mayer, pull yourself together!'

He cursed himself, cussed himself; cajoled, scolded, pinched, prodded and slapped himself. Then he covered Ruby's body, blew out the candle and fell asleep.

When she awoke the following morning, Ruby was certain she had lost her virginity:

"By golly, darling, you'd better marry me now."

She kissed Mayer, climbed on top of him, and rode him like a horse.

*****

Ruby had wanted to sleep with Mayer just as much as Mayer had wanted to sleep with her. She hated the social convention which said women had to save themselves for marriage, and did not consider it immoral to sleep with one's future husband. She went on to do so on a regular basis.

Ruby and Mayer often talked about marriage, but they never made any plans; Mayer was far more concerned with making money than making vows. He made lots of money for Mr Bronze, and kept a small commission for himself. Everything was going well, until Mr Harmer stormed into the shop, red faced, with bloodshot eyes, chattering teeth, dishevelled hair and an untucked shirt. He pushed the other customers aside and began to scream:

"My man was robbed coming back from France. You said you would 'Protect our interests in that market'."

"Ah, actually," Mr Bronze began.

But Mayer stopped him short:

"No, no. We promised to protect Mr Harmer, and protect him we shall."

"We shall?"

"*Yoooo* shall?"

"We shall, my dear man, we shall!"

"Ah."

"Hmm. Now how much did you lose?"

"Seven pounds, twelve shillings and five pence."

"We shall repay it all."

"We shall?"

"*Yoooo* shall?"

"We shall."

"And a ha'penny."

"And a ha'penny!"

"Well then, we shall continue to do business."

"It'd be our pleasure."

"And we shall tell our clients just how trustworthy you are."

"That'd be grand, my dear man."

"Good day to you."

"Good day to you, Mr Harmer."

With that, Mr Harmer turned to leave. And, with that, Mr Bronze turned to Mayer:

"What did you think you were doing?"

"Taking things to the next level."

"The 'Next level'?"

"Yes, Mr Bronze, I've had an idea."

*****

Mayer's idea would occupy him for many years, make Mr Bronze a great deal of money, and encourage Mayer to dream of opening a goldsmith's shop himself.

Inspired by the men at his guild, who had already walked the path he was travelling, Mayer journeyed to France, where he established relationships with a network of goldsmiths. All those hours spent alone in his room, ignored by his family, reading about finance, trade and French, were finally beginning to pay off. Mayer was becoming a man.

But it was the old Mayer who really shone. His eager handshake and winning smile had as much effect on the other side of the channel as they had done back at home. The fact he carried references from some of the most respected goldsmiths in his guild only furthered his cause.

Mayer returned to London, where he met Jim McCraw in Mr Bronze's shop:

"You've caught the sun."

"Aye, laddie, I have."

"You look a million dollars! But that's not why I wanted to see you. Dear friend, I have a proposition: When you exchange British coins for French ones, so you can buy wine in France, we'll continue to exchange them. But then, instead of handing you the French coins, we'll give you the option of putting them in our safe. For a small fee, we'll issue you a promissory note; an official document, a bit like a receipt, which will state your name and the amount you've deposited.

"You can think of it as a tally stick. Your promissory note will be like a tally's stock, representing your credit with us. We'll keep a record of our debt to you, the gold in our safe, which'll be like a tally's stub."

McCraw shook his head:

"I dinnae get it. Why would I pay fur a bit ay paper an' nae take mah gauld, when I can hae mah gauld an' nae pay a thing?"

Mayer smiled:

"Because your gold could be stolen on route."

"Jings laddie! The promissory notes could also be swatched on route."

"It's true. Hmm. But if they were, you'd only have to tell us. We'd replace them and cancel the originals. It's just paper, after all."

"Aye, that's true."

"It is."

"And ye cannae jist replace gauld."

"You cannot."

"But what use is a promissory note in France? Mah merchants there want gauld, nae paper."

"They do."

"Sae?"

"So give them gold, dear friend, give them gold!"

"Haw? Pure, Mayer, you're doin' ma dinger. You're a right wee scunner."

Mayer laughed:

"I believe it's a part of my charm."

"It's nae."

"Yet you're smiling."

"I'm smilin' tae stop meself greetin'. Explain yerself boy! What good is a promissory note in France?"

"It's good for gold."

"It is?"

"Yes. We've established a network of goldsmiths there who'll honour our notes. They'll exchange them for the French coins you deposit in our safe."

"Fur a fee?"

"Naturally."

McCraw laughed:

"Okay, sonny boy. Robberies oor on the rise, sae I'll gie this a gang an' see where it gits us."

"I think you'll be pleasantly surprised."

"It's only 'coz I troost ye mind. Ye're all bum and parsley, but I troost ye."

McCraw and Mayer smiled.

Mr Bronze tapped his foot. It was four o'clock, and Mr Bronze always tapped his foot at four o'clock.

*****

If it were left like this, the goldsmiths in France would soon run out of gold. This is where exporters like Mr Harmer helped to balance the books. Mayer convinced those men to take the gold they received when selling goods in France, and deposit it with his French goldsmiths. In return, they were given the promissory notes which the likes of McCraw had left behind.

This helped the French goldsmiths to replenish their gold, whilst earning another commission. It ensured that exporters, like Mr Harmer, could return to London without any fear of having their gold stolen on route. And, of course, it meant that Mayer could charge another fee when those exporters came to cash their notes.

Like the other goldsmiths in his guild, Mayer had set up an elaborate system in which he offered extra services, and charged extra fees, without doing much extra work.

It did not stop there.

Having established a network in France, he established a network in The Netherlands. And, having passed business the way of goldsmiths in those nations, they repaid the favour; sending French and Dutch merchants his way.

Mayer charged those men for his services, earned more money, loaned that money out, charged interest on those loans, and made yet more money. Most of that money was reinvested, but Mr Bronze kept a share, and Mayer kept a small commission.

OF LOVE

"Perhaps some of us have to go through
dark and devious ways before we can
find the river of peace."
JOSEPH CAMPBELL

Three friends, united by nature, divided by nurture, were destined to chase three very different goals. We have seen Archibald chase power and Mayer chase wealth. This leaves Hugo. And this leaves love.

But what love did Hugo chase?

He had already been moved by philia, his love of his friends, and by eros, his lust for Lola. Having married her, two new types of love came into play.

Let us start with the first: Philautia.

Philautia, put simply, is the love of oneself. On the surface, it may appear a selfish sort of love. And, carried to excess, it can be disastrous. You may recall Narcissus, the Greek hunter who fell in love with his own reflection. On realising that his love would never be reciprocated, Narcissus took a blade and slashed his throat.

Self-love can lead to a selfish desire for pleasure, fame, awe, respect, wealth and devotion; even when such things are harmful.

But is it all bad?

Ask yourself this: Can anyone truly love someone else if they do not first love themselves? What sort of love would a self-loathing person be able to offer?

A little self-love can be a precursor to other, grander forms of love.

This was the case with Hugo.

Hugo had hated himself since the day his home burned down. He blamed himself for his family's deaths, and believed the hardships he endured were karmic retributions for that original sin; he believed that he deserved to be thrown into the workhouse, to be thrown out of it, to be made homeless, and to be trapped by Jonathan Wild. He blamed himself for his destitution, despised himself for becoming a thief, and pitied himself for needing Mayer's help. He became a dark shade of his original self; a boy who stole from life and cheated in love.

He lacked philautia.

Until, that is, he married Lola...

*****

Lola loved Hugo, but hers was the most foolish of loves: Love without due-diligence. She did not know Hugo at all, and so she accompanied him to work, to get to know him a little better.

Lola watched on, mesmerized, as Hugo removed an ingrown toenail with one painless swish:

"That was majestic."

"It was?"

"Yes, hubby, you're an artist. A master of your trade!"

Hugo was perplexed. No-one had ever called his work "Majestic". The adulation made him feel strange, but it was a nice sort of strangeness; as comforting as it was uncomfortable.

He smiled and continued his work; diagnosing ailments, performing surgery, prescribing and preparing cures.

"You're an intelligenius," Lola said. "I wish I had your smarts."

"You do?"

"I do."

Hugo could not quite believe that a woman like Lola, educated at one of the finest schools in the land, could covet *his* knowledge. His face burned with embarrassment and his ears slunk into his skull.

Lola blushed:

"You make such a difference."

"I do?"

"Yes, silly! Just look at everyone you've helped."

Hugo looked around. He saw a boy, who had come to say "Thank-you" for saving his mother; a girl, who had come to be saved; an elderly couple, for whom Hugo was their last hope; and two newlyweds, for whom he was their only hope. A prostitute looked at Hugo with grateful eyes, knowing she would be crippled without his assistance, and an orphan looked at him with affection, inspired by his path to success.

"See?"

Hugo paused:

"Yeah, I think so."

"I know so. You're a real life superhero, Hugo Crickets."

"Well, I wouldn't go that far."

"I would! You're *my* hero, and I'll not have you say otherwise. Now, if you'll excuse me, I really must go and eat some trifle."

* * * * *

Their cottage was modest compared to Lola's previous homes, and palatial compared to Hugo's. Bought with Lola's dowry, there were two bedrooms upstairs, a lounge and a kitchen downstairs, and a servant's room in the basement. A rock sat on the mantelpiece, Hugo sat on an armchair, and Lola sat on Hugo.

"Lola?"

"Yes."

"Can I tell you something?"

Lola nodded. She could tell Hugo was serious. He spoke with a pensive, almost timid tone. His eyes seemed to beg for compassion, plead for understanding, and scorn the idea of pity.

The smell of cinnamon wafted in from the kitchen. It reminded Lola of love. It reminded Hugo of cinnamon buns.

Lola gripped Hugo's knee.

"This is bad," he said.

"I'll forgive you."

"You won't."

"I married every little bit of you, Hugo Crickets; the good and the bad."

"But I'm just so imperfect."

"It's our imperfections that make us who we are."

"Yes, sorry, but..."

"Our imperfections make us human."

"I guess. But..."

"I'll still love you, hubby. You'll always be the apple of my eye."

"Well, the thing is. The thing... What happened... Sorry. The situation... So..."

Lola stroked Hugo's leg.

Hugo took a deep breath:

"The thing is... You see... I killed my parents and siblings."

Lola opened her mouth, looked at her husband, frowned, stopped herself from laughing, stopped herself from crying, straightened her back, and lifted her shoulders. Then she relaxed, inhaled, exhaled, went to speak, paused, and allowed Hugo the time he needed:

"I was three at the time, maybe four. It's a bit of a blur, but I know I did it."

"Did what?"

"Burnt my house down. My family. They... They... They all died."

Lola's eyes bulged open:

"What dramedy! How could a three-year-old burn down a house?"

"I don't know."

"You don't know?"

"No."

"You don't know, because you didn't do it, silly!"

"I did."

"You didn't."

"What?"

"There's no truthiness to what you're saying."

"Is too! It makes sense to me."

"Balderdash makes sense to the fool."

"What? Are you calling me a fool?"

"I'm calling you foolish."

"Oi!"

Lola laughed:

"Go on then, mansplain yourself."

"Sorry?"

"How did you do it?"

"I lit the fire in the pantry. I lit lamps, torches, ovens and stoves."

"When you were three years old?"

"Yes."

"At night?"

"Yes."

"How did you get out of your cot?"

"I don't know."

"How did you start those fires?"

Hugo shrugged.

"Why didn't anyone stop you?"

Lola looked at Hugo:

"I... I... I..."

"Come on, silly."

"I... I... I just know I did it."

"And yet you didn't."

"I didn't?"

"No. It doesn't make any sense. You misoverestimate yourself."

"Oh. Sorry."

"Now, if that's sorted I must be off. I have a hankering for scotch eggs which demands satisfaction."

Hugo looked up in surprise.

Lola gave him a hug.

*****

These two scenes transformed Hugo. He stopped saying "Sorry", comparing himself to others, and thinking negative thoughts. His self-hatred gave way to self-love.

Lola did not try to turn Hugo into another man, such efforts usually end in disaster, but she did enable the real Hugo, hidden for so many years, to be reborn.

Hugo had a limitless ability for being reborn. This, then, was nothing new. And yet it was, because, for this the first time in his life, Hugo was born of love.

*****

Able to love himself, Hugo was able to love others.

In time, he would come to truly love his wife. But first, he needed to get to know her. Because, despite stalking her, Hugo had never discovered the real Lola. And because, in their early days, they had not wished to jeopardise their relationship by getting to know each other *too* well.

Once they were married, however, they did not wish to jeopardise their relationship by leaving any stone unturned. This was why Lola had accompanied Hugo to work, and this was why they talked each evening.

Hugo watched on as Lola turned their small garden into an urban paradise; moving rocks into their home, and replacing them with plants.

"Plants are like people," she explained. "If their foundations are good they will grow. If you nurture them, they will love you."

This comment betrayed a strong maternal instinct, of which Lola never spoke. It is impossible to say why she kept silent on the subject of children; like most women, she had her little quirks; but it must be noted that this was the exception, not the rule. Lola was more than loquacious when it came to almost every other topic. Sometimes she said things which made Hugo stop and marvel:

"I knew something was amiss. My toenails didn't grow at all this morning."

"I can't wear green, hubby! People say it makes me look like a turtle."

"It's bad enough being a girl, when I like boyish pastimes and edutainment. I really can't get over not being a boy. And it's worse now than ever, for I'm dying to go hunting with daddy, but I'm forced stay inside like a poky old spinster."

Lola might have been called a feminist, if such a word had existed. Nicholas called her his "Son". He did so in all seriousness. And Lola, for her part, accepted it as a compliment. She *was* her father's son; she quoted him word for word, and often passed his views off as her own.

Hugo noticed this.

He noticed how Lola played the piano, which revealed a little of her soul, as music often does. The rushed notes revealed her fiery temperament, and the lightness of her touch revealed her inner grace.

He noticed Lola's eating habits; how she punched the table whenever she was struck with a new idea, how she always ate her meat before touching her potatoes, how she went to get food whenever she wished to end a conversation, and how she never gained weight despite eating that food.

He noticed the way Lola smiled in her sleep, the squeak she made when she got out of bed, and the shimmy she performed when she dressed.

And he noticed how Lola wore his shirts around their home. Hugo liked the way they stroked her thighs; hinting at mysterious curves, and leaving his imagination to do the rest. Those boyish shirts revealed Lola's femininity *and* her masculinity.

Lola was a contradiction, and Hugo would not have had it any other way.

*****

As Lola and Hugo grew closer, their love grew stronger.

But this was not philia, eros nor philautia. This was pragma.

Pragma is pragmatic. Pragma is the abiding love which develops when two lovers come to know one another; accepting one another, warts and all. Not so much loving a person in spite of their faults, but loving them because of their faults; seeing perfection in their imperfections.

Pragma is based on understanding, tolerance, work and patience. It is not about "Falling in love", but about "Standing in love".

Hugo and Lola stood in pragma. As the fug of romantic infatuation began to fade, the remnants of their eros were pushed into the shadows by something more beautiful; real compatibility.

It was as though they had hurdled every obstacle and reached the very heart of love; capable of enjoying their spouse's silence, reading their thoughts, and predicting their words. Perhaps, despite all the lust and lies, they really were soulmates. Or, perhaps, they had simply met at such a young age that their personalities were still malleable enough to bend to their partner's needs...

*****

Hugo changed; from surgeon to doctor, tradesman to professional, working-class to middle-class, seducer to lover, bachelor to husband, boy to man.

He liked the person he became; forged by the fire of misfortune, hammered into shape by the lightness of a woman's touch, and cooled off by icy Georgian Society.

Was he living a lie?

Hugo asked himself this question on a regular basis. A part of him said "Yes"; he felt more dishonest than when he was stalking Lola. A part of him said "No"; it was a natural part of growing up.

But Hugo was certain of one thing: His love for his wife.

That love made him want to become a better person; a person worthy of Lola.

Like many men, Hugo had a solitary streak; he liked his privacy and valued the time he spent alone. One might say he valued it a little too much. Before getting married, he had stalked Lola alone, studied alone, and spent countless nights alone in his flat.

Lola wanted him to be more social:

"We're going dancing, hubby. I want to hear some banjitar."

"Well, honey bun, dancing; it's really not my thing."

They were sitting in the lounge; Hugo in the armchair, and Lola on his lap. Two rocks rested on the drinks cabinet, and two drinks rested in their hands.

"Hugo?"

Hugo did not reply.

Lola did what she always did when her husband was being stubborn:

She scrunched her nose in condescension and smiled with her eyes. Hugo was seldom able to resist this concoction of menace and meekness, sugar and spice.

"You're looking radiant tonight," he said.

Lola raised her eyebrows.

"You look stunning when you don't wear makeup, and also when you do."

Lola squeezed his knee.

"I love you."

Lola almost smiled.

"Okay, okay. I'll get my coat."

Lola smiled.

Hugo took her hand, led her past a pile of stones, opened the door for her, hailed a carriage, and helped her up inside.

They arrived at the dance hall, entered, and began to dance.

Hugo felt just as lost as Mayer had when he first stepped inside the Almack Rooms. Lola felt just as comfortable. She danced in the most ridiculous way; shuffling and skidding with all the grace of a three-legged dog. Yet she felt great; set free by love and unencumbered by any desire to make a good impression.

Hugo loved Lola's carefree abandon. He did not even think she was dancing that badly. Uneducated in such matters, to him it was Lola who was majestic, and everyone else who was wrong; dancing pretentiously, with steps which were too stiff and postures which were too pointy.

To Hugo, his wife's dancing was so graceless it was charming. Every misplaced step and mistimed shimmy brought a sparkle of joy to her eyes. Every wobble which burst from her hips, involuntarily, possessed a natural sort elegance; out of place in high society, but at one with a higher nature.

So, the more her dancing veered from the script, the more lines Lola wrote in Hugo's heart. Her disdain for the contemporary style mirrored Hugo's disdain of that function. It united them. And so Hugo came out of his shell; he danced just like Lola, and looked just as goofy.

*****

Hugo, who had never danced before, became a regular dancer. Lola took him to plays, concerts, ballets and banquets. In time, he learnt to enjoy those events. Apart from the opera. Hugo never did understand the opera.

A new Hugo was born, this time of high society. He was rebirthing with increasing regularity.

Lola introduced her husband to her friends; endowing him with a new social circle. Hugo, on the other hand, hid Lola from the likes of Bib and Wilkins. This was not hard, since Bib and Wilkins tended not to appear at the ballet. In fact, there was only one occasion when Hugo recognized someone he knew at those events. He was at a ball, when he spotted Mayer dancing with Ruby.

Hugo felt Mayer's pride and Mayer felt Hugo's discomfort.

Hugo's discomfort was born of the guilt he felt for tricking his old friend. Whilst he felt his actions had been justified at the time, hindsight had burdened him with a thousand nagging doubts. Mayer felt Hugo's discomfort, but assumed it was the dancing, not his guilt, which made him feel that way.

Mayer's pride was born of the way he felt he possessed Ruby, as if she were a trophy. Hugo felt Mayer's pride, but assumed it was love, not vanity, which made him feel so proud.

Still, Hugo and Mayer were happy to see each other. They felt each other's happiness, embraced, talked for hours, danced together, and left in good spirits.

When Mayer took Ruby to bed that night, he saw Lola's face on her body.

When Lola went to bed that night, she spent hours thinking about what could have been.

*****

Hugo realised two things...

One: He truly loved Lola.

Two: His house was full of rocks.

It happened like this:

As soon as they got engaged, Lola stopped buying hats. As soon as they moved in together, she gave all her hats away. The first time Hugo walked into their marital home, he was overwhelmed by the sheer weight of their absence.

Lola had found a new outlet for her addictive personality.

From that day on, she accrued rocks; small rocks, big rocks, round rocks, square rocks; rocks of all varieties and forms. They started to appear, at a rate of about one per day, in place of the hats which had come before them.

Hugo was so preoccupied with work and study, and so focussed on Lola herself, that he did not notice those rocks until it was impossible not to. They were everywhere.

He felt he had to speak:

"Why all the rocks?"

"Collecting rocks is nanty narking: Great fun! They all have different shapes and sizes."

"But why?"

"Rocks are like people."

"They are, honey bun?"

"Yes, they all have different personalities."

"But why so many? I can hardly move."

"I suppose I can't help myself. I don't know which rock is which, and I've started to forget their names, but I do love them all."

"Can we move a few outside?"

"I don't think so. My rocks are like children to me, and one does not leave one's children outside. Now you'll have to excuse me; I really must eat some kedgeree."

Lola went to the kitchen, where she shoved her mouth full of rice, cream and smoked fish.

Hugo looked at the rocks between his feet, by his armchair, alongside the skirting board, and on the coffee table. It seemed to him that every inch of his house had been taken up by a rock or a plant.

He smiled, and laughed to himself:

'*My wife is perfect. Utterly, utterly perfect.*'

DELUSIONS OF GRANDEUR

"There are very few people who look in the mirror and say, 'That person I see is a savage monster'. Instead, they make up some construction that justifies what they do."
NOAM CHOMSKY

Archibald was battered, bruised and almost broken. He simply could not believe the way he had succumbed to Ursula:

'*How could I be so weak and feeble? Haven't I learnt anything at all?*'

He felt like a boxer, on the ropes, taking punch after punch; cowering, crouched, but just about standing. He required strength he did not have, and energy he had already expended.

He took a deep breath.

'*What do I lack?*' he asked himself. '*Power! What do I need? Power! What will I seek? Power! Power, power, power!*'

*****

Any run-of-the-mill genius can believe the truth. It takes a special sort of fool to believe a lie.

Archibald was a special sort of fool. He retraced his steps, telling himself to be '*Persistent*', '*Keep trying*' and '*Never give in*'. He believed things would get better.

Things stayed the same.

Archibald used park ladies, which gave him the rush of power he craved, but left him wallowing in self-pity thereafter. When the wrestling season began, he filled his pockets, moved on to a better class of prostitute, but was always left high and dry.

Sometimes he went with a street walker; ladies who would do anything to help a fellow prostitute, and anything to satisfy their men. He could spot those ladies with his eyes closed, purely on account of their perfume.

He visited the low lodging houses which filled the streets of Whitechapel, Wapping and Ratcliffe Highway. Run by Jewish entrepreneurs who overcharged their tenants, they were filled with prostitutes who seldom paid their rent. Archibald heard them call their landlords "Christ killers" and "Heretics" by way of justification.

And he visited night-houses; sellers of moonshine liquor, whose bouncers were always on the lookout for the local night watchman.

Archibald searched for prostitutes who looked like Lola. But, in the end, he seldom slept with those women. He normally ended up with what you might call "The rugged type"; muscular ladies with hairy armpits, whose thighs could crush a man, and whose sweat tasted of chicken broth.

Archibald refused to admit he found those women more attractive than effeminate women, but he was convinced that they made better lovers. He believed they were driven to satisfy their men, to make up for their compromised looks, whereas beautiful women were often lazy; acting as though the world owed them a living.

He moved on to girls of all ages and all races. Once, he was tempted into a Molly House, but he drew the line at sleeping with a man.

'*I need to have some sort of standards*', he told himself. And with that he stormed out, found a muscular woman, took her to bed, and imagined she was Lola.

*****

Archibald still felt Hugo's love for Lola as if it was his own. He felt it when Lola freed Hugo from his self-hatred, when Hugo watched Lola dance, and whenever Lola made Hugo smile.

This extreme form of empathy inspired an extreme form of infatuation.

Archibald imagined what Lola might be doing, how she might be doing it, how her marriage must be falling apart, how she would walk out on Hugo, and how she would run into his arms.

He continued to draw Lola's image, scraping his pencil with so much intensity it caused stray dogs to howl and cats to screech. This caused birds to rise up in clouds which obscured the sun.

He began to write those four innocuous letters, 'L-O-L-A', on autumn leaves, in the froth which rested atop his beer, and in the creases of his palms. He did it without thinking, unconscious of who might be watching or how they might react.

And he continued to dream of Lola. Whenever he slept, he entered an alternative realm in which he and Lola were married.

*****

It would be easy to judge Archibald harshly for the way he treated women, Archibald judged *himself* harshly for the way he treated women, but it should be noted that he never deceived an innocent virgin in the way that Hugo tricked Lola and Mayer tricked Ruby. He *did* have a moral code: He was always open and honest about his intentions, he always paid a fair price for sex, he never slept with anyone aged under eighteen, and he never used force or lies to get a woman into bed.

Sex, though, did not give Archibald the power he craved. If anything, sex held power over him. His desire for sexual conquest became an addiction; born of a need to escape from the burden of reality, and re-enter the world of his dreams.

It got worse.

The games he once played with Ursula no longer satisfied him. Discarding women no longer satisfied him. Satisfying women no longer satisfied him.

Archibald invented worlds of unreality: He got prostitutes to pretend to be his childhood bullies, then he ravaged them, silenced them, came inside them, lifted his arms, and cried out with glorious abandon. In that moment, he overcame his tormentors. In that moment, he took control.

It never lasted.

Archibald got his women to pretend to be the factory owners who ruined his village, the traders whose requests led to Raymondo's death, and the locals who failed to save his family from the flames. He pinned those women down, rose up, worshipped himself, and then crumbled.

He lacked boundaries. He treated women, not as people, but as need-fulfilling objects. He feared subjection, so he pretended to be powerful. He feared intimacy, so he replaced it with intensity. He feared solitude, so he slept with a different woman each night.

Unable to regulate his emotions, he felt shameful, exploitative, compromised, grim, joyless, distant, dishonest, despondent and depressed. Then he masked those emotions; denying their very existence.

Giddy with moral vertigo, his actions were not his own; they were compulsive and disconnected from his real self.

Archibald had become a sex addict.

Like any addict, he craved another hit. Another woman. Then one more.

Like any addict, he risked everything; his relationships, finances, shop and wrestling.

And, like any addict, he lacked satisfaction; the next hit always had to be a little more intense than the last. It was ephemeral; offering the illusion of love, tenderness, nourishment and belonging; briefly dulling the pain, but never resolving his underlying issues.

Archibald swayed from temporary euphoria to permanent malaise.

Sex, for him, was not about pleasure; he did not enjoy sleeping with women at all. For Archibald, sex was about a craving for shame, for the love which had been stolen from him, and for so many things which contradicted each other, yet which seemed to make perfect sense.

Finally, he admitted it to himself:

'*I'm a sex addict.*'

But he could not admit it to anyone else:

'*What would they say? People understand alcoholism and gambling addiction. But sex addiction? They'll say, "Yeah, right! We're all addicted to sex", and then they'll laugh me out of town.*'

*****

Archibald's mind was held captive by thoughts of sex. He worked, but he was never completely present; customers came and went without registering on his conscience. He wrestled, but his performances began to slip. His body, fatigued from sexual conquests, refused to do the things it once found so easy. His mind was slow to react.

The losses started to mount, Archibald's power slipped from his grasp, and the man in a hat stopped paying him to lose.

That bookmaker's agent, who had made thousands of pounds from Archibald's fights, vanished as soon as people stopped betting on Archibald to win. It was only then that Archibald realised he knew nothing about that man, because the void his absence created could be measured in pounds and pence, but nothing more.

Still, it was a large void. Archibald had lost his main source of income.

*****

Archibald's addiction to sex had cost him his money, sanity and friends. He regularly neglected his social commitments in order to get laid. His mood swings were deeply unpleasant.

He could not help himself.

So it was that he started to visit Soldiers' Women; prostitutes who were so low they gave their profession a bad name. They slept, as you might have guessed, with soldiers. But, since soldiers only earned a shilling a day, they were forced to sleep with several men each night, which left them plagued with syphilis and covered in bruises.

It was this sort of woman who Archibald visited on that cold summer's night. She presented a revolting appearance, her skin was covered in eruptions and rags, but she lacked shame, and Archibald was grateful for that.

They retired to her room, a rickety old box she shared with two other women. Everything in there seemed to be made of wood, including the windows, walls and ceiling. The only item not made of wood was a grubby hand basin which dribbled noxious water onto the rotten floor.

The stench of damp mingled with the smell of gin on Archibald's breath.

"Come on then me luvver," his woman said. "I'll be your bully. Whatever floats your boat."

Crouched in a corner, two other prostitutes snickered.

Archibald picked his woman up, pinned her down, pinched her, squeezed her, pushed her and pulled her. He screamed out with delight, and then collapsed on top of her flaccid form.

By the time he looked up, the two other women had gone, as had his clothes and money.

Archibald wore a glassy expression; at once appalled and, at the same time, completely indifferent. His life had been going so badly, it did not surprise him that things had just gotten worse. If anything, it made him feel grateful that he had not been robbed before. It seemed like a miracle, when he came to think about it.

"I'll get youse some clothes," his woman said, as if was the most natural thing in the world.

Archibald clenched his teeth.

*****

His woman did not return.

A midget did.

Everything about that man seemed to aspire to greater heights. His heels lifted him four inches off the floor, his hair stood on end, and his pink shirt seemed to scream, "Look at me! Look at me!"

He started to scream:

"Look at you! Look at you!"

Even his tone was high-pitched:

"Ooh, aren't you a strapping lad? You're just the sort of man we've been a-looking for, right down to your brass tacks and ribbed back. Why, I bet you could whip your weight in wild cats!"

"Eh?"

"Quite the specimen. Quite the specimen. Why, I bet you could be a boxer."

"Damn right. I'm a wrestler."

"Ooh, even better. Even better! I love a man who can grapple."

"Err, yeah. Who are you?"

"I, young wrestler boy, am what they call 'The Goose'. They call me 'The Goose'!"

"Is there an echo in here?"

"Echo! Echo! No, I don't think so."

Archibald raised his eyebrows.

The Goose placed a pile of clothes on the bed:

"You can have these for free."

"Certainly."

"A-nothing in life is free."

"What?"

"I said you could have these for free."

"Thank-you."

"But there's a price to pay."

"What?"

"For the clothes. You can keep them, they're our gift to you, we just feel it'd be nice for you to gift us your services in return."

"My services?"

"Your services! Your serve…. Yes. Protect and serve. Serve your country. Your country needs you. For king and country. God save the king. Send him victorious, happy and glorious. Make that sacrifice. Do your duty. Be brave. Take up the sword of justice. Become a better you. Be the best you can be. Be all you can be. Rule Britannia. Britannia rules the waves. Go army! Enlist now!"

"Bang on. So you're saying…"

"By Jove, I think he's a-got it. Give the boy a gun!"

"Nope, I'm lost."

"Well, you've come to the right man. We'll soon put you straight."

"Put me straight?"

"Give you everything you've ever wanted; a-training, money, girls and power."

"Power?"

"Loads of power!"

"I'm in!"

"That's my boy."

*****

The Goose was a crimp; a private citizen who earned a living by recruiting for the army. Crimps had a reputation for chicanery, cunning and outright coercion. It was a reputation they fully deserved. Crimps had been known to kidnap men, throw them in a cell, strip them naked, dress them in an army uniform, drag them onto a ship, and send them off to war.

The Goose was not so violent.

Unaverse to the odd trick or two, he preferred the "Friendly, friendly" approach. His signature move involved navigating a steamer down the Thames, inviting men aboard, plying them with alcohol, and sweet-talking them until they succumbed to his charm.

He was a favourite with the army's top brass.

He was a favourite with Archibald, offering our man everything he wanted; sex, power and money:

"You'll become a rich nabob; a member of high society, like Robert Clive. We'll give you a commission on whatever money you make. You'll travel the world. The world! You'll sleep with the sort of women you could never imagine. And just think of the power! You'll be like a king. With muscles like yours, no-one will dare to come near you."

Archibald smiled. He had no money, women nor power, but he had this opportunity, and he was determined to take it. He signed up for a ten-year stint, and went to say his farewells.

Mayer stood up to greet him:

"Can you believe this rain we've been having?"

Archibald shrugged:

"It's England, what did you expect?"

"Rain interspersed with showers!"

"Huh. Yeah, anyway, I came to say that I'm joining the army."

"What? The army? My brother, you could die!"

"A little death never harmed anyone."

"Are you sure?"

"Absolutely! Death is a piece of cake; it's life that's frigging hard."

"Well then brother, I must wish you good fortune. I'm sure you'll be a credit to your nation."

They drank some ale. Then Hugo had his say:

"I must say that this has come out of the blue."

"Out of the blue? No, it's come out of the you."

"The me?"

"Don't you remember? You once told me how you won Lola's affections by saving her from some muggers. Well, now it's my turn to be that guy; the knight in shining armour who always gets the girl."

Archibald believed what he was saying. He believed that if he proved himself abroad, he would be able to return, with his head held high, and win the girl of his dreams. He was becoming a soldier for Lola. He did not believe her marriage would last, and was determined to be worthy of her by the time she came back onto the market.

Thinking that Lola might *actually* be his, Archibald was overcome by a sudden surge of confidence, which made his abdomen feel deliciously warm. In the spirit of brotherly love, Hugo and Mayer also felt this warmth, which put their minds at ease.

They still felt each other's emotions because, deep down, they were still the same person; a person who just happened to have three separate bodies. Whilst their upbringings had driven them apart, they were still bonded by something thicker than blood; a shared nature. They took comfort in the way they looked the same, like Hugo's father, and they took comfort in their shared beginnings. They felt like they were stepping back into a lost life whenever they were together.

Hugo and Mayer looked at Archibald, and had the very same thought:

'That would've been me, had I been forced to endure what Archibald went through as a child.'

Archibald sipped his beer:

"I'm never going to be feeble again. War will sort me out. I'm gonna be sadistic! I'm gonna rain down a plague of fury on anyone who has the misfortune of getting in my way!"

Mayer grabbed Hugo's thigh.

Hugo replied:

"Just make sure to be true to your wondrous self. We'll always be here if you need us."

Archibald pushed Hugo off his chair:

"You big sissy. I'm never going to need you again!"

*****

Archibald sold his shop to the ironworks, spent every penny he received on prostitutes, packed his bags and went to sea.

MONEY GROWS ON TREES

"The process by which banks create money is so simple that the mind is repelled."
JOHN KENNETH GALBRAITH

Mayer saw Hugo and Lola on several occasions; howling with merriment at a "Punch and Judy" show in Covent Garden; scoffing jellied eels, with messy faces, at St Katherine Docks; holding hands, gawping at bearded ladies, at a freak show in Regents Park; riding in a carriage, with their heads on each other's shoulders; strolling, with perfect fluidity, and the grace of wild tigers.

Each time Lola saw Mayer, she acted with such serenity it seemed as though he had not registered on her conscience. If she greeted him, she did so with discipline which verged on indifference; never making the slightest gesture which might allow Mayer to suspect she remembered his solicitations.

Each time Mayer saw Lola, he felt Hugo's love. And, each time he felt that love, the unreasonable pounding of his heart convinced him that it was his own. Since Hugo's love was still at a nascent age, amplifying by the day, Mayer was sure that his own love for Lola was growing, and would continue to grow forever.

Lola's image took up residence in Mayer's mind, her scent lingered in his nostrils, and he heard her voice in every sound that flirted with his ear.

Ruby seemed second-rate in comparison: Her neck seemed less refined, her posture less dainty, her hair less shiny, her skin less smooth, and her step less precious.

"I love you," he told her.

"I love you too."

He gave Ruby a pair of earrings.

She blushed:

"By gosh, darling, I don't deserve you."

Mayer shrugged. Then he got to work…

*****

Clarky cut an awkward figure. His wide temples and narrow chin made his face look triangular, his skinny calves and fat thighs looked somewhat amphibian, and his feet were too big for his legs.

His appearance, however, had never been a cause for concern; Clarky looked so unthreatening, that he naturally inspired trust. So, when Mayer returned to find him with Ruby, it was easy to believe him when he said Ruby had approached *him*.

They were at a dance. Music played and couples glided by.

"No," Ruby protested. "He approached me!"

"Hmm. This man? He doesn't look the sort."

Ruby's face turned red:

"But darling, you simply have to believe me!"

Clarky put his hands in the air and backed away.

"Of course I believe you," Mayer replied. "Any man with two eyes and the semblance of a libido would want to talk to you."

Ruby threw herself into Mayer's arms and peppered him with kisses:

"Thank-you! Thank-you! Thank-you!"

"But promise me this. Don't ever talk to that guy again. I'll not have you cavorting with bachelors. I just... I just... I just don't think I'd be able to forgive you."

Ruby shook her head:

"Never! By ginger, darling, you have my word."

*****

A couple of weeks passed before Mayer saw Ruby with Clarky again. She was holding a diamond ring, which Clarky had just thrust into her hand.

"Ruby!" Mayer screamed. "How long has this been going on? What did I tell you?"

"But darling, it's simply not what it seems. This man..."

"It's exactly what it seems. Do you think I'm blind?"

"Well..."

"I expressly forbade you from talking to him."

"Yah, but..."

"And here you are talking to him."

"Yah, but..."

"But nothing. I told you I wouldn't be able forgive you and, well, I can't. We're done. Finished. Pack your bags and go."

"But darling!"

"But nothing."

"I..."

"Go!"

*****

Ruby went straight to a convent, where she vowed never to trust a man again.

She lived out her days as a nun, without realising the truth of the matter; that Clarky was a client of Mayer's, who had fallen behind on his repayments. Mayer had asked him to approach Ruby as a gesture of goodwill, in return for which he adjusted the terms of Clarky's loan.

*****

Mayer spent his twenties making Mr Bronze rich; managing relationships, exchanging coins, issuing promissory notes, making loans and charging interest. One day passed in much the same manner as the last, as days tend to do.

It happened slowly, but it happened.

Mayer became aware that most of his promissory notes were not being cashed. An increasing number of gold and silver coins were being left, abandoned, in Mr Bronze's safes. Mr Bronze had to purchase a third safe. It too filled with gold. Mr Bronze had to buy a fourth safe, then a fifth.

After much mental anguish, and several sleepless nights, Mayer decided to run an experiment behind Mr Bronze's back.

He placed some of the unclaimed gold in a sack marked with a winged pig, and lent it to Damian Black; a meticulously solemn man who wished to become an undertaker. A month later, the same sack of gold was deposited by Mr Grim; a retiring undertaker who had sold his business to Damian Black. Mayer issued Mr Grim a promissory note in return for his deposit.

Mayer lent the sack of gold a second time, this time to Baxter; a butcher who wished to open his own shop. A month later, the same sack of gold was deposited by Mr Scrooge, a landowner who had sold Baxter the land he required. Mayer issued Mr Scrooge a promissory note.

Mayer lent the sack of gold a third time, this time to Claude; a newlywed who wished to buy a marital home. A month later, the same sack of gold was deposited by Mrs Feather; a widow who had sold Claude her house. Mayer issued Mrs Feather a promissory note.

Mayer had created three new loans, each of which generated interest; he had three new creditors, each of whom preferred to hold promissory notes rather than gold; and he still had the original gold, just in case one of those creditors wished to withdraw it.

Somehow, he had created three new debts and three new credits; three new sets of money.

Feeling he had done enough, Mayer stopped the experiment. He considered it prudent to hold back, and see what would happen next.

*****

"Sixty five pounds, two shillings, eight pence," Mayer said.

Abe's reply was so loud, his cup spun in its saucer and tea spilled onto Sadie's favourite tablecloth:

"Really? That's more than normal."

"Hmm."

Abe gave Mayer an inquisitive look.

"I'm repaying my debt in full."

"Oh, well, yes. Hang on May, let me check my ledger."

Abe left.

He returned, wearing a yellow waistcoat which was a shade brighter than the one he had been wearing before.

He began to shout:

"You're spot on! Well this is jolly good, jolly good indeed. Let's crack open the bubbly."

Mayer tensed his cheeks:

"No thank-you."

"'No thank-you'?"

"I don't have any reason to stay."

"Do you need a reason?"

"Yes."

"Well... Err... Because I'm your father, I guess."

"You're not."

"Well, no, but..."

"We've wiped the slate clean."

"Yes, and..."

"So you don't need to offer me any champagne, and I don't need to accept it."

"I suppose not, but most lads..."

"Most lads feel a debt of gratitude to the people who raised them. It's natural for them to try to repay that debt, by maintaining a relationship and helping their parents in times of need. I, however, have repaid my debt in full. I don't owe you a thing, and have no reason to maintain a relationship."

"May!"

"Thank-you for the services you provided during my childhood. It's been a pleasure doing business with you. Goodbye."

Abe wore a vacant expression.

Mayer grabbed his hand, shook it enthusiastically, and left Buckingham Towers for the final time.

*****

Mayer had freed himself from Ruby and Abe, he had money, but he did not have much else. He had few possessions and no family. He had plenty of friends and acquaintances, but even there he felt short changed, having just waved goodbye to Archibald.

To fill the gap in his life, Mayer acquired a taste for mistresses. Not his own mistresses, please understand. No, Mayer acquired a taste for *other* people's mistresses.

'*If I can't be with a respectable lady like Lola*', he told himself. '*I'll just have to be with the mistress of a respectable man.*'

Mayer felt common cause with those women. Like him, they came from the working class. Without the help of a formal education, they had hauled themselves up by their bootstraps, using no little amount of cunning, and every ounce of beauty at their disposal. They had given themselves the appearance of respectability, and won themselves a place on the borders of good society.

It was an ascension Mayer had made himself, with just as much cunning, but far less beauty.

Mayer's first mistress went by the name of Sal. A portly girl, from thirty steps she looked like a grapefruit amongst satsumas; from twenty steps, she looked like a warrior from days of yore; but from ten steps, she looked divine. She had a magnetism which enticed the eye. Mayer could not help but explore her contours, curves, crevices and crooks.

Sal, the daughter of a tradesman, had always dreamt of escaping the drudgery of her father's shop. As she put it herself:

"My parents are stupid, easy-going, and extremely uninteresting to me. I'm fond of dress, also of theatre, and I could not gratify these loves in my village."

Without much resistance, she had succumbed to the desires of a local man and moved with him to London. When their relationship ended, she became a mistress to a gentleman named Raph.

She liked her life:

"I have everything I want, and my friends all love me to excess."

Raph put Sal in a townhouse near Regents Park, which came replete with a full wardrobe, maid, tutor, and the aroma of freshly cut grass. She was granted an annual allowance of five hundred pounds, which she spent on horses, a box at the theatre, jewellery and shoes.

Unlike Mayer, Sal lived for the moment. Like him, she had an invincible distaste of marriage, and an infinite desire for copulation. They shared a belief that the world was split into two groups of people: Those who screwed around, and those who would screw around if only they were less repressed.

Perhaps this is why Sal succumbed to Mayer's advances.

"I believe I'm loved by all the ladies here," he told her when they met at a dance. "And I'm certain that I don't love any of them apart from you."

Sal fanned her face:

"You love me?"

"I do."

"Then love me."

"Love you?"

"Love me all night long."

It really was as simple as that.

Mayer visited Sal whenever Raph was with his wife. They ate that man's food and frolicked in his bed, without a guilty conscience, safe in the knowledge it would never last; that Sal could discard Mayer at any time, and that Mayer would discard Sal if he were to ever get a chance with Lola.

*****

Mayer finally saw Jim McCraw.

"Hello dear friend," he cheered. "Long time no see!"

"Aye laddie, ah cannae argue wi' that."

"The weather has been grim."

"Aye, pure Baltic; all pish-oots and dreich."

Mayer exchanged some coins, penned five promissory notes, and asked McCraw about his family.

"They're jist bonnie," he replied before turning to leave.

"One more thing," Mayer called out.

McCraw stepped back towards the counter:

"Aye?"

"Your promissory notes: Are you cashing them in France?"

"Nay."

"No?"

"Nay, sonny boy, there's nay need. Oor suppliers hae been acceptin' them fur years."

"They have?"

"Aye. They ken they can cash them if they need tae."

"So they exchange them for gold themselves?"

"Nay."

"No?"

"They spend them."

"Spend them?"

"Aye. A nod's as good as a wink tae a blind horse: Fowk ken yer notes oor good, sae they spend them, as if they were gauld, without ever cashin' them."

Mayer nodded:

"Hmm. Yeah, I knew that."

LOVE THY NEIGHBOUR

*"When you see a man drowning you must
save him, even if you cannot swim."*
IRENE SENDLER

Hugo qualified as a doctor and started to work for Nicholas. But, for Lola, it was not quite enough:

"Hubby, you really shouldn't just be a doctor, you should also be a person."

Hugo raised his eyebrows.

"It really won't do."

"What won't, honey bun?"

"I'm telling you, it won't. Now you'll have to excuse me, I simply must eat some bubble and squeak with broccoflower."

Lola went to the kitchen, where she ate some periwinkles.

Hugo stared at one of Lola's dolls, until he saw the bible his wife had left open on the table:

"People do not despise a thief if he steals to satisfy his hunger when he is starving."

It was the verse which rang in Hugo's ears the first time he stole.

He kept on reading:

"But when he is found, he must repay his debt sevenfold. He must donate all the wealth of his house."

This was Lola through and through. She seemed to know what Hugo was thinking, even before he had the chance to think it himself. It was as though she did Hugo's thinking for him, and then nudged him along, to help his mind to catch up with his thoughts.

In that moment, Hugo reconnected. He did not feel guilty for his thieving, his days of negativity were behind him, but he did feel a duty to repay his debt to society.

He waited for Lola to return, smiled, and then spoke:

"I'm going to give something back."

Lola kissed his cheek:

"Yes, hubby. Yes you are."

*****

So it was that Hugo, ignoble by birth, became noble by deed.

He headed for Brown's Bakery, where he exchanged some pennies for a number of nails equivalent to those he had once deposited. The look of surprise on Mrs Brown's face was something to behold; her forehead advanced on territory previously only held by her skull, and her ears retreated towards the backwaters of her cranium.

"And twenty-one loaves of bread."

"Twenty-one?"

"Yes please."

"That's a lot of bread."

"It's seven times the amount I bought with those nails."

Hugo flung a hessian sack full of bread over his shoulder and headed to the docks, where he asked for Honest Jim. Most people ignored him; some laughed, others sighed. Finally, a hunchbacked geriatric answered his calls:

"Honest Jim, youse say? Aye, I knew Honest Jim. Weren't so honest, mind. I'm not even sure his name was Jim. I can't even says I truly knew him, comes to think of it. Not sure anyone truly knew Honest Jim. Well, wheres was I?"

"I was looking for Honest Jim."

"Ah yes, Honest Jim. Weren't so honest, mind. I'm not even sure his name was Jim."

"Where is he?"

"Swimming with the fishes. We gave him a salty grave. A salty grave for a salty sailor."

"He wasn't a sailor."

"No, he wasn't. I'm not even sure his name was Jim."

Hugo gasped:

"Where's his crew?"

"That'll be them over there."

"Thank-you, you're a star!"

"That I am. Oi! Where are you off to in such a hurry? What d'ya say ya give an old codger some bread. Oi! Wait up! Over here!"

Hugo pivoted, chucked the man a loaf, and headed on his way. He returned the nails to Honest Jim's crew, before snaking back through the East End; giving bread to a homeless mother, a crippled veteran, some pickpockets who looked nothing like Hugo, and some orphans who were his spitting image.

By the time he reached the Old Bailey, his sack contained just one loaf.

The shadow of Newgate Prison loomed large.

It whispered to him in a voice which harked back to another age:

"Hugo..."

Hugo stopped walking.

"Hugo..."

He shook his head.

"Hugo…"

He turned around.

"Psst! Mr Ah Cricketty, over here."

Hugo glanced in every direction:

"Dizzy?"

"Jiminy Crickets! Ize ain't seen ya since youse was knee 'igh to a grasshopper."

"Dizzy? Fizzy Dizzy? What happened to you?"

"Ize got meself banged up, didn't I?"

"No shizzle."

"Yep."

"What for?"

"Dunno."

"You don't know?"

"Nah."

"Really?"

"Wells, some ol' codger saids it was for sellin' my body, didn't he? But I dunno. Leastways, it's my body to sell. That's hows Ize sees it."

Hugo nodded:

"Can I help?"

"Youse got any food? Ize is so famished I could eat bow wow mutton. Ize is halfway betwixt an ant and a string bean."

Hugo took his last loaf of bread, tore it into pieces, and stuffed it through the bars:

"I mean, can I do anything to help get you out?"

"Nah, Ize expects they'll release me once they've had their fill. They'se is always quoddin' us dollymops, but it's only ever for a drag. Now if youse could return each night with some bread, that'd be grand."

Hugo winked:

"You can count on me. We're brother and sister after all."

*****

Hugo ran straight into Lola's arms:

"I did it. I only went and did it!"

"Amazetastic!"

"I love you honey bun."

"I love you too."

"I repaid Mrs Brown, gave bread to the poor, and helped my old friend Dizzy. It felt great, like the jammiest bit of jam!"

Lola smiled:

"There's luxury in doing good."

Hugo paused. In that moment, he was overcome by love for his wife. In the next moment, he was overwhelmed by three dolls. One, with thick yellow hair, was sitting on the stairs. The others, one freckled, one eyeless, were standing by the door.

*****

Having learnt to love himself, Hugo had been able to love someone else: Lola. Now, he was beginning to love *everyone* else.

Hugo had discovered agape ('*Ah-gah-pay*').

Agape is benevolent love, based on goodwill to all humankind. Known as "Loving kindness" by the Buddhists, and "Caritas" or "Charity" by the Latins, it is a radical kind of love.

The more Hugo felt comfortable in Lola's company, the less he felt the need to impress her. He still told her he loved her, brought her flowers, baked her cakes, opened doors for her, and told everyone how wonderful she was. But he no longer felt a need to stalk her, trick her, dress in fancy clothes, boast or show off. As a result, he could reallocate his energy into performing benevolent acts, safe in the knowledge that Lola would be by his side. She was his biggest cheerleader and fiercest critic. She was the rock upon which he built his love.

*****

Each year, Lola asked Hugo what he would like for Christmas. And each year, he asked for twelve pencils.

This left Lola a little unsatisfied. She would have liked to have given Hugo something grander. But, such was her love, she respected Hugo's wishes and never bought him anything else.

Hugo used those pencils, one for each month, until only the stubs remained. He stored those stubs in a box. He said they each possessed a soul, made from the stories they had told, and that it would be wrong to discard them.

It was around this time that Hugo began using those pencils to document the hardships he saw in London's East End; a place where everything merged and nothing stayed the same; where rich pushed up against poor, and migrants pushed into locals.

Hugo saw the seeds of good and evil, the fruits of hard labour, and the mulch of unfulfilled potential. He made a note of all the children he saw abandoned in doorways or left at the poor house. He documented scammers, shirkers, thieves, conmen, prostitutes and pimps.

His heart swelled, his mind raged, and his body marched on; propelled by two flames: The flame of anger against injustice, and the flame of hope for a better world.

He trawled the streets after work; stitching, vaccinating, medicating and healing the poor. He gave bread to the hungry, hugs to the unloved, and company to the lonely. Then he opened his notebook, found the person he had helped, and put a line through their name.

It was a losing battle. Hugo saw so much suffering, he filled his notebooks with entries at a far faster rate than he could cross them off. As a result, he suffered from a nagging feeling that should be doing more. Much, much more.

*****

Hugo felt a duty, first and foremost, to help the people who had helped him.

He visited Dizzy in prison each evening; stuffing an abundance of treats through the bars, whilst the other inmates showered him with a superabundance of profanities and praise. When she was released, Hugo took Dizzy to every dock in town, until they found a captain who was willing to recruit her. Finally, she went to sea, just as she had dreamt of as a child.

Hugo took Izzy to Mr Orwell, to learn to read and write, and then employed her as a receptionist. He rented Jo a stall on Billingsgate Fish Market, he convinced Bear to apprentice Wilkins, and he bought Bib a cart full of apples, so he could become a costermonger. Then he headed to the docks.

Back when Hugo was a mudlark, the Royal Admiralty had owed twelve months' wages to the labourers at Deptford Docks. As a result, those men had been allowed to take whatever scraps they could. Hugo had seen people like Crafty Chris take "Cabbage", leftover cloth; "Chips", short pieces of timber; "Thrums", "Sweepings", "Buggings", "Gleanings", "Knockdowns" and "Tinge"; hemp, canvas, bolts, cod and, of course, those ubiquitous iron nails.

When the government began to pay those dockers on time, they smeared the previous arrangement, rebranding it as "Workplace pilfering". They set up a police state; spying on workers from a giant surveillance tower, and punishing anyone who left with state property. Some dockers were whipped in front of their fellow workers. Others were put in jail.

Above everyone else, Hugo felt a debt of gratitude to those dockers. Without them, there would have been nothing for him to collect in the mud. He might have starved.

So, having heard of their predicament, Hugo felt compelled to act. He took food to any docker who found himself in jail, cared for their families, and stitched their wounds. He helped them, but he also benefited himself. Whenever he looked into a docker's eyes, he briefly glimpsed their inner-child; mute, silenced by vanity, but able to speak a mellifluous language which was dripping in emotion.

The love he felt brought Hugo a certain sort of peace, but it was still not enough; his notebooks continued to grow, and he still felt an urge to do more.

* * * * *

Hugo came face to face with the reality that his home had been invaded by an army of porcelain dolls. He stared at their unnatural faces, free from warmth; with googly eyes, dishevelled hair, puckered lips and bulging cheeks. He stared at their stiff limbs, misshapen bodies and tired clothes:

"Your rocks have all gone."

"Yes, silly."

"Thank-you, honey bun. I love you more than words can express."

"I love you too."

"But what's with all these dolls?"

"I just like dolls, I suppose. They make me happy. You can dress them up in skorts and shackets, frocks and hats. I've had dolls ever since I was a baby."

"But you're a fully-grown woman."

"Yes, I suppose I am."

"So what's with all the dolls?"

Lola scrunched her nose in condescension and smiled with her eyes. This proved an irresistible concoction for Hugo, who spoke without realising what he was saying:

"We should have a baby."

Lola nodded:

"Yes, we should. And now, hubby, I'd like to eat a treacle tart."

"We're out of treacle tarts."

"Well then, some biscuits topped with strawberries and cream will have to do."

Lola headed to the kitchen, ate some Eton Mess, returned, took Hugo by the hand, led him to bed, and remained there until she was pregnant.

* * * * *

This, then, was Hugo's life.

Over the course of the next nine months, Hugo helped ninety more people, and Lola bought nine hundred more dolls. Bulbous dolls' eyes spied on Hugo from every nook and cranny. Wherever he looked, he saw mouths without teeth, feet without toes, and noses without nostrils.

Perhaps this was why Hugo spent more time in town. Perhaps this, in turn, was why Hugo's skin became coarse, and the first strands of grey appeared in his hair. Perhaps. Perhaps it was the natural aging process.

Then Lola gave birth to a baby girl, who they named "Emma" after Hugo's mother. In that instant, Hugo's hair turned completely grey.

Emma came out the womb laughing. Then she sneezed. Then she hiccupped. Then she burped.

The noises did not stop.

Even when she slept, Emma snored, smacked her lips, or blew frothy bubbles. She was a nonstop engine of motion; always making noises; sometimes making new noises, the likes of which neither Hugo nor Lola had ever heard before.

To them, it was magical; their very own genius was inventing a whole new language of her own. To everyone else, it was an unbearable annoyance. Still, Hugo and Lola did not care what anyone else might think. They had a new mouth to feed, a new body to cuddle, and a new person to love.

WHAT SHALL WE DO WITH A SOBER SAILOR?

"Those who can make you believe absurdities, can make you commit atrocities."
VOLTAIRE

There were a lot of new recruits on Archibald's ship. A lot of them contracted tropical diseases. Some of them were not even interested in becoming soldiers. A spotty man named "Biggins" openly admitted that he expected to be rejected on physical grounds as soon as they reached India. He wanted a new life, and so had enrolled to get a free journey.

Not everyone on that ship was a new recruit. That ship, in fact, was a merchant ship. It just happened to be filled with soldiers, and protected by more cannons than an average warship. When it returned from India, however, it would be filled with cotton and silk. The lines between commerce and conquest, money and power, had long since been blurred.

As well as soldiers, that ship carried clerks, shipbuilders and nuns. Cooks had come to cook, nurses to nurse, and traders to trade. A vicar with small teeth had come to ease people's consciences; telling anyone who would listen that they could do anything they chose, so long as it served the empire, because the empire served God.

Archibald tried to talk to all those people. He did not quite succeed.

He tried to adjust to the boat's harried panting. He did not quite succeed. He could often be found, with his arms outspread, spewing purple vomit into the ocean.

Archibald did, however, make his uniform his own. Whenever he put it on, he felt the same thrill he felt when wearing his Morris dancing costume; brushing down that skimpy white suit, and tying bells to his knees. That same thrill he felt when dressing up to wrestle; wearing long johns which caressed his thighs, and a vest which gave him an air of flamboyance.

He took pride in his long red blazer, tight white trousers, and tall black hat. He cleaned, pressed and ironed that uniform every day. He loved the way it hugged his skin. He loved putting it on and mincing up and down the deck like a model on a catwalk, wearing perfume which smelled of shoe-polish, barber shops and grease.

There was another soldier who also took pride in his uniform. Named "Delaney", that man also walked and spoke like Archibald. The similarities, however, ended there. Delaney's muscles, whilst pert, were not nearly as large as Archibald's. His hair, whilst brown, was not nearly as long. He did not come from London, speak in a deep voice, wrestle or dance. He had never lost a parent, worked in a shop, or slept with a prostitute.

Their similarities bonded them. Their differences bonded them too. They talked for countless hours and, whenever they docked, they went ashore together, hand-in-hand.

It was never long before Archibald sought out the nearest brothel.

Filled with native women who had been kicked off their lands and left with nothing to sell but their bodies, those places introduced Archibald to a type of sex he had never known before. It was animalistic, passionate and verging on the violent. Archibald orgasmed harder than ever before and, as soon as it was over, he felt even more depraved.

Delaney never entered those brothels himself. Instead, he waited for Archibald outside.

"I'm waiting for the right person," he explained.

Archibald nodded. He considered Delaney's words to be a thing of both utter beauty and utter naïveté:

"What if you never find her?"

"I'm more worried that I will,"

Archibald gave Delaney a knowing look, as if to ask "And?"

"And," Delaney replied, "I'm worried they might not love me back."

Archibald tensed his cheeks and thought of Lola:

'*What if <u>she</u> never loves me back?*'

He shook his head, closed his eyes, saw Lola, placed his hand on Delaney's thigh, and gave it a gentle squeeze.

*****

Everyone has a beautiful angle; an angle from which they look transcendent. Even the ugliest of people possess such an angle. Briefly glance at them, when standing in the right place, in the right light, and you will believe you have seen an angel. Then they will turn, or you will move, or the light will change, and you will realise your mistake. But that image, that tiny glimpse of heaven, can linger in your mind. If you allow it, the resonance of that hidden beauty can stay with you forever.

Delaney had a beautiful angle. When seen from behind and from below, in the half-light of dusk, Delaney's face seemed so smooth, sharp and sensuous, that it seemed wrong to compare it to other faces. Michelangelo's David and da Vinci's Mona Lisa did not possess such an allure.

When viewed from any other angle, however, Delaney looked distinctly average. It would be just as wrong to say he looked exquisite as it would be to say he looked vile; he did not approach either extreme. There was nothing wrong with his face, but, then again, there was nothing right with it either.

It would be easier to describe Delaney's face by speaking of what was absent. There were no blemishes, marks nor scars; his nose was not bent; his lips were not crooked. It was almost impossible to find fault with his facial features. Yet his face lacked something: Character. There were no wizened lines, quirks, mysteries, imperfections, or battle wounds. Delaney's face, put simply, was just a face. His body was just a body. He had one beautiful angle, as we all tend to have, and that was it.

For Archibald, however, this was a grand thing. To him, Delaney's anonymity was comforting. He felt he could open up to his new friend:

"I have a problem."

Delaney nodded.

"I'm a sex addict."

Delaney squeezed Archibald's thigh.

"I'm going cold turkey. No longer will my penis overpower me; I'll overpower my penis!"

It was easier said than done.

Archibald still slept with prostitutes whenever they docked, but he did not sleep with quite as many. He knew he needed to abstain from sex completely, like an alcoholic going teetotal, but he also needed to find an alternative outlet for his addictive tendencies.

He tried running. Then he decided it was too much like hard work. He tried eating the spiciest chillies he could find, reading, playing cards, whipping himself, writing about his experiences, and talking to Delaney. Then he decided that running had not been such a bad idea. He ran around the deck, sprinted up the stairs, scrambled up the netting, and climbed up the mast.

Having run himself into the ground, Archibald realised that he had been right before; running *was* too much like hard work.

Instead, he decided to masturbate. It was easier; he did not even have to leave his room. And it was more effective; it extinguished his desire for sex.

He thought of Lola each time he masturbated. He told himself that if he wanted peace, he needed to stay loyal to Lola; that to sleep with anyone else would be a betrayal. Then he spoke to Delaney.

Archibald spoke to Delaney about everything that passed through his mind; that man became his rock; his biggest cheerleader and most loyal companion. His abstinence acted as a shining example for Archibald to follow. And, in time, Archibald did follow; he became abstinent himself, just like Delaney.

*****

Before arriving in India, there was the small matter of a few thousand miles at sea. This gave Archibald a few hundred hours in which to think.

It was during these hours that Hugo helped his friends. Whenever Hugo performed a kind act, he filled with love for Lola. Archibald felt that love as if it was his own. He opened his notebook and opened his heart; writing the sort of love letters he was incapable of writing when they might have made a difference. He poisoned himself with the smoke of his lamp, stayed awake throughout the night, made confetti of his letters, and then scattered that confetti across the ocean.

The ocean gleamed like a mirror for the sun.

Archibald was living a lie; denying the hopeless of his situation with Lola, his feebleness, and his pent-up sexual urges. But, then again, all the new recruits on his ship were living a lie. They had all listened to the lectures hosted by a loquacious Recruitment Officer; a man with high buttocks, buttery skin and a miscellaneous aura of priggishness. They had all allowed that man to convince them that they would be serving a higher cause, "King and country", and that they would be acting with untold "Heroism" and "Honour".

Deep down, they knew they were driven by their own selfish ambitions; to see new countries, have adventures, gain power, get laid, find the means to settle down, and then live comfortable lives. Still, the idea that they were going to fight for a greater good did help to bond them.

By the time they arrived in India, Archibald and his comrades had allowed themselves to be convinced that they were on a moral crusade, serving humankind, and that they would find glory on the battlefield. They were ready to "Take no prisoner", "Give no inch", and "Neutralize the threat".

*****

Archibald was struck by three things when he stepped foot onto Indian soil…

One: The smell. It was contradictory; both sickly and sour, hot and humid, wretched and regal. At one moment, Archibald wanted to suck it down into the depths of his lungs. At the next, he was forced to choke.

Two: The language. It seemed to Archibald that the locals were fluent in two distinct languages: English and Gobbledegook. He preferred to speak English. They preferred Gobbledegook.

Three: The dazzling colours and magnificent shades; the majestic yellows, reds and greens; the sparkling silvers and golds.

India was far from the uncivilised backwater Archibald had imagined. Everywhere he looked, he saw palatial homes, psychedelic temples and multi-coloured robes. There was an abundance of poverty too, but no more than back in London.

Although Archibald did not know it, India had been one of the richest nations on earth for many centuries. When the British first landed there, in 1608, the Mughal Empire had produced twenty percent of the world's wealth. Britain, by contrast, had produced just two percent. The natives had looked on in bewilderment, as their nation was slowly conquered by a people from a poor European backwater, who just happened to have lots of canons.

*****

During the weeks and months which followed, Archibald was drilled relentlessly, and turned into a lean, mean, killing machine. He enjoyed the process. It reminded him of when he had trained to become a wrestler.

But Archibald did not live for that training. He lived for his strolls with Delaney.

Each evening, just before the hazy hour, they weaved their way through the labyrinthine streets which wrapped themselves around their garrison. They ran their fingers along the walls of mud huts and painted palaces, inhaling the scents of jasmine, patchouli, ginger, garlic and dung.

They visited Hindu temples, prostrated themselves on the floor, and prayed to the Christian God. They skipped, hand in hand, making faces at little children, and dodging the cows which moseyed about like kings. They ate samosas and pakoras, and choked on the spice. The natives laughed at them, and they laughed back. Then they beat them at cards, chess and draughts.

*****

As soon as the Mughal Empire began to fall, in the early 1700s, British Governor Generals began to pick up the pieces. Slowly but surely, they reunited that empire; creating a new nation of their own.

Where necessary, they fought bloody wars. Where possible, however, they formed diplomatic alliances; winning the right to collect taxes and manage foreign trade.

Britain's armies grew strong. Between them, they employed hundreds of thousands of soldiers, mostly natives, and thousands of officers, mostly British. Dressed in red coats, they looked daunting. Armed with a wealth of weaponry, and backed up by naval support, they inspired fear and awe wherever they went. The natives spoke of their magical prowess; some said they possessed demonic powers, whilst others compared them to vicious fallen gods.

Most natives succumbed on sight. A few put up a resistance.

So it was that Archibald found himself in Delhi. He had already helped to conquer several small villages, but he had not yet encroached upon a city.

He inhaled that metropolis.

Domed mosques, shaped like giant bulbs of garlic, rose above a sea of rickety huts. Pigeon-towed hawkers strolled through the dusty streets. The Red Fort, standing bold at the heart of the city, seemed to push everything else aside.

"Faith!" the locals called.

French commanders and freewheeling local soldiers came charging forth, wielding antique swords, spears and matchlock guns:

"Die, infidel, die! Let's banish these pork-munching goons for good!"

Their calls echoed to infinity, carried by the wind, ricocheting off every surface.

'*Die!*' the wind hummed.

'*Die!*' it whistled.

'*Die!*' it sang; crooning a lullaby so sweet, it would have rocked a crying baby to sleep.

Nimble feet danced a jig through the burnished soil. Swords swished the spicy air. Spears stabbed sepia skies. The cries!

"Die, infidel, die!"

Archibald's nerves raged, his lips quivered, his eyebrows flickered, and a solitary bead of sweat formed atop his temple. His hair turned completely grey.

A native man hurtled towards him; ribs protruding, head bobbing, muscles tensing.

The dust parted. Brilliant cinders rose up on either side, dripping fantastic light in a million shades of black and gold.

The man's feet seemed to pound in slow motion; fudding, like a muffled drum:

'*Boom*'. Long pause. '*Boom*'. Long pause. '*Boom*'.

Archibald's heart beat in time:

'*Boom*'. Long pause. '*Boom*'. Long pause. '*Boom*'.

His enemy held his spear in front of his body, with his knees bent; crouching whilst running; drifting through the air. Ready, raging, poised; he sprung high, lifting his spear even higher, before thrusting it down towards Archibald's chest.

Archibald froze.

The spear's point accelerated towards his flesh. Metal was ready to pierce meat. Life was ready to succumb to death. The ground was ready to rumble, the dust to shatter, and the earth to split.

Boom! Archibald did not even think. Instinctively, his elbow lifted itself, and nudged the spear to one side. His enemy, following through, landed beyond Archibald's shoulder.

Archibald found himself above that man, with his legs spread, and his bayonet held high above his head. He paused, on the verge of doubt. Then the Recruitment Officer's words echoed through his mind: "Bravery". "Heroism". "Forget your doubts and crack on".

Archibald watched on as his bayonet darted past his eyes, pierced his enemy's chest, and found a home in the cosy warmth of his palpitating body.

His heart beat in time with his enemy's:

'*Boom*'. Long pause. '*Boom*'. Long pause. '*Boom*'.

He felt the blood flow through that man's arteries as if it were flowing through his own. He felt a thrill which reached every atom of his being; an ejaculation of pure, hedonistic fantasy; a screaming orgasm which satisfied him in a way that neither sex nor wrestling ever had.

He stood over his enemy; the master of life and death itself; decider of fates, writer of destinies, and author of histories. He embraced the eternal now, stepped beyond the limits of his humanity, and burst through the constraints of his physical form:

"Hallelujah! Praise the lord!"

His bayonet gyrated inside his enemy's flesh; in and out, in and out, in and out.

It felt warm and cosy and right.

*****

Archibald remained on that battlefield, stabbing that corpse, for what might have been hours, days, weeks, months or even years. He could not be sure. His mind was consumed by Lola. He felt he was serving her; becoming her knight in shining armour; readying himself to save her from Hugo.

His victim's body disintegrated, but its eyes remained whole. There was no life left in them, only the pain of death.

Hours. Days. Weeks. Months. Years.

An arm wrapped itself around Archibald's shoulders.

"It's okay," Delaney whispered. "Shush. Don't worry, I'm here for you, I'm here."

THE PAPER ALCHEMIST

"While traditional alchemists attempted to turn lead into gold, in the modern economy, paper was made into money."
JENS WEIDMANN

You may recall that Mayer garnered many of his ideas from the other bankers at his guild; "The Worshipful Company of Goldsmiths". Those uncle-like figures showered him with affection and advice.

Among them were two men who took a particular shine to young Mayer. The first, Bumble Blumstein, was a hairy man. The second, Timothy Tyrrell, was a hairless man. Bumble had hair where you would not expect to see it; in the very depths of his earholes, on the undersides of his wrists, and on the soles of his feet. Timothy did not have any eyebrows.

Both were goldsmith bankers. But both held very different positions.

Bumble started his career in Goldsmiths' Hall, where he inspected precious metals and marked them if they passed muster. Adding such a *mark*, whilst in that *hall*, was known as "Hallmarking". Bumble, however, soon left that position to establish a bank of his own.

Timothy, on the other hand, was a banker until 1793, when he became the City Remembrancer. It is the Remembrancer's job to sit in parliament and whisper in the ears of politicians; encouraging them to pass laws which serve the interests of the nation's financial institutions.

Despite their different appearances and backgrounds, Bumble and Timothy had both been known to make the same claim:

"What I don't know about banking isn't worth knowing. What the public know about banking isn't worth a thing."

*****

Whenever Mayer arrived at one of his guild's functions, he made a conscious effort to avoid Bumble and Timothy, so he could make small talk with the other bankers first. He knew that once he met his favourite mentors, it was unlikely he would have time for anyone else.

After two glasses of champagne, he finally approached those men:

"A grand day! There's not a cloud in the sky."

They smiled, nodded, sipped champagne, and returned to their conversation.

"We were just talking about the Bank," Bumble explained.

"The Bank of England," Timothy corrected.

"Yah, the Bank of England. Now, Sonny M, the Bank of England was formed in 1694, when a consortium of merchants lent King William £1.2million to wage war against France."

"And to fund his womanizing."

"Yah. Well, it was Charles the second who was the real lothario; he had several mistresses, and bore fourteen illegitimate children. But William took on Charles's debts. So yah, he needed money for women as well as for war."

"For love as well as for power."

"Yah, for love and power. And, in return, the consortium of merchants was given the right to issue official banknotes."

"And to charge the king eight percent in interest per year."

"Yah, eight percent. But the most important thing was the banknotes. They were promissory notes, just like ours. They said, 'I promise to pay the bearer on demand the sum of x pounds'.

"Well, laws were passed which made forgery of those notes punishable by death. Other laws were passed which allowed those notes to be used to pay tax. So, people accepted them when selling things, before using them to pay their taxes. They circulated as money, much like tally sticks had done before."

Mayer raised his hand:

"So, the Bank of England's notes are promissory notes, like the ones we make? Like tally sticks?"

"Yah."

"And the Bank of England is owned by merchants? It's a private bank, like ours?"

"Yah."

Mayer paused. He looked around at the champagne flutes which seemed to be floating above their heads, the men in tuxedos who looked like giant penguins, the canapés, chandeliers and crystalline light.

"Of course, Sonny M, it was the Chinese who first issued paper money."

"Back in 806."

"Yah, 806. Like us, they issued promissory notes to merchants who were worried about travelling with bullion. But it wasn't until the twelfth century that such money appeared in Europe."

"In Venice."

"Yah, in Venice. The Venetian government issued bonds to fund a war."

"Money for power."

"Yah. Well those bonds also began to circulate as money, so we weren't the first to do it."

"But we were the best."

"Yah, the British always cap the climax. Why, some of us are even issuing notes without receiving any gold!"

"Unsecured notes."

"Yah, unsecured notes."

Mayer raised his hand:

"What if people exchanged those notes?"

Timothy and Bumble guffawed:

"We wouldn't have the gold to pay them! The state would have to bail *us* out, I suppose. It sure would make a change for power to rescue money."

"It would. Hahaha! But it'd never happen."

"No, never. People seem happy to leave their gold in our safes and trade with our notes. Tell me, Sonny M, do people collect their gold from you?"

Mayer shook his head.

"Of course they don't! Sonny M, we provide a service to this nation. We funnel wealth from the idle rich to the industrious poor. We're democrats; we help grease the wheels of industry. And, if we can fuel more industry, by issuing more notes, then we have a duty to do so. A duty, I tell you! We're on a righteous crusade!"

"It's a beautiful thing."

"Yah, a truly beautiful thing!"

*****

Mayer thought about his experiment; how he had lent gold to Damian Black, Baxter and Claude; and how that same gold had been returned to Mr Bronze's shop. Then he had a thought:

'Why couldn't we lend notes instead of gold? People seem happy to use our notes as if they were money; McCraw told me so himself. If folk insist on depositing the gold we lend, and then taking our notes, we might as well lend notes instead of gold in the first place.'

His conversation with Bumble and Timothy had filled the brain in his head with thoughts like these. But, like most men, Mayer had two brains. And, like most men, it was the brain in his pants which controlled most of his actions.

So it was that Mayer took Sal to the Haymarket Theatre. They were standing outside, between two pillars, when Raph approached.

Sal took the initiative.

"My love!" she screamed; throwing herself into Raph's arms. "This is my cousin, Mayer."

Raph wore an expression which fell halfway between suspicion and surprise:

"Jolly good to meet you old bean!"

Mayer engaged his winning smile.

Raph continued before Mayer had the chance to speak:

"Well, you two have a grand time. I must be off."

With that, he left. And, with that, Mayer's hair turned completely grey.

In the weeks which followed, Raph had Sal watched by a team of spies. When one of them caught Mayer kissing Sal in Regent's Park, Raph dumped Sal, gave her five hundred pounds in hush money, and kicked her out of his townhouse.

Mayer kicked Sal out of his life.

*****

So began a period in which Mayer fell from one woman to another; loving them all, but loving them in the shallowest of ways.

He became a regular at Mrs Hamilton's Dining Rooms, a place full of "Prima Donnas"; girls who gave themselves superficial airs and graces in order appeal to vain men. Mrs Hamilton's prices kept the riffraff out, Mayer had to spend five pounds just to enter, but he always snared a lady, using the same charm he used to woo clients. He had a talent for spotting loose women, and cut such a modest figure, because of his antiquated attire, that they often slept with him out of pity.

Mayer moved on to "Introducing Houses"; satin-clad abodes, dulled by catholic light, where the staff matched men with women. It was a cordial arrangement, apart from on the rare occasions when a husband was paired with his wife. Girls sold their virginity several times over, and men consummated their libidinous desires, with a flute of champagne in one hand and a woman's breast in the other.

Finally, Mayer moved on to "Female Operatives"; women who occasionally asked for money, but usually went to bed for their own self-gratification. Mayer slept with straw bonnet-makers, furriers, hat-binders, shoe-binders, silk-winders, tambour-workers and slop-women. But by far his favourite were the ballerinas; women with low incomes, high expenditures, and a natural penchant for gaiety. He made love to them in any place he could, and some places in which he could not.

One woman insisted he listen to her play the accordion before he kissed her, one threatened to cut off his hair whilst he slept, one ripped all the buttons from his shirt, one made him wear a baby's bib, one insisted that her dog watch them undress, one sang whilst they made love, one hummed, one recited poetry, one cried, and one whistled.

On one occasion, Mayer climbed through a woman's window before sleeping with her in the dark. When they awoke, and that woman saw that Mayer was not her fiancé, she screamed so loudly that Mayer jumped straight out of bed and straight through the window.

On another occasion, a woman who wore a garland of nettles told him: "You should probably know that I'm doolally". Mayer considered this a thing of pixyish self-depreciation, and never did find out that she had escaped from Bedlam just an hour before.

Once, Mayer awoke from an afternoon snooze on a park bench. He immediately declared his love to the woman who roused him, before taking her back to Mornington Palace.

"I shall never consent," that woman giggled, whilst Mayer kissed her neck.

"I shall never consent," she gasped, whilst they walked through the park.

"I shall never consent," she groaned, whilst Mayer kissed her lips.

"I shall never consent," she panted, as they hailed a cab.

"I shall never consent," she wailed, as she lay naked in bed. "Never! No! No! No! Yes!"

*****

Mayer's love for Lola grew more intense as she slipped further from his grasp. This was why he became a regular Don Juan; deciding that if he could not love *intensely*, like Hugo, he would have to love *extensively*;

replacing abstract love with carnal passion.

He did not *want* to love extensively, he felt that he *had* to:

'*It's Lola fault I'm like this. If she'd married me, I'd have become a loyal husband and a loving man, like Hugo, and he'd be the one sleeping with half of London. As it is, what choice do I have?*'

*****

Mayer was everything to everyone and nothing at all; submissive for the bold, confident for the shy, young for the old, experienced for the youthful, sensuous for the sensitive, and risky for the debauched.

He became a proficient lover, as if by mistake, for he never gave love nor received it. He saved his love for Lola, considering it an act of infidelity to love anyone else. As a result, he was able to focus on giving and receiving pleasure; doing whatever it took to please his women.

If you had spoken to Mayer, he would have been keen to use one of his tried and tested lines: "I like men who have money and women who do not".

This erred somewhat from the truth. Mayer liked all women, regardless of their wealth. It just so happened that women with money tended not to like Mayer.

Mayer seduced without discrimination. He found dazzling beauty in every woman he saw, irrespective of her appearance. He lavished them with attention, mirrored their personalities, chased their bodies, and declared love to their hearts.

For Mayer, sex was a battle. It was a matter of power; the power to seduce and to conquer. But Mayer never found contentment; he always felt an unquenchable desire to launch a new mission, just as soon as the resistance had been crushed. Possessing one woman was never enough; Mayer wished to possess the whole of womankind.

*****

Distracted by his libido, Mayer's talk with Bumble and Timothy did not inspire him to act. It took a further conversation to kick him into gear.

He was in the pub, with Hugo, when a drunken sailor began to argue with the barmaid:

"This… woood… neveeer… happen in China. No sir-eee!"

"Well, me duck, this ain't China, is it?"

"It isn't?"

"Nah, it ain't."

"But in China, I could just write you a note likey this, and all would be good."

"Well, we ain't in China. Here you have to pay with real money."

"Eeees real!"

Mayer interceded; pulling the sailor aside, inhaling his mustardy hair, and supporting his lackadaisical limbs:

"I'll pay for your beer if you tell me your tale."

"Now why'd you do that? I may be half-rats, 'arf and 'arf and 'arf, but I ain't no coot."

"Because I'd like to hear your tale. And because sailors like yourself are a credit to this nation; you deserve our support."

"Well, my friend, come 'ere!"

The sailor grabbed Mayer's head, and ran his tongue up Mayer's cheek.

"Hmm. Really, there's no need for that," Mayer said whilst pulling away.

"Nooo… Nooo… I insist."

"Please just tell me about China."

"The food stinks."

"Tell me about how you paid for your beer."

"Oh, yes. We paid our tabs by adding endorsey-ments on the back of receipts issued by bankies in Ing-ger-land. Those notes passed round and round and roundy-o! I once had me own note passed back to me with thirty names on the back."

"Thirty names?"

"Thirty!"

"So, you just wrote your own money on paper? That was that?"

"That was that. A, bee, see, dee, eee! Who's your uncle? Who's your aunt?"

"Hmm. Yes. You've been a great help. Have yourself another drink."

Mayer paid for the sailor's beer.

The sailor licked Mayer's cheek.

* * * * *

That conversation kicked Mayer back into gear.

He realised that if a drunken soldier could make money out of nothing, simply by adding a signature to a banker's draft, then anyone could make money out of nothing. *He* could make money out of nothing. He could become wealthy beyond his wildest dreams, without producing anything valuable at all.

He pushed through the crowds, jinked around the flaring gas jets, and skipped over the multifarious debris of unsanitary life.

He burst into Mr Bronze's shop:

"I've got it! By Jove, I've got it!"

"Got what?"

"The idea which will make us a fortune."

"Ah, but we already did amass a fortune; of gold, pure; diamonds, exquisite; and jewels, fine."

"We're small fry, Mr Bronze, we're chicken feed. We could be giants!"

Mr Bronze slowly closed his eyes. As always, he was the epitome of modesty; neither energetic nor lethargic, stressed nor placid.

"Ah," he said. "Tell me your idea."

"We create money out of nothing."

"Out of nothing?"

"Nothing!"

"Never."

"Why?"

"Man did never have the ability to create things out of nothing."

"So we'll make it out of paper."

"Out of paper?"

"Yes, out of paper. We'll issue notes, like our promissory notes, only we won't ask for any gold."

"No gold?"

"No, Mr Bronze, it'll be unsecured. We'll lend people notes, to spend on businesses and houses. Then we'll ask them to repay us over time, either with our notes or gold coins. And, of course, we'll charge them interest. There won't be enough of our notes in circulation to cover the interest, so people will have to pay it using coins which contain real silver or gold."

Mr Bronze shook his head:

"Ah, but you can't just create money out of nothing."

"You can."

"No, money doesn't grow on a magic money tree."

"It does, Mr Bronze, and we bankers are its gardeners."

"I don't believe it. One cannot turn chickens into cows."

"You could trade them."

Mr Bronze shook his head again:

"Ah, but the people who take our notes will use them to buy businesses and homes. Then the people who did receive them will come here and demand gold. But we won't have the gold, if we didn't receive it when issuing the note. We'll owe more than we possess."

"We have gold; our safes are full."

"Ah, but what if people did ask for it? What if they asked for more than we have?"

"They won't."

"They might."

It was Mayer's turn to shake his head:

"Give me *some* credit, Mr Bronze. Look, people have been leaving their gold in our safes, untouched, for years. Why do you think they'd start claiming it now? Coins which contain gold are a gamble; people can doubt their weight and purity; they're easy to lose or misplace. People would much rather use our notes than carry gold. We just need to make the denominations small enough to circulate. The Bank of England only issue large denominations; we'll have an advantage if we issue small ones."

Mr Bronze raised his eyebrows.

"Think about it," Mayer continued. "How much gold has Abe deposited here?"

"Ah, three hundred pounds, give or take."

"And when was the last time he had less than two hundred pounds?"

"Why, no such time did exist."

"And Zebedee?"

"He had eighty pounds the last time I checked."

"And has he ever had less than sixty?"

"Not that I can recall."

"Mr Harmer?"

"At least one hundred and fifty pounds."

"And McCraw?"

"At least one hundred."

"So that's five hundred and ten pounds right there. We could keep that money in our safe, issue notes worth the same amount, and see what happens. If the notes are cashed, we can pay for them using Abe's and Harmer's gold; gold which seems to have been forgotten. Chances are, however, that they won't be cashed; they'll circulate as if they were real money.

"Then our debtors will repay us, and pay us interest, either using our own notes or actual gold. It's a cash cow, Mr Bronze; it's the golden goose which will keep on laying!"

Mr Bronze smiled, as if enlightened, and then frowned, as if unsure. He nodded, as if in agreement, and then shook his head, as if unconvinced:

"You'd be making money out of nothing; giving receipts and taking gold."

"Exactly! What could possibly be better than making money out of nothing? It's so much more productive than making money out of something. The world is full of people who make things out of other things; that's just human. But creating things out of nothing? Well, that's superhuman. It'll set us apart!"

Mr Bronze gave Mayer an inquisitive look.

Mayer continued:

"It all comes down to trust. If people trust our notes, they'll use them. If they believe they'll be accepted elsewhere, they'll accept them themselves. It's the same as with gold coins. People accept those coins because they believe they'll be able to use them to buy things, not because they have any intrinsic value. They don't. Gold is just a simple metal.

"It all comes down to trust. If people believe they can cash your notes for gold, that you'll honour them, then they'll accept them as currency, and never actually cash them.

"It all comes down to trust. And who's more trustworthy than you, Mr Bronze? Why, even old Zebedee trusts you, and he wouldn't trust an angel of God if it appeared to him surrounded by golden light!"

Mr Bronze chuckled, Mayer chuckled, they embraced, and Mr Bronze coughed. It was twenty past six, and Mr Bronze always coughed at twenty past six. You could set your watch by it.

*****

Mayer saw a future for himself. If he could turn Mr Bronze's shop into a great bank, he reasoned, then he would be able to create a great bank of his own. He was preparing for his future; for prosperity and fame.

Mayer felt great. He did not just walk to the printer's shop, he positively skipped. He skipped through a jumble of airless, unlit alleys; surrounded by buildings which had been patched up, stitched up, divided, subdivided, and crammed full with more people than could possibly fit inside. Bodies dangled from windows, and laundry dangled from bodies.

He skipped through a honeycomb of temporary dwellings, hovels and shacks; past shops made of crumbling bricks and knotty timber; and beneath heavy, pendulous signs, whipped by the wind, which looked as though they would fall at any minute.

He opened his nostrils and sucked down that syrupy London air; that raw sewage in open drains, sickly, sweet and nauseous; that smell of wet dogs and wet horses; that rubbish, left to rot; those flea-addled rats, who banqueted on the remains; those chamber pots, emptied from second story windows; those innards, thrown out of butchers' shops; that manure, dirt, dust and human waste.

He loved that fetid odour!

In that moment, as he entered the printer's shop, he loved everything in existence.

*****

Mayer left the printers with a bag full of fresh notes. Boy did he love them! He ran his fingers over their textured surface; that thin, durable cotton, which felt like paper and smelled like success.

"Bronze's Bank" was written in ceremonious lettering, above a pastoral sketch of Regent's Park. In the top corner was a picture of a bronze pig with angel's wings, and at the bottom was an empty space where a date could be added.

Those notes came all sizes: Large, larger and massive. Some were worth as much as ten pounds, others as little as a shilling. All, however, included a simple pledge:

'We, Bronze's Bank, promise to pay the bearer of this note £x.'

This was a departure from their promissory notes, which had always been made out to a single individual:

'Receipt for £___ deposited by ___ at Bronze's Goldsmiths.'

But the most important line was a modest one. Written in the simplest of fonts, a mere four words long, it cut to the very heart of the matter:

'In God we trust.'

*****

Mayer lent those notes to anyone with a business plan, a reputation, or half an ounce of sense. He lent to Abe's sons, so they could move into their marital homes; to Randel, the roguish shoeshine, so he could open a cobbler's shop; to people in Camden Town, Kentish Town and Hampstead Heath; the young and the old; inventors, entrepreneurs and speculators.

Mayer's notes passed from one hand to another: The people who took them used them to buy things from other people, who used them to buy things for themselves. Businessmen used them to pay their workers, who used them to buy things from businessmen. And Mayer used them himself; he rented a townhouse, employed two cooks, two maids and a butler.

Occasionally, those notes were returned to Mr Bronze's shop; either by people repaying their loans, or by people who wished to cash them for gold. This was never a problem for Mr Bronze, since he continued to receive more gold than he was ever asked to pay out, but it was a problem for Mayer.

Up till this point, each of the bank's promissory notes had been balanced by a deposit of gold. But that had ceased to be the case, there was no balance, and so Mayer questioned his actions, his system, and his entire existence:

'It simply doesn't add up. It's bound to fail. And, when it does, my reputation will be in ruins; I'll never be able to establish a bank of my own.'

Doubts like these swirled around Mayer's mind. He did not trust his system and so, to compensate, he sought the trust of others....

*****

'The challenge in banking', Mayer told himself, *'Is to convince other people that your money is real. The challenge in life, is to convince them that your love is not.'*

Mayer did not have a problem hiding his one burning love, which was not a love of money, as people supposed, but a love of Lola. He locked his secret love deep within his heart and threw away the key.

To convince others to trust his money, however, took a little more effort; he had to make sure he was both likeable and respectable; proficient but also human.

To seem proficient, he persuaded Mr Bronze to move to a grander premises, with tall doors, polished counters, brass railings, a team of tellers and an open foyer. That place spoke of respectability; of stifled decorum and inaudible grace. Mayer lined its walls with references from the great and good of London society, commissioned paintings which depicted businesses the bank had funded, and placed a statue of Mr Bronze outside. Mayer, himself, began wearing clothes which made him look even older than before; adding a tiepin to his tie, cufflinks to his cuffs, and collar buttons to his collar. He walked with an ivory cane, which was more of a nuisance than a help, but which gave him a rarefied air of antiquity.

To seem human, Mayer deliberately made little mistakes; dropping his pen, spilling its ink, or tripping on the edge of a carpet. He hummed out of tune, and told terrible jokes:

"Bankers never die. We just lose interest."

"My jacket doesn't have any pockets. Well, whoever heard of a banker with his hands in *his own* pockets?"

"During a robbery, I gave orders to block the exits. The thieves escaped! I asked my staff what happened. They said the thieves had left through the *entrance.*"

In this manner, Mayer's new clients first saw his competence, then they saw his humanity, and then they learnt to trust him.

Mayer grew richer by the day.

*****

Whenever Mayer helped his clients, he felt the same "Luxury in doing good" which Hugo felt whilst helping Dizzy, and the same ecstasy which Archibald felt on the battlefield.

At the very instant Archibald's bayonet pierced his enemy's flesh, Mayer dashed a young man's dreams; rejecting his application for a loan. Like Archibald, he felt a thrill which reached every atom of his being.

At the very instant Hugo first helped a docker, Mayer helped a businessman who had fallen on hard times. Like Hugo, he felt a certain sort of joy.

Like his friends, he experienced a small amount of happiness. But, like his friends, it was never enough. He thought back to when he saved Hugo from Jonathan Wild, and Archibald from his bullies. He longed to be that selfless, innocent boy once again. He wanted more. Much, much more.

THE DO GOODER

"You have not lived today until you have done something for someone who can never repay you."
JOHN BUNYAN

Fragrance is a force that can pierce the most belligerent of armour. Lola's perfume possessed such a force.

The scent of rose water, rich and fresh, whisked Hugo into a balmy trance; the woody tones of patchouli cradled his flesh, and sweet aromatics wound him around Lola's little finger.

"I really think we should open a charity," she said.

They were canoodling on the sofa. Emma lay on their laps, burping and babbling. She felt so light, she seemed to defy gravity.

"You do, honey bun?"

"I'm thinking of cutting off my hair."

"You are?"

"Yes, hubby, a charity. It'd be nice to do something together, as husband and wife, don't you think?"

"Well, yes. But your hair? Your hair is exquisite, just like you."

"Yes, a charity it is. And not your everyday charity either. One really must dream big. Be as crazy as a loon. Ridonkulous! Make it so unbelievable, that people will have no choice but to believe it for fear of appearing absurd."

*****

As is the way of the world, those who do good judge themselves harshly, whilst those who do evil consider themselves righteous.

So it was with Hugo. Hugo was already doing more good than most, yet the more he did, the more suffering he saw; the more his love shone a light, the more it cast a shadow. Hugo was convinced that he was not doing enough, and so he was more than receptive when Lola suggested he do more.

It was as if Lola was reading his mind. Perhaps she was doing his thinking for him, Hugo could not be sure. He could not be sure where his mind ended and hers began.

Hugo had always been this way. He had spent his life spinning in a whirligig of other people's influence; shaped by the Drillmaster, who drilled him into shape; Dizzy, who trained him as a mudlark; Wild, who turned him into a thief; Mayer, who saved him; Bear, who apprenticed him; Nicholas, who funded his studies; and the professors who made him a doctor.

Met with ill intents, he had been battered down. Met with a loving hand, he had been raised up.

Hugo was never truly himself and yet, in a sense, Lola was helping him to become himself. It was a contradiction. But, then again, it is our contradictions which make us human. And Hugo, if nothing else, was certainly human.

*****

Charity was all the rage. To be a bona fide member of high society, one simply had to have one's foot in a benevolent institution or two.

Such charities were popping up like lilies on a lake. Grandiose mansions were transforming into hospitals, homes and refuges. Do-gooders were caring for the unfed, unclothed, deaf, dumb and blind.

At one moment, a body would lie dying in the street, its lifeblood ebbing at a shuddersome rate. The storm-clouds of doom would close in overhead. Then a wealthy gent would establish a charity, and save that nameless soul. High society would cheer, palms would pat backs, glasses would chink, and good tidings would be washed down with brandy.

"Ra, ra, ra," the gentry would sing.

At least that was how Hugo imagined it. So it was natural for him to feel confident as he went in search of benefactors. They would, he reasoned, be easy to find.

Yet, as is so often the case, the cumbersome reality deviated from the diaphanous dream. Hugo went cap-in-hand to landed gentry and prosperous merchants, to the rich and the even richer, but he was met with rejection wherever he turned:

"I pay my taxes."

"Charity begins at home."

"I don't want my money going to the undeserving poor."

A little part of Hugo died with each such remark. Then Lola consoled him, Emma blew a raspberry, and Hugo bounced back.

He approached the mansion of a man Mayer had recommended to him: Rudolph Reginald Ruben Roland Reynolds. He waited, surrounded by begonias which softened to the touch of weightless flies, before Reynolds finally opened the door.

Known simply as "R", that man was pugnaciously intoxicated; drunk on a mixture of homebrewed apple brandy and the fumes from white spirit. He was showily dressed but not well-attired; wearing a shirt which had been dabbed with sherry vinegar, creased with cigar ash, and made cruddy by long since evaporated tears. His face reminded Hugo of a cadaver he had once dissected whilst studying medicine; puffy, ghostly, yet filled with thousands of life's stories.

R led Hugo inside, where Hugo tried to make his case.

R responded as if he had not heard a word:

"My Richard recently died."

"It pains me to hear that."

"A right royal romantic he was. A real rascal; rousing, resolute and reckless till the end. Alas! Now he rests, reposed, retired, repositioned; ready to rise to the rapturous roars of the remotest reaches of the ever after. Alas! Removed from this realm. Alas! I remonstrate with regret, ruing the wrongs which rock us. Alas! Wretched, wretched world."

"Ahum," Hugo sputtered. "I realise I should recount... that it'd be reasonable to return... at the required hour. In reality, I should really return... it'd be right."

R glanced at Hugo with an expression which was curious, unsure, honoured, wise, weary and circumspect. His eyebrows seemed to puff with voluminous abandon, and his skin seemed to melt:

"No, no. I refuse to reject your request. Alas! Royalties must be reinvested. Alas! The rat-race does not rest; neither for royalty nor for the rabble."

So it was that R embarked on a monologue in which he used seven hundred and sixty words beginning with the letter "R", and said "Alas" on no less than eighty-four occasions. With a sparkle in his eye, he told Hugo that his dear friend Richard had been a wealthy man ("Rich", "Refined" and "Rolling in it"), and a generous man ("Reverent", "Responsive" and "Righteous"). He said that Richard had put his fortune in a trust fund, the interest from which was to be given to good causes. R, as executor of Richard's estate, would be the principal trustee.

Hugo spoke of his plans in exquisite detail.

"Righty-o!" R cheered. "If you realize these results, and if you're remotely as reliable and righteous as Mayer reckons you are, we'll have ourselves a rewarding relationship. I've every reason to rest assured that the ramifications will be ravishing! Right royally resplendent!"

*****

Hugo opened his notebooks and inhaled their greasy pages, which were slowly crumbling to dust. He sorted forgotten entries, before concluding that he should open a foundling hospital in London's East End; that hotbed of squalor and vice, where paralysed houses, rotten from chimney to cellar, cast black shadows over even blacker roads, sticky with slime, and grody with decay; where gruel-fuelled bodies, with ill-covered skulls and charcoal-rimmed eyes, flickered and vanished at the behest of indifferent lamplight; where brothels, gin palaces, small workshops, large workshops, music halls and lodging houses jostled for position with an overabundance of charitable institutions. Where pious matrons from the "The Society for the Suppression of Vice" walked by, ignoring intoxicated vagabonds and pregnant teens; and where religious missions competed, claws bared, with more malevolence than any private business.

Hugo stepped forth into this world. Behind him stood R's money, and in front of him lay a future blinded by hope.

He sourced an abandoned building on Stepney Causeway, which was perfect in every way apart from the ceilings, which were missing; the walls, which were crumbling; and the floors, which were cracked. They had been cajoled into veiny swathes by the roots of an aristocratic oak, which stood imperiously at the centre of the courtyard, from where it had covered that ruin in an ocean of leaves.

It took quite an effort to convert that arboraceous shell into a functioning space. Hugo, Lola and a team of builders worked night and day, whilst Emma lay in her cot; chortling, chattering, creaking and crying.

By the time they had finished, their bodies were a stone lighter. Curtained windows faced outwards towards the oak, and inwards towards rooms which Lola filled with plants; placing forget me nots in the dormitories, snake plants in the halls, and areca palms in the dining room.

All they needed was children. So Hugo went, notebooks in hand, to round up all the guttersnipes who sheltered in London's hidden nooks. He took them to "Saint Nick's", having named the charity after his father-in-law, and he provided them with everything they might need; food, accommodation, clothing, healthcare, education and apprenticeships.

As the years ticked by, the dormitories filled to capacity. They kept on filling. So many babies, abandoned to the wilds, found it to Saint Nick's that Hugo felt compelled to turn older children away.

One such child was known as "Carrots". His features had been disfigured by disease; his face was famine-stricken, his eyes were bloodshot, and his hair was the colour of dried apricots.

Carrots was turned away one snowy December evening. Left to trawl Stepney's frost-kissed highways and glistening lanes, he slept alone beneath the niveous sky, exposed to the northern chills.

When he saw Carrots the following morning, Hugo leant down to touch his brow, which had frozen rigid. Carrots had died.

Hugo, bitten by shame, placed a sign above the door to Saint Nick's, which read "No Child Refused Admission", and sent Lola to find new backers.

*****

It was in fundraising that Lola came into her own; raising more money than even she thought would be possible. Still, for her, it was not quite enough:

"Hubby, I've decided to become a doctor."

"Nothing would give me greater pleasure," Hugo replied. "But you know as well as I do that women can't be doctors."

"Well, in that case, I'll simply have to become a man."

"A man, honey bun?"

"Yes, a man. I don't mean to blow my own trumpet, but if you and papa can be doctors, then so can I. We're a partnership, that's what a marriage is, and it goes without saying that any self-respecting woman should be able to do anything her husband can. Now, I really must devour a ginormous bowl of tapioca pudding."

With that, Lola left in search of food.

She never did become a doctor, although she did become a proficient nurse, an exceptional fundraiser, and a doting mother. She bore two more daughters. Then she gave birth to a stillborn son, and a son who died in infancy. Then she bore two more daughters.

Each time she gave birth, an extra line formed on Lola's stomach. She liked those lines, since they reminded her of her children. She was not so enamoured with the lines on her face; the laughter lines which poked fun at her eyes, and the cracks which lay siege to her lips. But she accepted them, and so aged with a dignified grace.

Their family moved into a townhouse, which filled with daughters in much the same way their cottage had once filled with dolls. Wherever Hugo looked, there were mouths without teeth, feet without socks, and noses with more mucus than seemed possible.

This was not a problem for Hugo, who still considered himself to be a child, and believed he would remain in this Peter Pan state for just as long as he kept the company of real children. He preferred infants to adults, since they said what they wanted to say, whilst adults could be painfully deceptive.

Hugo's love for his daughters was a new sort of love, "Storge"; a tender love, based on devotion and respect, which bonds parents and children.

Hugo and Lola possessed storge in abundance. As Lola once put it, whilst cradling Maddie in her arms: "I love you so much I could kill you!"

Yet Lola was hesitant to smother her daughters. She never lavished them with false praise; she complimented them when they were kind, but not when they were clever. She never overindulged them with affection or treats, but she made sure they knew who they were. There was no flattery to spoil them; no vanity with which they could be deceived. Lola never commented on her daughter's looks; she allowed them the space they needed to grow. She never bought them toys nor games; she encouraged them to create their own.

She did, however, buy her daughters books. So many books, in fact, that they pushed Hugo's notebooks off their shelf, and formed piles in the most unlikely of places; in plant pots, drawers, the breadbin and the laundry basket. She read them to her daughters each night; using zany voices and pulling wacky faces. Then she took them to Saint Nick's, where she read them to the orphans.

*****

Lola seemed to be hoarding perfume.

Hugo had once told Lola that he thought she was beautiful without makeup. She took it as a compliment, but continued to wear makeup nonetheless. So although Hugo had thought about telling Lola that he liked the way she smelled without perfume, he knew she would still wear it, and so he had kept shtum.

Lola still wore perfume.

She collected perfumes in every scent known to the human nose, kept them in bottles of every imaginable shape, and wore them for every imaginable purpose; to signal her authority to her employees, blend her into good society, lure Hugo to her bed, and entice wealthy men into parting with their money.

Lola had a natural talent for getting men to part with their money.

She went from door to door, establishing a network of subscribers around their Fitzrovia home; she approached new donors at banquets and balls; and she welcomed a vast array of potential benefactors to an annual fireworks gala, which she hosted herself.

As a result of her efforts, Hugo and Lola were able to build another floor on top of Saint Nick's, add six more dormitories, set up a soup kitchen, and establish a ragged school which served jacket potatoes to every pupil.

*****

Unlike Archibald and Mayer, who dressed to impress, donning false identities in order to earn real respect, Hugo wore the clothes he found most comfortable.

It cost him.

When people saw him with his shirt untucked, he immediately went down in their estimations. His crumpled trousers caused one potential donor to walk away before they had exchanged a word. His ill-fitting waistcoats and odd socks lost him the respect his actions deserved.

Lola felt compelled to act. She took control of Hugo's wardrobe; replacing the clothes she disliked, and ensuring that everything was ironed. She dressed Hugo each morning; whistling as she rolled his pants up his legs, put his socks on, buttoned his shirt, and brushed down his chest. She ended this performance by kissing Hugo's cheek.

Hugo enjoyed this ritual, but his new attire did make him feel like a fraud. Like Archibald and Mayer, he had also borrowed an identity to impress borrowed friends.

*****

Hugo was wary of Lola's perfumes.

It was not without good reason; he recalled how Lola also wore hundreds of scents when she was a debutante. It was part of her allure; titillating her suitors' noses and sending shivers down their spines.

'Who is she trying to court now?' he asked himself. 'Is it me? But why? I'm already hers. Has she got her eye on another man? Perhaps she's already got herself another man! Has she made a cuckold of me? Will I ever know?'

It drove him mad.

He was relieved, therefore, when she sat on his lap, free from any aroma:

"Grownups never have any fun. It's all just dowdy work, silly clothes, pesky wrinkles and paperwork."

She pulled a face at baby Sylvia, stretching her lips out wide and waggling her tongue.

Emma, aged six, tore around the room pretending to be a horse:

"Neigh! Giddy up! Giddy up! Woah boy! Yee-hah!"

Hugo smiled at Lola.

"I feel as weak as water. It's as if I did that pull up last year for nothing. Well, anyhoo, I've been looking through our accounts, and it appears we've been receiving anonymous donations."

"We have? How wonderful!"

Lola scrunched her nose and smiled with her eyes.

Hugo replied without thinking:

"I'll look for a second premises."

Lola squeezed her husband's knee:

"Well, hubby, I'd love to stay and chatter, but there's a turducken manwich with my name on it..."

*****

Deep down, Hugo was still the same little boy who was thrown out of St Mary Magdalen's; unsure where to go, what to do, or what to say. He did not feel like an adult at all. He looked in the mirror and asked himself: *'How am I getting away with this massive lie?'*

But Hugo felt confident, as the man of the house, the boss of a charity, a doctor and a father, because of Lola. She had his back.

Lola felt the same. She also felt like a child pretending to be an adult. She also survived because of her man.

This arrangement seemed to work. At least, it worked most of the time. Then Emma stopped talking. That little ball of noise stopped sneezing, hiccupping, burping, coughing, clicking and clapping.

Lola and Hugo asked her questions, read her stories, made silly noises, coughed, clicked and clapped. But, no matter how hard they tried, they could not get Emma to speak.

Hugo liked the peace and quiet.

Lola prayed for noise.

THE HERO

"The greatest crimes in the world are not committed by people breaking the rules, but by people following the rules. It's people who follow orders that drop bombs and massacre villages."

BANKSY

Archibald had tasted power, but it had not satisfied his cravings; it had only made him want more. His addiction to violence came to dominate his being.

Whenever he heard that a battle was afoot, Archibald requested permission to head to the front. In the first place, he and Delaney went after the Marathas; the only major obstacle standing between Britain and total domination of the subcontinent. He killed a second man at Asirgarh Fort, a third in Laswari, and a fourth at Adgaon. He was branded a "Hero", "Brave" and "Daring". He was told he was "Protecting Great Britain" and "Serving the British people".

But it was in the south Indian town of Vellore that Archibald's star truly rose.

Hindu soldiers there had been prohibited from wearing religious marks on their foreheads, and Muslim ones had been made to shave their beards. When they protested, they were whipped.

They fought back, hoping their rebellion would lead to the liberation of their homeland. They killed fourteen British soldiers, took the fort, and raised the flag of the Mysore Sultanate.

A British officer escaped. He found Archibald's troop, who came to the rescue; riding through the dust, which formed a halo of zippy light above their heads.

Accelerating ahead of his troop, Archibald and Delaney arrived alongside eighteen other men. They lassoed ropes to the ramparts, and helped their comrades up.

Unseen and unheard, Archibald led a bayonet charge, picking off every rebel in his way. Blood sprayed from torsos, forming an exotic monsoon; a celestial fountain of claret rain.

"Gotcha!" he cheered, as he stabbed a doe-eyed sepoy.

"Atcha!" he cheered, as he stabbed a pug-faced youth.

"Have it!"

"Take this!"

"For Britain!" he wailed, as he whipped the breath from the mouths callow insurgents and grizzled malcontents, diminutive and rangy, barefoot and black-eyed: "For mutton-shunting Britain!"

Blood fell like rain, screams roared like thunder, and bayonets bolted electric.

Archibald felt almighty.

His chest exposed, his brow furrowed, he dreamt that Lola was cheering him on. He stabbed and slashed and shunted for her. He did not care that he might die; he thought that dying for Lola would have been the ultimate expression of love.

"Die, devils, die!"

"Ungrateful infidels, die!"

"Unappreciative savages, die! We've civilised you. How dare you repay us like this?"

*****

By the time the dragoons arrived, Archibald had beaten a bloody path to the gates, which he blew apart from the inside.

The cavalry charged, striking everyone in their way, before dragging everyone else outside.

As they left, Archibald made one mutineer lick up his daughter's blood, and another one kick a dying comrade. He left corpses in the midday sun, bent at nauseating angles, scowling with twisted lips; attracting flies, maggots and worms.

It was impossible to discern Vellore's garlicky scent beneath death's impassioned vapours.

Archibald paraded across a field, where the grass prostrated itself in shame, and leaves fled on the wings of a sheepish breeze.

After a series of mock trials, he and Delaney helped to tie the rebels to cannons, before firing one themselves.

'*Boom!*'

A thousand tiny birds exploded from a tree.

A thousand tiny body parts blew to smithereens. Skull fragments flew upwards, leg fragments shot downwards, and pieces of arm blasted left, right and centre. No vestige of life remained to be buried.

For every Muslim and Hindu, the message was clear: Without a body there could be no burial, and without a burial there could be no afterlife. The punishment would last forever. The British ruled supreme.

For Archibald, it was glorious. He had the power he craved; power over life, death and the afterlife; over every shattered splinter of human existence.

The old Archibald had died. The new Archibald had become a man.

This Archibald would not allow his loved ones to be driven to their graves, his bullies to call him a "Sissy", or a girl like Lola to get away. This Archibald drove *others* to their graves, called *others* "Sissies", and never let anyone get away!

He killed hundreds of people that day.

His pride swelled to epic proportions.

*****

As is the way of the world, those who do good judge themselves harshly, whilst those who do evil consider themselves righteous.

So it was with Archibald. He was convinced that he was righteous; everyone told him he was a "Hero"; that he was "Serving his country" and "Making his nation proud". Delaney patted his back. His superiors made him an officer:

"Well, you acted like a brigadier in Vellore, don't think the top brass didn't notice! The least we could do is make you a Rupert."

Yet Archibald was still unfulfilled, he still wanted more, and so he was delighted when he was sent to collect tax.

*****

The British inherited a functioning taxation system from the Mughals. Then they changed it; introducing a Land Tax, equivalent to two thirds of a peasant's income, believing it would encourage them to work harder and become more productive.

But, even at full capacity, growing rice and grain could not generate enough income to pay that tax. So farmers were forced to shift production; to grow valuable crops for export, such as indigo and cotton, instead of growing food for themselves. What grain they did produce was often seized by force. Levies were placed on salt, leaving the poor vulnerable to dehydration and cholera.

The consequences were tragic. When a drought arrived, in 1769, so little land was left producing food that ten million people starved to death. Had it not been for the shift in production, caused by the Land Tax, most of them would have survived.

But, rather than reduce their tax, the British increased it to make up for their losses. They took land from farmers who defaulted, forcing them into debt peonage, and issued land-rights to farmers who paid, thereby winning their loyalty.

*****

Archibald helped to maintain this system. He went from house to hut, collecting taxes and beating anyone who refused to pay.

In time, he was given a second responsibility; managing the textile trade, which Britain was in the process of monopolizing.

So it was that he was sent to mete out justice on a mauve-haired weaver who had sold cloth to an Indian trader.

Even many decades later, Archibald would still recall the hollowness he felt as he flung back the door to that man's suburban shack. He would still sense the ginger, resonant and rich, which pockmarked the inside of his throat; the vapour of chopped onions, which dilated his nostrils; and the garbled bubbles of a baby's saliva, which popped cheerily in his ears.

Archibald would still recall how he and Delaney dragged that family out into the savage sun; how they made them stand there for several hours, with their backs bent, and their feet buried in the sand; and how they placed hot stones on their spines, whilst their men sat in the shade, chomping on macadamia nuts, and drinking that weaver's milk.

That image seared itself onto Archibald's memory. As if painted by a master artist, he saw the burnt flesh on a young girl's back; pyogenic, crisp and raw. He saw veins pop through her mother's skin. He saw anguish in bloodshot eyes.

Each time he applied a new form of discipline, he would come to recall the scene in vivid detail; every colour would seem bright, every smell would seem pungent, and every sound would seem pronounced. Yet, whenever he repeated that punishment, he would forget it straight away. Those events, of which there were too many to mention, all blurred into one.

The first time Archibald rubbed chillies into the eyes of a rogue weaver, the scene burnt itself into his memory. He could not escape the image; the cornea washed maroon, the eyelids inflamed, the lashes entwined. In the end, however, Archibald rubbed chillies into so many eyes that it became the norm. He could not distinguish one such event from another.

The first time he saw his men bugger an elderly Indian, Archibald winced. The second time it happened, he merely shrugged. The suspect confessed to a crime he had not committed, and so Archibald was happy to believe that the ends had justified the means.

His men tied suspects to branches, with their arms stretched high above their heads; they clamped women's nipples in spiked vices; they confiscated property and possessions.

Archibald shrugged.

*****

This period in Archibald's life lasted for almost a decade.

Although he never accumulated much wealth, such were his meagre wages, you would never have guessed it had you seen him. Whilst his men stole anything which was light enough to carry away, Archibald only ever stole clothes. He cut an extravagant figure; wearing a stolen plume of eagle feathers, a stolen gold medallion, and a stolen velvet cloak. Delaney followed suit; adorning himself with a plume of canary feathers, a silver medallion, and a cotton cloak.

But Archibald's pièce de résistance was his necklace, which he wore night and day, even when he was still in uniform. Made from thumbs he had removed from rogue weavers, to stop them from weaving, it earned Archibald a new title: He became known as the "Thumb Taker General".

*****

Whilst Archibald flourished, India floundered. It transformed from a rich, self-sufficient nation, into a subservient state; producing low-value raw materials instead of high-value processed goods.

The Indian textile industry was crushed. Indians were forced to export their cotton to Britain for a low price, and buy back British cloth for a high price. British textile producers prospered, but Indian weavers did not. Their larders emptied, their bellies shrunk, and their skeletons bleached the plains. Archibald trod on their crumbling bones, as if stepping on seashells. The population of Dhaka fell to one seventh of its previous size.

Overcome by guilt, Archibald went to speak to the Governor.

The Governor was a distinguished, arrogant man, with an indefatigable owl's beak and sculptured contours which were held rigid by stiff man's disease. He lived at the mercy of his prejudices, which may explain his response:

"If we are to create a modern, civilised country, we must accept there will be growing pains. A little force can be justified in the name of the greater good. And anyhow, if we weren't here, the fuzzy wuzzies would only abuse themselves. We're maintaining *their* wog customs after all."

Archibald wore a blank expression, as if to ask for more.

The Governor obliged:

"It's as Martin Luther once said: 'Christians are rare in this world. Therefore, we need a strict government which will compel and constrain the wicked, in order that the world not become a desert, peace may not perish, and trade may not be destroyed; all of which would happen if we were to rule according to the Gospels'."

These words cleansed Archibald's conscience.

'*I have power,*' he told himself. '*Who am I to complain? Who am I to let my selfish moral doubts get in the way of the greater good?*'

*****

The Chinese believed they had a heavenly mandate to spread justice and harmony worldwide, the Romans believed they were endowing the barbarians with peace and refinement, and the Babylonians believed they were responsible for the welfare of the people they conquered. So it came to be with the British. They too believed they were on a moral conquest; spreading Christianity and free-trade.

Archibald reminded himself of this whenever he was plagued by guilt. Then he went to church, where he listened to his vicar; a man whose skin was the colour of raw cod, and who suffered from sudden bouts of blushing:

"Be humble, be meek, be kind! Rise above temptation, and follow in Christ's footsteps. Love thy neighbour, love thy enemy, and turn the other cheek!"

Listening to these sermons made Archibald feel even guiltier than before:

'*Should I not turn the other cheek when a peasant is unable to pay their taxes? Should I not love the Indian weavers? Should I not treat them as I would wish to be treated?*'

Doubts like these plagued Archibald whenever his vicar spoke. He always left church in a pensive mood, before changing into his silk cloak, feasting on roast meats, and downing copious amounts of liquor. As he talked about chivalry, pride and honour, the vicar's words would fall from his mind.

"We're serving God," he would tell Delaney. "We're his noble bloody henchmen!"

They would fall into a drunken slumber, awake hungover, and leave to enforce the law. A week would pass, and this cycle would repeat itself once more.

*****

For ten years, Archibald collected tax, chased rogue weavers, and meted out justice. Things, in general, followed a steady course: Archibald worked during the week, doubted himself at church, and then got drunk. Whenever he was overcome with guilt, he spoke to his superiors, who reassured him that he was a "Hero" doing "God's work". Whenever he was unconvinced, he blamed Lola:

'It's her fault I'm like this. If she'd married me, I'd have become a loyal husband and loving man, like Hugo, and he'd be the one in the army.'

One thing, however, did change over the course of this period: Archibald's dreams.

They changed in two halves...

Over the course of his first five years in India, the image of Lola which visited Archibald each night evolved; her face stiffened, taking on the granite contour of Delaney's cheek; her nose took the shape of Delaney's nose; her shoulders widened and her breasts hardened. Her aura, as undisciplined as the wind, slipped from Archibald's dreams and also from his portraits. In time, those sketches began to look less like Lola, and more like Delaney. On one occasion, Delaney caught a glimpse of such a picture, and exclaimed: "Oh, how nice of you to draw me!" Archibald was so shaken, he did not eat for days.

Over the course of the next five years, the faces of Archibald's victims began to appear in his dreams. They flickered in and out of view, but never impinged upon his imaginary marriage to Lola.

By his tenth year in India, those characters were appearing with increasing regularity. There was a weaver, whose dislocated arm dangled from its socket, discombobulated, as if baffled and confused; a farmer, whose brow held canyons full of blood; and a dead baby, whose face was a picture of innocence lost.

Slowly but surely, those figures came to the fore. One smiled. One spoke. Archibald rocketed upwards; awake, alert, and more than aware that his demons were launching an attack:

'Where's my power? Why can't I control my dreams? I need more power. Give me more power! I need to control my mind!'

MUCH, MUCH MORE

"Money often costs too much."
RALPH WALDO EMERSON

The king was declared insane.

A bankrupt banker assassinated the Prime Minister.

Mayer lined his pockets.

At the very moment Hugo felt an exquisite thrill from finding his second premises, and Archibald felt that same thrill whilst evicting a farmer from his home, Mayer was making thousands of pounds.

He was approached by three Frenchmen in Bourbon uniforms, who told him that Napoleon had been killed. He immediately invested in government securities, whose value shot up. But he had second thoughts, and so sold those stocks for a tidy sum.

The whole thing had been a hoax; the "Great Stock Exchange Fraud". Mayer had been right to sell when he had, which made him feel greater than words could express.

*****

Mayer became richer by the day; creating more bank notes and claiming more interest; earning a pay rise and even higher commissions.

He made it his mission to own more than Abe and Sadie. He bought himself a house which contained one more bedroom, one more living room, and one more dining room than Buckingham Towers. He filled that place with more cooks, maids, horses, carriages, chintz, chinoiserie, doilies and drapes than Abe and Sadie had ever owned.

He felt good, but not complete. Happy in life, Mayer was unhappy in love. He still slept with any women who took his fancy, using his money to his advantage. He even housed two girls of his own, like Raph had done with Sal. Yet, now in his mid-thirties, he considered himself to be too old for the bachelor lifestyle. He felt that he was not so much playing the field, but being played by the field itself.

Mayer wanted to grow old gracefully, with his one true love by his side. But there was a problem: His one true love, Lola, was happily married.

"Come on Hugo!" he muttered beneath his breath. "Why can't you hurry up and die?"

His situation was hopeless, yet he still had hope.

'*Flee where you will,*' he told Lola during an imaginary conversation. '*Go to the ends of the earth. I will still be yours. Marry whoever you like. Marry a hundred men. You will still be mine. Love me or hate me, bless me or curse me, live or die, sleep or wake, speak or stay silent; I will still be yours, and you will still be mine.*'

Mayer was convinced that Lola was his soulmate; the other half of his tally; the stock to his stub. He was certain they would unite.

The universe had a way of bringing Mayer the right people at the right time. It brought him Abe, through whom he met Zebedee and Mr Bronze, and it brought him Archibald, through whom he met Sammy and McCraw. These people had made him rich.

Mayer was sure the universe would come up trumps again, and throw Lola into his arms when the time was right; he just needed to wait, patiently, and everything would fall into place.

*****

Like Archibald, Mayer considered celibacy. Unlike Archibald, he decided that it would only make matters worse:

'*At least I can pretend to be with Lola when I'm with someone else. The illusion of love has got to be better than nothing.*'

Mayer stopped his womanizing, split up with one mistress, and stayed loyal to the other: Nicola.

"Nicola!" he sang out loud. "Even her name sounds like 'Lola'. Nick-O-Lola!"

Like Mayer, Nicola was a heartbroken wreck; haggard in appearance, although ladylike to the eye; tawdry, yet also bright. Several years Mayer's senior, and more sympathetic by several degrees, she had found true love, only to lose her husband to scarlet fever.

The house Mayer rented for Nicola was filled with the trinkets her husband had bought her, besotted by his belief that he had to give her something new every day to keep their love alive. Decorative plates covered every wall, Russian dolls covered several shelves, and handcrafted African masks hid in at least two cupboards. Nicola cooked for her husband every evening, just in case he happened to return from the dead; she scrubbed his shirts to the point of distraction, and encouraged Mayer to wear his clothes. She imagined Mayer was her dead spouse, whilst Mayer pretended she was Lola. She did not wish to speak of that man, and Mayer did not wish to speak of Lola, so they found a mutual understanding in their shared silence. Their relationship did not need words, because it transcended the limits of human speech.

Their silence had its own flavour; a subtle flavour, more vanilla than chocolate, but a flavour nonetheless. Mayer inhaled that silence, swilled it around his palate, and let it drip down his throat.

Nicola and Mayer found sanctuary in each other's arms.

Sometimes, one of them would think a funny thought. The other person would laugh. Then they would both laugh together. Mayer would laugh so much he would snort. Nicola would laugh so much she would fart. Then she would cover her face with a pillow, to hide her shame. Then she would laugh even louder than before.

Sometimes, one of them rubbed the other's back at just the moment they needed to feel an empathetic touch. Sometimes they left, at just the moment the other person needed some space. They sat with entwined fingers, watching lachrymose sunsets. They hugged for timeless spells; soothed by a love that could never be born.

*****

This was how the years ticked by: In the silent embrace of a proxy spouse. Mayer grew rich, but he remained poor in love; he felt young, but he looked old.

He waited, with the stubbornness of a statue, for Hugo to die and for Lola to be his.

CHEEKY REBEL

"Here enters Satan; the eternal rebel, original freethinker and emancipator of worlds. He makes man ashamed of his bestial ignorance and obedience; he emancipates him, urging him to eat from the tree of knowledge."
MIKHAIL BAKUNIN

Hugo walked into a stuffed beaver, steered himself around it, and made his way into the lounge. He had long since learnt that it was best to act naturally, even in the most unnatural of situations.

He kissed Lola.

She spoke:

"There're such a lot of different Lolas in me: There's a mum, daughter, wife, fundraiser, bookkeeper, gardener, woman and girl. I'm a real mumtrepreneur. If I was just the one Lola, things would be much simpler. But then, I suppose, things would also be pretty dull."

Having spoken herself silent, Lola looked at her husband:

"There's something wrong."

There was, indeed, something wrong. Regardless of how much Hugo did to help the needy, he still felt an urge to do more. He had so much love left over that he did not know how to use it.

It was around this time that Hugo read about the Haitian Revolution. The black slave population on that island had risen up; massacring their overlords before taking control of the island. Fearful of similar uprisings in their own colonies, the British abolished the transatlantic slave trade. The actions of a few rebels had improved the lives of millions of people for good.

Hugo realised that he had fixed the symptoms of poverty; homelessness, nakedness, starvation, sickness and illiteracy; but he had not fixed the root cause. He realised that he needed to take a leaf out of the Haitians book and challenge the system itself. He needed to do more.

"You need to do more," Lola told him. "You need to challenge the system."

Hugo furrowed his brow:

"I should. But, then again, maybe I shouldn't."

Hugo was afraid; well aware that rebels were being deported to Australia.

Lola was not afraid:

"Stop being such a nervous Nellie and listen to your wife."

"What? That's not how it works."

"That's not how most marriages work, but this is not a normal marriage. Most women serve their husbands, but most husbands make their wives. That never happened with us. I raised *you* up from the gutter and gave *you* a position in society. In this marriage, I'm the husband and you're the wife."

"Oh."

"You do what I say."

"Yes, honey bun."

"Now act like a man and take me to bed. I want to lick some whipped cream off your chest."

*****

Not wishing to be *too* radical, Hugo turned to radical charity. He joined the board of the Needlewomen's Institution, promoted the Metropolitan Early Closing Association, and gave lessons at the Metropolitan Evening School.

It was not enough. Hugo still felt an urge to do more, and so he became a Luddite.

✳ ✳ ✳ ✳ ✳

Things had been good in the good old days. Skilled weavers had been their own bosses; taking pride in their work, producing quality cloth and receiving ample compensation. They had supplemented their incomes by growing their own food.

Then their land was enclosed, which stopped them from cultivating crops.

Then factories were established, which churned out low-grade cloth for low prices; putting the weavers out of business, and forcing them to find employment in factories. They worked longer hours, with less artistic integrity, less freedom, and lower incomes.

At the same time, crops were taken from the British people to fuel the government's wars. Food became scarce and costly.

Dedicated to a laissez faire economic doctrine, the government ignored the people's petitions. So, when the harvest failed, the peasantry felt that they had nothing to lose. Riots spread across the land. Workers, demanding better pay, broke into factories and destroyed looms. They formed a national movement, led by Ned Ludd of Sherwood Forest; a feared leader of unseen armies, who whose face was ghostly white, and who did not actually exist.

This was not important. The myth meant more than the man.

The myth inspired bands of rebels; organized from below, cross-dressing, masked and anonymous. Like the Haitian rebels, they sang revolutionary songs, wrote threatening letters, mocked the establishment, attacked factory owners and assaulted merchants.

The state fought back; ordering soldiers to attack the Luddites, and making machine-breaking a capital offence. Seventeen rebels were hung in a single year, but thousands escaped; protected by the mutual aid of their brethren.

✳ ✳ ✳ ✳ ✳

This, then, was the world into which Hugo stepped.

After travelling the nation, he arrived at a mill near Manchester. He was met with universal suspicion. The locals said he looked like a spy.

That mill had a sad face; all red bricks and tall windows, sorrow and frost.

Two thousand protestors had mad faces; all chiselled foreheads and granite chins.

A solitary chimney stabbed the sky.

Five windows shot open, instantaneously; sliding in unison, at exactly the same rate, and making one solitary '*Click*' as they hit the tops of their frames. Then a sixth window shuffled open, struggling and squeaking, jostling from side to side.

Hugo chuckled.

Six rifles poked through; hovering in mid-air, as if held by ghosts.

Hugo stopped chuckling.

The crowd stopped cheering. Overcome by an omnipotent silence, eyes glanced inwards and feet shuffled back.

'*Bang.*'

It was simple as that. There was no warning, no call for order, no negotiations, no sympathy, no inch given and none expected.

Six bullets flew as one.

'*Bang.*'

Six more bullets kissed the air.

'*Bang.*'

Round followed round followed round.

Hugo stood his ground. Blood-flecked, mud-specked, fearful and faithful; he got to work, skipping through the wreckage; stitching gashes, setting bones, removing bullets, tying wounds and amputating legs.

He breathed life back into eighteen injured bodies. Three people died.

He returned the next day, and saved twenty more lives. Five people died.

A part of Hugo felt he should have done more, a part of him felt he had done enough, but one thing was certain: Hugo was no longer met with suspicion. He had become a true Luddite.

*****

In the days which followed, Luddites retaliated by killing the owner of that mill. In the weeks which followed, protests met bloody ends all across the land.

Hugo was always on hand to pick up the pieces...

He cared for protestors at the Food Riots, at which fifty people were killed. He saved several lives at the Corn Law Riots; a protest against tariffs on grain, which were starving the peasantry to death. He helped at the Littleport Riot, where protestors called for poor relief and a minimum wage. He attended the Spa Field Riots, where protestors demanded electoral reform. And he treated wounds at the Blanket March, where weavers demanded to keep their legal rights.

Whenever people made a stand for justice, Hugo made a stand for them. He was the doctor to a protestor generation; the yang to Archibald's yin, ready to ride away on the spur of the moment, with a flask in his hands, and radical pamphlets sewn into his blazer's lining. He only ever returned once it was clear he was no longer needed, which meant that he often spent months away.

This put a strain on Hugo and Lola's marriage.

Sometimes, when she had not seen Hugo for weeks, Lola began to doubt their love. It was as if she needed Hugo by her side, to remind her that she was adored.

In those moments, Lola questioned her choice of spouse: *'Wouldn't I have been better off marrying a rich or powerful man; an Archibald or a Mayer?'*

She recalled Archibald's muscles, the doll he left on her doorstep, and the way he had looked at her with such timid love. She imagined the hero he had become; a real knight in shining armour.

She recalled Mayer's courting with phantasmal nostalgia; laughing at his innocent idiocy and puppy-dog eyes. She reminded herself of how she might have married him, if their date had not been such a disaster. She thought about the times she had seen him, alone and lonely, as if he wanted to be by her side. She thought about his money and all the things it could buy.

Then she thought of Hugo; neither heroic nor rich, incapable of defending her in battle or buying her the world. It made her mad. She lost her appetite, spoke sarcastically, contradicted herself, snapped the pages of her books, and paced around like a caged tiger; her claws bared and her eyes steamy with hate.

The more she thought of Archibald, Mayer and Hugo, the angrier she became.

Then Hugo would return, and Lola's anger would disappear. Her husband's presence made her so happy, that Hugo never realised she had been sad.

There was something else Hugo did not notice: Lola's latest addiction. She had turned their house into an Aladdin's cave of stuffed animals.

Hugo did not notice the dead fox which seemed to shoot out beneath his feet as he walked across their hall, nor did he notice the outstretched claw of a brown bear, which slashed his cheek as he fell. He landed with a thud, which knocked a boar off balance. Rocking one way, before wobbling the other, it crashed down upon his back.

'*Smash!*'

"Ouch!" Hugo wailed. "That's it! Enough! This is a home not a jungle."

"Is there a difference?"

"A tremendous difference."

"But need there be?"

"Whatever do you mean?"

"I want a stuffed jackalope."

"A what?"

"And a sharktopus. And a zonkey. I feel we should move to Africa."

"Sharktopus? Zonkey? Africa? You're as mad as a March hare!"

"Most certainly. But insanity is a virtue, and true madness is next to godliness. So let's move to Africa. I hear their mangos are bang up to the elephant. Divine! Talking of which, let's have some fruit."

Lola went to the kitchen, where she ate some black pudding.

Hugo remained on the floor, shaking his head in frustration.

*****

Something changed, without anything changing at all.

Lola still massaged Hugo's feet whenever he returned home, Hugo still hugged Lola from behind whenever she cleaned her teeth, Lola still shaved Hugo's face, and Hugo still brushed Lola's hair. They still loved each other, but theirs was a sane sort of love, built on routine rather than thought.

Even their conversations followed a tried and tested path. Hugo spoke, then Lola spoke. Hugo smiled, and then Lola left to eat.

They always spoke about the same things: Their daughters, friends, and home.

It came as quite a surprise, then, when Lola said their funds had dwindled:

"R's endowments have gone missing, and the anonymous donations have stopped."

Hugo bolted upright, as if yanked by his tie:

"What?"

"I said R's endowments..."

"Yes, honey bun, I heard. What an absolute bummer."

"Yes hubby."

"I wonder what we should do."

"You should talk to R."

"I should talk to R."

"Yes. Now, I fancy some toad in the hole. I really am rather hangry."

*****

"The endowments have gone missing," Hugo told R.

They were sitting on rocking-chairs in R's reading room.

"Alas! Right you are."

Hugo nodded sympathetically:

"Well, as I'm sure you can understand, this is far from ideal. It's a delicate subject, I know, but the charity has been doing some masterful work, as you yourself have been keen to point out, and it won't be able to continue with your generous support."

R's face flushed ruby and red:

"Right you are. Repeatedly, recurrently and reiteratively; right, right, right! I revere your righteous remedies, and request to reward them royally."

"But?"

"Realise this: I rail for you, really I do, but I'm just a representative of the rank and file. Alas! I have remarkable rivals whose rangy arms reach beyond my own."

"Rivals?"

"Right. Rivals! Rivals who are ripe and ready to reveal the reports you require. I recommend you rap with them."

"With whom?"

"The treasurer."

"The treasurer?"

"The treasurer."

"And where my I find the treasurer?"

"In his rooms near the registry on Regent's Row."

Hugo paused, smiled, shook R's hand, finished his rosé, drunk some rum, ruminated on the troubles of the world, and then departed.

He had never met the treasurer, and had always considered him a rather shadowy figure; more fictional character than living, breathing soul. So he hesitated before he set off for Regent's Row. Then he ran there as quickly as his feet would allow.

THE LONG ROAD HOME

"Doubt… is an illness that comes from
knowledge and leads to madness."
GUSTAVE FLAUBERT

Archibald felt a temporary wave of euphoria whenever he hurt an Indian; his position gave him the power he craved. But, as we have seen, his joy was contaminated; he questioned his actions whenever he went to church; his nightmares grew gnarlier by the night.

Rather than just appear, menacing but still, the characters in his dreams began to act. The dead baby beckoned Archibald down into its grave, the girl with pus-covered scars blew flames towards his body, and the man with tangled eyes rubbed chillies into his face. His vision turned dark with blood.

It was not so much their actions which horrified Archibald, but the way those characters slowly took Lola's place in his dreams. The longer they stayed, the less time Archibald spent with his imaginary wife. By the time those figures featured in every scene, Lola had completely vanished; their overwhelming presence had created an overwhelming void.

Archibald had not seen Lola in his dreams for several months when her ghost reappeared, rising from the floor of his subconscious; remote, but still alert. She looked at Archibald's victims, and then turned to face Archibald.

In that moment, Archibald realised he had not become a knight in shining armour who could save Lola from Hugo, but a villain from whom Lola needed to be saved.

He awoke with a jolt, feeling as though it would be his last day on earth.

*****

It happened in a pungent alley, in a fragrant town.

His fingers clenched the shoulders of a rogue weaver, whose broken shirt was darkened by hard work, and whose broken skin was charred by the sun. An uppercut to that weaver's abdomen made him choke on his paan. A backhanded slap sent betel juice spraying from his mouth.

Before the weaver knew what had happened, his body had turned and his back had been pressed against a wall. He stood face to face with Archibald; swallowing the meat on Archibald's breath; his belly filling with rancid flesh.

Four other soldiers stepped out of the shadows, cracking their knuckles and gnashing their teeth. They each had putrid odours of their own.

"Curry nigger!" Archibald mocked in a voice which was both whiny and vainglorious. "How many laws have you broken this week?"

The weaver did not reply.

Archibald's fingernails clamped the weaver's throat, pierced his skin and squeezed his larynx; inflicting a devilish sort of pain which was both physical and emotional:

"Civilisation and Christianity not good enough for you, eh?"

The other soldiers joined in:

"Cloth lubber!"

"Smell-fungus!"

"Flap-doodle!"

"Horn-swoggler!"

Archibald shook his head:

"You'll be executed for your treachery, if we don't finish you first."

He fisted the weaver's stomach so deeply that knuckles penetrated lungs and tobacco fired out of the weaver's mouth. Winded, the weaver gagged. And, as he gagged, Archibald's vision blurred.

In his mind's eye, he was back in Warwick Lane, some minutes after the hanging of Jonathan Wild. He had become his own tormentor, Donald Donaldson, and he was bullying himself; inflicting the same pain on the weaver that Donaldson had inflicted on him. Only it hurt more, in that moment, than it had ever hurt before. Archibald's throat clenched so tightly he could barely breathe. His spine screamed, as though it was crumbling, as though his very soul was about to rot.

In this scene, however, Hugo and Mayer did not come to the rescue. In this scene, that duty fell to Archibald, who turned and held up his hand.

Delaney moved to his side.

"Three on three. That's a fair fight. What do you gutter-rats say?"

Archibald's subordinates furrowed their brows.

Archibald ushered them away with a pompous flick of his hand:

"Off you trot, with your tails between your tallywags, and don't ever pick on this man again!"

Archibald turned to face the weaver, whose face was a mixologist's blend of gratitude and horror:

"Don't worry. Everything's going to be alright!"

The weaver composed himself before he replied:

"Please join me for dinner. It'd be a privilege to host you kind gentlemen in my home. Please! My wife's biriyani is famous; it's the talk of the village."

*****

This left Archibald in a quandary. His guilt left him feeling powerless, despite all the power he held; the power to command soldiers, mete out justice, and decide men's fates. His guilt bled into doubt, which bled into despair. His nightmarish visions appeared during the daytime, and he began to feel his victims' pain as if it were his own.

Word got back to his superiors, who took Archibald to one side. They had planned to discipline him, but one look in his eyes told them all they needed to know: Archibald was a broken man.

They sent him home.

Archibald boarded his ship, with Delaney by his side, happy to believe he had a large dividend awaiting his return.

"Head to Regent's Row," he was told. "You can claim your commission there."

LET'S GO ROUND AGAIN

"Everything is repeated."
UMBERTO ECO

The entrance to the building on Regent's Row led to a waiting-room, inside which a receptionist sat between two doors; one red, one black. Red settees flanked one side of the room, and black settees flanked the other.

Out of shape, Hugo arrived there out of breath. His eyes were out of focus. When he saw Archibald, he thought he was out of his mind:

"Archie? Ghost! Ghoul! Aaagh! Him. This man! He's not real. Who are you, what are you doing here, and why are you wearing my friend's skin?"

Archibald was just as shocked to see Hugo:

"Hugo? Is that really you?"

Hugo opened his mouth, but no words emerged.

The receptionist cut through the silence:

"Sir, we're ready to see you."

She showed Archibald through the black door, and gestured for Hugo to sit on a red settee.

*****

The first thing Archibald noticed when he entered that office was just how large it was. It was larger than any apartment he had ever called home.

The second thing he noticed was just how large the desk was. It was larger than any desk he had ever seen. It was larger than most *rooms* he had ever seen.

The third thing Archibald noticed was the man behind that desk: Mayer.

"Huh?" he said.

"Archibald?"

Archibald nodded.

"My brother! I rejoice to see you. Please take a seat. Make yourself at home in front of the fire."

Archibald sat down.

"Did you order this snow we've been having? It must make a change from India."

Archibald's jaw hung open:

"Eleven years. India. Money."

Mayer smiled, poured two brandies, and opened a grandiose ledger.

A speck of dust hopped off the water-damaged page.

"Hmm. Here you are. Officer Archibald. Yes. Eighteen shillings and nine pence. Very well, I'll have someone get that for you right away."

"Eighteen... Eighteen shillings... Eighteen shillings and nine... Nine pence? Nine pence, for eleven years' service? You've made a terrible mistake! My dividend should be one hundred and thirty pounds; I've done the maths."

Mayer nodded.

"One hundred and forty-three pounds, fifteen shillings and thirteen pence."

"That's more like it!"

"Minus twelve pounds and three shillings for your journey to India."

"Oh."

"That makes one hundred and thirty-one pounds, twelve shillings and thirteen pence. Minus seventeen pounds and six shillings for your journey home. That makes..."

"Hang on a minute! Why did my return journey cost more?"

"You had an officer's cabin."

"I'm an officer!"

"Oh yes, I heard. Bully for you! Woop-di-doo!"

Archibald puffed his chest.

"No, I really must give credit where it's due. Brother, you're a bona fide hero; protecting king and country; serving your nation. Bravo!

"Now, where was I? Hmm. Yes. Minus forty-three pounds, sixteen shillings and four pence for food. That makes..."

"Hold up! For food? They're charging me for scran?"

"You did eat, didn't you?"

"Of course I ate. But..."

"But what? You thought food was free? What, did you think it grows on trees? That you could just pick it, and '*Voila*', there it is?"

"Certainly not. Don't treat me like some sort of Jilly five plonks. But..."

"Then there was the small matter of twelve pounds for weapons and ammunition, thirty-two pounds for accommodation, six pounds and twelve shillings for medical care, and nineteen pounds for horses."

Archibald waited for more.

There was no more.

"And that leaves..."

"That leaves eighteen shillings and nine pence."

"Eighteen shillings and nine pence."

"I'm appalled."

"You should be grateful, brother."

"Grateful?"

"Yes. Most men return in debt. You've done marvellously well to keep your head above water."

"'Well'? I've done blimming well amazing, but that's neither here nor there. We're here to talk about my money."

"Hmm. Yes. There really is very little money of which to speak."

"No money?"

"No money for you, only for the rich and powerful."

"Listen here, and listen up good: I am powerful. I'm an 'effing boss!"

"No, you're not nearly rich enough to be powerful."

"'Not rich enough to be powerful'? Good god man, whatever do you mean? You're as tight as a boiled owl."

"I'll explain."

Mayer poured Archibald another brandy, patted his back, rubbed his back, massaged his back, smiled, and then told him about the British East India Company...

*****

The company was founded in 1600, when a group of merchants, determined to make *money*, were granted a royal charter from Queen Elizabeth, the holder of *power*. They were given a fifteen-year monopoly on trade in the east, as well as the right to wage war.

This arrangement was known as "Mercantile Imperialism". Run by merchants rather than kings, it was financed by investment rather than taxation:

Cloth merchants made investments, which financed explorations, which founded new colonies, which produced cotton, which the cloth merchants turned into cloth, which they sold for money, which they used to make further investments.

In time, joint-stock options were issued, to help investors spread the risk across several small investments. The first stock markets were created so those stocks could be traded.

Mayer, who held influence over cloth merchants such as Mr Harmer, managing their investments through his bank, decided to take advantage. He bought stocks in the British East India Company, and used his position to secure some of the company's accounts.

*****

Things were good for the British East India Company until famine hit Bengal. Having lost a third of its workforce, the company's debts mounted. It was unable to pay its taxes, and had to ask the government for a bailout.

It got its bailout for two reasons: Firstly, it was too big to fail.

Secondly, its *money* had bought it *power*.

Throughout the eighteenth century, members of the company had bought politicians and parliamentary seats, especially in the "Rotten Boroughs"; constituencies where it took as little as one vote to elect a member of parliament. The company had made donations to the treasury whenever the state faced bankruptcy and, in 1767, it had agreed to pay the exchequer £400,000 a year.

In return, the government backed the company with state ships and soldiers, maintained its right to govern India, and extended its monopoly on trade.

This private business had merged with the state.

By the time Archibald joined its ranks, the British East India Company had become the de-facto government of India. Tax collection, not trade, was its main concern. It employed more soldiers than merchants, had more arsenals than warehouses, and more tax rolls than business ledgers.

*****

"So you see," Mayer continued. "Armies serve one god: Money. Wars are only ever fought to open up new markets, control resources and amass wealth. All wars are bankers' wars."

Archibald frowned:

"If war is so profitable, then the company should be able to pay their soldiers."

Mayer smiled, shook his head, took a sip of brandy, poured two more brandies, tapped his desk, and sighed:

"The company needs to reinvest its profits to maintain its power. Just think of all the gifts it must buy for ministers, lords, judges and bankers. That doesn't come cheap!

"The company did once make its employees rich; nabobs used to return home coated in gold. Alas, dear brother, those days are gone. After paying the government to maintain its monopoly, and paying dividends to its shareholders, there's nothing left over for anyone else."

Archibald clasped the air, attempting to catch the right words:

"Nothing? Sweet Fanny Adams? But I'm a soldier. A blimming war hero! I have power over life and death. I have dignity, honour and chivalry."

"There's no such thing as honour. Dignity and chivalry aren't real."

"And you think your money is real?"

"I know it's not."

"And..."

"It doesn't matter. My money, real or not, grants me power."

"What?"

"We bankers can create as much money as we like; people will always have to deposit it in our banks, so our ledgers will always balance. You, on the other hand, are subject to our whims, beholden to money you can't create yourself, and shackled by the debts we create in your name. In short, brother, you work for us. Despite your weapons, position and subordinates, it's us, with nothing more than our quills, who hold the real power."

"Your tatur-trap don't half spout some mumbo jumbo; argufying the topic. But, at the end of the day, you're nothing more than a lily-livered desk wallah. I'm a man of action."

"You are, brother, you are. Your actions are truly delightful."

"I have honour!"

Mayer shook his head.

Archibald filled with doubts. He doubted his power, his dignity, his honour, his everything. He even doubted his love for Lola:

'Can love be real? Is that not also just a trick of the mind?'

He let the thought go. As the years had ticked by, he had come to trust in his love for Lola like nothing else. It was his god and religion; a matter of unflinching faith.

Still, he was rattled:

"How can you have money without power? Mother of pearl! You need soldiers to protect you."

Mayer laughed:

"Truer words have never been spoken!"

"You need us."

"We do."

"And?"

"We buy you. We own shares in your company. We pay your wages. It really is as simple as that."

"But…"

"But nothing. Look, I love you, brother; you made me the man I am. If you hadn't introduced me to Sammy, Abe wouldn't have expanded into south London; Mr Bronze wouldn't have heard of my involvement, and wouldn't have taken me on as a goldsmith. If you hadn't introduced me to McCraw, I wouldn't have started to exchange money, I wouldn't have become a banker, and I wouldn't be rich.

"Without you, I'd be nothing. It pains me to see you like this. So let me make you an offer: Cut your losses and switch sides. Become a banker. It'll give you the power you so obviously crave."

Archibald's cheeks inflated, his eyes bulged, and his skin turned from white to beige, to magenta, pink, crimson and red:

"No way! Absolutely not! There's no honour in bilking and cadging. Banking was conceived in iniquity and born in sin. Unlike you, I have moral standards."

Mayer guffawed:

"Perhaps. Perhaps you're right. Hmm. But we bankers own the earth. Take it from us, and with the stroke of a pen we'll create enough money to buy it back. Think of the power!"

"Power without honour isn't worth jack."

"It's worth the world."

"Ballcocks."

Mayer swilled his drink:

"Hmm. Please allow me to take you to the pub. This conversation, well, it's not becoming of brothers. Come, let's have civil words. We've got a lot of catching up to do."

"We do."

"And I'm buying."

"You are."

Archibald left the room.

Mayer shook his head.

'In all human history', he thought. 'There's never been anything as deadly as simple men with an abundance of good intentions.'

*****

Archibald saw Hugo in the waiting room:

"We should catch up."

"We should."

"The pub?"

"The pub!"

The receptionist interrupted:

"Mr Crickets, the treasurer is ready to see you."

Hugo smiled at Delaney, shook hands with Archibald, walked through the red door, and entered Mayer's office:

"Huh?"

"Hugo! What brings you here?"

"Mayer?"

"Brother, I'm heartedly glad to see you. Please take a seat."

Hugo sat down.

"What about this weather? Isn't it horrid?"

Hugo's jaw hung open:

"You? You're the treasurer?"

Mayer smiled, nodded, and poured two brandies:

"I suppose I am."

"And the anonymous donations?"

"Guilty as charged."

"What? Why didn't you say anything? Those donations were phenomenal!"

Mayer tilted his head, closed his eyes, broke into a modest grin, opened his eyes, looked at Hugo and nodded:

"True charity should be anonymous. The left hand shouldn't know what the right hand is doing."

"But you? *You* care for charity? You're a banker."

"I am."

"You care about money."

"I do."

"And?"

"I'm human too."

✶✶✶✶✶

It all started when Mayer thought about how he had saved Hugo from Jonathan Wild, and Archibald from his bullies. He longed to be that selfless boy again, and he recalled how *he* had been the recipient of charity when he was adopted.

"It's the responsibility of the wealthy to help those with less than themselves," Sadie's friend had opined. "It really does soothe one's conscience to know one is not *only* spending one's money on oneself."

Mayer had wanted to soothe his conscience. He felt guilty beyond compare.

He felt guilty for earning so much, whilst others earned so little. He felt guilty for rejecting loan applications, for his usury, and for discarding girls. He felt guilty for pretty much everything he did.

He decided to make amends.

When Hugo told him of the difficulties was having, sourcing funds for Saint Nick's, Mayer saw an opportunity. He sent Hugo to meet R, his client at the bank and, when R agreed to fund Hugo, he became his charity's treasurer. R would not have it any other way:

"I repeatedly request that you regulate the charity's reports and records. I am resolute! It's only right. Alas! All other realizable realities are redundant."

So Mayer became familiar with Saint Nick's and, when he saw it had become a success, he was more than happy to donate to it himself.

Mayer bathed in the reflected glory of Hugo's goodness. It cleansed his blackened soul, and lifted the burden of guilt from his shoulders; giving him the peace of mind he craved, and giving him a certain sort of power over Hugo. Mayer became a puppet master, able to stop his donations at any time, and send Hugo running to him for help…

*****

Hugo sipped his brandy:

"Since when did you care for charity?"

"I don't," Mayer replied. "Hmm. I find people who seek to please others rather dull. People who seek to please themselves are far more interesting, for it is they who reveal their true character."

"Eh? So why did you donate?"

"To please myself. In an age where poverty and plenty rub shoulders, the rich must do everything they can to protect their interests."

"That's selfish."

"It is."

Hugo stared.

Mayer chuckled:

"Brother, only the artist dreams of selfless acts; the realist knows that great things are always a little selfish."

"What?"

"We need charity; it compensates for the worst excesses of capitalism, without challenging the system itself. It's an investment which pays dividends; protecting capital from civil unrest."

"So that's why you donated to Saint Nick's?"

"Yes, and that's why I stopped my donations, and convinced R to do likewise."

"What?"

"Your behaviour got a little out of hand."

"It did?"

"Yes, brother, it did. Rather than compensate for the worst aspects of the system, through Saint Nick's, you challenged the system itself."

"I've been an activist for donkey's years."

"You have."

Hugo paused, scrunched his eyes and nose together, and then gestured for Mayer to continue.

"We liked your opposition to tariffs on grain. My clients wanted food prices to fall, so they could get away with paying their workers less. Yes, brother, you deserve credit for that. But you took it too far. You're helping people who are destroying my clients' investments. My investments! I'd love to support you, but this has got to stop."

"But…"

"But nothing. Everything you've achieved has been down to the philanthropy of people like me; the capitalist class. You can't attack us and expect us to help you. Do you think we're as mad as hops?"

"I think you need me as much as I need you. You're nothing more than a loan-shark. A usurer! Jesus overturned tables in the temple to save us from your sort. You're betraying the Lord!"

Mayer guffawed:

"Perhaps. Perhaps you're right. Hmm. I sure do need charity to save my soul. God knows it, you know it, and I know it. But there are plenty of other charities I can support; you can bet your bottom dollar on that!"

Mayer paused:

"Brother, your choice is simple: Cut out the rabble-rousing or lose your funding."

"I won't do it."

"Think of the children."

"What good is it to save a few children today, without challenging a system which'll impoverish thousands more tomorrow?"

Mayer smiled:

"I admire your chutzpah."

Hugo stared back at him with rage, which mellowed to anger, then disdain, dislike, indifference, warmth, affection and, finally, love. Looking into Mayer's eyes, he recalled how that man had saved him from Jonathan Wild, introduced him to Mr Orwell, and got him his apprenticeship with Bear. He acknowledged that without Mayer's introduction to R, or his anonymous donations, Saint Nick's would have never even opened.

"I think we'll have to agree to disagree."

"We will."

"But I see no reason why R's donations should stop."

"Hmm."

Mayer swilled his drink:

"Allow me to take you to the pub."

"I'll allow it."

*****

The pub smelled stale. The sweat of London clung to clothes, flecks of sawdust drowned in spilt beer, and the aroma of burnt coal crept in through the cracks in the windows.

Everything seemed smaller, more wistful and white, than when they last drank in that pub. *They* all looked smaller, more wistful and white. It hit them, at the same time, in the same way; how Hugo had stopped saying "Sorry", Mayer had started to wear archaic clothes, and Archibald's eyes had grown hollow; how they had all been subdued by the gravity of age, and how they all looked alike.

The resonance of their shared roots still reverberated within them.

They still felt short changed by the fire which took their families. They still felt as though they were stepping back into a lost life whenever they met up.

They still felt each other's emotions because, deep down, they were still the same person; a person who just happened to have three different bodies.

When they looked at their friends, they all thought the same thing: *'That could have been me.'*

Seeing their childhood companions made them feel old.

To counter their discomfort, they blabbered about the time they had spent apart. They seemed happy for each other; clinking glasses and stamping feet. To the naked eye, their conversation bore all the hallmarks of a joyous reunion.

Beneath the surface, however, Hugo and Archibald resented Mayer for the grip he held on their lives. Archibald and Mayer resented Hugo for marrying Lola. Archibald had clung to the hope that Hugo's marriage would fail, and Mayer to the hope that Hugo would die, but that hope had turned from a dream to a fantasy to an outright delusion. Seeing him only rubbed salt into their wounds.

Still, no-one resented Archibald, who had never done Mayer or Hugo any harm. Their love for that man kept their friendship alive.

They smiled, cheered, clinked glasses, drank too much, and then stumbled home.

*****

Hugo returned to his wife and five daughters.

Emma was silent; she had not uttered a word in six years. Maddie only spoke when she was spoken to, Sylvia only spoke when she was not spoken to, Peta answered questions which were not meant for her, and Natalie questioned everything:

"Since your eyes are brown, does that mean you see everything in brown?"

"Are there more leaves in the world or blades of grass?"

"Why do spiders run away when I fart?"

Hugo told Lola about his conversation with Mayer.

Lola sighed:

"Never trust a man to do a woman's work."

"What was that, honey bun?"

"Oh nothing, hubby. I'll sort it out. Now, let's eat some faggots."

*****

Mayer's heart skipped a beat when Lola entered his office:

"Lola! What a pleasant surprise. Please take a seat."

Lola sat down.

"Horrible day, isn't it?""

"Snowmageddon; all mizzle and snice."

Mayer laughed.

Lola fluttered her eyelids:

"How are you, sweetie?"

"Well, you know me, I get by."

"I can see."

Lola crossed her legs, uncrossed her legs, twiddled her hair, pouted her lips and arched her back:

"We used to have something, you and I."

"We did?"

"Yes. You were ever so cute when you took me to dinner. It was sweet how you went to all that trouble."

"Hmm. Thanks. You did walk out during the first course."

"Yes, I wanted to apologize for that."

"Apologies are for ugly people; you don't have anything to be sorry for."

"Perhaps not, although I do often wonder how things might've worked out."

"You do?"

"Yes, silly, we could have been special."

Mayer smiled. For the first time in years, he believed he might actually have a chance with Lola. He regressed into his adolescent state; filled, once more, with graceless enthusiasm and baseless hope.

'*I just need to give her what she wants*.'

"I just want you to continue to donate. Those donations were ever so kind. When I heard they came from you, I felt like I loved you. Well, that I would have loved you had I known. I'm not so sure I love you now that the donations have stopped."

'*I just need to give her what she wants. Come on Mayer! Don't mess this up!*'

He shrugged:

"Your Hugo has been sabotaging my investments."

Lola smiled, stared into Mayer's eyes, and touched his hand:

"I'm not asking you to donate to Hugo. I'm asking you to donate to Saint Nick's."

She paused:

"Don't do it for Hugo. Do it for me."

A solitary tear formed in Mayer's eye.

"Okay," he said, without believing what he was saying. "I'll do it."

Lola beamed:

"You will? Oh Mayer, that's fan-dabby-dozy! You're my knight in shining armour."

The tear ran down Mayer's cheek:

"I just ask for one thing in return."

Lola frowned.

"Each time you receive a donation, I want you to think of me."

Lola giggled:

"I'll do it! You have my word."

They stood up and embraced.

Mayer ran his finger down Lola's spine, as if she was his lover. Lola patted Mayer's back, as if he was her fool. Yet a small part of her did warm to Mayer in that moment. When she left it was her heart, not Mayer's, which skipped a beat.

TALLY GO

"I must finish what I've started, even if, inevitably, what I finish turns out not to be what I began."
SALMAN RUSHDIE

As bankers like Mayer produced more banknotes, so tally sticks fell out of circulation.

In 1782, an act of parliament declared that the Bank of England would destroy its tallies as soon as its two chamberlains retired. They stayed in position for decades. By the time the last of them hung up their quill, a large room, needed for a bankruptcy court, was filled with those wooden sticks.

Orders were issued for them to be destroyed.

Two men set to work before dawn, one clear October day. They transported those tallies across town, before burning them in iron stoves beneath the Palace of Westminster.

The sun rose and the sun set, but the pile of tallies still stood tall. Growing impatient, the workmen threw caution to the wind, and threw handfuls of tallies to the flames. The heat grew so intense that it could be felt through the carpets above. Within the hour, those carpets had caught fire. Within minutes, the House of Commons was ablaze.

It was a sight to behold.

The skyline was usurped by a giant ball of fire; crowned by wispy smoke and misty soot. The Thames glowed crimson and gold. Crowds gathered on Westminster Bridge; huzzaing and hurrahing, as firefighters waged war with bloodthirsty flames.

The tally, therefore, did not die tamely. Nor did it die alone. After years of feudal struggle against death, Zebedee also died that night; choosing to die with his dignity intact, rather than live on in a society he believed had fallen to hellfire.

BOOK FOUR

AND SO TIME ACCELERATES

FRIENDS REUNITED

"Maybe one day I can have a reunion with myself."
SEBASTIAN BACH

Our friends had reunited. They would soon be divided, such was the ebb and flow of their lives.

In the meantime, they all went bald, three seconds after the other, whilst doing exactly the same thing: Filleting fish.

As innards and carcasses detached, hair fell, and thoughts fell through their minds. Archibald realised he could not have power without money, Mayer realised he could not have money without power, and they both realised that neither power nor money were worth that much without love.

Hugo had love, and he was happy with that, although he would not have said "No" to a little more money.

*****

All three friends developed their first wrinkle, just above their left eye; they were all forced to wear glasses, and they all headed to St Peter's Fields, Manchester, for three very different reasons.

Hugo, as he had done for years, went to protect a group of protestors; Archibald, considering a job in the local infantry, went to protect the town; and Mayer went to protect his investments.

*****

One person's beauty is another's vulgarity.

Hugo saw beauty. He saw multifarious souls, dressed in their Sunday best; miscellaneous faces, draped in smiles; and multitudes of people, united as one.

Archibald saw vulgarity. He saw the enemy's rank and file, jostling for position on the battlefield; their leaders above them on a cart; and buildings above them, casting a long shadow over proceedings.

Mayer saw potential; the opportunity for profit, tinged by the risk of loss.

The air filled with the sound of trumpets, trombones, drums, claps, cries, cheers and calls:

"What do we want? Living wages! When do we want them? Now!"

"Down with the rotten boroughs! Down with tariffs on grain!"

"Votes for all! Votes for all! Votes for all!"

A pasty-skinned, bristly-haired, flamboyantly-dressed politician, known simply as the "Orator", took to the stand. Arching his back, he paused to appreciate the scene, before fleshing out the slogans which adorned a sea of homemade banners:

'Love'. 'Universal Suffrage'. 'Equal Representation'.

At the front, the Orator's words were well received. Further back, however, they were lost to the wind. Walls groaned, shutters clanged, and eighty thousand protestors did not hear a word he said.

Nor did they hear the waspy voice of a dog-faced magistrate. With Mayer's hand on his shoulder, that man leant through a window and read the Riot Act:

"Our sovereign lord the King chargeth and commandeth all persons, being assembled, immediately to disperse themselves."

Unheard, he was ignored. Ignored, he was enraged. Enraged, he was vengeful.

He called for reinforcements.

Six hundred Hussars, four hundred cavalrymen, four hundred constables and two canons joined Archibald's unit. Then came the Yeomanry: Local business owners intent on revenge. Riding on horseback, with cutlasses and clubs in hand, they knocked a baby from its mother's arms, and charged on through the masses.

Soldiers raised their guns.

For a millisecond, the world stood still. It felt like an eternity. The silence was the loudest noise Hugo had ever heard.

Then the panic turned outwards.

The Yeomanry charged inwards, their sabres drawn, slashing their way through the flags.

"Drive them through!" an officer bawled.

"For shame!" Archibald bellowed. "The people cannot escape!"

*****

Our three heroes were unaware of each other's presence, yet they sensed their friends in the most insoluble of ways.

Hugo almost felt horrified and almost felt emboldened, without feeling either emotion at all. He felt compelled to help, but incapable of doing so.

Archibald did not feel compelled to help, even though he could. He felt duty-bound to stand with his comrades, not the protestors.

But Archibald felt Hugo's despair, and was helpless to resist the tender power of that emotion. He raised his sword and bellowed:

"For shame! The people cannot escape!"

*****

Mayer saw the crowd encroach on his vantage point. Believing his time was up, he also felt Hugo's despair.

That despair melted into fury, which gave way to an exquisite surge of bliss. Because, as soldiers slashed and stabbed, spraying claret across the ground, Mayer saw his enemies fall before his eyes; helpless and hopeless, outflanked and overpowered.

It was murder. Sabres skewered whichever body took their fancy, horses trampled flesh into the concrete, and limp torsos were crushed and thrown.

*****

As Archibald led the counter-charge, a channel opened up through which the crowd was able to escape.

Seeing this turn of events, Hugo felt Mayer's bliss. He felt empowered.

*****

Archibald, in leading that charge, also felt Mayer's bliss. It bubbled within him, spicy and raw, like chilli pepper for the soul. He felt empowered; the leader of men; a hero amongst villains.

*****

All three men luxuriated in the glow of their personal victories.

Archibald and Mayer left.

Hugo trudged through rivers of blood, with sodden shins and stained ankles. He stitched, sewed, and saved as many lives as he could.

Glory flowed through his veins.

Mayer felt that glory, whilst sipping champagne with his clients. Archibald felt that glory whilst dining with Delaney. But it was incomplete; tinged with sorrow, and diminished by pain; watered-down by a vision of infinite loss, and made toxic by the gaseous embers of death.

That scene would live long in our heroes' collective memory. They would each feel responsible.

They all shivered in time.

HERE, THERE, EVERYWHERE

"Travel is fatal to prejudice, bigotry and narrow-mindedness."
MARK TWAIN

The "Peterloo Massacre", as it came to be known, inspired national outrage. It was okay, so the logic went, to massacre black and brown people in the colonies, but the military's shoot-first approach was simply not tolerable at home.

Sir Robert Peel was tasked with forming the first national police force, to control the population in a more civil manner. Archibald was invited to join its ranks.

He simply could not do it. Archibald wanted to serve his people, not contain them. He believed in traditional policing, from the bottom up; by the people, not by the state.

The "Police".

To Archibald, they looked ludicrous; patrolling the streets in those stupid uniforms. They even sounded stupid: "Po-lease". "Po", as in a chamber pot. "Lease", as in a long-term loan. "Po-lease"; a long-term loan of a chamber-pot. Ugh! Archibald shuddered.

He was not alone. The entire nation opposed that force. The upper classes feared it would end up like the French Policers; Napoleon's spies. The lower classes feared it would stifle their protests; keeping them impoverished forever. Hugo feared it would spawn an infinite number of Jonathan Wilds.

Archibald still craved power, but he was determined to use his power for good. He wanted to become a righteous man, worthy of Lola, and he wanted the "Honour" and "Dignity" he had been promised during his army training. Joining the police, therefore, was out of the question, as was returning to India or becoming a banker. There was just one problem: Archibald did not have any other options.

*****

We humans have a habit of repeating our mistakes. We return to restaurants we did not like, flit from one inappropriate lover to another, and blame others for our problems at work.

Archibald, struck by the arrogance of the well-intentioned, did not learn from his mistakes. Certain that he could change the British Army from the inside, he and Delaney reenlisted. For them, it was the best of a bad bunch of options.

Archibald still wished to become a knight in shining armour for Lola, he still longed for real power, and he still believed he could win that power, by eschewing his malevolence, and finding it in the smallest of acts.

He believed he had learnt from his mistakes, even as he repeated them.

*****

Archibald and Delaney sailed to Vandemonia with the Van Diemen's Land Company; a mercantile corporation with a royal charter to turn that island into a wool colony. They beat back the wilderness; climbing mountains and fording rivers, before employing convicts to build infrastructure, grow food and raise sheep.

There was one major problem.

Amongst the colonisers, there were about ten men for every woman. Without partners to satisfy their sexual urges, their longings grew by the year. Tens of thousands of convicts, slaves in all but name, looked outwards for gratification.

A group of shepherds crept up behind two Aborigine women, dragged them into the forest and ravaged them. Those women passed out, but still the violations continued; unsatiated desires still demanded satisfaction, and lovelorn minds still demanded proxy love.

The Aborigines responded; spearing a captive in his thigh, before killing one hundred sheep.

The shepherds responded; killing thirty Aborigines.

As native game disappeared, the Aborigines were driven to hunger. They launched new attacks; clearing sheep from their hunting grounds.

The settlers responded with mass killings.

The natives sought revenge; considering themselves a resistance movement against an occupying force.

The settlers sought revenge; considering themselves a civilising force against a savage foe.

The deaths mounted, the fear mounted, and the Lieutenant Governor declared martial law; granting immunity to anyone who murdered a native, and offering bounties for their capture. He launched the "Black Line"; a moving human cordon, hundreds of kilometres wide, which drove the native population into the northwest corner of the island.

It was doomed to fail. Archibald let it fail. He turned a blind eye as they swept past one Aborigine, and threw his lunch to another. For

Archibald, this was a success of sorts. It was power. A whole new kind of power: The power to disobey.

Yet it was fleeting. Archibald needed help, a saviour; someone like George Augustus Robinson...

*****

Everything about Robinson was tall. He had a long face, which was made to seem ridiculous by the hat he placed upon it; his umbrella was four inches longer than the norm, so it could be used as a cane; his trousers reached his stomach, and his overcoat reached his toes.

A builder by trade, Robinson moved to Vandemonia in search of fame and fortune. Instead, he found Archibald.

In a dusty tavern, on a ghostly lane, in a forgotten corner of town; inebriated by one too many gins, and dehydrated by one too few tonics; he slurred as he spoke:

"Yooo sir-eee, I seen yooo. Yes sir-eee. Yooo ahr like me, yooo ahr!"

Through eyes turned hazy by liquor, Archibald saw a man whose head seemed to touch the ceiling, and whose feet seemed to be buried beneath the ground:

"Like you?"

"Yes sir-eee. Yooo think the natives ahr alright."

"Don't tell me what I think."

"But you do!"

"I darn-tooting do."

"We shall help."

"I'll do what I want."

"Yes sir-eee!"

*****

As that conversation descended into incomprehensibility, it inspired a collective resolve. Those men felt a new sort of power, power in numbers, which enabled them to form a plan...

Step one:

They approached the Lieutenant Governor's office; a coal-stained building which rested on an indigent slope, near snoozing emus and sun-bleached grass. Its wooden walls had once been painted bright white, to represent the wool the first settlers had hoped to produce. As that enterprise floundered, that hut began to fade. In the space of three years, it had been repainted yellow, when someone tried to farm wheat, and green, when someone tried to farm lettuce. When both projects failed, the Lieutenant Governor's office was left unpainted, and no longer could be said to possess any discernible colour at all.

Inside, the image of the Lieutenant Governor, in a uniform pressed so viciously it had razor-sharp edges, was enough to resurrect in Archibald the torment of long morning runs, the egregious discipline of military drill, the monotonous hush of sentry watch, and the ghoulish images which had once usurped his dreams.

Archibald was surprised, then, when his senses judged the Lieutenant Governor in a way his preconceptions had not permitted; seeing that man's romantic gaze, which bore no resemblance to his militaristic tendencies; replete with a wandering eye which lacked the discipline for which he was famed. Archibald realised that the Lieutenant Governor was more inclined to listen than talk; reacting to his appeals without so much as a word, but with a vast array of nods, blinks, winks, frowns, puckers, flickers, smacks, tenses, spasms and twitches.

The rain sounded like diamonds falling from heaven.

Archibald sounded bombastic:

"You must give us permission to feed the natives. A satisfied stomach is a satisfied mind, and a satisfied mind will not seek conflict."

The Lieutenant Governor thumbed his nose.

Robinson stepped forwards:

"I believe the natives on Bruny Island would be receptive to our advances."

The Lieutenant Governor stroked his chin.

"Sir?"

The Lieutenant Governor nodded.

*****

Step two:

Our three renegade heroes headed to Bruny Island, where they set up a ration shack, learnt the local language, and observed the natives. They saw young girls massage the calloused feet of old men, adolescents trek miles for water, and women whistle to the birds. Those birds whistled back, which encouraged marsupials to prick their ears and flowers to bob.

The sun seemed to have a different hue when seen from that place; slightly greener and slightly less aflame. The whole island seemed to hum. The ocean was so clear, Archibald was able to reach in and pick up fish with his hands. The sun refracted in chaos theory; shimmery in pools, still above coral, turquoise near coves, and navy near caves.

Delaney insisted that the ocean was made to look at; "If God had wanted us to swim, he would have given us fins"; but Archibald ignored him and dived in whenever he could. He became one with the rhythm of that island, winning the trust of the natives, and encouraging thirteen of them to surrender. He wrote to the Lieutenant Governor, claiming he could secure the surrender of the whole population:

'It'll be for their own good. It'll be the Christian thing to do!'

*****

Step three:

Determined to save the natives from extinction, Archibald and Delaney traversed Vandemonia, set up ration shacks, and persuaded the remaining Aborigines to surrender; promising them food and safety, before sending them to a refuge Flinders Island.

*****

To Archibald, the water on Vandemonia tasted of the forest, the berries tasted primeval, and the fruit was freedom-flavoured.

He enjoyed a pitiful happiness; suffocating in the nefarious sun, and stewing in perspiration, but only ever a few steps away from real contentment. He believed, once again, that he had power; that he was deciding fates, controlling destinies, and writing history. Only this time he was benevolent; he was both powerful *and* righteous.

For Archibald, ignorance was bliss.

That bliss lasted just as long as his ignorance...

Firstly, he discovered that his ration shacks had been turned into military posts. Soldiers had used them to launch attacks.

Secondly, he discovered that three quarters of the Aborigines on Flinders Island had perished; ravaged by pneumonia and savaged by influenza.

Thirdly, he discovered that the survivors had been enslaved in a concentration camp; forced to wear European clothes, use European names, study Christianity, learn to read, write, farm and sew. They had grown melancholic and stopped having children.

After ten thousand years of blissful isolation, the genocide was complete.

This knowledge hit Archibald at once; in an unlit room, in the Governor's office, in an overheard conversation, in the bitterest of winters.

He fell to the ground, hugged his knees, and prayed for release.

*****

Back in Britain, Mayer recalled the thought he had many years before:

'*In all human history, there has never been anything quite as deadly as simple men with an abundance of good intentions.*'

*****

The Vandemonian Aborigines were extinct, but the settlers did not profit. Crops failed, supplies went missing, convicts rebelled, and workers absconded.

Things were hardly any better for the Van Diemen's Company. It lost thousands of sheep, was forced to curtail wool production, and saw its share price fall by sixty percent.

And things certainly were not any better for Archibald. In search of a remedy for lovesickness and guilt, he sampled one medicine after another. He awoke every day before dawn, rubbed whisky into his gums to soothe his toothache, swallowed morphine to settle his bellyache, and drank tincture of opium to alleviate his heartache. He took pills throughout the day, always in secret, because he did not want the world to know. He took drugs which he thought he needed, and drugs which he knew he did not. He drank a concoction of potions whenever he wanted to die, and chewed dried chillies whenever he wanted to feel alive.

Archibald spent a decade on that island, in a druggy haze, marching on into middle age. His eyebrows became scraggly, hair grew on top of his ears, a small crack formed in his glasses, his muscles started to ache, his body-fat reduced, and his skin became thin. He began to groan whenever he bent over, lose his sense of smell, do crosswords as if they were a religion, drink sherry and twitch.

He still dreamt of Lola.

He still coveted power; some new sort of power he was yet to experience. He did not know what form that power would take, or how he would get it, but he knew he would not find it on Vandemonia. So, when they heard of an opening on the HMS Hyacinth, he and Delaney set to sea. They spent several years surveying the Australian coast, and then they headed for China...

*****

Europeans had been importing tea, porcelain and silk from China for many centuries. The Chinese, however, had not been importing from Europe. This meant that silver, used to buy Chinese goods, had flowed from Europe to China without ever flowing back.

The British East India Company decided to make amends; producing huge quantities of opium, which they sold in China. In return, they earned enough silver to buy considerably more tea than before.

When the British East India Company lost its monopoly on trade, a raft of other British firms began selling opium in China.

Millions of Chinese people came to depend on two plants; rice to keep them alive, and opium to make them forget. Their lives were lived from day to day, without energy in the moment, nor money for the future. Productivity declined, the Chinese economy floundered, and the death count mounted.

The Chinese fought back. They killed native drug dealers, seized opium supplies, closed the Pearl River Channel, and destroyed opium abroad.

British traders rallied British politicians, many of whom owned shares in opium producing firms. Their calls were answered. *Power* was sent to rescue *money*. Archibald was sent to war...

*****

Floating atop crystalline waters, the ocean's salt in their hair, Archibald and Delaney loaded their cannon.

Clouds moseyed by at a lackadaisical rate, birds glided by in formation, and ripples lapped up against their hull. Archibald heard the squeaking of an unused hammock, but little else. He felt as though time had forgotten to exist.

The captain raised his arm, held it high, and brought it down with fury:

"Fire!"

'*Boom!'*

A line of cannonballs emerged from a line of cannons; parting the clouds, sending birds in disparate directions, and turning sleepy waters into tsunamic waves.

The Royal Saxon shook atop the rolling waters.

That British vessel had signed a bond, agreeing not to trade opium. Considered traitorous, the British navy was stepping in to protect free trade.

Beyond the horizon, the Chinese saw frothy vistas of white and dewy crescendos of blue. They saw an ally ship come under attack; rocked by fire and scorched by flames.

Back aboard the Hyacinth, Archibald saw their yachts come skipping over the water, like a swarm of bugs, with sails which flapped at the breeze.

Mistaking their red flags for a declaration of war, Archibald's captain raised his arm:

"Aim for the ships themselves. Hold it! Wait... Fire!"

A Chinese raft sank, throwing helpless bodies to indifferent waves. Its bow and stern shot up to kiss the sky, whilst its middle was swallowed by the ocean.

"Wait... Fire!"

Another raft exploded, sending sparks in every direction.

"Fire!"

A Chinese boat atomized in front of Archibald's eyes.

"Fire!"

A fourth boat took two cannonballs to its portside. It wobbled, as if unsure what to do, and then sunk in slow motion; retiring to a watery grave with the meekest of whimpers.

Surrounded by fire and failure, the Chinese retreated to shore.

Sensing a counter-attack, the British returned to Macau.

*****

British opium producers demanded that the Chinese government compensate them for their lost earnings, but their calls fell upon deaf ears. So they launched the Opium War, determined, once and for all, to secure access to Chinese markets.

The seas opened wide.

Armed with a magnificent arsenal of weapons, Archibald's fleet beat a capacious path; brushing Chinese vessels aside, and hurling them down into the deepest depths of the ocean.

Timber fell like rain. Sails flapped, unchecked, like the wings of demented birds. Tangled limbs and mangled torsos waved goodbye to the world with an awestruck kiss.

This scene extended for two years, unchecked by the whimsies of night and day. Battles merged into battles, cannonballs rapped an incessant beat, cities fell, and the British emerged triumphant; winning compensation for their merchants, securing access to Chinese markets, and taking possession of Hong Kong; a coastal territory which was transformed into a base for British drug dealers.

Above all else, they won one symbolic prize: Power.

Archibald revelled in the reflected glow of that omnipotence. But, deep down, he knew it was just a mirage; he was still serving money, fighting bankers' wars, and was not empowered himself.

He grew older and wiser, but he did not grow content.

*****

His fifties saw Archibald age at an accelerating rate. The skin beneath his jaw sagged, forming a hypotenuse between his chin and Adam's apple. Wrinkles crept out from his eyes, marched across his cheeks, and snuck back in towards his lips. His bald head, reddened by the sun, displayed an archipelago of liver spots; pointy like Cyprus, claw-shaped like Cuba, and ovoid like Sardinia. Fine grey veins crisscrossed his hands.

Archibald still cut an impressive figure, with wide shoulders and iron breasts; he still looked hardy, worldly, battle-worn and brutish; and he still dreamt of power.

He still dreamt of Lola. As well as sketching her image, he wrote her poems, letters and stories. Then he locked those things in a set of drawers, threw those drawers overboard, and began again afresh.

*****

Archibald, Hugo and Mayer thought of Lola at the same time, whilst doing the same thing: Reading a book about tapestry. All three put their book down. Whilst Hugo counted ninety-seven hairs on Lola's arm, Archibald and Mayer imagined the hair on her head. Mayer counted three hundred strands, but Archibald made it all the way to a thousand.

He grew addicted to counting. He counted the planks of wood on his ship, the dolphins in the ocean, and the stars in the night sky. Then, after thirty days and three hours, time which he counted, he vowed never to count again.

Without this distraction, life's clock rang loud in Archibald's mind. So, running on fumes, on hope rather than expectation, he decided to chase one last hurrah. He knew it was a case of "Now or never".

One thing drove him on: An image of himself as a child, beaten and battered and bruised. He had lost Raymondo and Ruthie, seen his village overturned, and was facing eviction from his shop.

Archibald wanted to be able to look that young version of himself in the eye and say: *'It's okay. One day you'll be strong. One day you'll be powerful. One day you'll be able to tell the world, "Look at me! I made it!" And, when that happens, Lola will be yours.'*

He packed his bags and sailed to Africa, where he was given control over a vast swathe of unchartered land. He could taste the power; it lodged between his teeth and made his eyes water.

He got to work, surveying his realm, determined to bring it to heel...

*****

Archibald and Delaney came across three sets of people in Africa: Citizens, tribespeople and hunter-gatherers.

The citizens lived in city-states, obeyed British laws and used British money. The tribespeople were agriculturalists, who lived in villages, made their own laws and rarely used money. The hunter-gatherers lived in the forest, had no laws nor money.

The citizens wore mad headdresses, printed shawls, bone earrings, rings with precious stones, rings with cheap stones, and a general air of restraint. The tribespeople wore different clothes according to their tribe,

gender and position. The hunter-gatherers barely wore anything at all.
* * * * *

Archibald would recall the first tribesperson he saw, vividly, for the remainder of his days. Even though he was familiar with the Aborigines, the image of that woman still cut raw to his eyes.

She stepped out of the jungle and then froze; staring at Archibald, who stared back at her. Red paint covered her face, and a leather wrap covered her waist, but her breasts hung loose and low. Her body was draped with multi-coloured beads, bracelets and bangles. She smelled of roasted meat.

That woman shot back into the forest. Archibald and his men stood frozen to the spot.
* * * * *

Familiarity breeds understanding. As Archibald became familiar with the tribespeople, he began to understand their ways.

He saw boys turn into venerated elders with so much speed it defied explanation. He saw people sleeping whenever and wherever they chose. He saw naked children rolling in puddles, and naked adults rolling in the long grass.

Some tribespeople fled on sight. One group of natives attacked his men, who were forced to shoot them dead. Most, however, offered up an array of presents; cowry shells, beads, cloth, meat, ornaments and paint. Archibald smiled. The tribespeople smiled. Then they took those presents back, using force if they were met with resistance.

At first, Archibald could not work out if those people were being hospitable or hostile; if they were acting as hosts, or treating him as a hostage. In time, however, he realised that it was their culture to share everything they had; giving according to their capacity to give, and taking according to their needs. In giving and taking those gifts from Archibald, they were treating him as if he was one of their own; attempting to integrate him into their group, and establish peaceful relations.

Only one person stood above this system; the village chief. They usually possessed less than the people they ruled; giving out everything they received as soon as they received it, in order to win the affection they needed to maintain their position. Knowing they could be overthrown at any moment, they used their *wealth* to maintain their *power*, leaving them with next to no wealth at all.
* * * * *

Archibald approached those people in their villages, safe in the knowledge that his guns would always protect him. Approaching the hunter-gatherers was more of a challenge. They ran away whenever he approached, which forced him to observe them from afar; hidden by a dark ocean of leaves, and deafened by the screeching of invisible bugs, the battle cries of diminutive mosquitos, and the thumping of crocodiles' tails.

He observed them hunting together; chasing herds of animals into narrow ravines, before slaughtering them en-masse. He observed them gathering together; picking berries, digging up roots, harvesting leaves and collecting mushrooms. He observed them cooking together, eating together, and washing together; owning nothing and sharing everything.

Those people spent less time working than anyone Archibald had ever seen; living for the moment, without toiling for the future. Unlike the people who lived in towns and villages, the hunter-gatherers did not have anything to defend, so did not need to build defences. They were happy to sleep in caves, so did not need to build huts. They did not farm, so did not need to sow seeds, clear terrain, or plough fields.

They spent most of their time relaxing; gossiping, telling stories, and playing with their children. They were as frolicsome as puppies and as carefree as cats.

Whilst their offspring often died in infancy, their adults lived longer than other Africans. They benefitted from a varied diet; dining on different delicacies every day, without forming a dependency on rice or grains. And, without property to defend, they were willing to flee when attacked, so usually avoided conflict.

The hunter-gatherers were talented, sensitive to the quietest of sounds and the slightest of movements; they were agile, able to move with the minimum of effort, and bend in the most improbable of ways; and they were sexual, sleeping with everyone in their group.

*****

Having surveyed vast swathes of land, drawn maps and reported back to the capital, Archibald was ordered to collect a "Hut Tax" from every man in his region.

No matter how hard he tried, he could not get the hunter-gatherers to pay. They did not have any money, they were not interested in money, and they ran away whenever he approached.

Things were simpler with the villagers.

They tended to have money either, self-sufficient people have never needed money, but they were static, and they did have possessions...

*****

Archibald held up a banner, laced with gold thread, which displayed the royal coat of arms and the cross of Jesus Christ:

"Comrades! Let us follow the sign of the holy cross with true faith, and through it we shall conquer."

His men wore expressionless faces.

"Allies, squaddies, undisciplined, repulsive things! You can keep a five percent of your plunder."

This offer had the desired effect. His men followed him into the first hut on his list, where they were met by a bull-necked villager who had misaligned pupils.

"You have to pay us sixpence, so we can afford to protect you."

The tribesman did not flinch.

Archibald repeated himself, slowly, producing sounds in instalments: "You."

He pointed at the tribesman:

"Need to pay us."

He pointed at himself.

"Six pence."

He held up six fingers.

"So we can protect you."

He hugged the tribesman.

The tribesman looked at Archibald.

Archibald looked at the hut. It was small, round, made from mud, with an earthen floor and a thatched roof. Six rocks surrounded the ashy remains of a thousand fires, and four children huddled in a corner, near three stools, a scythe and a pot.

Archibald pointed at the stools.

"Three pence for one," he said; holding up three fingers and then holding up one.

He pointed at the scythe, decided better of it, and shook his head.

He pointed at the pot.

"Six pence," he said; holding up six fingers.

He looked at the oldest child, paused, and held up six fingers.

The tribesman froze, unfroze, stared, shut his eyes, wobbled, recovered, ran his foot through the dirt, and then patted that dirt back down. He had never placed a value on his possessions, and could not fathom how anyone could have such a warped philosophy; considering this thing to be worth three fingers, and that thing to be worth six.

Delaney lifted his gun.

The tribesman panicked.

He sped across the hut, flicking up soot, shooed his family aside, crouched, and opened his palms to present the stools. One of Archibald's men picked up two stools and walked away. Archibald hugged the tribesman and smile.

"We," he said; pointing to his men.

"You," he said; pointing to the family.

"Protect," he said; making a circle with his arms, flexing his muscles and giving a thumbs up.

*****

It was easy work.

Divided by centuries of conflict and distrust, different tribes never came to each other's rescue. They stood back, allowing Archibald's men to march from one village to another; turning autonomous communities into subservient districts of a distant state, and forcing villagers to obey laws they had no say in making.

In most instances, the mere threat of violence was enough to impose control. Occasionally, Archibald's men were compelled to act; tying one dissenter to a tree, and whipping another.

Normally, Archibald took possessions as payment of the Hut Tax. Occasionally, he came across a village which used coins. After several months, he met a man who spoke English.

Like the rest of his tribe, that man wore a leather loincloth, dyed yellow, folded around his hips, and crescented between his legs. Unlike the rest of his tribe, he also wore sandals. He had straightened his hair, cut his nails and trimmed his nostrils. He smelled like a dandy lord.

When Archibald asked for his Hut Tax, that man nodded, sagely, and collected payment from everyone in his clan.

Archibald was stunned.

"One last thing," the tribesman said in an impeccable Surrey accent. "Please be so kind as to tell me: If you need silver and gold to pay your troops, why not dig it up?"

Archibald took a small step back.

"Our nation is rich with silver and gold; mining it would be a cinch."

Archibald's eyes turned milky white; a colour which was the absence of all colour. He could not answer. For several seconds, he could not even speak. Then he recalled something he had been told during his training.

He repeated it out loud:

"Ours is not to reason why. Ours is to do and die!"

*****

His answer, whilst abrupt enough to end that conversation, did not settle Archibald's mind:

'*Why couldn't we mine the gold? It'd be far easier than trawling this godforsaken land.*'

He was reluctant to admit it, but he felt he had no choice:

'*That savage had a point.*'

*****

When he returned to the city, Archibald's mind was awash with thoughts like these. So he arranged to meet the Governor General, entered that man's office, doffed his cap, and waited for permission to speak.

The Governor General appeared to be made of granite. His prodigious frame was covered in saurian scales, although his palms were as soft as kitten fur; his moustache smelled of molasses, and his voice rumbled like a miner's cart. He talked at a canter, whilst chewing tobacco; only ever stopping to sneeze or swig his chartreuse. He had consumed three glasses of the green liquor before Archibald had the chance to speak.

He explained his situation and waited for an answer.

An answer never came.

The Governor General picked up a bell so small it would have made a gnome look like a giant, held it between his thumb and forefinger, and rang it until a boy came hurtling into the room.

The boy saluted, stamped his foot, and awaited orders.

"Hail a carriage for Officer Archibald. He's to be taken to Bronze House."

Archibald saluted, left, and boarded his carriage. He rode past shanty towns painted in psychotic colours, markets bustling with trade, houses doused in mosaics, a woman with cats in her pockets, thirteen pink-faced monkeys, and a single ostrich.

As soon as he arrived at Bronze House, two doormen heaved open the imperious wooden doors. Archibald stepped into an atrium which was so large, and so vacuous, it took him seventy-three steps to traverse.

He entered an office.

At the opposite end of that room, a bald man sat with his back turned. He waited for Archibald to approach, and then he swivelled around:

"Hello, my brother, I've been expecting you."

Archibald froze.

Mayer guffawed.

THE BUTTERFLY EFFECT

"States created markets. Markets require states.
Neither could continue without the other."
DAVID GRAEBER

His ability to create money made Mayer rich, but it also inspired hundreds of other goldsmiths, who began to print notes of their own. This created a bubble. The bubble burst.

A great northern bank went bust, and had to be bailed out by the Bank of England. Gold reserves dwindled, forcing the state to borrow gold from France. A financial crash in America, where almost a thousand banks failed, meant that loans went unpaid, notes became worthless, and investors saw their fortunes wiped out overnight.

Interest rates increased, prices increased, and the government was forced to act. Sir Robert Peel, by now the Prime Minister, passed the "Bank Charter Act"; prohibiting banks from printing money.

It seemed like the good times were over.

*****

"The good times are over," Mr Bronze sighed. "It did go pear-shaped after all."

Mr Bronze had grown so old he had become ageless.

A gold monocle still hung from a chain attached to his blazer, and he still wore the same suits he had always worn; stitched, sown, washed, pressed and ironed so many times it was a wonder they had not fallen apart. His hair was snowy white, and his skin was as hard as rubber; this made him seem antique, although no-one could recall a time when he had looked any different.

Mr Bronze had attempted to retire several years before. But the day after he said his final goodbyes, he awoke at the time he always awoke, left home at the time he always left home, and arrived to open his bank at exactly seven o'clock. Such was the high esteem in which he was held, his staff did not dare to question his presence, and so he continued as if he had never retired. His staff, in turn, assumed that he would never retire again.

"No," Mayer replied. "The good times aren't over."

For the first time in his life, Mr Bronze forgot to have his eleven o'clock cup of tea. Mayer checked his watch thirteen times, unsure what had happened; sure that the world had stopped:

"Tea, my dear man?"

"It's over."

Mr Bronze looked relaxed; Mr Bronze always looked relaxed. He did not look flustered; he never looked flustered. He looked a little concerned, but no more; his emotions never overwhelmed him:

"I fear we're done for."

"No, we're not."

"We're not?"

"No. If the government stops us from printing banknotes, we'll create other forms of money."

"Other forms of money?"

"Yes, my dear man, other forms of money. Before we made money out of paper, we used tally sticks made from wood. In other nations, people have made money from whales' teeth, knotted cords, cowry shells, beads, feathers, and salt. Money can be made from anything. If we can't make it from paper, we'll just use something else."

"Something else?"

"Something else!"

"Ah, but what?"

"Who knows? Who wants to know? Ignorance is far more intriguing than knowledge, for it is ignorance that inspires the search for knowledge, whilst knowledge just hides.

"It doesn't matter what sort of money we create; only that we create it. And bankers will *always* create money; give us some credit! Why, I've already heard of a new invention called 'Cheques'. Those could take off. Maybe one day we'll create token money, electronic money, or money spent on plastic cards."

"Eh?"

"It doesn't matter. Whatever money we create, I'm sure it'll be delightful. And anyway, I think we'll be safe to continue as normal for now."

Mr Bronze tapped his lip:

"That'd be illegal."

"The law is unenforceable. People are creatures of habit; they trust our money, and so they'll continue to use it. The government won't be able to do a thing."

Mr Bronze nodded, patted Mayer's back, and performed his six o'clock stock-check.

*****

The Bank Charter Act did not prove an obstacle for Mr Bronze; banks like his continued to issue banknotes for many decades. Given time, Bronze's Bank would merge with a group of local banks. Given more time, they would merge with other, similar groups. They would form national chains, with names such as "HSBC" and "Barclays".

But the Bank Charter Act did have one major effect: It created a closed-shop. Bank owners like Mr Bronze were able to maintain their positions, but people like Mayer were locked out for good.

Mayer's dreams went up in smoke.

His eyebrows became scraggly, hair grew on top of his ears, his glasses cracked, his muscles started to ache, his body-fat reduced, and his skin thinned.

He still dreamt of Lola.

He still dreamt of money.

'*If I can't establish a bank here*', he told himself. '*I'll have to look elsewhere.*'

He looked to Africa.

*****

Leaving London was the hardest thing Mayer ever had to do; abandoning his acquaintances hit him hard, and saying "Goodbye" to Mr Bronze brought a tear to his eye.

Before he left, he spent one final night in Nicola's arms, imagining she was Lola.

In all their years together, luxuriating in their vanilla-flavoured silence, those two lovers had never uttered a word. Before he left, Mayer turned to Nicola, saw Lola in her eyes, and uttered three:

"I love you."

His words echoed:

'*I love you. I love you. I love you.*'

*****

Mayer left for two reasons: Hope and fear.

He *feared* a revolution; Hugo's comrades were gaining ground.

He *hoped* to set up a bank of his own; taking monetary control over a nation, and accruing the wealth he believed would win Lola's heart. He planned to return to Lola just as soon as Hugo died, and so took up subscriptions to all the London papers, whose obituary columns he read with religious fervour.

*****

Mayer sailed the crackled waves.

He arrived to a myriad of peregrine aromas: The smell of ashy smoke coughed up into the evening air; the smells of sweet cloves and burnt milk, burning ozone and unbaked clay.

He arrived to a scene of splendour and squalor; the seed of a city unborn; a castle on a hill, a palace within, and turrets spearing the sky; slums and shacks and shanties; mud and brick and stone.

He arrived in the Governor General's office.

"Get the buggers in the interior to use money," that man told him. "Then I'll grant you your charter to establish a bank."

*****

Mayer went on a reconnaissance mission.

He approached the Lele; a tribe who adorned masks which obliterated their identities; making large seem little, female seem male, and wise seem simple.

Mayer was enthused to see the Lele use lengths of woven cloth, made from raffia palms, as if they were money. He saw a boy give his father twenty cloths when he became a man, a husband give his wife thirty cloths when she gave birth, and a youth give a rival ten cloths to heal a rift.

Those cloths passed from one hand to another, helping to maintain order, console mourners and arrange marriages. But Mayer never saw anyone use them to buy actual, physical items.

Confused and in need of more information, Mayer observed the tribe which Archibald would later meet. Dressed in loincloths, their breasts were cajoled by the breeze, their calves were taut, and their skin was so dark it shone.

He observed their gift exchanges, and tried to join in; gifting a cow to a granite-nosed villager. The villager accepted the cow, slaughtered it, and shared it with his tribe. Then he gave Mayer a duck.

Unperturbed, Mayer returned a few days later. He pointed to a woman's bracelet and smiled. Before he knew it, he was wearing that bracelet himself. The woman pointed at Mayer's clothes. Before he knew it, he was as naked as the day he was born.

Mayer chose not to return a third time. Instead, he observed the Tiv; a tribe who wore robes adorned with zebra stripes.

Mayer was immediately drawn to a woman who was so dense she seemed to possess a gravitational field of her own. She had mountainous breasts, volcanic eyes and fiery breath.

Mayer followed her. He did not have a choice; his feet paced without instruction, his legs lifted themselves, and his eyes were drawn to the basket of eggs on her head:

'*Will she sell them? Or cook them? Or exchange them?*'

No such thing occurred. She walked to another village, where she met a woman who had the scent of a wild animal and eyes which touched. After an hour spent drinking tea, she left without the eggs.

Mayer returned the next day, when he saw the second woman give the first woman nine eggs.

This scene repeated itself: The first woman gave three fish, and the second woman returned four; the first woman gave twelve mangoes, and the second woman returned two. Nothing ever balanced.

Perplexed, Mayer returned to the city in search of an explanation...

*****

As was his style, Mayer was building a circle of acquaintances. Amongst them was an academic known as "Jumble"; a man who could wax lyrical about almost any society on the planet, recount its history, and then get lost in a tangle of words; a man who was a tapestry of musty smells, elbow patches, tweed, ivory pipes and sandals.

Only two things protruded from Jumble's two-dimensional face; a remarkable wart and an unremarkable nose. Of the nose, we shall say no more. The wart, however, merits further investigation. Viewed from one angle, it looked conical, like a fleshy barrel. Viewed from another, it looked spherical, like a gooseberry. It cast a long shadow, which rotated around Jumble's face. It had spawned seventeen hairs; each thicker than the last, and each more resistant to plucking.

"The Tiv, you say?"

Jumble swilled his vermouth:

"Harumph-grumph. Ah yes, the Tiv."

"I was just saying how their exchanges don't add up."

"No, they don't."

"Why?"

"Debt."

"Debt, my dear man?"

"Debt! And a jolly fine thing it is too, even if I don't say so myself."

"Say it."

"It's a jolly fine thing."

"Say why."

"Oh yes. Harumph-grumph. Where was I? Ah, Tiv debt. Spiffing! They never repay eight eggs with eight eggs, they return slightly more or slightly less in order to maintain a debt."

"Whatever for?"

"So that they have a reason to meet again."

"Hmm."

"It's really very simple: To not repay anything would be exploitative. Excuse me. To repay the exact amount would be an insult; it would suggest you didn't want anything more to do with the other person. Harumph-grumph. Yes. Pay a little less than you owe, and you'll have to meet the other person again, to repay the difference. You create a society. And a jolly good show it is too!"

Mayer was about to ask a question, but he stopped to think:

'*Would Abe and I still be on speaking terms, if I hadn't repaid my debt?*'

Jumble, however, did not stop to think. He was loquacious to a fault:

"Now the Gunwinggu, in Australia, will just walk up to someone, say 'Nice shoes', and be given those shoes right away. Excuse me.

"The Arabs have a similar custom. But they have a get-out. If they want to keep something, they'll say, 'Isn't it beautiful? Yes, it was a gift'.

"Harumph-grumph. Where was I? Oh yes, the Inuit. They refuse to make value judgments; to compare, measure or calculate; believing it would make slaves out of men.

"The Indians use a caste system; everyone has a role to play; a product to produce. Those products are distributed according to a hierarchy.

"Now the Iroquois, in the States, arrange things on a communal basis. Excuse me. They stockpile their produce in longhouses, where women's councils distribute it according to need."

Jumble stopped for air.

"Enough!" Mayer screamed. "My head's spinning."

Jumble laughed:

"Another drink?"

"Another time."

*****

Mayer had been guilty of the most common of crimes: Judging others by his own standards. He had judged stateless people as if they lived in a state, and human economies as if they used money.

His conversation with Jumble helped to clarify his thoughts.

He realised that the tribespeople did have economies; they did produce and consume, things did move from hand to hand; but their economies were based on relationships, on love, not on money.

To create an impersonal economy, in which strangers could trade using *money*, Mayer realized he was going to have to bypass those bonds of *love*. If necessary, he was going to have to use *power*, the occupying army, but first he tried to go it alone…

*****

Mayer gifted a decorative knife to a tribeswoman with sapphire eyes, and showed her how to use it. A few weeks later, he returned with five more knives, hoping to sell them to that tribe. He also took some bronze pennies, hoping to exchange them for grain, so the villagers would have the coins they needed to buy his knives. This, he reasoned, would get them accustomed to using British money.

Much to his delight, Mayer saw that his knife had proved popular. He found it, dripping with blood, next to a dead kudu.

When they saw him coming, the villagers pointed at the knife, pointed at Mayer, and smiled until their cheeks inflated.

Mayer saw a Medusan-haired woman use that knife to split a hide, before passing it to a bucktoothed woman, who used it to chop carrots, before passing it to an albino woman, who used it to cut her daughter's hair. Whenever anyone wanted that knife, they simply took it for themselves.

But when Mayer offered the villagers coins in exchange for their grain, they just shrugged; they did not consider his coins to be pretty enough to use as jewellery, nor practical enough to use for anything else. And when Mayer tried to barter his other knives, the villagers just shrugged again. They could not understand why their village would need more than one knife.

*****

Mayer realised that for markets to exist in that land, and for businesses to thrive, he was going to have to create demand for things people did not want or need. It was not good enough for a community to share a knife; everyone had to want their own knife, even if it spent most of its time, unused, in a drawer:

'Ah yes, we'll have to sell them drawers! We'll spread fear of knife crime. Then we'll tell them they need knives to protect themselves, leather pouches to protect their knives, and belts on which to clip those pouches. Walla! Job done!'

Mayer headed into the bush, recruited people from every village, taught them to speak English, and sent them home in western clothes.

"Haha! Look at you!" those agents told their tribes. "You're naked! You look so savage. Why don't you wear clothes like me?"

It seldom worked. Outnumbered, Mayer's agents were usually mocked themselves. But, on some rare occasions, they did manage to trade western goods and money.

Mayer encouraged his agents to persist:

"Tell the villagers to 'Be individuals'. Tell them to ignore their elders. Dear friends: Tell them to 'Be true to yourself', 'Follow your heart' and 'Just do it'. Then sell them more clothes than they could ever possibly need. Then sell them wardrobes."

*****

These years, his early fifties, saw Mayer age at an accelerating rate. The skin beneath his jaw sagged, wrinkles crept out from his eyes, and his bald head, reddened by the sun, filled with an increasing array of liver spots.

He was too old to chase women and too old to care, but still young enough dream of Lola and money. He had established a bank, and his agents were turning a profit, but he wanted more.

So Mayer went to meet Jumble in his favourite gentleman's club; a fusty place full of leather-bound books and leather-clad chairs.

"Well, you see," Jumble explained in his grandiloquent style. "Money has been used as a unit of account, to calculate taxes, for about four millennia. But coins have only been used as a means of exchange since 600BC.

"Harumph-grumph. Ahum. Yes. The first Greek coins were produced by wealthy families, vying for political supremacy. Emblazoned with seals and mottos, they were given away as gifts in an attempt to curry support.

"You see, those families aspired to self-sufficiency, they saw resorting to trade as a mark of failure, and so they didn't use their coins to buy or sell things. Oh no! They were more like military medals than modern coins. Spiffing!

"Well those Greek families coveted power, so they came together to form a state, replete with magistrates to protect their power at home, and soldiers to win them power abroad.

"Those public servants needed to be paid wages. Excuse me. Well, to pay those wages, taxes needed to be raised. It was agreed that they would be paid for with gold and silver coins.

"The families were forced to sell things like food and clothes, to receive those coins, so they could afford to pay their taxes. Excuse me. The public servants, in turn, were paid those coins, before spending them on the items the families had been forced to sell. Markets were created and money began to flow. It was jolly splendid. Taxes forced people to buy things, sell things and use coins."

Jumble sank back into the leather-clad embrace of his rumpled chair. He sipped his sherry and took in the bombastic ambience of that place.

"You haven't answered my question," Mayer said.

"Oh yes I have," Jumble replied. "Harumph-grumph. Jolly hockey sticks. Ra, ra, ra!"

*****

The Governor General was squished into a chair meant for a much smaller man. He was wearing an amazing array of accessories on what would have otherwise been an exceedingly dour blazer. Multicoloured medals feathered a striped sash, which was held in place by a white belt and a silver pin. He wore shoulder-pads, cuffs, stars, buttons, pips, buckles, and a collar which covered his neck.

Mayer stood to meet him, removed his rabbit-skin gloves, and shook his hand:

"How are your geraniums?"

"Dead."

"I'm sorry to hear that. Hmm. I suppose it must be this weather we've been having."

"True-ho!"

The Governor General had grown fond of Mayer, who gave him a bottle of chartreuse every month, and so he was happy to allow him to speak:

"We need a 'Moralizing Tax'; a 'Hut Tax' which will empower the state and force the natives to use British money. It worked for the Greeks, and it'll work for us. I tell you, my dear man, it'll be a gorgeous fine thing. Just delightful!"

"What-ho? How in the buggery would it work?"

"We'll print money."

"And then what?"

"We'll demand it back."

"Why?"

"To fund our magistrates and soldiers."

"When?"

"At harvest time. The tax will force people to be more productive; to create a surplus to sell at market. That's why it'll be a 'Moralizing Tax': It'll teach the natives the value of hard work.

"We'll use our tax revenues to buy their food at market, then we'll use that food to feed our troops, who'll help us to collect the tax."

The Governor General paused, tapped his foot, chattered his teeth, chewed a nail, tilted his head, untitled it, brushed something invisible from his sleeve, and then smiled:

"Good-ho! The natives *are* as savage as a meat axe."

"They are, my dear man, they are."

"I heard the buggers kill babies born without hair."

"Hmm. I heard they abandon their elderly."

The Governor General tapped his lower lip:

"What do you need?"

"Soldiers."

"Righty-ho! Consider it done."

*****

Mayer's soldiers forced the native population to pay British taxes.

African people worked harder than ever before; growing crops, breeding cattle, weaving, sowing and building; yet many of them were still unable to pay.

If they had crops to sell, Mayer's agents bought them and sold them on for a profit.

If they did not have crops to sell, Mayer's agents lent them money and charged them interest. When they defaulted, they were taken from their communities and forced to work in mines, extracting gold, silver and diamonds; or on plantations, farming rubber, timber and palm oil. They toiled day and night, turning African resources into British wealth.

So began Mayer's rise.

His bank lent money to businessmen to establish mines and plantations, charged interest on those loans, turned those interest payments into more loans, and reaped more interest.

He grew rich and, in a way, he grew happy. He had the bank he had always dreamt of and a mansion most people could not even imagine. He furnished that place in just the way he thought Lola would have chosen to furnish it herself, fit for a princess, with a walk-in closet, private spa, make-up room and ballroom. He had those rooms stocked with flower pots, ready for Lola to fill, and the most elegant outfits that century had seen. But those rooms remained in a state of mourning, gathering dust, waiting for the day when Mayer would hear of Hugo's death, travel to London, and return with Lola by his side.

His was the biggest house in the land; dazzling white, with ivy caressing the columns. It was an angel's playground of sculptures and statues, fountains and fish; with more rooms than he could count, and so many servants that he could never remember their names.

Yet, despite being surrounded by those people, Mayer still felt lonely. Despite his wealth, he still felt poor. He had money and power, but he did not have love, he missed Nicola, and he prayed to see Lola again.

"We used to have something, you and I."

Her words were repercussive, eternal, cherished and catastrophic.

Their tendrils reached the deepest recesses of Mayer's ego, with consonants in motion and letters in rhyme.

So began Mayer's fall.

He saw visions of Lola's face, conjured up in the mist, the clouds, and the steam which leapt up from his morning coffee. She was a mirage, spirit and enigma; whistling, humming, and emitting sparks; mocking him with a game which had no rules.

Once, Mayer could have sworn he saw a bloated version of Lola buying a lovebird at the market. He rushed across the street, pushing people aside, tripping, falling and rising, only to reach the stall and realise she was not there.

On another occasion, he thought he saw her buying a back-scratcher. He thought he saw her gliding through a convent with luxurious maturity. He was so convinced he had seen her in a café, he screamed her name out loud:

"Lola! Lola! Lo... o... o..."

Those visions appeared to him with increasing regularity. Mayer had to pinch, prod and slap himself just to keep his feet on the ground. It was all he could do to stop himself from going mad.

'*She's not real. She's not there. She's not real. She's not there.*'

And still her voice echoed:

"We used to have something, you and I."

"We could have been special."

*****

As if to mock his wealth, Mayer followed an austere routine, which was probably inspired by Mr Bronze's clockwork personality. Mayer, however, insisted that this routine was his own original invention, which he had developed to help himself escape from his visions.

He rose at the same time every morning; five forty-five. He ate the same breakfast; smoked fish and poached eggs. He drank at least fifty cups of tea a day, and spent every evening alone, on his marble patio, shaded by mango trees and fragrant blossoms.

Mayer got his best ideas in the stillness of dusk, when the silence was only ever disturbed by the distant cries of street hawkers and stray dogs; omnipresent creatures who engaged in bouts of doggy politics as soon as the sun began to set. Those dogs proudly displayed the scars of debates won, debates lost, and debates descended into bites and brawls; wearing half-eaten ears and tufty fur as if they were marks of distinction. If they ever managed to make it past Mayer's fences, ditches, sentry towers, security guards and servants, Mayer was always sure to reward them with a treat and a cuddle. They were the best friends he had.

Mayer was just as lonely as he had been in Buckingham Towers, and so he consoled himself by reading just as many books. He read classics which everyone had heard of but no-one had actually read, obscure books which no-one had ever heard of, and unpublished tomes which no-one had ever read. He read newspapers to keep in touch with reality, and works of fiction to forget; imagining that the characters in those stories were people he knew in real life. Whenever he read a romantic novel, he pictured himself and Lola as star-crossed lovers. But this only made matters worse; encouraging his subconscious to create even more visions of Lola than before. This, in turn, intensified Mayer's desire for Hugo to die.

*****

This was the state of play when Archibald stormed into Mayer's office.

Mayer, whose face curled into a smirk, was wearing a starchy suit from a bygone era. Archibald, whose face compressed, was wearing his army uniform:

"Tell me, if we need silver and gold to pay our troops, why can't we just dig it up? For Pete's sake man; the land is stuffed full of the stuff."

Mayer leant back in his chair, rocked slightly forwards, rocked slightly back, steadied himself, poured two brandies and smiled:

"It's a lovely day, isn't it?"

Archibald's eyes bulged.

"Mind you, it's always lovely here. 'Blue skies and sun pies', as I like to say."

Archibald opened his palms in desperation:

"Good god man! Why can't we just mine the gold?"

Mayer chuckled:

"That's your first question? No, 'How are you?' No, 'What are you doing here?' No..."

"No!"

"Hmm. Very well. To answer your question, we *are* mining gold. We're doing very well from it, thank-you very much! But an army cannot eat gold or wear silver. We need the natives to produce food for our troops to eat and clothes for them to wear. That's why the Hut Tax works so well. It forces the natives to sell food and cloth to our troops, so they can earn the money they need to pay our tax."

Archibald glared, grimaced, pouted, frowned, raised his eyebrows, lifted his chin, lifted his finger and puffed his chest:

"Blister of pearl! We're on the same blimming side!"

"We are, brother; we always have been."

Mayer gestured towards Archibald's brandy. Then he continued:

"I feel for you, brother, honestly I do. Your lands are sparsely populated, that's why they haven't been civilised before, and you're trying to impose a new mindset; forcing states and money onto free people. It'll take time. But trust me: You *will* change those people. They'll come to believe our way is the only way."

Archibald did not look convinced:

"Go on."

"Look at things back in Blighty. Ask anyone there about the police, and they'll tell you they've been around forever, that society would crumble without them. We both know that's not true. But the truth doesn't matter there, and it won't matter here. People will start to pay our taxes, use our money, and follow our rules. Before you know it, they'll forget there was another way."

Archibald replied with a single word:

"How?"

Mayer replied with several words:

"Myths, my brother, myths! Truths are so dreadfully bland, but myths are truly delicious; one simply cannot help but swallow them whole."

Archibald furrowed his brow.

"We'll create shared myths in an imagined order. We'll say that states are great, not because we say so, but because God has ordained them. We'll say that monetary economies are great, not because we say so, but because they're an immutable law of nature. Who'll dare argue with that? Who'll dare question the will of God and nature? No-one, brother, that's who! Not even the natives."

Mayer put his arm around Archibald and led him to the door:

"It sure is great to see you."

Archibald nodded:

"Let's go to the pub."

"To the pub!"

*****

The doors heaved open. Archibald and Mayer stepped out into the market square.

It sparkled with static. The setting sun glistened on silver roofs, cloaked only by the opalescent afterglow of a thousand friendly fires. Lustrous colours hung from the haze; iridescent, in flux, alive.

Buildings jostled for position.

Bodies jostled for position.

Bombastic rhythms beat from African drums. Banners, nudged by subliminal currents, seemed to kiss the clouds above. Feet stomped, hands clapped, and voices rang loud:

"What do we want? Freedom! When do we want it? Now!"

"No more taxes! No more state! No more government! No more hate!"

Archibald and Mayer moved their heads in unison, before fixing their gaze on a white man who had stood up to address the crowd. His scalp was bald, reddened by the sun, and covered in a vast array of liver spots.

"Hugo?" they whispered. "No, it can't be. Hugo? Really? No."

GOD'S GARDENER

"Take up the White Man's burden,
Send forth the best ye breed.
Go bind your sons to exile,
To serve your captives' need."
RUDYARD KIPLING

Hugo's daughters seemed to grow in instalments. At once, they were babes in arms. Then they were toddlers. In an instant, they were infants. Then children. Then teens. Then fully-grown women.

They grew so effortlessly. Baby fat: Gone! Legs: Longer! Hair: Shorter! Then longer. Then shorter. Then longer.

Spots marauded across their faces as if in time-lapse photography.

Breasts burst through the innocent restraints of their skin.

Their lives took place in constant motion; in fatness then thinness, smiles then tears, skips then jumps, this colour then that one, this dress then another, and then another.

Hugo scratched his head. He could not quite understand where the time had gone. To him, those fully-formed women were still his babies. Lola called them her "Kidults".

*****

In the space of just one year, Lola's parents both died, and her daughters all moved out.

Emma, forever mute, became a nun. Maddie, who only spoke when she was spoken to, married a man who spoke to her a lot. Sylvia, who only spoke when she was not spoken to, eloped with a man who barely spoke. Peta, who answered questions which were not meant for her, toured Europe with an inquisitive man. Natalie, who questioned everything, married a man who had lots of answers:

"Why did you come home half drunk?"

"Because I ran out of money."

"What ended in 1811?"

"1810."

"Can I ask you a question?"

"No."

*****

The ambient noise of Hugo's life had been replaced by a silence which was louder than sound. His eyebrows became scraggly, hair grew on top of his ears, and a small crack formed in the corner of his glasses. Lola bought him a new pair of glasses. She moulded his age into shape; massaging his aching muscles and rubbing cream into his rashes; stocking his wardrobe with frock coats, long boots and genteel hats; viewing him with different eyes from everyone else, and doing everything she could to make sure the rest of the world saw him the same way she did.

Lola still dressed Hugo, but she only did so every second day; Hugo dressed Lola on the days in-between. They had fallen into this routine out of a romantic notion of egalitarian love, they had continued it out of a force of habit, and they had never changed it because they could not conceive of any other way to act.

*****

Throughout this period, three things dominated Hugo's life.

One: Activism.

Hugo attended the Swing Riots, where protestors demanded higher wages for factory workers who had been forced off their land by enclosures. He was a founder member of the Chartist movement, which called for all men to have the vote; attending the Newport Rising and producing a giant petition. He assisted rioters during the General Strike, and protested against tariffs on grain.

His activism made a difference. Factory workers *did* get higher wages, men *did* get the vote, and tariffs on grain *were* abolished. His generation inspired future generations of activists: The Suffragists, who secured votes for women, and the Trade Unionists, who secured improved working conditions, a two-day weekend, maternity pay, paternity pay, paid holidays and more.

Two: Charity.

Hugo managed Saint Nick's. Aided by donations from former residents, he and Lola were able to open a girls' village in Barkingside, which his daughters helped to run.

Three: Marriage.

Hugo's love for Lola matured by the day. It was strong, but it was not without its little holes. Hugo grew frustrated whenever Lola muttered people's names in her sleep: "R". "Archibald". "Papa". "Mayer". Her habit of forgetting appointments made Hugo grind his teeth. During one brief moment, Hugo was overwhelmed by a flush of unmitigated hatred for his wife; hoping she would die the most violent of deaths. That feeling passed. As if he had never felt it, Hugo went back to loving Lola as much as ever before.

Hugo and Lola found romance in the minutiae of everyday mundanity: In the way Lola buttered Hugo's toast, with the grain, adding a square of marmalade to one corner. In the way Hugo hugged Lola from behind, with his arms around her waist, rocking her gently if it rained. In the way they bathed together, splashing water, spitting water, and rubbing each other's backs. In the way they strolled together, holding hands, supporting each other's weight, and helping each other around whatever obstacles stood in their way.

Lola still left to eat whenever she wished to end a conversation. She ate Scottie cakes, yarg, pigs in blankets, Welsh rarebit, rumbledethumps, stargazy pie and scouse. Despite her gluttonous appetite, she kept hold of her youthful figure. Then, overnight, she put on all the weight she should have gained over the course of several years.

As if it were contagious, Lola caught old age. Her hair silvered, her eyes lost their light, and her skin took on a sour odour. This was not a problem for Hugo, who viewed his wife through biased eyes. To him, she looked splendid in her maturity; her weight suited her, and her roundness seemed even rounder than before. Hugo took pleasure in the folds of Lola's wrinkled skin, the uneven contours of her crumbling bones, and the elasticity of her breasts. But even Lola's buxom form could not fill the void left by their daughters' departures. Their home felt like an empty nest.

"I never see you these days," Lola complained. "You're always off protesting."

Hugo clutched his wife's thigh:

"I love you."

"I love you too, hubby."

"And I'd like for us to spend more time together."

"But how?"

"We could retire."

"Yes, let's grow old in the sun."

"Yes, let's sell the house and move to Africa."

"Africa? You're as mad as hatter!"

"Assuredly so. But insanity is a virtue, and true madness is next to godliness."

Lola giggled:

"Okay, Africa it is. I hear they do the most divine mangos. Talking of which, let's eat some mushy peas."

Lola left the room and Hugo fell asleep, holding his cup of tea.

Lola returned and took it from his hand.

Hugo bolted upright:

"What in the blueberries? I was only resting my eyes."

Lola laughed, tuned Hugo's cravat into a bib, and then ate some piccalilli.

*****

Lola collected three things in Africa: Back-scratchers, lovebirds and plants.

She bought her first back-scratcher because of a genuine need to scratch her back, her second because it was far prettier than the first, and her third because she did not like to own two of anything. For Lola, two was an unlucky number.

Having bought three back scratchers in three days, Lola did not see any reason to stop. Habits, she supposed, should only be broken if they cause harm. And where was the harm in owning a few back scratchers? Or a few hundred?

Lola bought her fourth back-scratcher from a hawker named Kali, whose face was almost perfect. It was ruined by a beauty spot, which would have been a vision of divine grace had it been placed a centimetre higher and a centimetre to the left. In its actual position, however, it made her look absurd.

Kali visited Lola every day. Lola invited Kali into her home, made her tea, gave a banana to each of her children, and then bought a back-scratcher.

Even when Hugo used a hundred of those backscratchers as firewood, it did not dampen Lola's enthusiasm. She simply started again afresh, as if nothing had happened.

Lola was not interested in owning vast quantities of back scratchers, only in buying a new one each day. The thrill was in the newness; in new possessions, new conversations, new friends, new cups of tea and new bananas. It did not matter what it was new, so long as it was new.

This may explain Lola's obsession with rosy-faced lovebirds.

She fell for those birds whilst meandering through the market, viewing every stall with leisurely delight; captivated by the snake charmer who tried to sell her magic potions, beguiled by the runaway slave who painted hieroglyphics, sampling crushed leaves, swaddling herself in patterned cloths, buying what she needed, and buying what she did not; all whilst her ears were caressed by the airless hubbub of banana fritter vendors and shoeshine boys.

The stall which sold pets stocked six of everything: Six iguanas, six parakeets, six house snakes, six egg eaters, six pygmy hedgehogs, six pouched rats, six aardvarks, six lemurs, six of this, six of that, but at least sixty-six rosy-faced lovebirds, if not six hundred. They were crammed together inside a cage, with pale green bodies, dark green wings, yellow chests and tangerine faces.

Lola was hit by a sudden urge to free those birds as soon as she saw them. Instead, she bought one, took it home, fed it and stroked its belly. Then she released it, whilst praying for its return.

It did not return.

So it continued. Each day Lola bought a new lovebird, tried to woo it, and then released it. Each day she was left disappointed when it failed to return.

*****

Hugo and Lola lived in a bungalow outside the city.

They chose that place for one reason: Space. Space in which to breathe, live and garden.

Lola explored the land, made cuttings of every plant she found, took those cuttings home, fed them, watered them, grew them, and planted them inside and out.

Vines slithered up pebble-dashed walls, forming porches where none had existed; canopies of green upon a canvas of white. Soil-filled shelves turned her home into a library of grasses and herbs; every wall was verdant, no surface escaped the touch of a curious leaf or a clumsy stalk. The air was a potpourri of pollen and perfume; an aromatic wonderland ready to tantalise the nose.

But it was outside where Lola's gardening really impacted the world. As the years ticked by, so her garden expanded in waves. Dancing grass formed undulating contours, trees reached over bushes, and succulents crawled across the earth.

Those plants made delicate steps, large and silent, like thieves in the night. Cautious to avoid detection, a finger held to their lips, they tiptoed towards the nearest hamlet.

Poised, ready and waiting, they launched their attack in the witching hour; submerging every structure beneath a carpet of bodacious leaves and petals. Vivid colours stole the show; presenting a thousand shades of neon blue, fluorescent yellow and electric green. There were the jazzy reds and lemony blobs of the Rafflesia Arnoldii, the sun-blushed mauves and sun-kissed pinks of spiky Proteas, the claret mouths of Venus Fly Traps, and the flaming petals of fiery Gazanias.

That delicious sea of colour lured the eyes of everyone who passed by. It drew commuters into its flowery embrace, intoxicated by sweet perfume, and bewitched by blossomy enchantment. The people who encountered that flirtatious Shangri-La were seldom able to leave.

That community grew; turning from hamlet to village to town.

Inadvertently, without seeking money or power, Lola had become the unwitting queen of a magical kingdom.

*****

Hugo had become an unwitting stray in an alien land.

In search of purpose, he explored the nation, sizzling in his Georgian suits, until the hellish sun became too much for him to bear. He returned home, burned every item of clothing Lola had ever bought him, and replaced them with African robes, covered in incredible patterns and images of elephants. He swapped his shoes for sandals and headed out again.

*****

One balmy February afternoon, as the sun lazed on the horizon, Hugo saw a tribeswoman in the grip of pneumonia. Green mucus kissed her snarled lips, and cold sweat covered her skin. She was hugging her knees, rocking, and muttering indistinguishable words.

Hugo got to work. Using an improvised form of sign-language, assisted by a youth who spoke a little English, he cradled that woman in his arms, carried her to her hut, laid her down, covered her, wiped her brow, spoon-fed her some soup, gave her some medicine, held her hand and whispered sweet nothings.

After three hours, that woman began to recover. After three more hours, she was back on her feet.

As Hugo left the village, a group of tribespeople blocked his path. The woman approached, pointed at Hugo's wedding ring and smiled.

Hugo smiled back.

The woman frowned.

Hugo frowned.

The woman grabbed the ring.

Hugo yanked it back.

The youth who spoke English called out:

"Well indeed! White men have no shame!"

*****

Hugo was perturbed. He wanted to help, but he did not want to endure that sort of reaction again.

'*I'll have to go undercover*', he decided. '*Well, it worked for Santa Clause, patron saint of thieves, and it worked for Robin Hood. Why can't it work for me?*'

He filled his bag and snuck off into the night.

He felt a phantasmagorical thrill; the thrill of youth revisited. He felt he was stepping back in time; sneaking into gardens to steal laundry, clambering up onto ships to pilfer nails, and double-teaming shoppers with Wilkins; running from the law, running from old age, and running from the lightness of life.

He felt alive!

He felt alive as he crept into a hut, serenaded by snoring snouts; the whistled concerto of the night. He felt alive as he saw the purple-red flush of malaria on a small girl's skin, and as he placed some lotion by her hand. He felt alive as he placed a wooden spoon by that family's pot.

He felt dead!

He felt he had died when a set of manicured fingers grasped his shoulder; when they spun him around and presented him with two shining eyes, as bright as stars, and larger than distant planets.

"Sir," that man whispered. "What in the buggins do you think you're doing?"

*****

That man went by the name of Moha.

Moha looked exactly the way he was supposed to look. His afro, whilst neither sleek nor stylish, was a perfect fit for his head. His lithe torso complemented his skinny limbs. His was not a beautiful body, but it was pleasing to the eye; to see it was to experience a warm sort of satisfaction.

Moha was one of the first men Mayer had recruited. He had been taught to speak English, to eat with cutlery, and act like an English gent; wearing western clothes, following English etiquette, and embracing English culture.

When he turned eighteen, Moha travelled to Cambridge to study law. On returning to Africa, dressed in a suit and tie, he boarded a first-class coach. It did not move. Hooves remained fixed to the ground, and faces remained fixed in contorted variations of disgust.

A solemn man tapped the sign above his head:

'No coloureds'

Moha paused, stared at each of the passengers in turn, tutted, disembarked, returned to his native village, adorned his native clothes, and spoke his native language.

He did not utter another word of English until he caught Hugo in his uncle's hut.

*****

Legend has it that an angry god hurled the first ever baobab tree into the earth, leaving its branches in the soil and its roots up in the air.

Hugo and Moha sat beneath such a tree. Above them, branches appeared like roots; gnarled and tangled. They cut the moonlight into shards.

Hugo explained what had happened.

"I'm bamboozled," he concluded. "Why would that woman grab my ring? If anything, she should have given *me* a gift for saving *her* life."

Moha grimaced. Then he smiled:

"Our ways are different to yours, old chum. Not better, not worse, just different."

"Oh."

"Here, when one saves a person's life, one becomes like their sibling; bonded by blood. Well, in our society, brothers and sisters share everything; when they have more than their siblings they hand it over.

"When that woman asked for your ring, she was asking you to act like her brother; to confirm your bond. When you refused, you shunned her, and insulted her entire clan.

"One can't expect payment here, old bean. Golly gosh; you're barking up the wrong tree there! Taking payment would be like saying you didn't want anything to do with the person you saved. In these parts, one needs to maintain a debt."

*****

Hugo had made a friend. He visited Moha as often as Kali visited his wife; they drank just as many cups of tea and shared just as many conversations. Moha told Hugo about his tribe's culture, customs and religion. He taught Hugo his language. He taught Hugo three other African languages. Then he taught him two more.

After several years of friendship, Moha finally spoke about the Hut Tax:

"It's jolly beastly, old fruit. To pay it, we must sell half our crops when prices are low. When we run out of food, we have to buy those crops back for double the price we received. To pay, we have to take out loans, on which we're charged interest. To repay those loans, we have to send our children to work on plantations. It's a sticky wicket. Darned unsporting. Our children end up wearing the white man's clothes, consuming the white man's things, using the white man's money, and practicing the white man's religion."

Moha shook his head:

"It's killing our culture, old chap. It's hit us for six."

Hugo placed his hand on Moha's shoulder:

"We endured something similar back in England. My people were forced into factories by the Enclosure Acts. They also lost their land, freedom and culture."

Moha lowered his eyes:

"Golly gosh. I say, what did you do?"

"We fought back."

"Did it work?"

"A little."

"How marvellous! Can you be a sport and teach us how?"

*****

Hugo told Moha about his protests, and the results they achieved. Then they travelled the land, persuading the natives to rise up.

Stepping out of the shadows, Hugo became a figurehead for a forgotten people. The power invigorated him. He felt that his whole life had been leading him to that point; that it was his time, his crescendo, his final hurrah.

But, as he spent more time travelling the land, he spent less time with Lola.

Lola was proud of her husband; she loved the way she had moulded him; turning him from a scruffy charlatan into a loving, charitable man. She loved the power she held over his life; the way she was able to make him attend dances, set up a charity, become an activist, and give her children.

But Lola felt her power slipping away. She had encouraged Hugo to move to Africa so they could spend more time together, away from Hugo's comrades. And what had he done? He had found himself a whole new set of comrades! Once again, he had chosen to spend his time with them instead of her. He had burnt the clothes she had bought him, and ignored her needs.

As before, Hugo's extended absences left Lola feeling abandoned, helpless and alone. As before, she lost her appetite, spoke sarcastically, and paced around like a caged tiger. As before, she wondered if she would have been happier had she married Archibald or Mayer:

'Just think what sort of people I could have turned them into! Imagine if I'd made Mayer more loving, and gotten him to give all his money to charity. Imagine if I'd made Archibald more loving, and gotten him to use his power for good. Surely I'd be better off. Surely the world would be a better place.'

Lola dreamt of Mayer and Archibald, muttered their names in her sleep, and saw their faces in the crowd whenever she went into town:

'I chose the wrong man!'

Her love for Hugo began to wane.

Her flowers wilted, their petals fell, and her trees surrendered their leaves; vines broke through her walls, chalky fragments crumbled from her home, and her garden turned brown.

People abandoned her town.

Lola abandoned hope.

*****

A wave of hope surged through Hugo.

A wave of protestors surged through the nation. They marched on the city, shaded by grassy trees. They sang out loud, serenaded by birdsong. The mountains echoed. The ground shook.

The city thickened as they progressed, stacking structures on either side; with whitewashed walls and walls in festive colours; cobwebby, lethargic and Arcadian; bathed in light from another age.

A magnesium blaze welcomed their arrival in the market square. The sun glistened on silver roofs, cloaked only by the opalescent afterglow of a thousand friendly fires. Lustrous colours hung from the haze; iridescent, in flux, alive.

Buildings jostled for position.

Bodies jostled for position.

Bombastic rhythms beat from African drums. Banners, nudged by subliminal currents, seemed to kiss the clouds above. Feet stomped, hands clapped, and voices rang loud:

"What do we want? Freedom! When do we want it? Now!"

"No more taxes! No more state! No more government! No more hate!"

Hugo climbed onto a cart to address the crowd:

"It's time for a debt jubilee. It's time to abolish the Hut Tax. It's time to reclaim the streets. The time is now. The time is ours. We are history! We are one!"

Calls bled into cheers, claps and cries. But, before he could continue, two of Archibald's men clasped hold of Hugo's shoulders; forcing his head to fall back through the air, and his feet to lift out of their sandals. Held aloft by an indifferent breeze, he was about to land amongst a mélange of banana skins and pamphlets, when a soldier reached out and caught him.

Cradling Hugo, like a groom with his bride, that man ghosted past the assembled masses, indifferent to their derisory howls. He sailed past naked flames in doorways, the scramble of leaves in gutters, and the din of fireworks in a starless sky.

As he was kidnapped, Hugo gazed into the eyes of his allies. He felt defrauded by the limpness of his surrender. But, surrounded by soldiers, and handicapped by his antiquated limbs, there was nothing he could do.

Hugo felt his power ebb away; escaping like sweat through the pores in his skin. He felt fingernails dig through his flesh, pressing muscles against bones, as his embarrassment turned into despair, dejection, anguish and, finally, resignation.

By the time he had been dumped, bloody and bruised, in the subterranean depths of a prison cell, Hugo was so drained he did not feel anything at all.

TWIST AND SHOUT

"Mastering others is strength. Mastering yourself is true power."
LAO TZU

'*Carpe diem!*' Archibald told himself. '*Seize the day!*'

He had given the command to have Hugo arrested, and had kept him locked up for weeks:

'*The time is now! Lola <u>will</u> be mine.*'

*****

Archibald spied on Lola through a peephole when she visited Hugo each morning.

He saw her, inflating by the day, with a bulbous stomach and breasts which were impossibly pert. He saw her in shoes appropriate for a solemn occasion, dresses unsuitable for a prison, and necklaces made from pearls. He saw her, free from spots; her hair thin and grey, slanted, and bobbed at the cheek; her skin wrinkled, rough, meaty and matted.

He saw her berate Hugo, gaze at him, and sit in timeless silence.

For Hugo, that silence was golden.

For Archibald, it was the colour of hope.

*****

Archibald tiptoed towards Lola's bungalow, clutching ten thousand portraits; the fruits of decades of labour and a decadence of love.

It was the sunset hour. Tenuous light painted the sky a moody shade of red. Vines cast skeletal shadows across the cracked walls, which glowed amber; warm and melancholic. Flowers drifted off into a silent slumber. Only the Venus fly traps made a sound; snapping at the marshy air.

Archibald shivered with déjà vu.

Stalled by the overwhelming presence of Lola's home, he crouched down and placed his sketches by his feet.

He was stepping back into his youth; an adolescent once more, he was pacing down Hill Street, plucking up the courage to knock on Lola's door. Overcome by anxiety, he felt a sudden urge to run:

'No, Archibald, no! Haven't you learnt a thing? Haven't you won any power at all? No! The time is now. The time is ours. We are history! We are one!'

Archibald took a deep breath and lifted his fist.

'Knock'. Pause. 'Knock'.

It was a slow knock, fifty years in the making. Archibald did not feel a need to rush. Everything he had ever done, every ounce of power he had ever grasped, had led him to that place. It was his destiny. His calling. His time.

'Knock'. Pause. 'Knock'.

A servant opened the door and welcomed Archibald in a manner which suggested she had been expecting his arrival. She collected Archibald's sketches and disappeared.

Archibald entered a room which was heady with the fragrance of flowers melting in the heat.

Lola entered. She turned a pale shade of white. She had to squint, blink, and glare at Archibald before her mind could process the information her eyes were generating:

"Ah… Ah… Archibald?"

"Lola!"

Lola stepped out of the shadows. To Archibald, she looked divine. He did not see a wrinkled, grey-haired, bloated old woman. He saw the debutante he first saw in Covent Garden. He saw her luminous skin, luscious curves, lavish eyebrows and luxuriant hair; the way a ringlet of that hair skimmed her shoulder and then rebounded; the perfect roundness of her face, eyes and nose; the subtlety of her weightless dress, the bead of moisture on her lip, and the pearl which decorated her ear.

"Archibald?"

"Lola!"

Lola placed her hands on her hips, removed them, tilted her head, straightened it, shook it, blushed, smiled and screamed:

"Archie!"

"Lola!"

Archibald paused. Locking his eyes onto Lola's eyes, he meandered into her personal space. His nose almost touched her nose. Their breath merged.

"Archie!"

"Lola!"

Their hearts fluttered, their hands quivered, their skin shivered, their teeth chattered, and their nostrils filled with the scent of cinnamon; that aroma which, for them, was the very essence of true love.

"Archie!"

"Lola!"

It appeared to Lola like a vision: Archibald in a café in Covent Garden. Archibald in a shop in Lambeth. His body ripped, his muscles bulging, Lola's heart pounding, that feeling of animalistic attraction, that feeling of completeness.

Lola saw those same muscles within the outlines of Archibald's skin. She saw that same pert chest, which had filled her with libidinous desire; the same lips, trembling with fear; the same eyes, misty with love.

Then she saw something she had never seen before.

Lola was back in Hyde Park, led there by a trail of folded swans. She was lost and confused, wondering why no-one had come to meet her.

Someone was sitting behind a newspaper. Lola could not see who it was, but she was beginning to get a sense of that man:

'Could it be? Was it? No, surely not.'

"Archie!" she screamed. "Archie? Is that you?"

"Lola! It's me!"

Lola felt the same pang of attraction which Archibald felt. Her arms wanted to reach out and grab her man, her toes jiggled with excitement, and her hair fizzed with static delight.

She had finally found her soulmate! Here was a man who also had an addictive personality, who also tried to control other people, and who was also moved by the scent of cinnamon.

She had finally broken free of Hugo's spell!

She had finally gotten her man!

"Archie!"

"Lola!"

Archibald tore off Lola's gloves:

"This is for all the portraits."

He tore off her blouse:

"This is for all the notes."

He tore off her corset:

"This is for all the swans."

He removed her dress:

"I love you."

He removed her tights:

"I've always loved you."

He removed her underwear:

"I always will."

Deep breaths. Deep sighs. Deep groans. Deep stares.

They fell into the deep embrace of a helpless settee.

Bodies fell into bodies; crashing like neutrons and exploding like stars. Archibald took Lola's head, clasped it and pinned it down. He pressed his fingers through her thin, colourless hair, and scraped the surface of her scalp.

Lola removed Archibald's glasses, delicately, as if they were ageless lovers who had been united for aeons.

Archibald locked his lips onto Lola's. Cracked flesh met loose skin, pores opened, pores closed, and tongues stroked tongues in a frenetic dance; exploring new terrain; twisting, turning, sucking and swirling; momentum increasing, force increasing, contact increasing; fuelled by monarchical urges which did not appear to have a beginning, middle or end.

Neither Lola nor Archibald had ever felt so needed, coveted or alive. They were shocked to discover that another person could want them so much.

Lola's turkey neck swung and swayed, her breasts flapped against her waist, and creases formed on her belly.

Archibald's fingers snuck inside her vagina. It was deliciously wet. His thumb circled and pressed her clitoris. His fingers moved with sympathetic rhythm; building towards a rapture.

His tongue mirrored his fingers.

They panted in time.

Lola quivered and gasped. Her nipples hardened, her body convulsed, her dark spots lightened, and her skin flushed with the glow of youth. It was the sweetest pill; a stinging bite; a taste hedonism turned to flesh.

Archibald planted his palm on Lola's chest. Arching his back, he thrust his penis into Lola's vagina. He climaxed on entry. Decades of repressed semen and sperm came gushing forth, flowed for thirteen seconds, and then stopped.

Archibald pulled out, sighed, and looked at Lola.

Like the images in his dreams, her face stiffened, taking on the granite contour of Delaney's cheek; her nose took the shape of Delaney's nose; her shoulders widened and her breasts hardened.

It hit him, like an uppercut to the jaw: The realisation that he had never loved Lola; that the love he had felt was Hugo's, or Mayer's, but not his own.

Sex had set him free.

His words came gushing forth:

"I'm a homosexual. I'm a sodomite! I'm a catamite! I'm a buggerer! I'm a Molly, I'm a Madge, I'm a mandrake, I'm a backgammon player, I'm a sausage lover, I'm a bud sallogh, I'm a gal-boy, I'm a pathic, I'm a pansy, I'm an indorser! I'm alive!

"Thank-you Lola; you've shaken every last drop of heterosexuality out of my wretched excuse of a body. I love you, I love you, I love you!"

He grabbed his clothes and wrapped them around his waist; suddenly ashamed to be naked in front of a woman.

'She's _my_ knight in shining armour', he admitted to himself. 'And I'm _her_ damsel in distress!'

Lola smiled:

"It's what I do, silly: I help men to become the people they were always meant to be."

"Oh."

"I fancy some jam roly poly. Sexercise always makes me hungry."

"Yes, well, I should probably be going."

Archibald pulled up his trousers, tripped on their hem, steadied himself, and continued. He dressed in such a way that his shirt remained untucked and his hips were left exposed.

"Archie?" Lola called. "Promise me one thing."

"Anything."

"Please release Hugo."

Archibald nodded, turned and left.

Lola slipped into a chimerical sleep; dreaming of the Archibald of her youth; an Adonis; masculine, athletic and unreal.

*****

Everyone has a beautiful angle; an angle from which they look transcendent. Even the ugliest of people possess such an angle. Briefly glance at them, when standing in the right place, in the right light, and you will believe you have seen an angel.

Archibald saw Delaney's beautiful angle.

Looking at him from behind and from below, in the half-light of dusk, his face seemed so smooth, sharp and sensuous, that it seemed wrong to compare it to other faces. Michelangelo's David and da Vinci's Mona Lisa did not have such an allure:

"Dah... Dah... Delaney?"

"Archie!"

Archibald threw himself at Delaney; clutching him, embracing him, and kissing him hard.

He felt four kinds of love:

Philia: He would have died to protect Delaney.

Pragma: They had been partners for years.

Eros: Their loins were ablaze.

Philautia: Archibald was finally able to love himself.

He realised that his craving for power and his addiction to sex had both been symptoms of his repressed homosexuality. At last, he possessed true power: The power to be himself. He did not care if the world called him a "Sissy", he did not care what anyone might say. He was comfortable in his own skin. And that, it transpired, was all he had ever wanted.

"I love you," he screamed. "I love you, I love you, I love you!"

"I love you too," Delaney cheered. "I always have."

"You've been waiting all these years?"

"Yes."

"And?"

"It was worth it."

FORGIVENESS

"The weak can never forgive. Forgiveness is
the attribute of the strong."
MOHANDAS GANDHI

Hugo stumbled out of the prison compound with giddy feet. An oily wash of colours swept across his cornea. He swayed left, then right, then left.

With a shaky arm, he hailed a cab to take him home.

With a shaky hand, he fumbled with his key.

He shuddered. He could sense that something had happened; everything seemed one shade darker, and most of Lola's lilies had died.

Hugo entered his bungalow, looked for Lola in three different rooms, and then found her on the settee, naked, surrounded by an eruption of clothes.

*****

When Lola awoke, Hugo was on his knees.

Voices laid siege to her mind:

'He tricked me! He never wrote me those notes or drew me those portraits. The bugger tricked me! How can I love him? Did I ever love him? Should I break free?

'Have I done wrong? I have! I slept with someone else. Oh, damn it. The shame! Will he forgive me? Will I be able to forgive myself?

'I hate him! He's a fraud. I hate him, the wily fox.

'No! I shouldn't hate. I should've never betrayed my man.'

She looked at Hugo with bloated eyes.

Hugo whispered in her ear:

"It's okay, honey bun. I'm here for you. It's okay."

Lola closed her eyes.

She thought of sunshine days: The day they got engaged, the day they got married, the day they opened Saint Nick's, and the days they had children.

Hugo stood at the forefront of every scene:

'He's no trickster. He's my love.'

A rosebud turned into a rose.

Their garden began to bloom.

*****

The uprising failed.

This had two consequences: Hugo's power vanished and his love took its place.

Hugo and Lola were sitting at their kitchen table, which was made from wood, which had been reclaimed from an unused coffin. They were surrounded by a collection of birdcages, each filled with a collection of stuffed birds; a chessboard topped with a half-finished game; a jar of ivory pipes, left there by a senile man; a shelf of books, none of which had been read; and a vase, made from backscratchers, which contained flowers which smelled of citrus, wax, sugar and grass.

Flies tapped at a dusty window pane.

A candle winked.

"You didn't draw those pictures."

"No."

"You didn't write those notes."

"No."

"You didn't make those swans."

"No."

"You cheated, lied, and stole my heart. It was vomitrocious."

"Yes."

"I forgive you hubby."

"You do?"

"Yes."

"Why?"

"Because I suppose I always knew, deep down; the signs were always there. You can't draw, your handwriting didn't match the writing on the other notes, and the swan you gave me wasn't folded correctly. I accepted it. You clearly loved me. I clearly held power over you."

Lola lifted her eyes.

Hugo lifted his finger:

"You didn't feel violated?"

"Violated? Yes. But all love is a violation; a violation of rationality, a violation of perspective, and a violation of good manners."

"You didn't mind?"

"How could I mind? If you'd been caught, you'd have been hung. You risked your life to win my heart; it was the most beautiful thing in the world."

"Beautiful?"

"Yes, silly. And irregardless, I'm not so innocent myself."

"You are!"

"I'm not."

"Are too! To me, you'll always be perfect."

Lola winced, lowered her eyes, and replied in a hushed tone of guilt: "I slept with Archibald."

Hugo fell forwards. He laughed so fiercely that he sprayed a fine mist of spittle across the floor:

"Archibald? That Mary Ann?"

"You knew?"

"Wasn't it obvious?"

"Well, I suppose."

"You suppose? It was as clear as night and day!"

Lola let loose with a wet builder's fart.

Hugo ignored it:

"I told him, just before he left for India, that he needed to be true to himself. But no-one ever listens to old Hugo."

Lola frowned:

"And that's it?"

"That's what?"

"Your response. I just told you that I had a sexcapade with another man."

"Yes."

"And?"

"I love you."

"But I slept with another man!"

"I forgive you."

"Why?"

"Because you forgave me."

*****

The next day, Lola found a piece of paper on her doorstep.

She leant down to collect it, with one hand held flat across her back, and her other hand swaying like an elephant's trunk.

In the muffled seconds it took for her to capture that note, her heart fluttered with zippy rhythm; accentuating every third beat; appearing to quicken without actually changing pace.

Lola stepped back into her virgin youth. She felt the thrill of the chase; of unmasked suitors, untold stories and unchained love. Effervescence flickered between her nerves, and covered her skin in tiny fissures.

Her hands shook as they unfolded that piece of paper.

Her eyes watered as they feasted on the portrait inside.

It was not as subtle as Archibald's sketches; its lines were less delicate, and its contours were blunt. But what it lacked for in artistry, it made up for in heart. It screamed: "Forgive me! I'm sorry! Please love me!"

Lola blushed salmon pink:

'He <u>does</u> truly love me. I <u>am</u> truly blessed.'

"Hubby!"

She bounded towards Hugo, took him by the tie, and led him to their room. Empowered by a surge of vestal energy, she pushed Hugo onto their bed, ripped his clothing from his body, and rode him more fervently than ever before.

Hugo, set free from his lies, was able to give himself completely. Lola, no longer living in denial, was able to take him in.

She climaxed three times.

Hugo bit the sultry air.

*****

Lola found a new portrait every day. Their images were coarse, merging chiselled lines with scratchy shades; a symphony of violent pencil and love unchained. Their designs were primeval and raw.

Each time she found a portrait Lola dragged Hugo to bed.

Each time they made love, she climaxed harder than before.

*****

Lola found a note on her doorstep. She leant down to collect it, pinched its weathered corner, and read the message inside:

'You're even more beautiful now than when we first met.'

Lola dragged Hugo to bed.

Over the weeks which followed, those notes replaced portraits, but Lola's reaction remained the same:

'Lola is my favourite word.'

'You're so perfect it's weird.'

'You take my breath away.'

'You complete me.'

*****

It was a topaz dawn. It was an amber morning. It was the smell of dew. It was a concerto of birdsong. It was a leaf in the breeze. It was a lone star. It was a mud-kissed worm. It was a spiral of smoke. It was an ageless peace.

It was their wedding anniversary.

Lola stepped outside, looked down, and saw a paper swan by her toe.

She giggled. It was a churlish giggle; too timeless to be called "Youthful", but blissful enough to evoke a sense of innocence lost.

She unfolded the swan and read the message inside:

'You ran STRAIGHT into my heart, now run into my arms.'

Lola ran straight ahead.

She unfolded a second swan:

'My heart will CONTINUE to beat for you.'

Lola continued:

'I love you each day, I love you each night. You deserve that love, and to be treated RIGHT.'

Lola turned right.

She skipped from one swan to the next; springing over crumbled twigs, long forgotten puddles, and indifferent blades of grass. She traversed fields, forests, thickets, gardens and groves; covering miles as if they were yards.

She reached a clearing which faced a twinkling lake. Its waters had captured a million fragments of sun; its banks rippled; its shores came and went.

By that lake was a copse of trees, by those trees was a table, and at that table was a man.

Lola bounded towards him.

"Hu..." she cheered; certain she was about to see Hugo.

She could not finish.

Her mouth fell open, she squinted, and she whispered:

"Mayer? Really, Mayer? Is that you?"

PATIENCE IS A VIRTUE

"All things are difficult before they become easy."
SAADI OF SHIRAZ

Mayer took slow, tentative steps towards Lola's bungalow.

It was the hour after sunset. A soft, red light was retreating from the oncoming march of darkness. Vines cast no shadow. Flowers had fallen into a silent slumber.

Mayer was about to knock on the door, but something held him back. At first, he could not be sure what it was. Then he heard it:

"Archie?"

"Lola!"

His toes began to tiptoe before his mind had a chance to think.

From a narrow angle, side on to the window, he saw images in the glass.

He heard voices in the wind:

"This is for all the portraits."

"This is for all the notes."

"This is for all the swans."

Mayer succumbed to a whirligig of distraction:

'What portraits? What notes? What swans?'

He grimaced as he watched Archibald tear clothes from Lola's body, pin her down, and plant his lips onto hers. He choked on his tongue, turned, and departed.

*****

Archibald stepped into Mayer's office.

Mayer filled with rage. His face turned pink, then salmon, red, maroon and purple. His toes clawed at his socks, and his stomach tensed.

Archibald smiled:

"I'm in love."

Mayer teetered on the precipice of war.

"With Delaney."

Mayer froze, melted, laughed, screamed, howled, jumped up and punched the air:

"You are, brother? Well... Well... Well that's just delightful! Good for you, old chap. Whoop-di-doo. What a splendid fine thing. You deserve it! You jolly well do!"

Archibald was taken aback:

"Umm, well, yes. Thank-you."

Mayer hugged his friend so tightly he choked.

Archibald would have smiled if his skin had not been stretched so taut. As it was, he bided his time, waited for Mayer to loosen his grip, and then continued:

"The thing is, you know, two men living together, well, it's not really the done thing, what with it being punishable by death and all."

Archibald's speech had receded back into its pre-belligerent state. His body had receded too. Archibald no longer resembled the man who stormed into Mayer's office just a few months before. He could feel the movements of his internal organs; the coiling of his intestines, the frothing of his blood, and the changing shape of his lungs. He felt and looked transparent.

Mayer's face curled into a portrait of sage concern.

"So, you see," Archibald continued. "We need to leave the army."

Mayer nodded.

"And, well, we were hoping you might be kind enough to put in a word with the Governor General, to encourage him to release us. I believe you and he are close."

Mayer tapped his fingers:

"Hmm. I think I can help. I can even find you a safe-haven, beyond the reach of the state, with a tribe that embraces homosexuality."

"Thank-you! Oh Mayer, it'd mean the world."

"I didn't say I'd do it."

"Oh."

"Hmm."

"Please. It'd mean so much."

"Yes, I can see that. I just have one little issue: The older I grow, the more determined I become to stay young. I've become rather attached to the idea of becoming a geriatric child. Well, if I were to help you, you'd be in my debt, and debts *do* have an awful habit of making people old. So, brother, I'm sure you can see my dilemma."

"Is there a solution?"

"There's always a solution."

"What is it?"

"Don't stay in my debt. Repay me right away."

"I'll do it! Name your price."

Mayer chuckled:

"Tell me about your portraits, notes and swans."

"But... How... I mean why... I mean what... But, yes, of course... But..."

Archibald choked, gagged, turned puce, turned purple, held his hand to his chin, forced his jaw open, gnawed the air, and finally inhaled. Then he exhaled. Then he told Mayer about everything he had done to court Lola.

As he left, Mayer put his arm around Archibald's shoulder:

"Let's have a lads' night out; you, me and Hugo. For old times' sake."

Archibald smiled:

"For old times' sake!"

*****

Mayer drew Lola's portrait several times, and then left those portraits on her doorstep; he left her a collection of notes and swans.

Lola approached:

"Mayer? Really, Mayer? Is that you?"

Mayer turned.

The low-lying light pushed a shadow from his face, which softened, not into a smile, but into a mellow shade of contentment.

"Mayer? Bu... Bu... But what are you doing here?"

Mayer tilted his head:

"Isn't this the perfect weather for sunbathing? Simply marvellous! Not too hot. Not too cold."

"Umm. Snickerdoodles. Jingle bells. Ups-a-daisy. Mayer?"

Mayer gazed into Lola's eyes:

"I love you."

He paused:

"I've always loved you."

He smiled:

"I always will."

Lola frowned:

"But you're a bankster!"

Mayer held up his hands:

"Guilty as charged! But, before I was a banker, I was a man. Some of my humanity must have survived."

Lola drifted back through time.

She was in Covent Garden, approached by the keenest of suitors. She was at a ball, approached by the keenest of suitors. She was in Covent Garden, warmed by Mayer's innocence. She was at a masked ball, emitting a ditsy giggle. She was at home, moved to tears by her father's rebukes. She was on a date; in a carriage; on a rooftop; in love.

'No. I can't be. No. It can't be so. No! No! No! No! No!'

"I love Hugo! Hew-ooo-go. Not you, silly. Hugo!"

Tears fell from Lola's eyes like torrential rain. Her face was a monsoon. Her body was shrouded in mist.

Mayer leant forwards, clutched Lola's hand and shed a tear. It landed on Lola's knee, where it merged with one of Lola's tears. It twinkled, ephemeral, and melted:

"Like all women, you have an infinite capacity for love. I don't doubt your love for Hugo, but I don't believe it infringes upon your love for me. Why, you even said we could've been special; that you wondered how life would've turned out if you'd stayed on our date."

Lola shook her head:

"I didn't stay. You misread me that night; your nonversation made me cringe."

Mayer's eyes pulsed in the middle:

"I was tricked."

Lola pulled back:

"Tricked? Really?"

"Really! Hugo fooled me! He had me overhear two boys talk about how much you liked oysters and feathers; that's why I bought you those things. I'd planned to give you flowers and roast beef."

"I love roast beef!"

"You do?"

"It's my flavourite. But I really don't believe your story."

Mayer stopped himself from speaking. Then he spoke:

"Hugo staged your mugging."

Lola shuddered.

She was back in the alley near her childhood home. A raggedy figure stepped out of the darkness; his majestic blazer was full of worm holes, and his breeches were faded with dust.

Lola inhaled London's musty air, and felt London's rain on her skin:

"I don't believe it. Hugo's no frenemy."

"Believe it! The men who mugged you were the same people who staged that conversation. I spotted them one day, and paid them to tell me the truth. They said they'd never planned to mug you; it was all a dastardly ruse."

Lola's eyes glazed over.

"Hugo also took credit for Archibald's sketches, notes and swans."

Lola paused, pondered, looked down at the ground, looked up at the sky, looked out at the lake, and looked into Mayer's eyes:

"I believe you; it's all so clear to me now. Oh, golly gosh. My whole life has been a giant lie! I should've married you. I *would've* married you, if Hugo hadn't sabotaged our date. I could forgive him for claiming credit for Archibald's notes, but not for that. That was truly grotten. Oh, poopsicles! I wish Hugo was dead."

Mayer shuddered:

"Now, now; Hugo is a good man."

"He's a dastard and a fraud."

"He is."

"I love *you*."

"And I love you."

THE END

"Endings are not always bad. Most times they're just beginnings in disguise."
KIM HARRISON

The British have a habit of rebuilding Britain wherever they go.

With this in mind, let us now return to the opening chapter of this tome.

Our three heroes are sitting in a traditional, British pub. But this pub is not in Britain; it is in a litter-strewn alley, near a market square, in an African town; miles from the London streets they once called home.

Hugo sips his ale. He is still on his second drink, despite his friends being on their fourth.

Archibald spreads out across the booth. He takes up more space than Hugo and Mayer combined.

Mayer, swilling his glass of claret, twirls a diamond-encrusted ring around his index finger.

These three men were once three babies, born on three adjacent beds, a mere three seconds apart. They were once three toddlers, living in three adjacent homes. They were once three teens.

But these men are not toddlers, nor are they teens. Age has wizened them, serpentine scales have cut craggy ravines from their skin, grey has replaced colour, and baldness has replaced hair.

Nor are these men united.

Thrown together by fate, they have been cast apart by the whimsy of circumstance, and sent forth to chase three very different goals: Money, power and love.

Now their race is run.

They clink glasses and embrace. Hugo and Mayer wave Archibald goodbye, whilst laughing at the thought of him going native; fleeing from the authorities he served for so long.

Mayer turns to Hugo:

"You know, brother, I used to love Lola as much as you."

Hugo nods:

"You still do."

"Hmm."

"It's true; just like me, you never stopped loving her. Our love has always been one and the same; felt in the same way, in the same places, at the same time."

Mayer laughs. It is an uncomfortable laugh, verging on a whimper. Hit by a response he had not seen coming, his script torn to pieces, he is nudged towards discomfort.

He changes tact:

"Do you remember how I captured Jonathan Wild, which gave you the freedom you needed to court Lola? How I introduced you to Mr Orwell, who educated you enough to appeal to her? And how I introduced you to Bear, who turned you into a surgeon; the sort of person who could win her father's approval? You'd have never married her if it hadn't been for me."

Hugo nods.

"You said you were in my debt; that it'd be your duty to repay me."

Hugo nods again.

"Well, I fear our days are numbered. If you wish to settle your account, you must do so before it's too late."

Hugo keeps nodding:

"You're right; you gave me everything, and there's only one way I can repay you: I must step aside and allow you to be with Lola. I've already experienced love in all its forms; now it's your turn to love."

Mayer clutches his chest, as if stabbed through with a blade:

"No, brother, that's not fair! You can't just hand her over. Lola is your wife. Put up a fight man! Defend her honour!"

Hugo smiles:

"I love you."

He embraces Mayer:

"I love you."

He rubs Mayer's shoulders:

"I love you."

He backs away.

*****

It is not the reaction Mayer had been expecting. It almost makes him feel guilty for poisoning Hugo's ale. He almost feels guilty for buying that poison from a tribal witchdoctor; her face painted white; her head crowned by a lion's skull. He almost feels guilty for adding that poison to Hugo's drink, drip by drip, whilst Hugo was at the bar. He almost feels guilty for watching its colour dissipate and its scent waft away.

Mayer had decided to poison his childhood friend when he was struck by the realisation that Hugo might not die:

'*He might outlive Lola! He might outlive me!*'

He felt compelled to stop that from happening.

Whereas Archibald considered it valiant to die for love, Mayer considered such a belief to be romantically naïve.

'*No*', he told himself. '*It's far more pragmatic to <u>kill</u> for love.*

'*I need to learn from my mistakes. I can't just wait for the universe to come to the rescue; I need to take matters into my own hands.*'

But now he has doubts.

He takes a deep breath, and then he justifies his actions:

'*It's better to be safe than sorry. And anyway, Hugo <u>does</u> deserve to die; he's the villain of the piece. He stole Lola, with his lies, stalking, manipulation, cheating and tricks. Lola was falling for <u>me</u>; she would've been mine, would've purified my soul, and would've made <u>me</u> a stand-up guy. Everything Hugo is, everything he has, and everything he's ever done; all his love, affection and charity; it all should've been mine. I should've been the loving one; the charitable one; the activist. He stole my life! He's scum! He deserves to die. I only wish I'd killed him when I was young. I should've killed him for Lola; to free her from his spell. I was far too patient and forgiving.*'

He smiles:

'*Lola <u>will</u> be mine! She'll make me a better person, and help me to atone for this sin.*

'*Lola <u>will</u> be mine! She'll help me to love again.*'

PARTING IS SUCH SWEET SORROW

"As a well-spent day brings happy sleep, so a life well spent brings happy death."
LEONARDO DA VINCI

There is an old story which may or may not be true...

Once upon a time there lived a girl who loved her dog more than anything in the world. But, when her dog died, that girl did not shed a tear.

This is what she told her parents:

"We are put on earth so we can learn to love. My dog had already learnt to love, so there was no need for her to remain here with us any longer."

This same sentiment could be said of Hugo: He had already learnt to love. There was no need for him to remain on earth any longer.

*****

Hugo returns home and falls into a drunken slumber.

He does not wake up.

Doctors, if they were to find him, would say he died of a broken heart; aorta crashing against ventricle; nerves strangling flesh.

We know better.

We know that Hugo dies of a satisfied heart.

He dies in a state of grace.

Within seconds, orchid petals begin to blow in through the open window. Within minutes, they begin to submerge his body.

By the time Lola returns, her marital chamber has transmuted into a tremendous flower; a potpourri of every colour known to humankind.

Hugo is nowhere to be seen, but the aroma of cinnamon tells Lola that he lives on.

She sits on the floor, feeling lightheaded, and sees one of her lovebirds return. It perches on her knee. A second lovebird perches on her shoulder.

By the time the sun fades, all her lovebirds have returned.

Their lullabies rock her into a blissful slumber.

HURRAH!

"Try not to become a man of success.
Rather, become a man of value."
ALBERT EINSTEIN

Lola dedicates an hour to each of the seven stages of grief; an hour denying Hugo's death, an hour blaming herself, an hour blaming Hugo, an hour wallowing in despair, an hour recovering, an hour organising her thoughts, and an hour accepting her situation. Then it dawns on her: She has spent those seven hours, not thinking of Hugo, but thinking of Mayer:

'Hugo defiled me. I would never have fallen for him if he hadn't staged that mugging, or taken credit for Archibald's notes. I would've fallen for Mayer, if Hugo hadn't sabotaged our date. And how did Hugo even get

the portrait he gave me in Hyde Park? That was one of Archibald's portraits. I know it. Yes, it was. He must've broken into my room and stolen it. What a creep! What a fudge-nugget! He tricked me into marrying him, held me prisoner for years, and raped me on a nightly basis.

'*No! It was Mayer who was always the one. It's* <u>Mayer</u> *I love. How could I not see that? Ugh! I need to make amends.*'

*****

An hour later, Lola finds herself on Mayer's veranda.

Mayer freezes a little, chokes a little, and puffs up a little. He laughs, immaturely:

"I bet it's raining back in London."

Lola smiles. Without needing to be asked, she explains her presence as simply as she can:

"Well, we've waited for half a century, it'll be for the best if we don't wait any longer. We could die at any moment."

Mayer smiles and leads Lola inside. He gives her the grand tour; showing her the chambers he has prepared for her, the spa and walk-in closet. The ballroom makes Lola recall the Opening Ball at the Almack Rooms. Then she thinks of Covent Garden.

"My love for you is like Aeolus," she mocks. "The Greek god of the winds, who imprisoned his sons in a cave."

Mayer laughs:

"I think you've been imagineering. Your love is not born of nature; you've created it out of thin air."

And now Mayer is back in Covent Garden, open-mouthed; betrayed by his tongue, and only able to blurt out three measly words:

"Be my girl!"

Lola replies just as abruptly as before:

"No."

"Hmm?"

"No, silly, I won't be yours. You're not you. Not now. The person in front of me is not a man, he's an idea; a manifestation of money. Yes, that's all you are: Money."

"So…" Mayer stutters; his thoughts tied up in a thousand tiny knots:

'*She loves me? But she doesn't love me? She wants to be mine? But she can't? I'm not me? I'm money? Who am I? What am I? Why?*'

Mayer stands here, rigid, blank-faced and helpless.

"You were love," Lola explains. "And I loved you for it. I still do."

A catty smile flirts with Mayer's face.

"So…" he stutters again. And again his thoughts collide:

'Should I protest? Should I claim to be the same person? Am I still love? Was I ever love? Can a person be love? What is love? Why love? How?'

"So," Lola replies. "Give your money to charity."

"All of it?"

"Yes. Take this swapportunity: Swap your money for love and I'll be yours."

Mayer does not react. He does not stutter. He does not even think. He simply stands here in a state of living rigor mortis.

Lola continues:

"You need to umble-cum-stumble that I fall in love with broken men. My love heals them; it helps them to become the people they were always meant to be."

Lola runs her fingers through her hair:

"Surrender your money, surrender to me, and I'll help you to become yourself."

Mayer opens his mouth, ready to consent, but it is Lola who speaks:

"You're not rich, you're just a poor man with money. To be rich, you don't need lots of wealth, you just need to be content with what you have. And you need love. And food. Talking of which, I fancy some spotted dick."

- - - **THE END** - - -

AFTERWORD

"Most of the money in our economy is created by banks, in the form of bank deposits – the numbers that appear in your account. Banks create new money whenever they make loans. 97% of the money in the economy today is created by banks, whilst just 3% is created by the government.

The money that banks create isn't the paper money that bears the logo of the government-owned Bank of England. It's the electronic deposit money that flashes up on the screen when you check your balance at an ATM. Right now, this money (bank deposits) makes up over 97% of all the money in the economy. Only 3% of money is still in that old-fashioned form of cash that you can touch.

Banks can create money through the accounting they use when they make loans. The numbers that you see when you check your account balance are just accounting entries in the banks' computers. These numbers are a 'liability' or IOU from your bank to you. But by using your debit card or internet banking, you can spend these IOUs as though they were the same as £10 notes. By creating these electronic IOUs, banks can effectively create a substitute for money."

POSITIVE MONEY

www.positivemoney.org/how-money-works/how-banks-create-money

THE LITTLE VOICE

"The most thought-provoking novel of 2016"
Huffington Post
"Radical... A masterclass... Top notch..."
The Canary
"A pretty remarkable feat"
BuzzFeed

"Can you remember who you were before the world told you who you should be?"

Dear reader,

My character has been shaped by two opposing forces; the pressure to conform to social norms, and the pressure to be true to myself. To be honest with you, these forces have really torn me apart. They've pulled me one way and then the other. At times, they've left me questioning my whole entire existence.

But please don't think that I'm angry or morose. I'm not. Because through adversity comes knowledge. I've suffered, it's true. But I've learnt from my pain. I've become a better person.

Now, for the first time, I'm ready to tell my story. Perhaps it will inspire you. Perhaps it will encourage you to think in a whole new way. Perhaps it won't. There's only one way to find out...

Enjoy the book,

Yew Shodkin

OCCUPIED

"A unique piece of literary fiction"
The Examiner
"Darker than George Orwell's 1984"
AXS
"Genre-busting"
Pak Asia Times

SOME PEOPLE LIVE UNDER OCCUPATION.

SOME PEOPLE OCCUPY THEMSELVES.

NO ONE IS FREE.

Step into a world which is both magically fictitious and shockingly real, to follow the lives of Tamsin, Ellie, Arun and Charlie; a refugee, native, occupier and economic migrant. Watch them grow up during a halcyon past, everyday present and dystopian future. And be prepared to be amazed.

Inspired by the occupations of Palestine, Kurdistan and Tibet, and by the corporate occupation of the west, 'Occupied' is a haunting glance into a society which is a little too familiar for comfort. It truly is a unique piece of literary fiction...

INVOLUTION & EVOLUTION

"Flows magnificently across the pages"
"Great, thrilling and enlightening"
"Quick paced and rhythmic"

This is the story of Alfred Freeman, a boy who does everything he can; to serve humankind. He feeds five-thousand youths, salves-saves-and-soothes; and champions the maligned. He helps paralytics to feel fine, turns water into wine; and gives sight to the blind.

When World War One draws near, his nation is plunged into fear; and so Alfred makes a stand. He opposes the war and calls for peace, disobeys the police; and speaks out across the land. He makes speeches, and he preaches; using statements which sound grand.

But the authorities hit back, and launch a potent-attack; which is full of disgust-derision-and-disdain. Alfred is threatened with execution, and suffers from persecution; which leaves him writhing in pain. He struggles to survive, remain alive; keep cool and stay sane.

'Involution & Evolution' is a masterpiece of rhyme, with a message which echoes through time; and will get inside your head. With colourful-characters and poetic-flair, it is a scathing critique of modern-warfare; and all its gory-bloodshed. It's a novel which breaks new ground, is sure to astound; and really must be read.

www.joss-sheldon.com

If you enjoyed this book, please do leave a review online. Joss Sheldon does not have a professional marketing team – he needs your help to take his books out into the world!!!

25398228R00174

Printed in Great Britain
by Amazon